The Heroine in the Bus Stairwell

Bryan Meadan

Summary: The Heroine in the Bus Stairwell is a story of Anna, and the women who fought with her, the role of youth movements in resistance and their struggle to survive one of the most horrendous periods in human history: the Warsaw Ghetto Uprising.

ISBN 979-8-9857815-0-2

Printed in the U.S.A.
First Edition, March 2022

Inspired by actual events

The Warsaw Ghetto

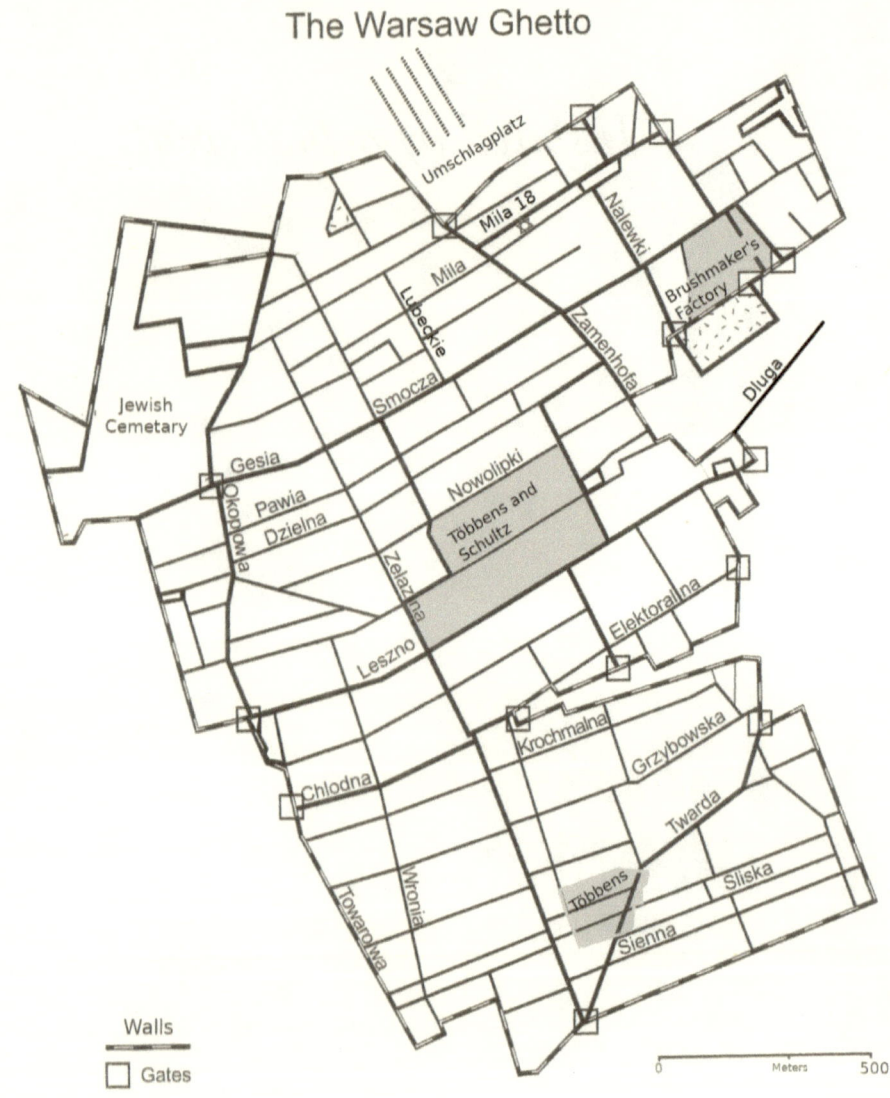

Umschlagplatz

Mila 18

Nalewki

Mila

Lubeckie

Zamenhofa

Smocza

Brushmaker's Factory

Jewish Cemetary

Gesia

Okopowa

Pawia

Dzielna

Nowolipki

Tobbens and Schultz

Dluga

Zelazna

Elektoralna

Leszno

Krochmalna

Grzybowska

Chlodna

Twarda

Wronia

Tobbens

Sliska

Towarowa

Sienna

Walls

Gates

0   Meters   500

One

July 3, 1976

Anna had witnessed war, lost more than anyone need suffer, written manifestos, led battles and killed enemies. She shouldn't have been so worried about missing a bus. As she entered the station, she distinctly saw her bus fill up and the driver prepare to shut the door. With two full bags of fruits and vegetables burning her arms as she waddled through the crowd, her elderly frame aching with each stride, she made a dash for the door.

The central bus station in Jerusalem was a sociological phenomenon, and it was always an absorbing experience to observe the bustling waves of people from around the planet that frequented the lines, each in search of their truths and havens, spellbound by Jerusalem. So much diversity for such a small place. The city may have mystical significance for three major religions, but to the impartial bystander, it looked more like an insane asylum. They even named a psychological disorder after the city, the Jerusalem Syndrome, the state of being so mesmerized by the center of religious zealotry that you go nuts. Those nuts were wandering the streets of Jerusalem en mass, envisioning God and Jesus and Moses and Mohammed, and even Buddha seemed to make a cameo appearance in their heads. These chimerical characters would instruct them to preach or act or dance or pray, and they would follow, for, after all, it was a deity speaking to them.

Many felt proud of this eclectic collection of differences – of this unrest. Many were proud back then. For despite all of its rawness, all of its wry sense of disorder, and all of its abnormal creatures, Jerusalem was the capital of the State of Israel and represented an entity that instilled in its inhabitants the desire to fight for her. On this particular cloudless Friday morning, the passengers on bus number 405 from Jerusalem to Tel Aviv were to witness a scene that was to profoundly affect each one of them and help them all understand what it was that they had been fighting for so long.

The chaotic station forced the morning crowds to pack the isles between the buses, leaving barely enough room to navigate a path to the stalls that were dragging thousands to their homes for the weekend – the short, far too short, weekend. Buses filled with lots of all ages and colors – soldiers and nuns, Jews and Muslims, sons and mothers, professors and beggars – filling up and driving off, leaving scores more of anxious weekend commuters to continue their unbearable, stifling, anticlimactic wait in the hot and sticky line. Soldiers who had just finished long weeks in the mud, or in the scorching desert heat, charging hills and eating out of cans, or in smoke-filled rooms learning about operation why-the-hell-would-we-want-to-do-that, anxious beyond sanity to get home to their girlfriends, their warm beds, their girlfriends in their warm beds, and yes, to get home to their mothers. A meal would be waiting at the end of the trek. It would be hot and more importantly, it would have seasoning. That was what the soldiers seemed to miss most of all, spices. Bland may have been good for the British during the mandate, but the mandate had been behind them for over a quarter-century, and now they could use a bit of salt. The Dead Sea was loaded with salt – even called the Salt Sea in Hebrew – let's just start giving some of it to the army, can't we? The soldiers eagerly awaited the arrival at a dinner table loaded with warm, salted food. Ah, but prior to that spiced up meal lingering in mom's kitchen, they must endure the drone of Friday afternoon bus travel in Israel. Often, after more than 45 minutes of not so patient waiting, the bus would arrive and those brave, mouth-watering souls, following a week of the harsh training, would be suddenly pushed from behind by a barrage of zealous old ladies trying to ensure their places on the ride to Tel Aviv, Ashdod, Beer Sheva, Haifa or even Tzfat. For they too had to get home, not for food, but to make certain that there is enough salt in the cholent.

"Stop pushing! Wait your damn turn. Try a little patience won't you," yelled a soldier. He was trying to enter the bus to Tel Aviv. Patience was a word many would have trouble understanding, but he yelled nonetheless – maybe they'd catch on. They didn't. "Could you get your damn gun out of my back! Idiot!" There was no queue, just a writhing mass moving forward toward the slim doors of the poor red bus. One would think that there was only one spot available, and like sperm reaching the egg, once that one spot was filled, the door would close. The gutter between the landing and the first step of the bus was wet even though it hadn't rained in two months. Water had flowed from the rinsed vegetable stalls up the path and brought with it the smell of rot with a touch of sage. A soldier elbowed his way through the door, oblivious to the people he had to maim in order to secure a position on bus 405; once up and over the crowd, he would pull out his wallet to pay the driver, who was wearing the typical Egged summer attire, short khaki pants, a light blue, short-sleeved, button-down shirt and sandals. The driver had a young-looking, round face with a slightly receding hairline and very slight graying near the temples.

On this particular summer day, while they all breathed a sigh of relief as the newly installed air conditioning hit them in the face, this particular driver, on this particular bus seemed anything but pleased by the prospect of dealing with this particular Friday rush. However, once the bus was filled with the full gamut of Israeli society, they'd have a quiet hour and a half ride down the hill and out to Tel Aviv. So they thought.

2

The illusion of a quiet ride in peace through the foothills of what was once the kingdom of Judea, home of David, a few short kilometers from where he had audaciously flung a stone into Goliath's forehead, was what caused the officer to smile. A moment later, he sighed as he looked down the long corridor of bus number 405 at the people who had managed to survive the attack at the front door and scrambled to find seats and rack space.

More and more people filled the red seats of the Egged bus. Each traveler had his distinct way of greeting the driver, paying and searching the bus for a suitable seat. One man even smelled his money before handing the bill over to the driver, drawing a glare. Window or aisle, find a nice young man or woman who won't fall asleep on your shoulder. People-watching was a favorite pastime for those lucky enough to get seats near the front of the bus.

A lieutenant with paratrooper wings on his uniform and a red beret on his shoulder slid into the inside seat in the first row. Of course, he had no way of knowing. He was just taking the first available spot. He was just going home after a week of drills and dust and insubordinate soldiers. All he wanted, like all his comrades, was to fall asleep until the driver woke him in Tel Aviv. He had no way of knowing that he would bear witness to an event that would stun even the most experienced of them. He was quite oblivious to the fact that by grabbing that particular seat on that particular bus on that particular Friday he was in for an experience he would never forget.

It was 1976, thirty-one years after the Jews of Europe had been liberated from the Nazi death camps. The officer looked down at the ragged bunch of people entering the bus.

The bus continued to fill until all of the seats were occupied. Chatter came from the back row of seats as two men argued about who had control of the overhead rack – as if it was a possession inherited by right. It was settled after one decided he preferred to have his bag on his lap, but they were seconds from punching it out, and their voices resonated throughout the cabin.

The driver pressed the button that started the folding front door to close as the last of the seats were taken. However, the door would not reach its destined position of shut, as Anna finally showed up. She shoved her foot over the threshold, jamming the door ajar and preventing the driver from continuing.

"There's no room to sit," yelled the driver. "Get off the bus. We have to get moving."

"Wait, please wait," she pleaded. "I want to get on. I must get on this bus."

"I said there's no room. Can't you understand? There's no room!"

By this time Anna had managed to get her entire left leg over and onto the first step of the bus and was attempting to swing the rest of her body through the half-closed door. Her stocking leg and half an arm reached amusingly around the rubber stopper on the edge of the door and into the bus. With one foot still firmly placed on the ground, slipping into the grime in the gutter, and the other halfway up the stairs, her head still mostly outside with the bustling crowd, she yelled into the bus through the crack she had solidified.

"I beg of you," she said with a strong Polish accent. "I must be on this bus to be in Ramat Gan on time." She swung her shoulder around to the inside of the bus, all the while pushing the door open, her strength no match for the simple hydraulics of the automatic door. "My sister from Megiddo, up north – she runs the factory there – oh, I am so proud of her, is coming for the Shabbat. She doesn't come very often, you know?" By the look on the driver's face, he didn't want to know. "And when she does finally come, how much time can I spend with her? I must get home in time to prepare. I must. You see, I bought so many nice things" she said, pointing down at the bags that had been left outside the bus, "and I'm going to make such a dinner for her and my other sister who lives with me. She used to be a doctor – a surgeon. Now she just sees patients when she's called in by the army. Can you imagine, a girl like her…"

"Listen, lady, no room means no room! I don't think that you'd want to stand. In any case, I don't want you or anyone on my bus to stand. And you sure as hell aren't taking any of my passengers' seats." He was so determined to close the door in her face and get going that he didn't even look at her as she spoke. "What's your problem? What's your deal with riding this particular bus? There's another one coming in just a few minutes, and you'll still make it to Tel Aviv in time to prepare a proper meal for your sister. Get off, so we can start going."

But Anna just remained stranded between the asphalt and the stairwell. She looked at him with pleading eyes framed by the black rims of the bus door and a resolve that made it clear she would not be moving any direction but up. Her hand was wrapped around the side of the door like a snake would grip a tree branch, and she was panting as she held her ground and kept the door from closing any further.

"She's going to faint," said the officer to the driver.

"You heard the boy," she said. "But I'm not going to faint. I may be old, but I'm sturdy."

The driver looked down at the lady stuck in his door and then up into the mirror as if the passengers on the bus would save him. He was beginning

4

to show signs of despair. It became clear that he wasn't going anywhere until he settled this. By now, as if his glance at them triggered a response, the rest of the passengers on the bus were becoming involved. Each had an opinion that needed to be aired. "Let's get out of here already," one yelled. "You can take the next bus. Can't you see this one is full?"

"Get the hell down from there. Who do you think you are?" cried another.

And then there were the sympathizers. "If you're gonna ride with us get on the damn bus. And if not, get lost."

The driver looked down at his steering wheel in defeat.

"All right, lady," he said in a sedate tone. He opened the door and the stubby woman grabbed her bags and stood in the open doorway. "I'll let you on the bus. But you'll sit here in the stairwell and you won't take any of the other passengers' seats. Do you understand? And I don't want to hear a word out of you the entire trip. Not a sound. I know your type. The minute you start, a war couldn't shut you up."

"I've seen my share of war," she said quietly as she ascended the short stairwell. The red handkerchief covering her grey hair fell slightly forward, causing her to set down the two large bags and readjust it. The bags, filled with fruits and vegetables, were old and torn and seemed to weigh at least as much as she did. She was poorly dressed and her face looked experienced and used. But beyond the wear of time, was a beauty that radiated through her eyes.

She tottered up towards the driver, one rung at a time, dragging the bags along and sighing with each step. "Thank you, thank you so very much," she said to the driver. She had a worn, tired look, but a youthful smile. "You're so kind. You should live a long and healthy life, you should. My sisters would just platz if I didn't make it ..."

"Just sit down and be quiet." He pointed sharply to the stairwell as he would command a dog to stay. "Sit here, and if you as much as say one word, I'll kick you off this bus without even stopping. Understood? So shut up, and enjoy the ride."

Rolling her eyes, she agilely plopped herself onto the top stair. The woman fiddled in her purse, she pulled out a few coins and handed them to the driver. He lazily tossed them into the small tray by his money bag and put the bus in gear, muttering something under his breath.

The officer laughed. The driver's stern threat to toss her off the moving bus did not faze Anna in the least. It was a pathetic sight. This poor woman, forced to plead to get a seat in the stairwell, was so defiant that her unrelenting drive to be on that bus was strong enough to slay the cold-hearted driver and win the battle. It was clear to everyone that even if he tried to throw her off the bus it would take physical abuse to do so. He seemed to know that his threat was futile – and so did she. She would surely keep on babbling.

After taking her seat in the stairwell, she put her bags behind her in the aisle and sat faced straight ahead with her knees in front of her like a schoolgirl. Many of the passengers in the front rows could clearly see the reflection of her face in the mirror. The dashboard of the bus blocked her view of the road ahead so that all she could see was the driver, who still wore a sour face.

"So, where you from?" asked the woman.

"I beg of you," whined the driver. "Shut up and let me drive."

"I only asked you where you're from. It's not such a big question. You could just answer you know. You don't have to get all upset. I don't think that you are ashamed of where you're from unless you're from prison perhaps then I could..."

"Okay, Okay," said the driver impatiently. "I'm from a kibbutz in the south."

"Oh, you're a kibbutznik. That's nice. That's very nice. Kibbutz is a good place for a young man like you. My sister, I told you about her, she's a factory director on Kibbutz Megiddo...that's very close to Har Megiddo – the hill near Megiddo. That is where our Christian friends prophesize the last battle between good and evil will take place – if you believe that stuff. Armageddon, the word Armageddon, comes from Har Megiddo, the hill near my sister's kibbutz. Oh yes, my sister will have a great view of that war. It's an awful thing to have a great view of a war. I can tell you that. Just horrible. Don't ever do it – not that you can avoid such a thing. So, do you work hard?"

The bus rolled down the main Jerusalem-Tel Aviv highway, a swerving, bumpy ride past Arab villages, recently planted pine trees, and shells of abandoned armored cars from the Independence War that had become monuments on the side of the road. The cars represent the battle to control the corridor to Jerusalem and were part of convoys bringing supplies to the besieged city prior to and during Israel's War of Independence in 1948. Two groups of four vehicles were on either side of the road. They had been ambushed by bands of Arab fighters who blocked the road with stones, forcing them to stop, and then attacked with snipers hidden in the hills and behind rocks. Most of the cars had belonged to the Kibbutz movement's transportation department, and their drivers had been volunteers. In the summer heat, the vehicles with little ventilation were rolling ovens, traveling the day-long route from Hulda to Jerusalem – a trip that now only took forty-five minutes in an air-conditioned bus.

"Would you please just let me drive?"

"Again with the attitude? I just asked if you work hard."

"My god…. Yes, sometimes."

"Yes, but you drive a bus. My brother drove a bus. That was in Poland before the war – *the* war, the World War, not *the* war we just had. He had a bus that he would bring home every night and park in front of the house. My son, rest his soul, loved to play on it. He thought it was his fort. Moishe, my brother would always yell at him, 'Get off of there, you little monkey. It's not a toy, it's my job.' But what did my son know? He was just a child, sheine yingele meine. Just a child."

The woman stopped talking and looked straight ahead at the dashboard. She had been smirking while recalling her son's escapades and the smile had not completely faded, though it had turned a bit sour as if forgotten there. These days she thought about her son often, as it was summer, and her son could play outside. In the winter months, back then in Poland, he was restricted to the house, as the biting cold was far too hostile. Had they lived in Israel back then, he could have played as much as he desired outside in the warmth of the Middle East winter – unless they lived in Jerusalem, where it snowed several times each year. She had tried to live in Jerusalem but ironically could not get used to the winters. Growing up in Poland where sub-freezing temperatures were the norm, she should have found Jerusalem quite toasty. But Jerusalem had a different type of cold than Poland. She had often thought it had to do with humidity, but she never found confirmation of that theory. So she moved to the coastal area, where it never snowed and she could imagine what her son could have done – only if. Thoughts of the boy, the little she could recall after over thirty-five years, ran through her mind. She could still picture his smile.

She sat staring blankly at the bus console for several minutes, not noticing the armored cars left by the roadside. The driver occasionally glanced down at her, as if to check if she was still among the living – as she had ceased to ask him annoying questions.

Two

"I told you to get off of that, do you hear me? Shimi, get off!" yelled Anna.

"He's just playing, don't worry about him," said Moishe without taking his eyes off the newspaper. He turned the page and peered through the glasses on the tip of his nose to see the headlines that made him sit up. "Did you read this?" he asked.

"If it's in the paper I read it," she said sharply.

"It's frightening, no?"

"Life is frightening. Shimi on that bus is frightening. The Germans are cowards. They'll all rot in hell. They may try to invade Poland, but they'll never touch Warsaw. They wouldn't last the winter anyway. Too cold here."

"But look at these agreements. The Russians already have given up Poland. They're massing troops. It looks like the British and French are making threats too. We could have war. Who will protect us?"

"Shimshon Avraham Kapalevitz, get off that bus right now!" she yelled again after being ignored most of the morning. Through the kitchen window, ajar just enough to let a breeze in and her cries out, she was able to observe the street in front of her first story flat. The building was on a side street, so traffic was light, but it was still a street, and her son was playing on it. The building across from hers looked almost vacant, as no one ever seemed to exit or enter it. Like hers, it was grey, unpainted for years, except for the doorposts at the front entrance, which looked as if they had been repainted a wheat color to clash with the walls. She didn't know those neighbors, if there were any at all, but looked at the decaying facade day after day as she washed dishes. The only sign of life in the complex across the quiet street was a window sill with red geraniums overflowing their white flower pots. Someone must be watering them, she thought, but whoever it was he rarely showed his face.

She was a small woman with high cheekbones, fair, smooth skin and short curly brown hair parted on the side. Her apron and light flowered dress made her look ten years older than she was. At age 22 she seemed too young to have a four-year-old child, but then again, she seemed too young to have written one of the most controversial manuscripts the Jewish community of Warsaw had ever read. In her blazing attack on the heads of the Jewish community, she claimed that actions by Jewish leaders, particularly the rabbis, have enflamed anti-Semitism in the city and brought Jewish-Gentile relations to an all-time low. The Jewish leadership was enraged and would have happily ejected her from any and all organizations she belonged had she belonged to any. She was a graduate of the Hashomer Hatzair youth movement, the left-wing of Socialist Zionism, and many of her friends had encouraged her to write the article in the local Jewish paper. She had expected the editors to bowdlerize it beyond recognition, but someone had fallen asleep on the job. It was nothing for her to redact a striking proclamation that would have a resounding influence on her community. It was just a matter of choosing the words that would have the most impact. As a socialist, somewhat disillusioned by Soviet socialism, she was now asserting that only through "social justice and economic equality" will the Jewish community be worthy of its place in Polish society. "Without it," she wrote paraphrasing Karl Marx, her favorite Sociologist, "the Jew becomes poorer the more wealth he produces. We are constructing a community built on the exploitation of the working class, our own people, our own family, and the result will be alienation and suffering. Even if we succeed, and we have, hence my trepidation, the Poles will view us, as they have shown outright, as the source of their civil society's woes. Our only recourse is to withdraw ourselves from our secular god, money, and create an emancipated Jewish society, freed from the god of practical need and self-interest. 'Money is the jealous god of Israel before whom no other god may stand.' It is our place in history to lead the world toward true freedom and equality," her scathing began.

"These are the true Jewish values," she had argued, "and our people must be the vanguard bringing about this crucial change." These were not new claims; Hashomer Hatzair and other Zionist youth movements had been making similar declarations for ages. What had particularly infuriated the Jewish leadership was the blame she had laid on the local rabbis, naming them individually. She was proud of her work.

"Leave him be. He can't do any damage," said Moishe

"If you're so concerned about the war, why don't you join me in Palestine?"

"I don't see you going anywhere right now."

"As soon as Shimi is strong enough to travel, we're going."

"How long will that be? He's four years old. Yehuda would never have it."

"Yehuda will do what I ask him to."

"Have you even talked to him about it? Or are you guessing." Moishe had never liked Anna's husband. Too bourgeois for him – not that he was any brilliant Socialist. But Yehuda was a banker, and Moishe could never understand how Anna could tolerate him and his anti-Proletariat job. There was an unspoken contradiction in the house that would surface through cynicism and occasional fits of anger, but for the most part, Yehuda and Anna were a happy couple, primarily due to Yehuda being an uxorious husband with few demands. There was an implicit agreement between them that political topics would not be mentioned; for Yehuda had complained that when they argued, Anna inevitably would turn to her bookshelf and recite one of the many scholars who had influenced her so. Anna had retorted that by removing politics, there was nothing else of consequence to discuss. Her friends had never mentioned their feelings, but Anna was sure that most of them had found her vapid husband quite lackluster and lifeless.

"I know Yehuda. There is a lot you can say about him and his backward politics, but he'll leave with me, you'll see." She moved over to the sink and rinsed the three potatoes she had removed from a small straw bag on the wooden countertop. For a Jewish family in Warsaw, they were considered well off, mainly due to Yehuda's cushy job – heavily criticized privately by Anna's friends, but never to her face. They were afraid of her response. They knew that few in the movement had as sharp a tongue, and no one wanted to get her started. But Anna justified her marriage to a "stuffy old money hog," as Moishe had described him, by saying he would change and she would change him. He was, after all, a kind and generous, loving man, who was not bad in bed, which was a combination hard to find in the Warsaw Jewish community. Moishe's reply to Anna was always the same.

"Serves you right for marrying a capitalist. You know what they say about the difference between men and women? Men marry women and hope they never change. Women marry men and hope they do. They're both always disappointed."

"Is that why you aren't married, Moishe dear?"

"Partly."

"And the other part?" she asked with a smirk on her face.

"I haven't found the right girl."

"You mean the one that will never change and never try to change you."

He did not reply. He looked back down at the paper now spread across the small kitchen table and just shook his head. Long ago he had learned that he could not win an argument with his younger sister. He could not even win a conversation. She was far too skilled an orator to let anyone outtalk her, and he was far too experienced to try.

Moishe was the eldest of five children, the first four being born one after the other with breaks as short as biologically possible, and the last born when he had just turned thirteen, which in Jewish tradition would make him an adult. He, therefore, had often been held responsible for the mistakes of

11

his siblings. His parents, who worked relentlessly but had little to show for it, were fairly progressive, but too busy to raise their own children. When something went wrong in the house lacking adult supervision, the finger was usually pointed at Moishe. This made him hard and controlling, and perhaps one of the most responsible people in Poland. He had virtually raised their youngest brother by himself – with a great deal of help from Anna. Their little brother needed constant care and watching from birth, as he was born with a hole in his heart. He died at the age of six, and for years Moishe blamed himself until finally, after an ongoing discussion that lasted most of their teenage years, Anna convinced him that there was nothing he could have done. Once convinced, when Moishe turned twenty, his guilt turned to resentment and he cut off all contact with his parents until they both died of broken hearts within a month of each other. Moishe and Anna's other two siblings left Poland for Canada when the youngest of them reached eighteen. They had hardly been in touch since their departure, but from what they knew, they had made it to Montreal and were working for a Jewish family making hats. They had tried to convince Moishe and Anna to join them, but Anna's ideology and Moishe's fear of boats kept them in the old country. Out of all Moishe's siblings, the only one who cared for him, appreciated him and although often prodded him to silence, cherished him, was Anna. He could not have treasured and loved her more.

"You know I hate you," he said.

"You're in good company," she replied and started slicing the potatoes.

She enjoyed having him live with them. Yehuda was not too keen on the idea in the beginning – possibly because Moishe intimidated him. He stood a full head taller than Yehuda, who was not a short man, and could easily have crushed him at will. His voice was deep and awe-inspiring, although it was anything but awe that Yehuda felt. Yehuda had often told Anna that he knew how Moishe felt about him, but he never once asked him to move out. Anna was convinced that having Moishe around made him feel safe; someone would always be protecting his precious treasure, and no one could be trusted to guard Anna more than Moishe. Anna, of course, thought it was the other way around.

"Look, he's on the bus again. I sure will be happy when he goes back to school next week. This summer has been too long. I'm lucky he survived it in one piece."

"You worry too much."

"You're the one worrying about the Germans. I'm just worrying that my son will fall off your bus."

"My worry is more logical."

"Logical?" she asked, turning to look back at him. "Just keep reading about the British and the Americans and all their diplomatic efforts. Do you think that kind of energy can end in nothing? Everyone, including Hitler, knows that the Great War is over. And it was a nightmare the likes of which the world had never seen. Why would anyone in their right mind want to start it again?"

"That's just it. We're not talking about people in their right minds. We're talking about the Germans."

"Could you please worry about something realistic for a change? We have nothing the Germans need right now, and if they invade, the British will go wild."

"You are banking on the British? You of all people."

"Don't underestimate the British. They made good...well, boats."

"I can't believe you are siding with the British. Supporting the guys that let your Karl write for so long?"

The Nazis invaded and occupied Poland the next morning. It had only taken one day to prove Anna wrong; although her optimism continued until the day the Germans entered her city. On September 3rd, Anna joined the crowds in the streets, Poles and Jews alike, to celebrate Great Britain's entering the war. The streets were electric with enthusiasm as they all sang Poland's national Anthem. It took only two more days for the Germans to take the city and a total of three weeks to devastate the sectors of Poland the Russians had agreed to let them plunder. Of course, Anna, with all her contacts and streams of information, like much of the Jewish community in Poland, did not know, or did not want to know, the ramifications of the non-aggression pact that Russia and Germany had signed. Known as The Molotov-Ribbentrop Pact, it would keep Russia from interfering in the German invasion of Poland. The Jewish press had played it down, and with an ostrich style mode of thinking, pretended that it was all going to pass soon enough.

Now with Poland securely in the hands of the Nazis, there was finally something that would keep Shimi off Moishe's bus. Some consequence, thought Anna, who would receive unremitting reports of what was happening throughout the country from her multiple lines of communication. Ruthless killers roamed the streets of their homeland, dressed and acting like soldiers; like Roman soldiers in lands where the law was suggested by greed and guilt, perpetrated by the whims of slave fighters; willing to die for a cause they knew little about, for a leader who promised salvation, for a Fatherland they had loved before it sent them to a new hell. She heard of the horrors of the first days of this new war and she knew that nothing would be the same. With the help of her brother's bus route, Anna's kitchen became the unofficial Hashomer Hatzair information headquarters for the Warsaw area. The kitchen was busier than usual, with drinks and food being prepared like never before. Anna received a great deal of assistance from her friends, who would never attend a meeting at her house empty-handed.

The Nazis wasted little time implementing plans that had obviously been created long before the invasion – plans that would bring governments of great countries surrounding the new superpower of the era, Deutschland, to their knees; plans that would destroy families, childhoods and livelihoods. No one would be spared the wrath of this inhumane, albeit human, act against human skin and bones; no one, no blood, not that of the Jews, not that of the Gypsies, nor that of the Homosexuals, the crippled or the Poles; all who stood in the way of the new National Socialist machine would be crushed, painfully and as gruesomely as humanly possible. The news arriving from the countryside only enhanced Anna's feelings of imprudence as she tried to forget her foolish pre-war optimism.

She would never again underestimate the enemy.

By late October 1939, it was already too late to find easy passage to Palestine. Palestine, Eretz Yisrael, a desolate piece of land on the shores of the Eastern Mediterranean, somehow, by some historic error, had become the last salvation for a small part of European Jewry retaining the dream of Zionist existence for forty years. The other Jews, "the smart ones with their senses," Anna's father would say, had their hearts set on the real Promised Land, America – or Canada if the Americans didn't want them. There was always a compromise available to the Jewish People, except maybe in Nazi Germany – and in Nazi Poland, as Anna began to understand. It had not taken long for Anna to recognize that the ossified Jewish community of Poland could no longer be viewed as home, but the rest of the community was ignoring the new reality that was becoming more apparent each passing day. Jewish assets had been frozen and families were limited to withdrawing only 200 zlotys a week – far too little to support a trip to the outskirts of the occupied areas. Anna had spent hours scanning maps of Europe trying to get information about where the Nazis were and what routes were available to reach the Mediterranean Sea. Since the publication of the British White Paper that restricted Jewish immigration to Palestine, the youth movements of Poland could not stop discussing the repercussions of this senseless document. Now, even if they were able to get past the Nazi posts that had sprung up throughout occupied Poland, with their strapping young soldiers with black berets, waving machine guns and laying barbed wire all around, they would never get past the British, another group of strapping young men, only with Red Berets, who had made draconian agreements with the Arabs and had seemed prepared to do whatever was necessary to prevent Jews from reaching Palestine – particularly the Jews running from the Germans. Why? Anna's friend Hanna would ask. No reason, it's just the fate of the Jews to be chased. The wandering Jew never wandered by choice; there was usually someone with a weapon not far behind. Anna was well aware that her fate was now in the hands of a few world leaders who would have to free her country from the hands of the Nazis; then those same leaders would have to allow her passage to her homeland, or else they would have to deal with her. But she also knew that once that happened, there would be important work to be done to ensure that the immigration, illegal or not, continued. Nowhere in Anna's mind was the thought that Jewish life in Poland could soon cease to exist.

Although Hashomer Hatzair was a youth movement, as a graduate of the movement, Anna had a significant leadership role to play in this time of crisis. She had mouthed the dictum that "Through crisis comes creativity," and would tell her fellow Zionists that she saw her job as the creative leader of the movement's communications center. It was nothing for her to juggle the chores of motherhood and the newly emerging leadership role she would play in the movement. Pressing issues needed tending, and she was lucky to have Hanna, a childhood friend with a guileless personality, to take care of her son while she fulfilled her self-assigned duty. The Jewish community had begun organizing their own schools after many had been removed from the public system soon after the Germans entered the city. Hanna had taken it upon herself to take care of Shimi, as he was not able to enter any of the existing educational frameworks available. Hanna was slightly shorter than Anna and presented herself in a manner fitting to a young child. When Anna introduced her to new friends – and in the Kapalevitz home new friends would arrive daily – she would almost expect Hanna to grab her leg and hide behind her like a shy little girl. Hanna had dirty blonde hair and blue-green eyes. It was hard to distinguish the exact color; sometimes they were green and sometimes they were blue – depending on the light and the color of her dress. Unlike Anna, Hanna always wore a dress. She was not overweight by any means, but neither was she slim, her round face looked plump at first, then just Slavic.

Anna's daily routine was unchanged throughout the first few weeks of the war. Considering the amount of activity she alone was generating in the movement, she created an impressive balance between movement leader and mother. Hanna would come early in the morning to fetch Shimi. She lived alone in the same building two floors above and enjoyed taking Shimi up to her place on cold days. When it was sunny, they would walk around the city

15

or visit a park, although it was already cold enough to limit their outdoor playtime. Anna would do simple household chores, read books by Borochov, Gordon and Weisman, stare at maps and hold meetings – scores of meetings. There was not a morning that someone from the movement wouldn't come and discuss plans, rehash ideas or just talk ideology with her. She would fold the clothes, wash the dishes or dust the dressers while discussing Bolshevik failures, the future of the Labor movement or Zionist thinkers. "The less their ability, the more their conceit," she would quote Ahad Ha'am. "He was talking about Hitler." The movement leadership loved visiting Anna. She would welcome them with open arms and never did they feel they were intruding. Most of all, they reveled in her thoughts – and there were many. One young movement leader once said of her, "I can't figure out how so many words can come out of such a small body." She loved to talk, and they loved to listen. Her day would press on and soon the house would fill with normal, family matters. Moishe would return and park the bus in front of the house; Hanna would bring Shimi in for a bath and some bread and butter; and finally, late in the evening, Yehuda would arrive exhausted and grumpy. It was good for Anna not to have him around all day. She needed her time away from him. She never let herself ask questions about her decision to tie her life with him. By the time she realized that they had little in common, it was too late. They were very young when they married, and Anna got pregnant as soon as they intimacy became a part of their relationship. That had sealed her fate. But she always enjoyed the financial security he provided. She could organize the overthrow of the government, but when it came to money, she knew nothing; he was the one who handled their finances. And then there was Shimi. Her incompatibility with Yehuda was a small price to pay to have a father for her child. Nonetheless, she loved being married to a man married to his work. Polygamy worked for her.

So there was nothing to prepare Anna for Yehuda's early return home one winter day. The inclement weather had brought hard snow upon the city all week, and the roads were covered with mounds of powder and ice. For Yehuda, it was a short trip to the bank, but in weather like this, he usually had to walk and would arrive frozen and gasping. In the summer, he would never arrive home before sundown, which in the long days of the Warsaw summer could be quite late. In the winter, he would arrive hours after the light had left the streets and cold night winds would blast through the slits in the roof. It was quite surprising for Anna to see him walk in the house at one o'clock on a Monday afternoon.

"What are you doing here?" she asked, mistaking his motionless demeanor for that of an iced face – the result of the walk in the elements.

"I was fired," he said.

"Fired? But you're a senior employee. You fire people."

"The bank was threatened by the authorities – the Nazis. If they don't fire all the Jews they'll close the bank."

Anna stood facing her frozen husband and felt somewhat removed from the moment. There was something pathetic about him standing there in his seven layers of garb, looking dejected and dismal, red cheeks and all. His hands fiddled with his gloves as he tried to remove them. She knew that he would not be able to overcome this blow, and she knew that she was now the head of the household, whatever that meant. In addition to the fate of the Jewish community of Warsaw, she would now have to take full responsibility for her family's welfare.

"Our lives are over here," she said. "We have to prepare to leave."

"We can't leave," he said. "There's no safe way out of here. You've heard what's happening. They're shooting people all over the place."

"We'll leave, and we'll get to Palestine safely. The movement has developed an underground that can get us out to the forests and from there to Soviet-occupied Poland. Things are happening. We now need to get more information. If we plan right, we'll make it. We have to. There is no more life here. Poland is dead to us."

Her stare was blank as she said those words that sent additional chills down his spine. It had only been a few months since the Germans had destroyed the freedom Poland had enjoyed. Polish Jewry, the largest in the world, had tasted the last of its autonomy. They had been forced to wear Stars of David, been stripped of all electronic devices, including radios, and now kicked out of their jobs.

The eastern areas of Poland that had been annexed to the Soviet Union were the last hope. The Soviets were bad, but the Germans were worse. At least from there, they could make their way to the Mediterranean and Palestine. She was sure of it. She sensed what was to become of her city, and she had to leave it before it was too late. The thought excited her. She never expected to feel invigoration from desertion, but that was not how she saw the departure of her city and country. No, it was not desertion, it was Aliya, accent, immigration to Eretz Yisrael, and it would be their rebirth as a free people in their homeland, the Land of Israel, Jerusalem. She would never underestimate the enemy again.

Anna moved into mission mode. First, she brought together the representatives of the Zionist youth movements, Hashomer Hatzair, Dror, Akiva, Halutz, and Gordonia. This was not the official leadership since it was feared that movement leaders had already been tagged and were being watched by the Nazis. Most were acquaintances of Anna's and had either worked with her on joint projects in the past or had just heard of her skills and wanted to do something. They all valued her efforts and respected her brilliance and were sure she would not lead them astray. They discussed plans for a mass evacuation from the city as soon as the snows ceased. They all figured that attempting to escape to the forests before the spring was suicide – particularly for those with small children. It was clear that the elderly would not be able to make the journey, and some even had doubts about the children. Smaller committees were formed and the escape date was symbolically set for May 1, May Day.

"Do you think we can survive out there?" asked Yehuda one morning while Anna was washing a few dishes that had accumulated from the evening before. Several youth leaders had been over for a late afternoon chat, deciding bravely to ignore the five o'clock curfew and risk their lives. But they knew the streets better than the Germans and had little fear of getting caught.

"I know we can," she said. "We have no choice. Every day there's a new decree against us. We can't have radios, own telephones, go to theaters or go to the post office. I can't even work as a prostitute for god's sake. Does that mean that the Poles can? Look, there is a strong network of support out there. Once we get out of the city, which actually isn't that hard, we'll be fine. We just have to stick to small groups and stay off the roads. Are you worried?"

"Of course I am. Do you think the idea of leaving my home, taking my child, wandering the wilderness for god knows how long, doesn't worry me? Of course, it does. Do I look like Moses to you?"

He absolutely did not, she thought. There was little leadership quality in Yehuda, let alone leadership quality of biblical proportions. She smiled at the thought of Yehuda trying to lead the Israelites out of Egypt. Had it been Yehuda out there in the Sinai desert, they would have turned back as soon as they reached the Red Sea. That parting of water would have been too much of a chore for him, and if any other miracles were needed he would have had to make sure the appropriate forms were filled out in triplicate.

"Don't worry," said Anna still smirking. "We have some great people waiting for us out there."

"But you have heard that even in the east under the Soviets the kibbutzim are closing down. And even if we do get to them, you've heard the Polish-Soviet border has been closed." The kibbutzim were small movement camps used to prepare Zionist youth movement members for the transition to life in Palestine. In the camps, they would learn agricultural skills, Hebrew, and Jewish history.

"Not all of the kibbutzim are closed; many have just changed their activities. There is still a strong support group out there and we'll reach them. As for the border, if the Soviet border is closed, the Romanian border will be open, you can be sure of that. In any case, Romania is closer to Eretz Yisrael."

Anna's confidence provided solace to everyone around her. Her optimism was contagious, and throughout the movement young men and women were repeating her statements as if they were from the mouth of God himself, or herself, in Anna's case.

"It is our fate to be free in our land," she would tell them, "and the Germans are just another catalyst to bring us closer. They are pushing us out of old Europe to our new homeland."

Wherever one went within the Jewish community, her statements were showcased like trophies of Jewish pride and promise. Most of the people uttering her philosophies had no idea from whose radiant mind they had been conceived, but that mattered little when her words brought so much light and strength to the youth of Warsaw, as life became gloomier and despair seemed the only sane option available. Polish winters were hell in a normal year, but when rations were light, and even lighter for the Jews, winter was unbearable, which made Anna's bright outlook all the more spectacular. As each day of struggle intensified, Anna became stronger. Even her physical appearance began to change. As winter progressed, she seemed to harden like the lakes, and her pale skin tone acquired a glow that made people think she had been sunbathing, an incredible feat in a land with no sun.

February 9, 1940

On a dark February morning, while the flat was empty and Anna was completing a morning routine that included nothing to be proud of, she received a visit from a young man who had just arrived in Warsaw from the East. He was thin and pale, with Arian features, but his Star of David armband and deep-set, starving eyes removed any fear that he was a spy. He appeared to be in his thirties, but it quickly became clear to Anna that he was no more than twenty. He was probably very handsome, she thought, before he had let the occupation curdle his face and soil his clothes. He introduced himself as Tuvia and had brought word from the eastern kibbutzim of Hashomer Hatzair. Hesitantly, he entered the house, looking around as if he was awaiting an ambush, but once seated on the flowered sofa in the main room, he wasted no time getting right to the point.

"The Russians are worse than the Germans," he said to her, nervously fiddling with the ends of his sleeves.

"No one is worse than the Germans," she replied. "You have just arrived. Soon you'll understand."

"They have blocked all exits from Poland and are dismantling our kibbutzim. We hear that you are planning a mass escape of movement people and their families. Russia is no option."

"I know that. We'll head for Romania."

"I have just returned from there. I spent several nights in jail after failing to cross the border. I was lucky. My friend Miriam did not make it. She was taken by the Russians. I don't know where she is now…" he paused and looked up to the ceiling trying to use gravity to prevent the tears from rolling out of his eyes. "Who knows what they did to her. As they pulled her away from me, she was screaming. They threw her into a truck with a few Russian soldiers. I heard the screaming for a few more minutes and then it just stopped."

"I'm sorry," she said.

"The Romanian border is not easy," he said, trying hard to regain his composure. "I was sent to suggest to you to look into the Lithuanian option."

"Lithuania? That's the wrong direction."

"If there is no way out of Poland to the south, you'll have to go north. In Vilna, we have some people who may be able to get you to the Scandinavian countries."

"Listen, I have one goal and one goal only, and that is to get these people to Eretz Yisrael. You, as a movement person, must understand that. There are more and more Jews returning to Warsaw each day and we need a viable plan to get them out of here. There is no future for us in Warsaw. What can you tell me about the Romanian border?"

Tuvia sat still for a moment and looked down at his knees. His pants looked as if they had not been washed in weeks and his shirt bore stains from his last several meals, which most likely consisted of little. He wore a black beret that he did not remove in the house, giving Anna a sense that he had not intended to stay long. "Anna, you are a smart woman. You know what is happening here. You also know the dangers of trying to leave. In Lvov they have begun organizing an underground to help us get through this period…"

"This period? This is not a period, it is permanent. Even if someone, God knows who, could do something to remove the Germans, there is nothing left for us to build here. It will happen again. Herzl was right. We have no choice but to get as many Jews out of here as possible. I just don't understand why the Jews of Vilna are waiting around."

"Do you know what winter is like in Vilna this year?"

"Do you know what winter is like in Warsaw? Look at me, I am disappearing. The rations are so small that even if I combined my entire family's rations I could not feed my son properly. The spring is coming, and we all have to start packing."

"I wish it was that easy," he said in a tone of despair that caught Anna off guard. "We need to reorganize and be prepared for the worst."

Anna looked directly at Tuvia as if he was the occupying enemy. "If there is anything worse than this, then I prefer to die."

"No you don't," he said quietly. "Because no one has given more life to the Jews of Warsaw than you."

Her eyes turned downward, almost embarrassed by her previous statement. No, she did not want to die, and she knew very well that she could endure a great deal more than she had had to bear the past few months. She had known for a long time that it would just continue to get worse and had no illusions about the Germans and no expectations about the allies; they were impotent and hopeless, and the Jews of Warsaw had only themselves to look toward for salvation. Statements like that were not in her nature, and she began to think that this whole ordeal was starting to get to her. She knew her weaknesses and knew that if she let herself imagine any form of desolation or dejection, any hint of hopelessness, then she was finished. Her optimism was her only weapon.

"You are right," she said. "Would you like to drink something?" Tuvia removed his beret.

Throughout the rest of the morning, the two talked of the evolving underground in the east. Anna asked question after question about the routes out of Poland, the movement activities in Lvov, Lublin, Vilna, and Bialystok, and Tuvia did his best to answer all of them. He had gathered more information in three months of travels than Anna imagined possible. Few Jews had been able to visit all three borders, and the details he provided seemed vital to Anna's plans. What had troubled Anna more than anything else was why he had come to Warsaw at all. She understood the visits to the borders; she could see why stops in Vilna and Lublin were necessary, but why come this far west when the dangers were so great. It seemed foolish to voluntarily enter a city that was so obviously doomed.

Tuvia was quick to tell her that the concern of the rest of the Jewish community in Poland over the plight of the Jews of Warsaw was serious enough for them to send emissaries just to provide encouragement and improve their mood. Many had already come and more were on the way. Besides, they were establishing the foundation for infrastructure within

German-occupied Poland, and only frequent visits to the center of Jewish life in Poland could complete that base.

"This is our community," he said proudly, straightening his chest as he spoke, "and this is our movement. We are coming back here to be a part of the rebuilding of Jewish existence in Warsaw. Many of the movement's counselors have kids here who look up to them. The movement leaders who have left are beginning to feel they have abandoned their children. They feel responsible for the future of the movement. That's why they have to come back to German-occupied Warsaw."

That Anna understood. Well, most of that. She was not so sure that there was anything to rebuild. Jewish existence in Warsaw was not to be resurrected – not now, and not ever.

"Did you mean that thing about rebuilding Jewish existence in Warsaw?"

Tuvia's eyes said everything to her. He did not need to speak; neither of them believed there was much of a future, and both felt that it was better for all that the future for Jewish existence be elsewhere.

The following week, Tuvia returned to Anna to tell her that he was leaving Warsaw to pass on some vital information about the city's organization to the movement council in Pinsk. His mission had been to transfer information from the east to Warsaw and return with a report.

"We are both so young," she said. "How did we get here?"

It was a strange question, but Tuvia understood it better than she could have ever known.

Tuvia removed his cap and wiped his brow with the back of his hand. "I heard that you once said that out of crisis comes creativity. Not all people have the strength to be creative. We are young…way too young for the tasks that have been bestowed upon us. Did you know that the average age of leadership of the Vilna underground is 21? There is a reason for that. We are here because we have been trained to be here. That is the essence of the movement."

"That's what I thought," she said. "I just wanted to hear you say it. When will you return?"

"In the spring. Even with all my motivation, any more winter traveling may kill me." As he headed for the front door, he removed his armband and stuck it in his pocket. "Time to become Polish," he said.

"Remember us Jews," she said sarcastically.

As he stood in the doorway he looked back at Anna. "You have inspired me," he said to her with a smile she had not seen in occupied Poland for months.

"And you have inspired me," she replied. "We will meet soon on the shores of the Kinneret."

But Tuvia's face expressed doubt that that would ever happen. He tipped his beret and left Anna.

As the winter cold lifted and the streets turned soggy with brown melting snow, Anna's preparations to leave Warsaw were moving ahead steadily. Her colleagues in the movement had received news of significant successes crossing the Romanian border, and although things could not have been harder for the Jews of Warsaw, her optimism was still a driving force for the youth of the city. However, her family was far from ready for the journey that lay ahead. Yehuda had found work in a Jewish bakery in their neighborhood but was more dejected each passing day. As much as she fought the new situation that had plagued her community, she also fought his depression. He would eat little, as there was little to eat, and other than leave to work in the morning and return at night, he had no activity whatsoever. He had few friends as it was, but since losing his job at the bank, he only socialized when Anna forced him to. Her movement friends had little in common with the ex-banker-become-baker and he felt belittled by them. They all seemed to ridicule him with their expressions, although no one ever said a word to his face. For the most part, the youth that frequented their home to be close to Anna ignored Yehuda when he was among them. He knew how important it was for Anna that he made an effort, but everyone could readily see that he had little energy to do so. At night he would close himself off in his room and try to fall asleep among the chatter from the adjacent room. When he did find the extra energy to leave the bedroom after work, he would spend it caring for Shimi who went through the winter with cold after cold. Anna, on the other hand, was indomitable.

There was an advantage to knowing that they would be leaving the city for good; Anna was able to increase the family's feeble income by slowly selling off all of their belongings. By her calculations, by May first, they would have sold almost everything they owned and left Warsaw empty-handed. Anna viewed it as a fresh start, Yehuda as a catastrophe.

Anna's only real concern was the health of her son. Shimi's colds turned to fever in April 1940. Anna was convinced that it was simply a nutritional deficiency that could be cured by finding the right produce – goods that were hardly available to the gentile community, let alone the Jews. In one of her ad hoc meetings with the movement members, she expressed her wishes to find onions, garlic and certain spices for Shimi. The movement took on the task as if it was a mission from the Zionist Congress. Plans and ideas and contacts' names were thrown about the room, and Anna knew that they could pull off the task. The group's commitment to Anna was stronger than any other tie they had, and Anna knew it. She would never have taken advantage of their dedication for her own good, but for Shimi, nothing was too much to ask of her friends. Within the week they had found a variety of foods that no one in Warsaw had seen for months. The lessons learned by the movement smuggling these commodities into the city would prove valuable once the Jews of Poland were herded into the walls of the ghettos. But for now, they were simply helping a child recover from malnutrition.

Anna slowly integrated the food, particularly vegetables, into Shimi's measly diet. However, this was not the miracle cure that she had hoped for; Shimi remained weak and limp. Finally, she had no choice but to call in a doctor. Several Jewish doctors were making the rounds at the time. So many of the Jews of Warsaw were suffering from malnutrition; they had little supplies to assist them, but it was always encouraging to hear that a doctor says it's not fatal – even when it so often was.

"He's had fever on and off for weeks now," she said to the doctor who himself looked sick from overwork. "I've tried everything."

"Yes," he said while examining Shimi's fingernails and testing his reflexes. He pierced his lips and curled down the ends of his mouth.

"What?"

"There are many infectious diseases that we are seeing here. He has one of them. Keep him cool and keep him hydrated."

"That's it?"

"I'm sorry, but that's all I can do right now."

Anna took Shimi's hand. It was so emaciated now. With all the efforts Anna was making to keep Shimi strong, for months he was not able to keep down the little food he was ingesting. She could clearly see him thinning and that was the most difficult part of this whole ordeal. She could live without many of the comforts she had been used to. She could tolerate the curfew and the fear the Nazis were thrusting on them. She could bear the hunger pains she had endured all winter, but seeing her son ill and withering away was too much for her. While she was trying to remain upbeat with her friends and family, inside she was dying as each day Shimi remained moribund with fever and lost so much of his vitality.

"Doctor, is he going to get through this?" She did not want to ask that question, but it just slipped out. It was the kind of question that produced only an irrelevant answer – at least for Anna. She knew what was going on around her; so many of the children of Warsaw were suffering similar fates – so many of the adults as well. She had witnessed more death that winter than in her entire life, and she knew well enough that Shimi was far from safe. However, she, as always, was optimistic and was worried more about traveling with a sick child than anything else. So she asked the question quite confident the answer would be satisfying enough.

"I have seen this far too often to give a sure answer," he said, "but Shimi is a strong boy and is receiving excellent care. As I said, you need to keep him warm, give him lots of water, and let me know if it gets worse."

Anna wanted to ask the doctor about traveling with the boy but was not sure she could trust his discretion. Too many professionals had been discovered collaborating with the Nazis, and no one could be trusted with information like that. So she phrased her question differently.

"When will he be able to play outside?"

"I don't know. If he starts showing signs of improvement and you manage to get him the right nutrients, which is terribly difficult to do here, he could be up and about in a few weeks. But I would not rush it. He is still very weak, and I would not let him run around or stay on his feet more than a few hours a day until he regains his full strength. Even if he improves, with the way things are going here, he could easily have a relapse at any time, and the next one may even be worse."

She thanked the doctor and for the first time began to understand the gravity of her situation. There would be little chance for them to be able to join the departing group on May 1. She was hesitant to ask her friends to postpone the exodus as she was sure that they would accommodate her wishes. She understood clearly that the departure had to be in May. The decrees were getting worse and it was only a matter of time until the Germans had full control of the roads.

Shimi's condition deteriorated over the following weeks; neither the doctor nor Anna had a solution. Anna had tried to reach a specialist, but no non-Jews were willing to make the visit. She had asked her friends in the movement to see if they could get someone to help, but as hard as they tried, nothing could be done. By mid-April, Anna had moved Shimi to the sofa in the center of the main room. The room had been designated the meeting area for her friends in the movement, and now with Shimi taking up most of the seating, the kitchen became the main venue for the meetings – which had the result of making them much shorter. There was a feeling of discomfort in the house. Slowly her friends stopped coming, some stating the truth that they were afraid of catching whatever it was the Shimi had, others cited reasons ranging from increased work searching for lost members to difficulty traveling the distance to her home.

Rumors were starting that the Germans were planning to move all the Jews of Warsaw into a small area of the city, but no one believed that it was logistically feasible. Anna was one of the few who did believe.

"I swore," she said to Hanna one afternoon, "that I would assume the

25

worst when it came to the Germans. Putting us in a giant cage will be the least of our worries. We can survive that. But I am afraid that their next step will be to bomb the entire area."

"Don't be crazy," said Hanna. "The Germans want us gone, but they wouldn't do something as dreadful as that."

"You will learn to understand what we are up against."

Anna was normally gentle with Hanna. Throughout the winter Hanna had maintained her innocence and rarely seemed concerned about the big picture. She continued humming as she did chores or tended to Shimi, and if by looking at her one was to judge the state of affairs, they would seem quite rosy. There was a comfort to being around her. With Shimi in the state he was, Anna's chronic optimism was receding and she would have been the first to admit that the winter had taken its toll on all of them.

But although the winter was coming to a close, the toll was still outstanding, and on April 30, 1940, the ultimate toll would be paid.

"Anna! Anna!" yelled Hanna from the Shimi's side on the sofa. All morning his fever had been spiking, and Hanna was wiping him down with a wet towel. "Keep him cool," she whispered to herself as he breathed irregularly, almost choking as he tried to drag air into his damaged lungs. His face was as white as the sheet that covered him, and his hair was matted from weeks of lying on the couch. Hanna could no longer smell the odors coming from the sullen den, once-bustling with guests and now as vacant as Shimi's eyes.

Anna came running in from the kitchen where she had been preparing a drink for him in hopes that something would remain in his shriveling stomach.

"Hanna, what is it?" Anna's eyes were wide as she bent over her son. "Shimi. Slowly dear. Breathe slowly. I'm here." She placed an arm around his back and lifted him upright. He felt as light as when he was born. There was little left of her young angel. He wheezed lightly as he tried to push and pull the air past his shriveled lips. His cheekbones were clearly visible as Anna brushed the left one with the back of her hand.

Looking down at Shimi, she could no longer see the boy climbing on the bus. She wondered how she could have ever been angry at him for just wanting to play. She closed her eyes and imagined that she was staring out the window and watching him grab hold of the side mirror and lift himself onto the hood of the dirty bus. Then she recalled the last time he had spoken. It had been over ten days since Shimi had uttered a single word, and the last phrase to leave his lips had been, "buses are good." Moments later he fell asleep, and by the next morning, his breathing had become too heavy for words.

"What should I get him," asked Hanna. She was shaking and fiddling with the damp towel.

"There is nothing more to get him," Anna said in a manner that turned Hanna's face white. Anna continued brushing his face with her hand, and she held him in her lap, swaying slightly as if she was humming a lullaby. But no sounds left her trembling lower lip.

It was then that the small spurts of air entering and exiting his frail shell ceased altogether. There was silence, except for Hanna's quiet sobbing. Anna was holding a lifeless child. He had stopped gagging, and she knew that he was gone. She held him tight for the last time. His arms were limp as if they were being pulled down to the floor by an imaginary weight. Anna thought she could feel the warmth leaving his body, but she knew that it was the warmth in her life that had left. So often over the past months, she had heard of parents losing their children, but she never could imagine the emptiness that overtook them. The recalcitrant woman who had defied her community leaders, her invaders and her own husband, could not beat the wills of nature. As she cried, Hanna hugged her.

Time was incalculable for Anna for the next few minutes, or perhaps hours. It was a loud bang at the door that finally woke her from her daze.

Tears streaming down her face, Hanna went to see what it was. As she opened the door, there stood one of the movement leaders holding a note in his hand.

"It is starting," he said without questioning the tears on Hanna's cheeks. "They have closed the Jewish area of Lodz, built a wall and everything. We are next."

Hanna stepped out of the doorway and shut the door behind her. Holding back more tears she explained, "Shimi died. He just died. It's terrible. Could you… could you come back tomorrow?"

"We will be gone tomorrow. You know that. We came to ask Anna to come with us. We didn't know about Shimi. I'm so sorry."

"I'll tell her, but I don't think she is ready to leave."

"She must leave. The Germans have already given notice that the Jews of Warsaw must live in restricted areas. If she doesn't leave now she will never leave."

Hanna returned to the living room and found Anna still hugging Shimi as she had before. "Let me call someone to help with the arrangements," she said whimpering like a distant siren."

"The arrangements," Anna whispered. "These were not the

arrangements that I thought I would be handling on May 1. Oh god!"

Hanna moved over to hold Anna who was still holding her son. She took Anna's arms and helped her place Shimi back down on the sofa. Anna sat up and looked around the room. So much had been sold over the past months that the vacant look seemed almost oppressive now. It appeared as if they were moving or had just moved in. The large pieces of furniture, like the 18th-century dresser she had inherited from her great aunt, were still there. It was made of oak assembled from Georgian timber with a large pot board shelf, open shelved racks with dentil cornice and perfectly crafted drawers on top. She looked at it and thought that it would likely make good firewood next winter. The mahogany dinner table had served them well, she thought. It too would burn nicely when the Germans force them to find their own heating supply.

"Anna. That was Mordechai at the door. He said they have closed the Jewish section in Lodz and that we were next. He wanted you to go with him."

Anna turned her head sharply as if there was some news in Hanna's statement. She had not thought about the departure for a long time. It had been impractical while Shimi was sick. She said nothing, just nodded.

"They are leaving tomorrow."

"I know."

"We can't go," she pleaded.

"I know."

"Anna, you have to tell Yehuda." She began crying again.

Anna's tear marked face was blank now. She looked in a daze. It was as if only her eyes had the strength to cry. The rest of her face was somewhere else entirely.

"I know."

There had been no way to contact Yehuda during the day, and both girls dreaded his return. Hanna stayed with Anna for the duration of the day, not only to lend support to the stricken mother but to avoid having to be alone herself. Outwardly, she had taken Shimi's death harder than Anna, but inside, Anna was consumed by an emptiness that only a grieving mother can understand. By the time Yehuda had arrived, Shimi's body had been removed from the house. As soon as Yehuda opened the door and looked into the empty living room he fell to the floor, holding his head. He said nothing as he cried on the rug like Shimi often did when he could not get what he wanted.

Three

"Shimshon Junction," yelled the driver to the passengers of his bus.

"Shimi?" said the old lady.

The bus pulled into a small dirt parking lot just off the two-lane road that had taken them down from Jerusalem. The lot was empty, except for the kiosk made out of the shells of two old shipping crates. The face of the kiosk had an open window with a makeshift shelf for the patrons to buy drinks, snacks, or cigarettes.

"I said we are at Shimshon Junction."

"My son's name was Shimshon," she said. "He didn't make it through the war."

There was a gasp from the seat behind the driver. She had spoken louder than she had intended and although her voice was as frail as her body looked, once the driver turned off the engine it was quiet enough for the front of the bus to hear.

"I'm sorry," said the driver.

"It was long ago. So much was lost back then."

"I know. I too lost my family," said the driver."

"But you're so young."

"Excuse me," said one of the passengers. "How long will we be stopping here?"

"Ten minutes," answered the driver. "Ten minutes people!"

He opened the back door of the bus and the passengers all filled out. The woman was still seated in the stairwell in the front of the bus, blocking the passage out, so most of them took the long route through the back door.

"You should get something to eat as well," he said to the lady as he opened the front door.

"Okay. I would like a drink." She picked herself off the floor as a small number of the passengers near the front of the bus waited for her to let them by.

She stepped off the black stairwell onto the dirt parking lot and sighed. "Oh, the dust here. When will they pave these places?" she asked no one in particular. Before she began walking toward the lone building set before her, she stopped, took a deep breath and looked around. The parking lot had two other cars, two buses and a truck, all parked next to each other. Aside from a few newly planted pine trees off in the hills and several eucalyptus trees that lined the edge of the lot along the highway, everything else was tan colored. Even the trees had a film of yellowish-brown dust covering the leaves closer to the ground; and the kiosk, like a huge cardboard

29

box set in the center of the dirt lot, was painted ochre in an apparent attempt to blend into its surroundings.

After taking a moment to assess her milieu, Anna took a deep breath, momentarily enjoying a faint scent of lavender coming from somewhere. She quickly realized that it must have been the perfume of one of the passengers from the back of the bus passing her on their way to the kiosk. Most of those who had left the cool air of the bus had lit up cigarettes and were utilizing the shade provided by a small awning protruding from the side of the block building.

Around the side of the kiosk was the entrance to a tiny eatery with three small round tables and a four-stool bar table. Behind the bar table were shelves of candy, bags of snacks and a half-sized refrigerator with drinks — mostly the local soft drink, Kinley. The falafel stand supplied a minimal amount of salads, pickled cauliflower and cabbage, tahina sauce and a chopped tomato and cucumber salad.

The lady waddled into the restaurant with the rest of the patrons and stood with the crowd of people waiting to order. Cigarette smoke and the smell of burned potatoes filled the confined quarters. There was no line, just a mass of about fifteen bodies pushing forward toward the counter where a young girl with dark brown eyes and hair in a ponytail tried her best to serve the impatient crowd. She must have been used to those tense ten-minute rushes when the buses traveling to and from Jerusalem stopped and passengers would rush the poor girl, all worried that they would not have time to grab that needed bite before the bus pulled out again. The girl looked flustered but professional. She had smooth olive skin and wore a flowered apron over a khaki shirt and blue jeans. Occasionally, she would attempt a smile, but it never remained on her face for more than a few seconds. After ordering, the passengers would scuttle away from the counter, as if someone was trying to snatch their newly acquired stash; they would struggle to break apart the mass of contracting bodies filling the void they had left and slip out back to their rides. As one large, sweaty man with a tight t-shirt and short black hair pushed his way back through the crowd, he unintentionally whacked Anna in the face with his elbow. He continued away from the mass of people waiting to order as if nothing happened. But he didn't get far, as he was soon to receive Anna's wrath.

"You! Stop right there," she said shouting in a way that silenced the raucous crowd. Her cheek seemed to have reddened where it had made contact with the brute's arm. "Not even an excuse me. Not even an, are you alright. I am just dirt like the dirt on the floor? You should be ashamed, and if you are not, I am ashamed to be part of the same people as you. Shame on you! Now come back here right now and apologize to everyone here that you mangled on your way out! Now!"

The man stood in the doorway holding a falafel in one hand and a soft drink in the other, staring back at the old woman in awe. He had most likely done that same maneuver out of crowds thousands of times and had never been called on it. Now, in front of the bus's entire passenger corps, with which he would have to continue to ride to Tel Aviv for the next hour, he was confronted by a petite tiger of an aging woman who seemed to be more powerful than he. His jaw dropped as if he had something to say, but nothing came out.

"Come on. We are all waiting."

He took a step in the direction of the lady and stopped. Then he continued toward her again, this time more forcefully. It seemed the insult had finally sunk in and it looked as if he was ready to save face. He walked right up to the lady, and some of the others in line backed away as if a brawl was about to break out. Her head reached the center of his chest, and if they were to bout, it would be a very short fight. The man glared down at her.

"I'm very sorry," he said gently. "No harm intended." He turned and left the room.

Anna smiled and said, "Better. Now, could we get a real line here?" But that was too much to ask. Within seconds the room returned to its previous state of organized chaos and people waiting to get their food continued pushing and cursing.

However, there was one gesture of goodwill within the mass that formed in the kiosk, and it was completely out of character for a mob of that sort. One young man, after seeing her valor, helped push Anna to the front of the blob of people and no one argued. They all seemed a bit terrified of her as it was – not risking upon themselves the same embarrassing fate of the large man. As Anna emerged from the crowd holding an orange Kinley soft drink, she was met by the driver.

"Nice work," he said to her. "He'll never do that again. Is your face okay?"

"Oh yes, I've endured much worse. He was nothing, but it's hard to educate people all the time.

"By the way, my name is Anna."

Four

November 4, 1940

"Anna!" Yehuda pulled the wagon into place at the bottom of the stairway in front of the door of the house. "We're here!"

Anna looked out the window and saw her brother and husband parking the wagon that was to assist them in dragging their few remaining belongings to their new quarters in the Jewish quadrant. There was so little to take now. They had been selling property for months to survive. It made the move a bit easier, but there was still a deep fear of the unknown. She was forced to sell items she had grown up with, some she had cherished but had known for a long time that she would not be able to take with her when she made her move to her new home. Anna thought that perhaps somehow there would be an opportunity here, a chance for them to rise out of these ashes and become stronger, more prepared for the journey to Palestine that would ensue at the end of the war. Whatever the outcome, she now saw happening what she had known was coming for years – what Herzl had warned about, what her movement had preached – that there was no future for European Jewry without enduring continued anti-Semitism and persecution. The Zionists were being proven correct; although not even in their worst nightmares did they imagine the judgments that were thrust upon them now.

Over the summer the decrees had continued. All Jewish-owned printing shops were closed and Jews were not allowed to mail letters abroad. Jews were no longer allowed to enter parks, municipal areas and specified streets in the center of Warsaw. Jews could not sit on public benches, and Jewish peddlers and merchants could not purchase goods in neighboring villages, or own bakeries, coaches or German books. Pilsudski Square was renamed Hitler Square and was entirely off-limits to Jews. Jewish doctors could not treat Polish patients and Polish doctors could not treat Jewish patients. Polish maids could not work in Jewish homes, and Jews were required to step off the sidewalk upon seeing a German. It was so much worse than what Anna had anticipated that relocating to the newly formed Jewish residential quadrant could only mean that things would still get worse.

The movement underground had kept Anna informed of the plight of Jews sealed off in ghettos in Lodz and other Polish cities. Smaller ghettos were established in villages outside Warsaw, and there were attempts to keep the lines of communication open between them and the capital. Throughout the summer, movement members acting as runners throughout the country had been transferring information between the Jewish communities in an attempt to find ways of either smuggling food or medical supplies into the closed areas, or if possible, planning mass escapes to the forests. The runners, particularly young girls since the boys had surefire ways of being identified as Jews, risked their lives for their communities.

The situation in all of the ghettos was dire. Reports of over-crowdedness, illness and mass starvation consistently reached the ears of the Warsaw leadership, and they knew that it was only a matter of time before they befell the same horrific fate. One-third of the population of Warsaw was to be squeezed into three percent of the city's area. Ten to twelve people per room would still leave thousands on the streets. Anna was determined to help find a solution, at least until the Allies could push the German's back and free Poland. Despite the news from the front of continuous German successes, Anna always believed that the Germans would eventually fall.

She had written a letter to the movement leadership in Krakow that was meant to help them organize for the trying period that lay ahead.

> *We have a grim challenge ahead of us like none other we have faced in our miserable history as a people in Europe – a history that must come to an end by choice – our choice to create a new Jew, free and proud. But this state of harsh malevolence and wicked malice is only temporary. Mind my words comrades, no evil as fervent as the Nazi's can last for long. We must organize our survival for no more than three years, for at which time we will be emancipated and will build our home in Eretz Yisrael. I know that in this current nightmare it is difficult to imagine a time when flowers will blossom in the spring and our people will be blessed with the fruit and spices of a new life. I urge you all to seize this as an opportunity to strengthen ourselves for the fights ahead in establishing our rightful place among the nations of the world.*

The letter was seen by many as a prophetic platform that would provide additional hope to a dying people. Unfortunately, only the youth of the Hashomer Hatzair movement ever had the pleasure of reading her sanguine writings. It was not Anna's optimism that took the movement leadership by surprise; although the suffering was great, they had come to appreciate Anna's demeanor during a crisis. No, what had shocked all of them was that the letter was written only a few short weeks after she had lost her son. They all dismissed this behavior as a defense mechanism and her only way to cope. The truth was that Anna did not collapse as many had predicted after Shimi's death. She took a week to mourn and then one day got out of bed and told Hanna that she was done grieving and had work to do. Soon she was busy preparing herself, her remaining family, which now consisted of her husband, brother and Hanna, and her community, for what was to be a horrendous period of trials beyond their worst imaginations. Without Anna's continuous prompting, many more of the movement members may have given up hope. Some had suggested that Anna was responsible for saving lives by brainwashing them into believing in a false messiah. She had responded that since there was no such thing as a messiah, the messiah was no threat to her, and belief in a false one was better than belief in death.

However, had it not been for the movement's support and their enduring plans for saving the Jewish People, she too, like so many around her, may not have had the needed outlet and let despair overcome her. It was terrifying for her to see so many having nothing to work for, no reason to get up in the morning and no light of salvation staring at them at night. Two days before leaving their home and moving into what would be known as the Warsaw Ghetto, Anna had a meeting with a few of her movement comrades.

"Do you believe in God?" asked Lifshe, one of the girls who had proven to Anna that strength had no connection to size. Lifshe was three years younger than Anna and showed promise of being a great movement leader. She was smart, energetic when she was eating, and understood her place in bringing about change to the world.

"I think the events of the past year have put an end to that discussion, don't you? Whether there is or isn't a god, I certainly don't believe in him. What kind of god would let this happen? We created God to help us through the difficulties of life in this wretched world. If there was a god that would put people through what we have been put through, the suffering and anguish that we endure here, then I want nothing to do with him."

"But that doesn't mean that God didn't create the world and then just left us alone."

"So, what if there was once a god? There was once a Roman Empire. It's no longer relevant to my life now, except as historical trivia. God as an icon is as relevant as knowing that in America there is a new movie that changes to color in the middle. It doesn't help me. It's over there. Here the movies, which we can't see anyway, are still just colorless, like so much of the world around us. God is a concept of the past. It's over there, we're here."

"That's depressing," said the girl. It was one of the first times that anyone had told Anna that something she believed was depressing.

Anna smiled and looked Lifshe directly in the eye. Lifshe shifted in her chair and prepared for Anna's decree. "There is nothing whatsoever depressing about a godless world. It only means that we are responsible for our fate, no one else. It means that if you believe that people are generally good at heart then the world will eventually be a good place to live. I think that we live in a world where half of the people still don't understand that. Once the world releases God as a solution, then we will all start treating each other better."

"Always the Marxist," said Yankel, a boy who had once been fairly overweight, but was now looking quite thin.

"I don't know about that," said Anna. "It's just the way I see the world. But I'm sure that Marx would agree with some of that, you know, the opium of the masses and all."

Within a few days, the entire community was talking about Anna's atheism. In normal times, she would have faced unbearable criticism from the community leadership, but that leadership had proved useless in this crisis and the youth movements of Warsaw were respected too much to condemn. It was never a popular move to remove God from the Jewish community, but Anna was never looking for popularity. She spoke her mind and cared little what those she did not admire thought. She was more likely to praise the theories of one of her seventeen-year-old movement friends than a Gabai from a synagogue.

On this November morning, with snow falling and dark clouds preventing sunlight into the world, Anna, with the rest of her displaced community, was to be tested again. As far as Anna was concerned, there was a positive side to moving. She would finally be leaving the house that had killed her son. She had often blamed the walls of the home for his death. She was very much aware that it was an irrational thought, but if the house was not to blame, who was? In any case, leaving the memories behind was not something that she would regret. She had always known that she would leave that place. Of course, she had believed that it would be under very different circumstances. It should have been by choice.

However, the result was the same. She was leaving the house and with it memories that needed to be suppressed, or better yet, erased. Yehuda and Anna had become distant since Shimi was taken from them. It was as if Anna had two roommates, Yehuda and Moishe, neither closer to her than the other. Yehuda was more like a brother than a husband. There was no intimacy between them, but they functioned well in the home. Some of her friends who had moved into the ghetto had told her that the conditions in the ghetto were appalling and she would have to find refuge with another family or possibly two. That did not bother Anna. She knew that she could not be much worse off, and, she was convinced, it was only temporary. Every time she said that Mordechai would say, "the most permanent things in the world are labeled temporary." She did not argue with him.

As the three began dragging what was left in the small three-bedroom flat to the wagon, she recalled that it had been a cold winter day when they had moved into the house several years earlier. She was still no more than a child, pregnant with Shimi and burdened with so much hope that her new life would be different. The difference she had been searching for was a separation from her parents' life. She loved and despised her parents simultaneously, a difficult task for many, but natural for Anna. Growing up in a Socialist – Zionist youth movement, she had acquired a values system that was opposed to her parents' traditional, status-quo lifestyle. She had argued with them throughout her teen years about the viability of the Jewish community in Europe. She thought they too should be moving to Palestine but knew that if she were to build a life there it would have to be without them. Her father was still quite religious, but her mother tended to cut corners. They had moved to Warsaw from a small village near Lodz when they were a young couple, well before they had children. The big city and the larger Jewish community had been what attracted them. It was a few years before the Great War, the pogroms had taken their toll and any young person who could leave the rural shtetl communities that had dictated Jewish existence for hundreds of years did so. There remained little sanctity or lore regarding their previous life. Anna had often told them that her desire to leave for Palestine was genetic. Her parents had left and now she would too. They were genetically nomads. Anna could only hope that she would be the last to wander. But her parents tolerated her talk with patience and love. They were not against sending Jewish youth to Palestine to build a nation, as long as it was not their own children. Anna just called them hypocrites, and they would reply that she would understand when she was a parent. She swore never to say that to her children.

Moishe and Yehuda had begun the chore of emptying the home of its contents. They thought they would leave the larger furniture and collect or sell it later. Anna had warned that they may be restricted from returning and what they did not take now would sit there unattended until after the war.

Within a few hours, the wagon was full and the men began on their long journey to the Jewish ghetto. Anna stayed at the almost empty home with Hanna who was planning on making the move with them. It would take the men over two hours to get there. Anna stayed behind to finish up and wait for them to return for a second load. However, that would not happen. As she was packing up the last few crates and gathering small items left in corners and on shelves, one of her movement colleagues came running to the door.

"Anna... they've been stopped!" he said out of breath. He looked as if he was no more than fourteen years old, but Anna knew that he would be turning eighteen next month.

"What do you mean?"

"The Germans stopped Moishe and Yehuda. They beat them and took the wagon. They just dumped everything on it onto the ground."

"Are they all right? What happened? Are they injured?"

"I think they are fine, although Yehuda looked like his side was hurting him. People came and helped them bring most of their belongings into one of the flats in the ghetto. You have to come now. It's not safe here."

"There is so much more to take," said Hanna, looking at Anna standing among the remaining items she had hoped to salvage.

"The Germans are rounding everyone up. They even shot some of the people who dallied behind. You have to leave this and come. We'll see if we can sneak some people over here tonight to get more or your stuff. Put what you really need next to the door. The rest you will have to part with."

"All I really need is already gone," said Anna.

The boy stood silent and shook his head. "I'm sorry."

"It's okay. Just help me take these two crates and we can go. The rest is junk anyway."

The three of them grabbed what they could and began walking. A few steps into the street, the boy pointed them down an alley in the opposite direction of their destination.

"We need to go around the roadblocks," said the boy. "They're hurting people just for fun down there."

"Is that where Moishe and Yehuda were stopped?" asked Anna?

"No, they were already inside the fence."

"The fence?" said Hanna.

"Yes. They're building a fence around the neighborhood. But don't worry, we have some tunnels planned. Some of us will always be able to get in and out. Even the efficient Germans won't be able to block all exits."

They walked down a back alley and around a group of buildings that seemed to be empty. Anna recognized the neighborhoods where some of the Jewish leaders had lived. They were close to one of the synagogues, and she knew that the houses had been cleared of Jews.

Even at their brisk pace, it took over an hour for them to reach the ghetto. As they approached one of the checkpoints into the quadrant, they joined the masses of people entering the area. The Germans had been rounding up the Jews for a few weeks already and there were still many to shove into the tiny neighborhood. Although Anna had heard a great deal about what was happening inside the newly established sector, she was shocked to see that in just a short period, the streets past the line were so packed with people moving about. Children without parents lined the sidewalks, some begging, some crying, and some just staring blindly at nothing at all. Close to the entrance, two dead bodies lay abandoned, shot by German guards either because they tried to leave or just for sport.

"What's going on here," Hanna whispered to Anna.

"Welcome home," the boy said.

Once past the checkpoint, it took the three another hour to locate Moishe and Yehuda. They had been brought to a home of one of Hashomer Hatzair's most colorful figures. His name was Isaac, but everyone called him by his last name, Peretz. He was tall and skinny during the best of times, now he was tall and vanishing. During the winter months, Peretz always wore a white knit scarf around his neck. Later, when he was too warm, he would tie it around his waist. He had himself arranged for Anna to stay with him saying, "If there is one person who will be able to get me through this hell it is Anna Kapalevitz." He then added, "We'll argue about Boas and Engels and anyone else who has written the kind of crap that is worth arguing about. I can't wait." He had also arranged for five other movement people to join them, knowing that by this time in the relocation process it would be very hard for any of them to find a place to stay.

The boy who had escorted the women into the Ghetto said that he had to move on to see if there was anyone else who needed help. Anna thanked him, saying, "You are what the movement is all about."

Anna and Hanna entered the house where they had been told that Yehuda and Moishe had been taken. They immediately saw Peretz standing with his bright blue eyes smiling at them; next to him stood Yehuda with a pouting look on his face as if he had been sucking on a lemon. Anna knew right off that Peretz had been the one to make the arrangements and she thanked him as well.

"I did not invite you here just to look at your pretty face all day," he said proudly. Yehuda made a face at him. "No, no, no. We have work to do. The Jewish quadrant won't survive without our help."

"Can I first get organized?" she asked looking at all their belongings scattered around the entry hall.

"Please, by all means. And who is this?"

"Oh," said Anna, "this is Hanna. She needs a place as well."

Peretz scratched his head. "I had planned for you, your husband, your brother and Ida to share the back room. It's crowded, but at least it's a roof. Right now there are eleven of us here, but I'm afraid there may be more, so perhaps Hanna will be able to squeeze in with you. Do you have a sheet to partition the room? No matter, we can find something. Privacy is a luxury that we all will have to do without." Hanna thanked Peretz without looking him in the eye; her head remained facing the floor the entire time he spoke.

Anna thought it would be fine to have five in a room. Just like the eastern kibbutz, she thought. She knew Ida well, and Peretz must have known that they got along well. Ida was a year younger than Anna. She had been active in the movement since she was a young child. She never married but was constantly pursued by the boys of Hashomer Hatzair. The joke was that the one who would catch Ida would be granted free travel to Palestine. Ida had short blonde hair, parted on one side, and tied with a ribbon on the other. That hairstyle, her bright blue eyes, and a smile that lit up the dark Polish skies were her trademarks. Once, while Anna and Ida were alone during a summer at the movement kibbutz near Radom, Ida told her why she had never connected with any of the boys who followed her every move. "I don't like boys," she said simply. "I mean, I like talking to them, but nothing more than that. I've always preferred girls." No one ever said things like that, and Anna, after a bit of a shock and a long silence, began to understand. From that moment on, they were close friends and Anna helped Ida fend off the wild beasts trying to court her. It would be a pleasure to share a room.

It would have been considered a grand flat for a young couple, or even a family with one or two children; there were two bedrooms and a large living room. The plan was to have four beds in each bedroom and three in the living room. The painted trimming around the ceiling gave Anna's new room a more regal look. None of the new occupants of the house had been able to bring furniture of any kind, but Peretz had arranged beds well ahead of the closing of the walls. With information regarding other Jewish residential areas reaching his always receptive ears, he knew what was to come and planned for what would be needed. Most of the material acquired had some connection to bedding: mattresses, bed frames, blankets, pillows and even some sheets.

As Anna dragged her personal effects into the back of the flat, she noticed that three people were standing in the side room off of the entry hall. As she looked a little closer she was shocked to see that she recognized one of them.

"Tuvia?" she said, placing the crate she had begun moving on the wood-paneled floor.

"Anna. Peretz didn't tell me you'd be here. Peretz! You pig. It's wonderful to see you. I thought you'd be gone by now."

He looked even thinner and paler than the previous time they had met. She had wondered what had become of him. He had not returned to Warsaw that spring, and her inquiries turned up nothing, except that he had reached Lvov that month but had left hastily. She had feared the worst but just held on to the hope that they would meet in Palestine.

"I couldn't," she said. "Things happened."

"May I help you with your belongings?"

"Yes, thank you. What are you doing here?"

"Oh, it looks like we'll have plenty of time to talk about what I'm doing here. Let's just get you organized now. Is your husband here? And your son?"

Anna's mouth curled down and she looked at Tuvia as a small child would look at a puppy.

"I'm sorry," he said looking down at the ground. "I didn't know."

"Yes. It was in spring."

"I see. Well then, let's get you set up here. We'll talk later." He lifted the crate and brought it into the room. She stood back and looked at him and a smile came over her face. She began thinking that between Tuvia, Ida and Peretz, this was going to be an interesting time for her. She knew that they would all be tired, cold and hungry, but she also knew that there would be constant discussions, planning and of course arguing. She looked forward to all of it – she was acutely aware of the irony.

Living with them in the tiny home was an array of people so different that it would have been unlikely for them to ever have crossed each other's paths. The movement people were Anna, Tuvia, Peretz, Ida, Nahum, who had been a student studying architecture, Miriam, Tuvia's friend, whom he had thought he lost to the Russians but had been released and found wandering the roads between the Russian and Polish borders, and Leah. The non-movement people were Yehuda, Moishe, Hanna and Emil.

Emil came from one of the smaller towns outside of Warsaw. He was medium height, with a lanky build, dark hair and the beginnings of what could eventually become a beard. It looked as if he had never shaved and the hair on his face was thin.

That first evening, after the curfew had begun and the group had nothing to do but sit around and chat, Emil told them his story.

"In my town," said the staid man, "there were maybe seven thousand Jews. We had two synagogues and little else. Many of the Jews didn't even come to synagogue. I did. I liked it there. It made me feel like I was close to God. When the Germans came, our Polish friends started acting differently. The Germans would randomly pull a few farmers out to the center of the town, accuse them of helping Jews and shoot them on the spot. After that, the other Poles wouldn't even talk to me anymore. I had a good friend who told me that his parents would no longer let him see me. Since we couldn't go to school any longer, I tried to find work, but there was nothing. Whenever I would lie and say that I was a Pole to get a job, they would ask me to drop my pants. 'You look Jewish to me,' they would say. So I decided to come here, to Warsaw. I told my parents that there was no reason for me to stay and that they would have fewer mouths to feed with me gone. So I left. I spent the first few nights avoiding the Germans in the forest. The Germans didn't frighten me, but their dogs did. I heard them barking every night and once I almost got caught. At one point I even once tried to enter a monastery, but I guess I wasn't the first there. They asked me to tell them some prayer, which I obviously didn't know, so I left. Eventually, I arrived here. I had no idea that it would be much worse in the city. So I stole food until the Germans started rounding up the Jews.

"One night, I was moving from building to building, trying to avoid the guards, when a small child came up to me and asked me if I had any food. He couldn't have been more than six or seven years old. He looked like he hadn't eaten in days. I answered him in Yiddish because I knew that he must have been Jewish. As soon as I spoke, five Poles jumped out from behind the building and beat both of us. I don't know how long they beat and kicked us, it felt like hours, and at one point I must have lost consciousness. When I awoke, two girls were standing over me. I thought they were angels. I was sure I was dead, killed by a few brutes who hated Jews – they weren't even Germans, I remember thinking. The girls helped me up and took me here. It was Ida and Leah. That was just over three weeks ago. I've been here ever since."

"What happened to the boy?" asked Hanna.

"He died," said Leah. "They crushed his skull."

"I still have headaches and a sore back," said Emil. "But at least I lived. I have bruises on my arms because I covered my head; and a few on my legs, because most of the time I was just curled in a ball. I keep thinking that had I answered him in Polish, this never would have happened."

"You can't blame yourself for the evil in others," Anna said.

There was a short silence as each of them thought about their personal losses. No one in that room was immune to the horrors of anti-Semitic persecution, whether it was on the streets of Warsaw or the shtetls they vacated.

"I left my family too," said Miriam. "But it was an ideological move."

"Ideological?" asked Moishe.

Miriam was the only girl in the group with long hair. All day it had been braided, and Anna could not take her eyes off of it. Even braided, her straight brown hair reached the small of her back; and that night she let it flow so they all saw how long it really was. She had striking features as well, a sharp nose and full lips. Her eyes were blue but in the dark twilight seemed almost green.

"Yes. I was moving to Palestine, where my real family would be. What can I say? I am a movement person through and through. When I said good-bye to my parents, I told them that if they ever wanted to see me again they would have to come to visit me in Tel Aviv." There was a gasp coming from Hanna as she heard that.

"Is that so hard to understand?" asked Peretz, turning to Hanna.

"Actually, yes it is," she said. "It's your family. How can you just leave them like that?"

"Well," said Miriam, "they weren't exactly angels. My father would drink a little too much Kiddush wine on the Sabbath and then hit me when I did something that disturbed him. Sometimes it was as simple as walking next to the Sabbath candles and having the air make them flicker as he was staring at them. I learned to stay out of his way when he was drunk. And my mother...well, let's just say that she had less of a spine than he did. I hated them both for that, and as soon as I was old enough, on my sixteenth birthday actually, I told them that I was leaving for Eretz Yisrael and never coming back. I told them Tarnopol was no place for Jews."

"What did they say?" asked Hanna.

"Nothing. My father hit me and my mother cried. I went to my room and did the most difficult thing in my life. I told my little brother that he would now have to fend for himself. He was twelve and he pleaded that I wait until after his Bar Mitzvah. I knew I couldn't. I knew that my father would have more reason to beat me. I explained that to my brother, but he didn't understand. He was treated differently. My father would never raise a hand against his only remaining son." Tears began to swell in Miriam's eyes.

"Remaining son?" said Anna.

"Yes. I had an older brother who died of tetanus when he was eight. I think my father always thought that it should have been me."

"That's terrible," said Hanna.

"No," said Miriam, "it's not. I never would have arrived here and found my real family."

"Yes, we are family now," said Peretz. "Even the lot of you who have yet to be exposed to the wondrous writings of the great Zionist thinkers. Don't fret. I'll take care of that."

"How did you get here?" asked Anna. "Tarnopol is really far."

"Tuvia found me. After I left home, I went to work on a farm before the trip to Palestine. I ended up staying there until the war. Soon after the Germans invaded, I decided to see if I could reach the Romanian border. It wasn't too far to Stanislavov, and from there I thought I could get on a train to the border. I was lucky to get a ride with a farmer out of Tarnopol, but my luck ended there. Just before we reached Stanislavov, he told me I would

43

have to pay him. When I said that I had no money, he said no matter, I could pay him with my body. He then jumped on me and tried to rip off my blouse. I struggled with him and then my hand found an empty bottle in the cart. I smashed it over his head and just ran. I ran into the woods and he must have been too stunned or injured to run after me. When I got to the woods I realized that he had all of my stuff. I had nothing but the clothes on my back – and they were a little torn. At first, I just sat next to a tree and cried. I wasn't sure where I was, how far to the nearest town, or if it was even safe to be there. I spent the next three days wandering the forest. I ate berries and covered myself in leaves at night. Eventually, I reached a village. I knew my clothes, which were now filthy, would immediately betray me as a Jew, so I stole a dress off a clothesline. I wandered the village looking for work, but no one would take me in. Finally, I ran into Tuvia."

"I thought she was Polish at first," Tuvia said. "I was just passing through that village by chance. I too had tried to reach the Romanian border, but when I got to Lvov I understood that the attempt would have been too dangerous, so I turned back. When Miriam told me that she was going from Tarnopol to Stanislavov, I laughed at her. She was a three days walk north of Tarnopol and Stanislavov was to the south."

"It turned out," she said, "that the farmer not only was going to have his way with me but had taken me in the complete opposite direction. Had there been any sun during that journey, I would have realized what was going on, but from the day I left home, it was just overcast. The ordeal didn't end there. Tuvia and I traveled again toward the Romanian border until we were spotted by Russian guards. They caught me, but I was thankful that Tuvia got away. I knew that if I could convince them to release me, Tuvia would be waiting for me in the woods. But they didn't, at least not right away. First, four of them… well, you know. I screamed in the beginning, but that only made them laugh. Then I just became passive until they were finished. They took me to their camp. I was sure I would just be used as a mattress there, but the commander seemed to have a conscience – as much as those Russian slimes can possibly have a conscience. He protected me from those filthy bastards and eventually let me go for no reason. I think they were going to be moving on and couldn't afford to take me with them.

"So I roamed. For weeks I roamed, really not sure where I was. And as hard as it is to believe, months later, Tuvia found me again! I should start believing in the Messiah, but I can't. I love you with all my heart, Tuvia, but you're not the messiah." They all politely giggled.

"Well, after that we didn't really go anywhere in particular – there was nowhere to go – so he took me to where he was staying. We spent the next few nights in this shack out in the forest. It must have been used for hunting in the past. Winter was coming, and we decided that the only thing to do was go to Warsaw and try to leave Poland in the spring. That's how we got here."

"Anyway," continued Tuvia, "Once I realized that she was Jewish…"

"He didn't believe me at first, I mean the first time we met," she said. "All this time I had been trying to convince people I was a Catholic Pole and no one would believe me, now I am arguing with Tuvia, and he doesn't believe I'm a Jew."

"You're just unbelievable," said Peretz.

"She is," said Tuvia. "She was dressed like a Pole; she talked Polish like a Pole…"

"Then why didn't you fear she would turn you in?" asked Anna. "If she was a Pole, you were risking your life talking to her."

"Her eyes," he said, turning to look at Miriam. "There was something wonderful in her eyes. I knew she was a good person. I thought she was a good Pole."

"There's no such thing," said Nahum suddenly. "All Poles are dirt."

"What is it, Nahum?" asked Peretz.

"Good Poles don't exist. They hate Jews, all of them. They just hate all Jews. Always have."

"But if it wasn't for the Germans, we wouldn't be here in prison, not the Poles," said Leah.

"Who are you kidding?" said Nahum. The Poles hated us well before the Germans got here. I'll tell you a story about those 'Good Poles.'"

Nahum was tall and slender and wore circular wire-framed glasses making him look about ten years older than he actually was. In his natural setting, he came across to people as urbane and refined. But the Nazi invasion had taken much of that suave eloquence away from him. He had been a student of Architecture and very active in the movement. He proudly showed off his drawings of concert halls, museums and art galleries that he planned on building in Haifa. All he knew about Haifa was that it was on a hill overlooking the sea. That was enough for him to let his imagination take over. Like the rest of the group, he knew that he would end up in Palestine, but the war had forced him to postpone his plans.

"When I was in school," he continued, "I had a study group. We were two Jews and two Poles. For two years we would find every opportunity to help each other. This was a fraternity that I felt closer to than my own family. We worked together, played together, shared our troubles with one another, everything. I thought it didn't matter to them that we were Jewish, but I was dead wrong. One day in 1938, the National Radicals, the Naras, decided to hold a demonstration on campus. We were concerned but did not take it too seriously. I figured there would be about ten to twenty demonstrators and the rest of the students would ignore them for the most part. Over five thousand people showed up. Jews were spotted and beaten right there in school. Needless to say, I stayed away, but the next day, my friends refused to sit next to me in public. I later found out that one of them had participated in the demonstration. But that wasn't all. Two nights after the event, our two Polish comrades asked us to come over to study. We thought nothing of it; we had been going there for years. Just as I was to leave, I was moving some junk around in my room and I dropped a box on my foot. It swelled up, so I decided to stay home. I had no way to contact Yatzik, and he went alone. Late that night, another friend of ours came by my room and told me that Yatzik was in the hospital. I quickly limped over there, figuring I would get my foot looked at in the process. When I arrived, I saw that he was hardly conscious. His face was bashed in and both legs were broken. The nurse told me that he had internal bleeding and they hoped he would make it through the night. He had trouble talking, but as soon as I arrived, he told me what had happened. Our two classmates had set him up. He said that when he arrived about five other Naras were in the house. They called him a dirty Jew and pounded him with sticks and their boots. When they had had enough they threw him out into the street. He told me that although our two friends didn't actually participate in the beating, they stood around and laughed. They also apologized to the other Naras for my absence. This was before the Nazis ever arrived. I never went back to school after that."

"I'm sorry to hear that," said Tuvia, "but it doesn't mean there aren't good Poles."

"I'm sorry to tell you that you have no idea what you're talking about. Either the Poles will stab us in the back or the Germans will shoot us in the back, either way, don't turn your back."

"Nahum, it's you holding the misconception," said Anna. "I know we're not all that connected to the Bund, but they have been fighting the Naras for a long time and most of the non-Jewish working-class Poles have supported that struggle. Polish workers have been on our side from the beginning. They understand that the Bund's battles are their battles, and they have proven repeatedly that they are more anti-Fascist than anti-Semitic."

"That doesn't make them good Poles," said Nahum in a tone that gave the impression that he was ready to end the conversation.

"Tuvia," asked Anna, wanting very much to move on to another subject as well, "how did you get to Lvov in the first place? The last I remember you were on your way to Pinsk."

"How much time do you have?" he asked.

"We have all night," said Peretz. "Although we should get some sleep eventually."

"We may have all winter," said Anna.

"I'll give you the highlights. I did leave for Pinsk, but I never made it that far east. I got lost. Can you believe it? Scores of journeys the width and breadth of occupied Poland and I got lost. It's still quite beyond me how I, Tuvia the wanderer, got lost. Anyway, I was in a village and trying to avoid the authorities. I came across a farmer who was hauling a load of vegetables to the local market in town. I asked him if I could help him, and in return, all I asked for was a few potatoes. He agreed, but I had a feeling he was not to be trusted. He kept looking at me like I was about to steal from him. I suppose I can understand that. I thought that maybe he suspected I was a Jew and was afraid of being stopped and questioned. When we arrived at the market he gave me three potatoes and told me to leave. So I did. But just as I left him, someone yelled, 'Jew! Jew!' I was sure they were yelling at me, but it turned out they were pointing at the farmer! He was the Jew. I saw him run out of the square and behind one of the buildings. He was lucky that no police were around. He escaped but left his entire crop sitting in the middle of the market. I ran after him and finally caught up with him. Needless to say, he was terrified of me and thought that I was the one who tried to turn him in. I told him that I was a Jew too and that I could help him. It took a few minutes of convincing, but I had him cornered and had his undivided attention. He finally agreed that we could help each other. He had explained that he had been working on a farm when the Nazis came. That was when I realized that I was still in the Nazi-occupied part of Poland, somewhere close to Brest-Litovsk. They killed the entire family on that farm, and he had escaped by hiding in a ditch for four days. Once the soldiers moved on, he took over the farm. He wore the owner's clothes, pretended he was Catholic and lived as they would have lived – except he never went to church since he feared his lack of understanding of Catholic prayer would have disclosed his Judaism. However, he always feared that someone would eventually recognize him and turn him in. Finally, it happened.

"So I offered to help him get some of his produce back, and then we could relocate farther east, but he refused. I told him that I knew how to get to Pinsk and he laughed. He told me that no one can get to Pinsk these days. The road was far too dangerous. The Germans had blocked all roads and even if they could reach the Russian front, they would not survive the Russians who were shooting everything that moved. He refused to join me and said that if he was going anywhere it was south to Lublin where he had some family. That was how I got off course.

"We left and headed in the direction of Lublin. It was there that I understood that the Germans had begun banishing the Jews from some of the cities. There was not a single Jew left in the small towns along the way. They had all been removed and non-Jews had moved into what were once the Jewish homes. I tried to visit some of the families that I had stayed with in the past, but they were gone. Solomon, the farmer, was so distraught by what we saw that I was afraid to stay around him. One night, we had been sleeping in an abandoned factory, when he began saying crazy things about the Germans and the Russians and the Poles. He cursed the Jews for letting the Germans remove them from their homes. I didn't know what to do, so I left him there alone. I figured that I could no longer help him and that he would have to fend for himself."

"You just left him there?" asked Hanna?

"Yes. I told him where he could get water and left. He was too dangerous to be around – although it was a great help to have someone who looked like a Polish farmer with me. I decided to try and continue to Pinsk. I began to doubt that the roads were as bad as he had said. After that night in the factory, Solomon did not seem as sane as I had previously believed. I doubted his word. So I started on the journey back north." Tuvia paused and put his hand over his mouth. He shook his head and continued.

"Listen," he said, "I have to tell you something that is going to be very hard for all of you to hear. A few days after I left towards Pinsk, I ran into your friends."

"What friends?" asked Anna.

"The Hashomer group that left here in May. They were on the way to the Russian border. I met up with them a few days' walk from Lublin. They must have strayed south a bit. It was strange how I found them...."

"How do you find people all the time?" said Miriam.

"The sun was out and it was a beautiful spring day. I decided to cut through a forest since I was easily able to see the direction I needed to go. While in the forest, I heard some crackling in the bushes. I froze, thinking it was an animal. I was not afraid that it was the Germans since they seemed to normally enter the forests with dogs. As I began to walk, I was hit from behind with a body blow that knocked me to the ground. Suddenly four guys were on top of me. It was your friends. I recognized one of them by a large mole on his cheek. ..."

"That's Ezra," said Ida.

"Right. So I immediately told them who I was. We were together for over a week. Each time that we got closer to the border, our path was blocked and we retreated to the forest. At one point, I told them that I still had to transfer information and that I was going to try to see if we can get help in Terespol. They were going to wait for me in the forest. Some of them insisted on joining me, but I explained that alone I had a better chance. I found my way in but was not able to get to anyone in the community. I have been to many of the occupied cities, but none was so guarded as this one, and eventually, I gave up.

"I returned to where the group had planned on waiting for me, but they were not there. Off in the distance, I heard the dogs barking and I knew that they had been found. I ran in the direction – why, I do not know, it was stupid, but I had to see what I could do. I never reached them. I heard screams and then gunshots. The dogs were barking and soldiers were yelling. Shot after shot rang through the forest and slowly the screams stopped. I moved deeper into the forest and waited in a hole. For most of the night I just waited for the dogs to find me, but they never came. In the morning, I walked over to where I heard the shots. The forest was silent, and I was sure the Germans had moved on. When I reached a clearing I saw the bodies."

"No!" said Anna.

"Oh my god!" said Peretz. "Were they all…?"

"Not everyone," continued Tuvia. "They had been 25 in all when I met up with them. There were 21 bodies. I was unable to determine who was missing. I really didn't know them too well. I only knew two or three of them, and they were among the dead. The others were gone."

Anna's thoughts were slowly turning to guilt. She could not help but think that had she joined them, this would not have happened. She was the one who had made the plans to get out of Warsaw; she had guided and instructed them, even though she herself had little information about the routes outside of the immediate area around Warsaw.

Sounds of quiet whimpering filled the room. Miriam was hugging Ida, who seemed the most distraught of the group. Moishe and Yehuda had been sitting at the table off to the side of the room, listening, but not participating in the conversation. They both hung their heads as if about to fall asleep on the table. These had been Anna's friends, but their acquaintances. Peretz placed his hands over his head and shook it back and forth.

"Who survived?" asked Hanna in tears. Although Hanna had not been in the movement, during the planning stages of the exodus, she had met most of the young men and women who left Warsaw for the forests on May first. They had all, at one point or another, broken bread with Anna. Anna, after all, was to be their leader.

"Whoever you want to have," said Anna. "Four are alive. Any four that you choose."

49

Five

"Anna, you can get on now," said the driver. "Everyone's aboard."

Anna glanced up at the driver from outside of the bus. She had been waiting for all of the passengers to pass over her seat, and for a moment it occurred to her that she would now have to sit where they all had walked. They had been trampling through the dirt parking lot, into the greasy floor of the kiosk and back over her seat. She laughed. "That should be the dirtiest place I'd ever had to sit," she whispered to herself. The driver had moved her two bags to the side to allow easy passage for the boarding passengers. There was an aroma of fresh fruits and vegetables drifting up and back towards the rear of the bus. It was quite amazing how strong the smell of onions and oranges can be. He had set them close to his seat as if he would guard over them while she was away – they were somehow his responsibility now.

The woman stood outside the door and sipped her drink, while the last passengers took their seats. She transferred her weight from one leg to the next, her flowered dress flopping about in the breeze. She watched as each of the passengers stepped up the first high stair and onto the bus. Most gave her a pleasant smile as they passed her – all seemingly pleased with her performance inside the kiosk. Finally, the last of them entered the bus, and she was alone in the lot, finishing her drink that began to taste too sweet and too bubbly for her liking.

"Let's go already," said the driver. "Don't you want to get to Tel Aviv. Your sister is waiting."

"You didn't tell me your name. Not very polite," she said, taking another sip.

"I'm Yaakov. Now get up here, already"

"Okay, okay. Don't push so much," she said as she waddled up the stairs, dropped the now empty can of soda into the small trash bin next to the driver, causing a loud clunk as the can hit the empty plastic bin. She adjusted her dress and readied herself to sit in the dirt.

"Here," said Yaakov, and placed a towel on the stairwell.

"Oh, thank you. I was worried I would soil my tush," she said and plopped herself down.

"Are you ready?" asked Yaakov. "Can we go now?"

"You need my permission?" said Anna. "What am I, your boss?"

"I just wanted to make sure you were comfortable. It's a bumpy ride."

"It can't be any bumpier than the way down the hill. That was terrible."

"I didn't design the bus," said Yaakov.

"Yeah, well you tell the people who designed the bus that it's bumpy," she said.

"I'd have to go to Germany for that."

"What? This bus is made in Germany? I thought all our buses were made in England, or Holland, or Belgium. And I thought they were put together here. I heard that somewhere. Wasn't there even a strike, and you had no buses for a while. I remember that."

"We used to get our buses from them, but now it's Germany. It may be painted here, but this one is made in Germany. It was the first bus Egged bought from them. So, the engine is German anyway."

It was also the start of a warm relationship between Israel's primary bus company and Mercedes-Benz of Germany. The bus had been purchased in order to upgrade the line from Tel Aviv to Eilat. It was one of the first air-conditioned buses in the Egged Bus Lines fleet and was soon used on several of the longer lines. The bus held fifty people (fifty-one if you included the stairwell), and was cordially known in the company as simply "302." The driver enjoyed the 210 horse-power, six-cylinder engine, and the passengers enjoyed the air – when the drivers didn't let it get too cold in the summer. The quality far surpassed the buses Egged had used previously. Everyone was happy with the deal.

"May I spit on the engine," she said.

Almost everyone was happy with the deal.

"I'll join you," he said. "I think it's a part of the reparations program that they give us for their guilt."

"Guilt. Yes, I know guilt." Anna paused and tried to look out of the front window. "Why do you want to spit on the engine? It's your engine."

"I have to admit, it's a good engine. Quieter than anything else we could get. I just want to spit on anything German. Just like you do."

"Who did you lose?" she asked hesitantly, almost as if she did not really want to hear the answer.

"Everyone. My parents. My history. I know nothing about anyone. I was an orphan by the time I was three."

Anna nodded and stared at Yaakov. There was a peaceful look on his face as he said that as if he had removed himself from the feelings attached to losing everyone. She had seen that look so often since the war. She had probably looked the same way at times. She knew there was absolutely nothing she could say that would penetrate that cold wall that he put up. So, in a moment completely out of character for her, she said nothing.

Just then the soldier in the front row decided to defy the driver's original request and offer his seat to the old lady. He lifted himself out of his seat in the front row, swinging his Uzi submachine gun on to his back. He had fought in wars, smelled gunpowder and death and had watched his closest friends get killed in front of his eyes. His name was Rami and he had signed on as a career fighter against his parents' pleas. He had also witnessed an American immigrant who had joined the army just before the Yom Kippur War in 1973, shot dead at his side. The American stood looking out over the landscape, while Rami bent down to pick up a dropped bullet. The immigrant's quick death, blown away by a sniper's bullet that would have hit Rami had fate not made his fingers ungainly, was just the first in a series of events that made Rami question his role in the Israel Defense Forces. "Why the hell do we need a state if it is going to cost us so many young lives?" he asked again and again. He did not sign on for permanent duty because of ideology. He was simply afraid to go into the workforce – and university just seemed boring. Now, with all the ardor and pain that he carried with him as he went to battle, there always remained the burning question of why. Of course, he was not alone in his disdain and condescension. Plenty of individuals, young and old, were leaving the country. It was a wave of an exodus from the Land of Israel, a consequence of the general disillusionment after the disastrous Yom Kippur War. He placed his red beret, symbolizing the elite paratrooper corps, under the flap on his shoulder. He had a set of paratrooper wings shining on the pocket of his shirt. "Excuse me," he said to her while beginning to stand. "Please have my seat. I need to stand. My back…"

"No, no, no. I'm very comfortable here, and you look very comfortable there. I'm sitting here next to this wonderful man and it's very comfortable, so just sit back down and enjoy the ride." She smiled and said, "You need to have a comfortable ride home. You are a fighter."

"And so are you," said Rami.

"Why do you say that?"

Rami was already out of his seat and standing behind Anna. He was holding the rack above him for balance and smiling down at her as she twisted her neck to get a better look at him. "I saw you at the kiosk. You are a fighter."

Anna smiled. What a strapping young man, she thought. She felt a sense of pride looking at him. Although she had seen thousands of his kind; Jewish soldiers, they still always made her smile, as they reminded her of some of the greatest Jewish fighters she had ever known – not in Israel, but in Warsaw, Poland during the war. Rami had blonde hair, bright green eyes and a strong face. Although he was neither muscular nor buff, he looked like he could take on the world. His hair was short, but his bangs were long, pushed to the side across his forehead. He was handsome and wore his uniform proudly. He could shoot back, she thought.

"And you have a scar on your arm that looks like a bullet wound."

"Very perceptive of you," she said. "I have several wounds, but I'm not going to show them to you."

"That's perfectly alright," he said.

"I hope you haven't been wounded."

"I've taken my share of shots, but nothing serious at all.

"That's good because I wouldn't want your mother to be upset."

Rami smiled. "Now will you please take my seat?"

Six

"Anna," said Moishe. "I think Yehuda is sick."

"What's wrong?" she asked.

"He has a terrible fever and he had dry heaves."

Anna moved into the bedroom and saw the skeleton of her husband. They all were looking thin and malnutrition was taking its toll, making them slower to move, slower to talk and prone to sleep a great deal. But Yehuda had been having the most difficult time. He had clashes with every disease the ghetto could muster up, and as he came out of one illness, another struck him down. However, this time was the worst. He had not left his bed for two days. These were two days when Anna was busy trying to find new sources of food outside the walls. She was hardly home and had no idea how severe his condition had become. Now looking down at his deteriorating body, she knew that he would not make it through this ordeal. She knelt down beside the bed, remembering how she had once loved him.

Anna had been spending most of her time organizing the runners who were smuggling food and medical supplies into the Ghetto. Children, sometimes as young as six years old, were risking their lives to climb over walls, steal a loaf of bread or some potatoes and sneak back behind the walls. The Ghetto had become a cesspool of bodies, some alive, some dead, most disease-ridden. The Germans were providing all of the food for the 300,000 Jews crammed into this one tiny space. But they were only bringing in enough for one-tenth of that number. It was already clear to Anna that the Nazi goal was to starve them to death. The easiest way to eliminate the entire Jewish population of central Poland was to stick them in a corner of the city, build a wall around them and let them die – and it was working. She just couldn't understand why they were giving them food at all. Wouldn't it have been faster to just lock the gates and let the Jews eat each other? It didn't make sense, but nothing made sense anymore. She knew that their only hope was smuggling – that and resistance, which was already being talked about by the movement leadership.

Anna reached out her arm across Yehuda's frail body, surprised that there was so little mass there, and grabbed a hold of his hand on the far side of the bed. She placed her other hand on his forehead and felt the heat through her slandering fingers.

He began to shiver.

"I know that I have not been good to you," she said. He was

conscious but seemed to be concentrating on the pain his body endured. "I know that I have not been yours since Shimi died."

Yehuda turned his head slightly toward Anna and opened his eyes.

"I just want you to know," she said as a tear trickled down her face, "that I loved you as best I could."

"You," he said swallowing hard, "loved me more than you could. And I...loved you more than you'd let me."

Anna let her head drop down onto his shoulder. They had been a couple that no one understood and in time, Anna the least.

It was Ida who took it upon herself to nurse Yehuda, although everyone had succumbed to the fact that he would not make it through the winter. The temperature in the house dropped close to freezing at night, and they were running out of things to burn. Had it not been for Peretz's preparations, acquiring a disproportionate number of blankets, they would have all shared Yehuda's fate.

In addition to the nine living in the house, two mattresses that were used for temporary residents were on the floor in the hallway. Occasionally, someone would bring home a friend or relative who was either new to the Ghetto or in need of shelter until they could find something more permanent. It was mostly movement people and smugglers who took advantage of the hospitality and despite the limited resources that would have to be split between more stomachs, no one opposed. "More bodies means more heat," Peretz would say. The plain truth was that as far as conditions in the Warsaw Ghetto went, this particular flat was doing okay. Between Anna's connections with the runners and Peretz's logistics skills, more calories per capita were between their walls than in most of the Jewish homes – and many of the Polish homes in Warsaw. On more than one occasion Miriam had argued that their extra rations should be going to the children, many of whom could be seen lining the streets in the bitter cold. The answer would inevitably be that they were the only ones who could save the ghetto, and if they died, more would die. It was estimated, by Peretz, arguably a bias source, that Anna's work was saving more lives than all of the doctors in the Ghetto combined. Anna would respond by saying that she was not alone and many were involved in the smuggling.

It was a warmer than usual winter night when Anna and Tuvia sat in the hallway on the vacant mattresses discussing the future of the war and the Ghetto. Yehuda was struggling to maintain consciousness, and Ida seemed to never leave his side. Anna, on the other hand, could no longer face him. It was almost as if she was waiting for him to die. She knew that he would never be up and about again, and that was too much for her to bear. This resilient woman could not stand to see her husband fade away.

"Are you okay?" Tuvia asked Anna while taking her hand.

"Am I?"

Tuvia just looked at her. The hallway was dark and the rest of the house was asleep. Her eyes reflected the dim lights from the street and her face was slightly lit by the white walls.

"I have not been able to care for Yehuda. It's like we left each other as soon as we moved into this place – actually, as soon as Shimi died. I was always a bit removed from Yehuda, but we were fine. We were married. He resented my activities in the movement. He was never a part of any of it. Now he doesn't understand how I can care for everyone in the Ghetto except him."

"Ida seems to be doing a good job," said Tuvia.

"Ida is not his wife."

"Are you?"

"What do you mean?"

"Are you his wife? If I were to come from outside this house and see you two, would there be any indication that you are married?"

"Do you mean do we sleep together?" she asked.

"Well, that's one thing."

"There seem to be conditions that make that quite impossible."

"You didn't answer my question."

"Love is a luxury that comes after food. We are too hungry to love."

"That's crap," he said sharply.

"Look at us," she said. "We are struggling to keep alive, to get a trifle of nutrients into our system so we don't all end up like Yehuda. And look at him. He's so sick that he could hardly hold me. And all I think about is my empty stomach."

"I am able to love on an empty stomach."

"Are you? And who may I ask is the recipient of that overwhelming love, that craving stronger than the urge to bite into a loaf of bread?"

"You know, Anna."

"I have not seen you courting any of the lovely maidens in this house or any other house for that matter. Come on. Who is it?"

"Anna, do you remember the day I left you, and you said to me that I inspired you?"

"Wait a minute. You said it first."

"Right. You inspired me. In fact, throughout my travels, all I thought about was getting back to you. I think that subconsciously I wanted to be forced back to Warsaw because I knew you were here."

"It's me?" she said, placing her hands on her cheeks.

Tuvia turned to face her and took hold of both of her hands. "For such a smart girl, you are not very perceptive. It has always been you."

He leaned forward and kissed her. She had not kissed a man for months. It had been even longer since she had made love, and she realized that if physical contact represents a relationship, then she had been out of one for some time. She did not resist and ten months of frustration and pain came bursting out of her like a dam breaching open as she returned her affection toward Tuvia. They made love that night in the hallway of the house where seven of their friends slept, no doubt dreaming of food, including one, her husband, who would die that very night.

Anna awoke in a panic as Tuvia lay beside her. They had fallen asleep, but providentially Anna was sensitive to noise and awoke as a cough came from the other room. It was not a simple clearing of the throat, but more of a choking sound, like a man gasping for air and quitting after failing the first two times. Within seconds, Anna realized that it was coming from her room and she woke Tuvia and asked him to return to his own bed.

She walked through the door and there was Ida, awake by Yehuda's side attempting to hold his head and pour water into his unresponsive mouth. Most of the water was trickling down the side of his face and onto the bed. From the doorway, without having to touch or see him in the light of day, Anna said, "He's gone," as a single tear worked its way down her face and onto the floor.

Peretz made the arrangements for the burial. They had all heard stories of the funerals. During some, SS officers would stand guard to make sure that no prayers were held. At others, they would take target practice during the procession. In one case, a German camera crew came to film the event in order to show that life in the ghetto was normal. They brought extras to act out scenes of mourning and even had Jews throw themselves on the ground in anguish over and over until they fell from exhaustion. Anna decided that Yehuda would not have a normal funeral, but a small service would be held in the house after his body was buried. Having grown penitent, Anna wanted to make sure that she could do justice to his memory, and fear of SS potshots was too much of a risk for them to take.

Her remorse also kept her from pursuing her relationship with Tuvia for the time being. He was very supportive of her, but she was distant, feeling the weight of the inappropriateness of their actions on the night Yehuda died. However, she knew that she cared deeply for Tuvia and realized that love and hunger could live side by side.

It was Ida who was most profoundly affected by Yehuda's death. Anna was grateful to her for all she had done, and Ida told her she had grown to love Yehuda "as a brother," she stressed. Anna, knowing Ida's secret, knew that was true and their bond only grew stronger.

It was shortly after Yehuda's death that Ida decided to become a runner and a smuggler. Her Arian look and beauty made her a perfect candidate. She could easily get by as a Pole and either smuggle food into the ghetto or transfer information to other Jewish communities. Since Yehuda was gone, she had told Anna that she needed an outlet for her energy and a purpose for her life. Anna, who had been organizing the many runners throughout their time in the ghetto, was hesitant to let her friend join their ranks. She knew it was perhaps the most dangerous job any of them could do and getting caught would surely mean death; if she was lucky it would be immediate; if not, she would first endure torture. Ida knew the dangers and agreed to leave the next day on her first mission.

"Take these," said Anna, handing her a new, clean dress.

"Where in the world did you get this?" asked Ida.

"Another simple acquisition courtesy of the Polish underground. Did you think we were just bringing food in here? This is just as important. You don't want to look like you haven't bathed in eight months."

"But I haven't."

"You will. Here is your first assignment," she said handing Ida a tiny piece of paper with a few words and a small map drawn in hand. "You will have to go to that address and meet a woman who goes by the name of Gretel. That's not her real name, but she is from the German area of Poland and speaks fluent German. She is Polish and has been working with the Polish underground since the start of the war. I met her several times and she is an angel sent to us by God himself."

"I thought you didn't believe in God."

"It's just an expression. Don't worry, I'm still sane. Now she will either have something for you to pass on to another community, in which case we won't be seeing you for a while, or she will give you something to bring back to us."

"How will I get back in?"

"Gretel will show you an entrance to the sewers. You will follow them south. Make sure you get your bearings before entering the sewer and keep track of all turns. After about ten minutes of walking, you will see a red X painted on the side of the tunnel. Next to it will be a ladder and at the end of the ladder a manhole. Knock on it once, go back down the ladder and wait. Knock only once, understand. Every hour afterward, knock once again and wait. There will be someone coming to open it for you. If for some reason a German opens it, you need to be hidden well enough for him not to see you. Once it is open, only if someone calls for Gretel are you to show yourself."

Ida looked very nervous, not the nervousness she had felt as an adolescent when a boy, who she found repulsive, would make a pass at her, but the kind of nervousness that one feels when she is about to dive off a cliff, not that Ida had ever thought about diving off a cliff. It was finally sinking in, and she understood that she would no longer be sitting in a flat taking care of a febrile man but would be facing the horrors of travel outside the ghetto walls – as if the horrors inside the walls weren't enough for her. But she was ready, and Anna would reluctantly send her on her way in her new dress with a hug that made both of them wonder if they would ever see each other again. As she was to leave the house and set out on her first mission, Anna meant to kiss her on the cheek. But Ida turned and her lips met Anna's. What was to be a friendly peck on the cheek, turned into a kiss on the lips. Anna's first romantic moment with another woman. They both laughed.

Ida was to leave the ghetto with another girl, an eighteen-year-old who had already been on countless missions. Rivka had straight blonde hair and looked Scandinavian more than Slavic. She had a long thin face and slender red lips. Even the harsh conditions of the ghetto had not taken her vibrancy from her. The night before the mission, Rivka and Ida spent some time going over coded messages and signals if they were to find themselves in peril. Ida was so impressed by her courage and maturity that she told Anna that night, "I think I found my savior."

Anna had known Rivka for years while they had worked together in the movement. In the summers, Anna had been Rivka's counselor at the kibbutz and had been molding her to become a future leader of Hashomer Hatzair. They had become friends, but the age difference was always significant. Only since entering the ghetto did Anna finally view Rivka as a peer and was so proud of her work.

The next evening, after Ida had set off with Rivka, and Anna's heart went with them, Anna talked of Ida with Tuvia.

"She's a special person," said Anna. "I don't think I could have made it this far without her."

I don't think she could have made it this far without you," he said. "Me neither."

Anna didn't respond to his comment. Throughout the days following Yehuda's death, while Anna was avoiding Tuvia, he was the perfect, understanding gentleman. There was nothing that could have upset Anna more since she found it so much easier to avoid him. She wanted to be angry with someone and Tuvia should have been the perfect scapegoat; just for a while, until she was ready for him again and ready to tell him a few secrets she had been storing. But Tuvia was charming, supportive and understanding, and Anna had no one to abhor.

"I don't know why I let her go."

"It really wasn't your choice," said Tuvia. "She needed to do something. There are so many women running around out there for the cause. How could she just sit in this despicable place and wait?"

"I hope she gets back soon. I should have given her something that would get her back here quickly. Gretel could send her to Lodz, and we wouldn't see her for months."

"She won't send her this time. It's too early. She needs some practice first."

"But she's with Rivka…. Oh my god," Anna stopped talking and stared directly at Tuvia.

"What is it?" he said alarmed. "What happened?"

Anna began to smile. "She's with Rivka!"

"So?"

"Do you know beautiful Ida has never had a boyfriend?" Anna had a sinister smile on her face. She knew that it was a secret she was never to tell, but under the circumstances, she felt it would be okay to let Tuvia in on it."

Tuvia just stared back.

"She likes her."

"Okay. So do I. Rivka's a great girl."

"No," said Anna. "She likes her."

"No!" said Tuvia, getting the idea now. They sat for a minute in silence, thinking about their new revelations. "How long have you known about her?"

"A long time. She confided in me one summer. You must keep this secret. I just knew I could trust you."

"Wow. That's, well…wow. I'll keep it to myself. But they would make a cute couple."

"Stop that! She kissed me goodbye, you know."

"So maybe she likes you."

"I know she likes me. What's not to like? It wasn't a bad kiss, but not for me."

Tuvia laughed. "I'm jealous."

"You have nothing to be jealous about."

"I've been waiting for you to say that," he said.

"I know."

It had been the first significant conversation that Tuvia and Anna had had since Yehuda died, and as the distant night caused all in the heavy, famished house to enter an escape world of dreams and wonder, the two lovers again spent the night together in the stuffy hallway. For Tuvia it was better than any of the dreams he had experienced, well, ever, and for Anna, it was a way of remaining sane. Love over starvation, passion over pain. Anna was ready for Tuvia again, ready to have him near her, to love her and most importantly, to let him join her in this world of loneliness and despair. It was so easy to despair for Anna. She had the world riding on her shoulders. "Beautiful, flawless, perfectly sculpted shoulders," Tuvia told her that night. He kissed them often that night, and she knew that each kiss was for support.

So she was ready for Tuvia again, although that did not matter, for what would have been a simple romance in hell, would turn out to be a commitment to save a life. Anna had been saving lives since the Germans invaded, a hobby of sorts, but one she would view as art. Tuvia saw it as a job. But the lives they had saved up to that point in time, that moment when life begins, in the heat of passion and the connection of hearts and biological beings deep within the body, her body, were nothing compared to the one life they would now have to protect. Anna was pregnant, and she knew it. She knew it because the last time something so colossal happened to her she had dreamed the same dream she had had when she conceived the previous night in the hallway.

As Anna fell asleep in Yehuda's arms on the night Shimi was conceived, years before she would learn the meaning of loss, and well before she would understand what crimes against humanity were humanly possible, what hate and fear could produce in man, years before all that, she dreamed of creation. And then, as Tuvia's arms held her in a damp hallway, surrounded by the only people left on earth that she could trust, while her husband, the man who gave her Shimi so long ago, lost consciousness, never to open his eyes again, on the night Yehuda left this earth, she again dreamed of creation.

Bands of clouds wrapped their way around sticks, or arms, or tree trunks, melting the outer layers of bark, or skin, of the mutant canes. As the heat rose from the burning mist, figures replaced the naked, bark-less, skinless, purposeless poles. Anna reached out to touch what had formed from the synergy and fusion before her eyes. Two figures stood before her watering eyes, for the heat seared her face as it retreated. She reached out to touch because it called upon her to touch. She was in Eden. What other place could cause her to cry from beauty? She did not reach for the head of the figures, now people in form and energy, nor for the eyes or the lips, but for the body, all of the body, all of the perfect, pale body, smooth as life itself. And she did not reach for his body, it was not hers to touch, she reached for hers because hers was more inviting. As her hands moved up and down the silken skin of who she knew without a shadow of a doubt to be Eve, the Eve, the mother of all mothers, the daughter of no one and the first to ever be pregnant, Anna understood. She stroked Eve up and down and as she did so, the serpent arrived at last, expected by all, even Anna, and his arrival marked the beginning of wonder. For the serpent split in two, one circled Eve, and one circled Anna. As they felt their blood boil and their bodies climax, the serpents entered them, in between their legs, and both their abdomens grew. She, as Eve, was with child.

Like so many years prior, she awoke holding herself, caressing her new child from without. She needed no doctor to tell her of her inception, and sure enough, within a few short weeks, she received her proof, first with a missed period, and finally the bulging stomach, satisfactorily deforming the figure she had learned to be so proud of.

The exact dream returned as Yehuda left her world, and it was just a matter of time until she would break the news to Tuvia. Included in the news would be the name of the child. She could not explain how she knew, but she did, that this child was a boy. He would be named Yehuda. But when to tell? She could no longer count on missed periods for proof, for her periods had been irregular since entering the ghetto. She was sure of the conception, but Tuvia was a man who believed faith was for the weak and she would need something physical to show. So she waited.

First, she waited for the period of mourning over Yehuda to end. Then she waited for Tuvia, and the second night they spent in the hallway was almost the moment she would reveal to him their eternal bond. Although she was ready for him physically, she was not ready for the disclosure. No one, absolutely no one was giving birth in the ghetto. Anna had once been told that people had children when they were happy. No one was having children in the ghetto. And those few who took the chance had slim hopes their child would survive; in many cases, the mothers would die as well. This was not a happy pregnancy, but it would be a happy birth.

Tuvia and Anna spent most nights together in the hallway when there were no guests, and the house was quite aware of the new couple in their midst. Every night Anna told herself that tonight she would tell Tuvia, but every night she made love to him and fell asleep with the secret.

One night, in her sixth week of pregnancy, Anna and Tuvia were together in the hall, naked under the blankets that Peretz had attained so long ago, when there was a knock on the door. It was a faint knock, almost as if they did not want to wake anyone up to let them in. Anna heard the knocks first, followed by a whisper coming from behind the door.

"Don't," whispered Tuvia as Anna tried to leave his grasp and go toward the door. But she ignored him, reaching for her nightshirt and slipping it over her head as she moved closer to the entrance. She approached the door as if approaching a seemingly dead animal – perhaps it is still alive and awake to strike. Again she heard the whisper, and this time she made out the words.

"It's me. Open the door."

Anna jammed open the lock on the top of the door and turned the gold handle as quickly as she could, swung the door open and vaulted out into the hall, where she wildly wrapped both her arms around the small figure stunned by the sudden lurch.

"Oh how I missed you," Anna said to Ida and she started to cry. She took Ida's head in her hands, tears streaming down her face, and kissed her.

Soon the entire house was awake. Tuvia almost forgot that he was disrobed, and had to jump back under the covers as Miriam and Peretz peaked out of their beds.

"Are you absolutely crazy?" said Peretz. "It's the middle of the night, you could die walking around out there."

"I hid the food," said Ida. "I was in that sewer since yesterday, knocking and knocking, but no one came. Finally, it just opened, and someone called Gretel... I thought I would have to go back."

Anna was still holding her tight, standing in front of all the housemates who had awoken to see what the commotion was about, and as Ida talked, Anna kissed her again and again.

"I need to go back and get the food."

"Where is it?" asked Miriam.

"There's an empty crate behind the orphanage. I put the bag there. I saw guards so I threw it there and hid in a dumpster until they left. Then I just ran here as soon as I could. We have to go back and get it."

"It's food," said Peretz. "If someone finds it they'll have something to eat."

"It's not just food," she said looking at Peretz. Her eyes darted around the room as if to make certain she could trust everyone. "There is a gun there as well."

The room went even more silent than it was and seven chins dropped to the ground.

"We have to get it tonight," said Anna, releasing her grip from Ida. "If that's found by the SS there will be mass executions."

"They don't need an excuse to have mass executions," said Emil.

"She's right," said Nahum, who tended not to involve himself in decisions of this nature. "I'll go. It's time I did something useful with my time."

"No," said Anna assertively. "Ida has to show us and I am not letting her out of my sight. We're going right now."

"Anna," pleaded Tuvia who had somehow found his clothes in the

64

dark.

"This is not up for negotiation," said Anna. "Get Ida something to drink and we're going."

Minutes later, despite both Tuvia's and Peretz's objections, Ida and Anna were gone, out the door into the jungle where the animals had no mercy and killed for sport.

They were two short blocks and two treacherous SS guards away from the orphanage. The streets were empty, except for occasional shadows of beggars sleeping on the walkways. Here and there those same shadows turned out to be dead shadows, but at night the dead and the living all looked alike. The girls crept through the streets of their dying Warsaw, the city they once knew and called home, but now call home as a corpse calls his grave home. They were continuously forced to stop and hide from the current rulers of this dark, evil, pain-entrenched concrete grave to be. Each time a sound was heard off in the distance they would jump behind something to escape death, often just behind each other, searching out a place to disguise their sins of vagrancy and loitering, behind a quilt that did not exist. Slowly, painstakingly slowly, they made their way through the grime of the once glorious, or perhaps never glorious, but civil, Polish Capital, until finally reaching the alleyway adjacent to the orphanage.

Ida pointed in the direction of a trash bin and Anna returned a questioning glance. She pointed again, shrugged and walked down the alley. There were closed windows on both sides of the street. No visible life could be seen or felt coming from inside the buildings that were sandwiching the asphalt road. Several large crates lined the sides and a rat scattered passed the girls. They had seen so many rats in the ghetto that they did not even flinch. As they approached the bin, Ida ran past it and stuck her hand inside a crate. Anna followed and as she reached her she heard the boots, German boots, an unmistakable click of hard, black German shoes on the cobblestone roads echoing down the alley. Before Anna could warn Ida of the approaching reaper, Ida knocked over the crate, causing the entire lane to ring with the sound of wood crashing. Anna and Ida kneeled behind the bin and froze.

"Anschlag!"

Were they seen? It was dark; their silhouettes could have been made out by the two young SS guards patrolling the night.

"Wer ist dort?"

The girls stayed frozen, trying not to breathe, while the alley walls began to close in on them.

Click, click, click, click…

The German slowly moved down the street, pistol drawn, his shadow absorbing the cobblestones between him and the crates. As he was steps from spotting Anna's legs, seconds from a disastrous moment that would kill her, her best friend and her unborn child, the rat scampered through the soldier's legs, like a tiny rupture in the asphalt progressing randomly towards the young German. He flinched, jumping back as if it was the entire military might of the Russian Red Army trickling past him. His finger tightened on the trigger of the weapon pointing at nothing in particular, just limp in his hands when it should have been taught, for he was less than trained, chosen perhaps in the haste of fulfilling personnel quotas and the search for ghetto guards. The trigger drawn back, the unheard click of the firing pin, drowned out by the tiny explosion of encased gunpowder. He fired. One shot. Bang.

The bullet had a mind of its own, which was necessary since the shooter gave it little direction; it knew where it needed to land. Although the shot should have been directed down the alley and should have, by all laws of physics, continued its travels to the end of the vacant street, hitting the stone wall, possibly ricocheting up into the air, possibly not, it sliced to the right, finding the edge of a drainpipe and rebounding across the concrete canyon, off the pavement and directly into Anna's perfectly sculpted arm. Her yell was muffled by none other than another set of shots by the second SS guard, who must have thought that the danger was significantly more pressing than an attack of a rodent, or maybe he was just making sure there was no one down the alley left to live. Ida instinctively grabbed Anna's mouth and held it shut as Anna winced in pain. Blood was damping the only blouse she had and dripping steadily onto Ida's already stained clothes.

Hearing and seeing nothing, thanks to Ida's strong grip, the guards moved on to search the rest of the neighborhood, or maybe just to return to their station and make a nice hot cup of tea. They had either killed the curfew vagrants, or not, or killed a rat, or not. One way or another they knew that they, the vagrants and the rats, would all eventually die anyway.

Anna groaned as Ida placed her hand over the saturated wound. The alley was getting darker to Anna, or maybe that was just her imagination. She was having a difficult time accepting the fact that she had been shot, but at the same time her life refused to flash before her eyes, signally clearly that she was not going to die – at least not today – she was happy that it was she and not her beloved Ida who had taken the bullet.

"Can you move?" asked Ida.

What a silly question, Anna thought. Shot in the arm, not the leg or the spine.

"I can't move my arm, but the rest of me seems fine."

"Does it hurt?"

"I was shot," she said, panting, "of course, it hurts."

"We need to go."

"Do you have the bag?"

Ida looked around as if the bag had perhaps decided to drift off into the night on its own, maybe to chase down the soldiers. "Yes."

"Why didn't you shoot him?" asked Anna.

"I said we had guns, not bullets."

Anna let out a chuckle between winces and signaled to Ida that she was ready to stand. Ida took hold of her torso from behind, and Anna could feel the warmth and malleability of Ida's breasts against her back. Something was soothing about Ida's touch that seemed to numb the pain in her arm. Leaving one arm around Anna and the other holding the bag slung over her shoulder, Ida led them out of the dreadful dead, almost dead, end street. There was a feeling that although they had barely escaped death, narrowly missed, just two fingers from her heart, the ultimate sacrifice, they had experienced a thrill from which they could grow. Perhaps it was just Anna's interpretation of the moment, a moment when there was pain and pleasure intertwined, when she realized that Ida was not just another movement person, but someone she was willing to protect with her life – like she would have Shimi had she been given the chance. Ida and Anna would bond like sisters, like lovers, like nothing Anna had ever experienced before. Just then, as she was rising from the battleground, she remembered Rivka. She hadn't asked Ida about Rivka. "What happened to Rivka?"

"You don't want to know," said Ida.

"I do."

"Quiet. This isn't the place." Ida kissed Anna on the cheek.

As they walked the short two blocks back home, they heard no clicking, saw no rats, to which they now owed a debt of gratitude, just the stillness of death in the Warsaw streets, a death they managed to postpone. Anna was thinking one thing the entire walk back. This would not be the last time a gun would be fired in her direction, but next time, she would make it a point to shoot back.

Seven

"Well now you listen," said Anna to Rami, who looked quite proud of himself. "If I had wanted to sit anywhere but here I would have asked you. Of course, mister bus driver here would have stoned me at the gates of the city for doing that. Wasn't that our deal? 'You can get on the bus, but don't take any of my passengers' seats.' That's what he said to me. His passengers. Are you his passenger?"

"I suppose so," said Rami with a smile. "If I'm anyone's passenger, I guess that today I am his."

"And I guess so am I," said Anna.

"I also told you not to talk to me," said Yaakov.

The discourse once again shut Anna down. She did not move to sit in Rami's vacant seat, neither did she return to her forward-facing position, grafted on to the black floor of the stairwell as if she was guarding something precious hidden under the floorboards. She stopped and thought, as did Rami.

The bus was still quite bumpy.

"Look," said Rami rolling up his sleeve a bit further. He was still standing, leaning on the seat next to him. There underneath the green cloth covering his body, the A uniform he was required to wear outside of his base, was a scar. "Shrapnel," he said.

"That must have hurt," said Anna.

"I was too busy dragging my friend out of harm's way. Wasted effort. He was already dead."

"I'm sorry."

"I showed you mine, now you show me yours."

Anna held up her arm and exposed an indentation in the shape of a heart.

"Great looking shape you have on that scar."

"It was a wound of love."

"What do you mean?" asked Rami.

"Never mind."

"Sounds heroic."

"Let me tell you a story of heroism, my dear boy. But first I would appreciate it if you would please sit back down."

"I told you I have a backache," said Rami, placing his hand on the swell of his back like a pregnant woman. "I need to stand for a while. What kind of story are you going to tell me anyway?"

"One you will never forget. From the war."

"My grandfather won't talk about the war. I thought that most

69

survivors don't talk about it."

"I am not most survivors. Now I don't believe you have a backache, but I never argue with people in uniform – although I have shot a few. So let me tell you a story of heroism," she said again. "I had a friend named Rivka. She was a camper of mine on Kibbutz in Poland. That's not a kibbutz like here. Kibbutz in Poland was a summer camp for the movement. Rivka was a beautiful, brilliant girl and I knew she had such promise. One day I sent her on a mission. Two girls set out on this mission. One returned. It was forbidden for Jews to travel outside the walls of the Warsaw Ghetto. You understand? To travel the trains, walk on the roads, work, nothing, all forbidden. If you were caught, you were killed on the spot. Butchers were waiting to strike down any Jew on the streets. These two brave girls were to go to a nearby village and get food to bring back to the ghetto. We didn't have enough food because of the barbaric rations the Germans placed on us. Barbaric. Hardly a piece of bread a day. The girls would escape the ghetto and meet our contacts from the Polish underground during the day; They dug pits in the ground to sleep in at night. Sometimes they would try to stay with families who needed workers, always fearing their true identity would be revealed. You know, only the women could do that, because the men had physical signs of being Jewish," she said pointing at the soldier's groin. He blushed and she smiled.

"Now Rivka and Ida, the other girl who left on the mission that I was responsible for, were sleeping in a pit one night when a German regiment stopped not ten meters from them. One of the soldiers went over to relieve himself when he saw the girls. He knew they were hiding, so he called his commanding officers. They looked at the two and one suggested that they must be Jews if they are sleeping in a pit. But the other said that they were too beautiful to be Jews and that they would make a nice prize for the officers that night. Ida was shaking so much that Rivka had to hold her up. You have to understand. If they were known to be Jews, they would have been killed on the spot. They had to pretend they were Aryans to blend in with the rest. Rivka even had a cross she was given by a family that hosted her. The skeptical officer decided that they had to be tested before he gave them away to the rest of the officers. This was Ida's first mission and when the officer asked her to recite some Christian hymns, she froze. Rivka, who had stayed with Christian families and had even attended church with one of them, crossed herself – you know, with her hand all over the place – and recited one of the prayers. That was good enough for the officers. They didn't kill them on the spot, but the girls still had the night to fear. As the German officers discussed what to do with the girls – which officer would get which girl for the night – Rivka once again intervened and said that she would be with all of them if they just let Ida go. There must have been something in the way that she spoke, or maybe they knew they couldn't keep two girls for very long, that convinced the officers and they let Ida go. Ida did not want to leave her friend alone with them and tried to protest, but one of the officers held a gun to her head and told her she could die or leave. I know, it didn't make any sense, but nothing made sense in Nazi Poland. So Ida watched in horror as she saw them take Rivka to a truck. She reluctantly ran away before they changed their minds.

"The next morning, after the battalion left the area, Ida returned to look for Rivka. All that she found was Rivka's torn dress in the dirt where the truck had been. Rivka was gone. She never returned to Warsaw.

"Heroism is not getting shot in the arm. It's not just fighting to the death. It's giving whatever you can give to save someone."

Only the hum of the engine could be heard over the silence on the bus. Anna looked up at Rami and awaited a response. Rami looked down at her with the sad eyes of a fighter.

"I understand," said Rami, and sat back down in his seat.

Eight

August 6, 1941

Several weeks after Ida returned from her first mission, Anna received word that after being held by the German regiment for over three weeks, Rivka had been placed in a work camp with Jews, Gypsies and mentally retarded Poles. One of the Jews in the camp had managed to get word out with a list of the prisoners, and by a stroke of luck uncharacteristic of the times, the list made its way to the Polish underground and into the ghetto. Anna was called to take a look at the list and help determine if any of the names were her operatives. When she saw Rivka's name, tears filled her eyes and she held her mouth. Her first thought had been that she needed to talk to Ida. She knew that what was written on that piece of paper would be devastating to Ida, and she was determined to be the one to tell her what had happened. Two symbols were next to Rivka's name, where most of the prisoners had only one. J meant Jew, G meant Gypsy, P meant Political prisoner and R meant mentally ill. The letter D on the side meant deceased. Next to Rivka's name, it said J-R D.

"I don't think that we can survive another winter like the last one," said Emil. "Look how weak we are already."

"We can survive five winters like that," said Anna.

"And we really don't have much of a choice," added Peretz, taking his white scarf and tying it around his waist. "But no, this is not an ideal situation. We need to find a way to increase smuggling."

Anna looked over at Peretz. "Have you heard about Mordechai's ideas?"

"To fight?" said Peretz.

"To set up Jewish resistance," replied Anna.

"What are you talking about?" asked Emil. "Fight who?"

"The Germans," said Anna. "He wants to establish a Jewish fighting organization."

"What will that do?" asked Emil.

"What kind of question is that," said Peretz impatiently. "You've heard the reports. 40,000 form Lodz gassed in Chelmno and another 40,000 from Pomerania. They are exterminating us like bugs."

"It's a rumor," said Emil. "Just a rumor."

"Don't be stupid!" said Peretz.

"Peretz! It won't help to get angry with Emil," said Anna.

"Emil is just regurgitating the filth coming out of the Judenrat's mouth. Most of the idiots out there dying in the streets seem to think the same thing. Believe it!" he yelled staring straight at Emil. "Why would those girls make any of that up? It's as true as my stomach is empty. We will fight before succumbing to that fate. Abrasha and Abramek have been talking about this for months. It's time we took action."

The Nazi assigned Judenrat, the twenty-four member Jewish Council of Elders in charge of the administration of the ghetto, was continuously under attack, first verbally, then physically, by the youth movements and Jewish underground. The perfidy of this council was undisputed among the movement leaders, but their course of action was continuously debated.

"Look what happened to Abramek," said Emil softly.

"Don't you dare speak of Abramek as anything other than a hero's hero! He gave his life to keep our work secret."

"He would have died anyway," said Anna, "But you are right about his heroism. He set an example."

Abramek was a movement leader who had been captured with illegal papers and tortured in ways that only the Nazis could have thought of. It was rumored that just a few words could have saved his life, but he resisted and died during interrogation. Peretz had been a close friend of Abramek and Abrasha, who led the charge to instill within ghetto youth the will to resist. Following Abramek's death, Peretz became depressed and then ill, and only after non-stop care and encouragement by Ida and Anna did he regain his zeal and once again take his place among the leadership of the house and the movement in the ghetto, swearing to continue the Abramek line.

"Where will he get weapons?" asked Emil.

"Even I can get weapons," said Peretz. "Ida got weapons. We just need to get more of them."

"Mordechai says we can make weapons as well," said Anna. "I heard that he has put together a science group to devise explosives."

"I heard that too," said Peretz. "We need to help him. Maybe Nahum could help."

"Nahum is an architect," said Tuvia.

"He has experience planning things. We need all we can get. We don't have the luxury of perfectly fitting each person to the tasks at hand. We need to improvise and compromise. I'm going to talk to Mordechai later today. I think we can help him."

Mordechai was a twenty-two-year-old Hashomer Hatzair leader who looked more like an accountant than a warrior. He had left Warsaw with one of the first groups of movement leaders, assuming the Germans would not get past the Polish defenses. It would be the last time he would let anyone else fight for him. He, of course, was not alone in underestimating the German military, but like Anna, he would never again underestimate the enemy. He was eventually arrested by the Russian army, and upon his release, after making a failed attempt to cross into Romania with hopes of reaching Palestine, he returned to Nazi-occupied Warsaw. He wasted no time preaching the need of the youth movement to turn itself into an underground organization, to smuggle food, people and arms. The same movement whose focal aim was to relocate the Jews of Europe to their only true homeland, now needed to fight, this time for the survival of body and spirit. He set out to Vilna to collect refugees who had been accumulating in the city. He had hoped to convince those poor souls, who had just been torn from their lives, that the smartest move at this point, after losing everything – home, family, country – would be to return with him to occupied Warsaw and set up an educational and political underground. He may have even told them that eventually, he would not hesitate to take up arms, but it was early in the struggle and even Mordechai was not looking that far ahead. Needless to say, this death wish did not seem smart, let alone sane, and although Mordechai did return with his girlfriend, Mira, he did not bring an army back to Warsaw.

Anna had argued with Mordechai at several stages of his activities. She was most perturbed at his reckless use of charisma to convince what she called "little boys and girls" that risking their lives was a good thing. She would change her mind after the Germans upset her even more, but early in the occupation, she saw his organization as a danger to the little innocence remaining among the children of the movement. However, she did approve of his educational activities. He learned and taught Hebrew, history and sociology. Both Mordechai and Anna enjoyed reading their favorite sociologist Karl Marx, who she thought should be taught to the young minds needing to understand the true workings of society and economics.

That summer there was more than just Mordechai's chatter about establishing a Jewish fighting force. Anna had received word that the Betar movement had sent 600 of their members out of Warsaw to become a partisan army of Zionist youth. As the summer progressed, she heard more and more stories of their capture, deaths, and eventual retreat back to the ghetto; but their training created an established army, and with it, not one, but two Jewish resistance organizations grew in the ghetto.

There was one thing that Anna always knew about Mordechai. He was smart. His travels in and around occupied Poland frightened many, but Anna knew that Mordechai, with all his cocky, post-adolescent overconfidence, would never get caught until he, and he alone allowed himself to be caught. That scenario was not out of the question. He was smart enough to know that there were advantages to getting caught at certain times. How else could he figure out how to rescue trapped prisoners? He was exceptionally bold, but luckily exceptionally patient.

In the summer of 1941, the Germans attacked the Soviet Union, ending the relative quiet the Soviet areas of Poland provided for the Jews, but of course, everything was relative. Most importantly, more Jewish centers came under Nazi rule, among them Vilna, in the city of Vilnius, Lithuania under Nazi-administered Reichskommissariat Ostland, where only 3,000 of the 60,000 Jews managed to escape. The rest were stuck and Anna knew that it would not be long before they too would become ghettoized. She felt something should be done. The movement in Warsaw had gained experience in smuggling, hindering German transports and developing survival skills, although those achievements were unseen on the streets of the ghetto. Anna felt it was necessary to share that information, and she would have volunteered to make a run to Vilnius herself had she not been in her eighth month of pregnancy.

Mordechai regularly frequented the house, since so many able bodies – if able bodies were what these skeletons could be called – were ready to take on what he termed "national tasks." One evening, when he had just finished his speech for the hundredth time on the need to bear arms and fight, and for the hundredth time Anna was making her ongoing plea to assist the Jews of Vilna before it was too late, Anna's water broke.

Like a well-oiled machine, the house moved into operation mode, with Mordechai leaving to see if there was a doctor available somewhere in the vicinity. Mordechai would return empty-handed, the only doctor living in a three-block radius had been transported to the Treblinka concentration camp during the first Aktion of the summer of 1941. It was no matter; Anna was strong and between Ida and Miriam neither a physician nor a midwife was necessary. Ida and Miriam worked wonderfully as a team, and Anna thanked and praised them again and again throughout the evening.

Within two hours of going into labor, Anna gave birth to the new Yehuda, a baby born out of the love of two bodies that fate just happened to bring together as bedfellows. Although the baby looked healthy at birth, Anna was weak and without uttering a word they all knew that in the ghetto the chances of survival for the baby were slim. There had only been a handful of births in the ghetto and most of the babies did not make it past their few months.

And life in the ghetto could not have been worse. Actually, it could have been, and would be, Anna knew, but at that moment, when a new life, a new Yehuda, was brought into the Valley of Death, it could not have seemed more hell-like, more gruesome a place to raise a baby. His innocence would be spoiled by the Nazi framework of terror and pain. Despite the hell surrounding her, Anna was determined to make this a happy birth, a victory for her and the newly formed resistance. She was tired of skulking in her city and this was just one more statement. It was the ultimate payback. While Germans were taking Jewish life, she was creating more. Why wasn't everyone doing it? Babies, we need more babies! Why not? Because babies need air, babies need food, and babies need Nazis to be far far away. And life in the ghetto offered none of that. Even the air was not fit for breathing. It contained Nazi in it.

Mordechai turned out to be the only one capable of saving Yehuda from certain death. Even Peretz, though not for lack of trying, could not muster up the right amount of nutrients to provide Anna the strength to produce that lovely liquid dripping off her nipples, that human dairy product that the whole group wanted to taste – and they did, once. Milk was scarce in the ghetto, no one in the house had had any for months. Suddenly, out of nowhere, they had their own supplier. Shouldn't human milk be better for humans? So one day, after Mordechai had arrived with Anna's extra foodstuff, smuggled especially for "The Mother" as she would henceforth be labeled, she fed Yehuda and when he was done, she fed Tuvia, then Peretz, Miriam, Ida, Nahum, Emil and even Hanna, who just put a drop on her finger to taste. Only Moishe refused to ingest his sister's breast milk. As risible a moment it was, they all knew that there was something unhealthy about the situation. "It's stealing from a baby," said Peretz. "When can we do it again?" For the men in the group, and Ida, it was a double treat: Food and stimulation in one sitting. But they never did it again. Well, almost never. Tuvia and Ida both decided that it was okay to finish off Yehuda's leftovers from time to time, but for the rest of the group, those who did not have the privilege of sharing a room nor sharing the body of Anna (who seemed to enjoy it more than any of them), it was the last time they would taste milk, any kind of milk, cow, goat or Anna, for a long time.

Mordechai continued to pamper Anna with extra food rations. He was saving Yehuda from certain starvation and, like so many others who crossed her path, had taken a liking to Anna. Unfortunately for him, she already had three people clinging to her breast which was crowded enough, for she was not a cow. They were all well aware and feared that without the extra food, Anna would not be able to feed Yehuda and he would eventually fall ill. Anna, Tuvia and Ida were like a family now. Tuvia moved into the back room with them, and Peretz built Yehuda a crib out of crates he found in the street. Their room was off-limits to everyone else in the house, for fear of bringing in some kind of disease. That provided a kind of privacy, even with four in the room, allowing for promiscuity in love and in bed that would have been frowned upon amid the reality in the ghetto. They kept the room sterile, as sterile as could be expected without cleansing materials. Mordechai smuggled in soap for them and they would diligently wash their hands before touching the baby. The room became known as "The Mother's Temple" and it would have been difficult for someone to believe that a room with a baby as healthy as Yehuda could exist in the ghetto in the summer of 1941.

Mordechai's food had also given Anna extra strength and weight. She was looking fit and strong, ready for what was to come. What was to come would become clear shortly as news of mass killings in Vilna shocked the house. Reports of 30,000 of the city's 60,000 Jews had been killed, slaughtered with machine guns into mass graves on the outskirts of the city. Mordechai was more determined than ever to build his army and he proceeded to move onto the recruitment stage. And he had allies. Most of the 3000 Vilna Jews who managed to escape made their way to Belarus, where things were still relatively quiet. But a few ended up in Warsaw, "From the frying pan into the fire," Peretz said. They came to spread the word and among them was an eighteen-year-old girl named Rachel, who became the eleventh roommate in the flat.

Rachel told of hell in Vilna, of the mass killings, the disappearances, the feeling of uncertainty and fear, which of course they were already familiar; after all, it was the same Nazi killing machine that ruled their streets. But she also told of plans to revolt. The remaining movement people in Vilna had had enough of Jewish passivity; they were on the warpath, with the aim of revenge. She explained how the Polish underground had supplied them with some guns, although they expected the Jews to carry out missions that only the underground leaders would approve.

Rachel had the saddest eyes anyone had ever seen. Even when she smiled, her eyes were sad. It was as if the world was dragging her temples down as they sank into a mysterious abyss that only she could see. There was abrupt pain in those eyes, a pain that no one as chaste and immaculate as she should ever reflect. She had long blonde hair, which enabled her to travel at ease as an Aryan, a sharp nose and blue eyes, sad eyes. And it was the sadness that struck Anna the most.

"Where is your family?" asked Anna one morning while she fed Yehuda.

"My parents are dead. I saw the SS guards take them away and I know that everyone who was taken that day was killed. I later went to see the mass grave. They didn't even bother covering up the corpses. I can't be sure, but I think I recognized my mother's ring on a hand sticking out of the mound of bodies. My brother, he's twenty, left one morning to Palestine and I have not heard from him since. He wanted me to join him, but my parents wouldn't let me. They said it was too dangerous. Look who's dead. I guess they were right too. Had he made it I would have heard."

"You never know," said Anna. Hundreds are being held in British camps because of the White Paper. Maybe he made it farther than you think. You haven't heard that he's been captured have you?"

"No, but…anyway, that's my family. I wasn't too close with the rest of them – aunt, uncles, cousins and whatnot."

"We're your family now," said Anna, reaching over and touching her pale face.

"I want to fight."

"So do I."

"We can inflict damage, and at least we won't go as my parents did. I won't go like them. I'll charge an SS officer and kill him with my bare hands before I let him pile me into a mass grave. We need to fight."

"We're taking care of it. We will need your help, but you must stay calm. This place will not allow you to make even one mistake."

Rachel quickly connected with Mordechai as the point person for establishing a stockpile of weapons that could be stored and saved for the fighting that awaited them. She proved greatly skilled in motivating other young girls to leave the ghetto walls and retrieve weapons and ammunition from the Polish underground. Her energetic nature galvanized tens of young women dedicated to the movement's cause. The Polish Underground viewed the attempts by the Jews in the ghettos as a diversion and a way to expend some of the German energy away from fighting them. But Rachel, along with Mordechai, Peretz, Anna and scores of other young warriors had their biggest challenges with the Jewish leadership in the ghetto, particularly with the Judenrat.

"Let's see how they react to the elimination of a couple of traitor bastards," said Peretz one day to Anna.

"What are you up to, Peretz?" asked Anna.

"Mordechai is ready to knock off some of the Judenrat who have been so devoted to destroying their own people."

"You want to take down the Jewish Council?"

"And the Werkschutz. And the Shops."

The Shops was a code name for German enterprises or businesses working on behalf of the Nazis. Peretz saw them as traitors, although it was difficult to convince many of their guilt. Like so many in the ghetto, the reality of starvation caused them to cooperate. But many in the movement felt they had taken their cooperation too far, helping the SS find informers and turn them in. The leaders of the resistance movement wanted to teach them a lesson, that their betrayal would not be tolerated by the new, young leaders of the resistance, who would take down the Judenrat once and for all, leaving a void that would only hurt the Germans.

Anna looked down at her child and realized what lay ahead for him. Yehuda had finished feeding and had fallen asleep, his head limping back into her arm keeping him from falling on the dirty floor. His lips still had white dots of milk from when he dozed off while pressing them against her warm body. Anna sat there, one breast exposed, the other leaving a milk stain on her blouse. There would be a war, she thought. Not the kind of war where two armies fight in the trenches, sending wave after wave of soldiers to their deaths, but a war of attrition, of real, true Jewish heroism. They would convince the young and able to fight, for either way they would die. She knew that in Vilna it was not honor that the Jews had been seeking, but salvation. For that reason alone, the resistance died, and with it the Jews. She took a deep breath and turned to Peretz.

"Peretz, we need a plan. Not just a military plan, but a political plan. We need to convince people to join us. It may take months, and we don't have months, but we need to start now. I want Rachel to talk to Mordechai and the others. We need a plan."

That was the start of what would make Anna the unofficial communications advisor for the Jewish resistance. Although no one ever granted her a title, and she never attended some of the most crucial meetings held by the movement leadership, her voice was always heard, echoed by Mordechai, Peretz and Tuvia, who all made it a point to make sure their views were voiced.

Anna personified pride and honor, as well as a tad of deviance and rebelliousness. It was well known among movement members that she viewed the birth of her son as a protest against German dehumanization. "What could be more honorable and insolent than to bring a new life into the world when our enemies, the enemies of the Jewish People and all of humanity, are set to destroy life after life." She used the word "humanity" when no one else bothered to look that far ahead, into a world where humanity would need to take some responsibility. Never ceasing to amaze her colleagues, she would often end her "ramblings", as Peretz jokingly would call them, by saying, "Make more babies!"

It was Leah of all people who decided it was her turn to make the ultimate gesture; well not ultimate, since ultimate would have meant death, and no one, not even Leah, wanted to die. She would get pregnant! It was a strange goal to set, particularly when Mordechai had made it clear that he would not be able to support another baby in the ghetto. But Leah was determined. She saw the vigorous travail that Ida was incurring, and Miriam, having the distinct advantage of looking like a Pole, had begun making runs as well. Rachel had carved herself a place within the resistance leadership. Anna was, well, Anna was Anna. And that left her, the only remaining movement female who could contribute by turning her body into the factory nature had intended to be. And Leah, like Anna, was still getting her period. For most women, the ghetto caused all chances of reproduction to remarkably cease. I was as if the body knew exactly what conditions life would have to endure. No period, period. In addition, the Nazis had made it illegal in many of the ghettos to bear children, and forced termination was common.

There was a transformation in Leah once she decided she would respond to the call to bear children – being capable, or as she said, "Blessed." She became happy. Leah had been quite depressed for the prior few months. She felt useless as everyone else found something that could keep them proud. As the previous winter wore on, Leah slowly lost her will to get up off the floor where she slept. Peretz tried to give her small tasks to instill some kind of self-worth, but by March, she would just do the tasks and return to bed. Often, late at night, she would whimper in her sleep. She had told Peretz that she missed her family.

But Leah was exceptionally weak, and Anna was the first to tell her that although she strongly believed that having children was the right thing to do, not everyone in every situation should do it.

"Anna, that's either hypocritical or insulting," said Leah. "I can bear children, which is more than you can say for any of the other women here."

"No, you just are not fit enough to bear a child. What good is it if you give birth and are too sick to care for your baby? The baby won't make it, and if you get pregnant now, you will have to survive the winter pregnant and Mordechai won't be able to help you as he did me. Do you understand the problem?"

"I understand that you do not want me to have the very children that you have been encouraging us to have. That is insulting. Who should give birth if not me? No one is fit in this place. The winter will be the same for everyone. Mordechai won't help any of those women you theoretically see as future mothers. They are all too weak, I suppose. Tell me, if you so believe in your statements, who should do the childbearing that you so adamantly push?"

Anna understood Leah's claims and realized the flaws in her theory. In addition, Anna's reaction was personal and she knew it because she did not think that another baby in this particular house would be such a good idea. It was not out of spite or jealousy, but out of fear. The house was already a den of programming and planning for the overthrow of the Third Reich, not that anyone in their right mind thought that there was a chance in hell that they could succeed, so why draw more attention to it. No babies in the ghetto, but here there would be two? That was sure to attract unwanted attention – particularly from the Judenrat. Those were the same traitors that now, for the first time, had been labeled by the youth movements as the enemy of the people, the Jewish People. They deserved to die. Anna feared attention, and she feared bloodshed in front of her baby, in her very home, because if one of the unlucky Judenrat volunteers would make a call to that home, he would be slashed open by a group of her protectors. That was her fear.

But Anna's inability to respond just increased Leah's determination. To make matters even worse for Anna, Leah wanted Moishe to be the father, not out of love or affection for him, but out of a simple process of elimination. She had told Moishe once, in a very candid and bold conversation that would run the course of one of their first nights together, that she, despite her movement background, felt inferior to the rest of the group. She wanted a non-movement person to father her child. Moishe wasn't sure whether to take that as an insult since he had considered himself as much a movement person as the next, even though he hadn't as strong an affiliation as Anna had.

"Listen to me," said Anna in the tone of voice that caused Leah to raise her eyes and look directly at her. "We need you to be strong and healthy. Things are happening here that will make our lives even worse than they are now. Next winter could be our last, and we need you strong."

"I won't stand the hypocrisy, Anna. You can't light the candle from both ends. I'm going to do this. You got me started, and now you're going to support me because I am doing what you know in your heart is right."

Anna knew she was beaten. The will of an aspiring mother was too much even for her leadership skills. The night that Leah and Moishe made their first attempt at conception was a sleepless one for Anna. And as if he too was concerned, Yehuda was more restless than usual, waking every few hours to whine and feed. Fearing that once would not be enough, Leah and Moishe would spend the next three nights together, and by the end of the week, Anna was a wreck. She had tried to convince Moishe that it was a bad idea, but he was feeling flattered and needed and this was something he could be proud of. Anna quickly realized that there was no point in pursuing the discussion with him.

A few short months later, after numerous attempts, Leah announced that she was carrying Moishe's child, unwanted by Anna, cherished by Moishe. Those many nights together caused Moishe and Leah to begin acting like a couple. There was no celebration at the news, although the housemates pretended to be pleased. Most knew that the upcoming winter would bring hardships that even the ever-darkening ghetto had not seen. There was fear for the new child and what it would do to the house – whether the baby survived or not. Most of the house members were living in a state of war, as opposed to the survival mode of the rest of the ghetto. In both cases, children do not fit in, and unless you were Anna, it was difficult to envision a nursery setting. The second baby was a distraction, and Anna, more than anyone else, viewed the pregnancy as her personal failure. From the moment that Leah announced her intent to have a child, Anna stopped asking women to make more babies in the ghetto.

Nine

"I never asked you," said Anna, "what is the name of your kibbutz."

"You asked me. And I told you."

"No, no. I'm sure of it. I may have asked you, but you just told me that it was in the south. And if it's in the south, why are you driving this line? Seems a bit out of the way. I mean, it's a major line, I would imagine that many drivers live in Jerusalem and Tel Aviv who would love to drive this line, and it's an easy road..."

"Okay, enough. I took this line just for today. I had to get the bus fixed."

"They don't have places to fix the bus in the south? I don't understand why you have to ride all the way to Jerusalem for a garage. Egged is big enough to have garages all over the country. I'm sure they have in Eilat, Beer Sheva, Ashkelon, and even Gaza City."

"It was a special piece for the door."

"The door seems fine to me. It trapped me in there pretty well. I think I have a bruise to prove it."

The driver glanced down at the lady, who was now glaring up at him, still quite sore about the earlier incident.

"You know that was not a very nice thing to do. I could have been injured."

"Well, I'm sorry. I just knew you wouldn't shut up the entire trip. I fixed it, so it's okay now. Strong enough to hold even you."

Now her glare turned wicked, and she shook her head from side to side to show her disappointment, her eyes remaining on Yaakov.

"You know, you are a disrespectful man, mister driver."

"I sincerely apologize. I did not mean any offense." Yaakov tried to concentrate on the road but continued to glance down at the woman who had taken over his ride.

"So?" she said.

"So what?"

"What's the name of your kibbutz?"

"Haven't we been through this already?"

"I'm beginning to think that you are a bit out of touch with reality. You can't even seem to be able to follow our little conversation."

"But I truthfully told you already."

"'Man must prove the truth,'" she said.

"What's that?"

"Someone smarter than both of us once said that."

"How do you know how smart I am?"

"I see how well you can follow our conversation. You may be smart, but you're not making much of an impression on me — except for your sandals." Anna had been staring at the driver's feet the entire ride. They were one of the few objects that had any motion whatsoever for her to look at.

Rami, who had returned to his original seat, chuckled. He had been listening to the conversation and was enjoying every minute of it.

"Who said it then?" asked Yaakov.

"Who said what?" asked Anna.

"Now who's not following the conversation? Who said whatever it was you said before about the truth?"

"You can't remember the phrase, can you? 'Man must prove the truth.' A sociologist named Marx."

"I should have known that," said Yaakov.

"How should you have known that?" asked Anna, stretching her torso.

"Because I grew up on a Socialist kibbutz, Yad Mordechai, near Ashkelon. We studied Marx in school."

"Well then maybe we should have been discussing Marx this trip. Perhaps you'd be able to follow the conversation."

"I hated studying that stuff. I wasn't the best student. What does it mean?"

"What do you think it means?"

"I asked you first," said Yaakov.

"I asked you second."

"Now you both sound like children," said Rami.

Anna turned to Rami and smiled. "What do you think it means."

"Don't bring me into this."

"I didn't. You brought yourself into it."

"Well," said Rami, scratching his chin, "I think it means that we shouldn't take what people say at face value. We should examine their statements."

"You see," she said to Yaakov, "you could have given an answer like that."

"I'm not as smart as he is," said Yaakov.

"That was a fairly good answer. What Marx meant was that objectivity and particular points of view of right and wrong need to be tested against experience. Marxism isn't going to accept a dogma based on faith alone. Truth, whatever we may perceive it to be, needs to be checked."

"I don't understand," said Rami.

"I'm not sure that I want to understand," said Yaakov.

"Don't you want to expand your knowledge of the world?"

"Not at the moment. I have a daughter who is constantly reading things and asking questions – an inquisitive mind like that has never before walked this planet. Sometimes I want to learn more just to be able to help her understand. But most of the time, I prefer to live with my ignorance."

"I see," said Anna. "So, you prefer to change the subject?"

"Yes."

"Okay, so you're from Yad Mordechai?"

"Yes."

"I too was in Hashomer Hatzair, in Poland. I knew Mordechai. A good man, Mordechai."

Yaakov hit the brakes. Eyes wide and mouth gaping, he looked down at Anna.

"Keep your eye on the road! You'll kill us all!" Anna yelled.

Ten

When Leah was only in her seventh month, she went into labor. The winter had not been what they expected, it was much worse, with corpses piling up in the streets, the movement in disarray over plans for more assassinations and illness after illness plaguing the streets of Warsaw – on both sides of the walls. No one was prepared for the baby, least of all Leah, who was not faring well that winter. She had fallen ill in December and had never fully recovered. All were concerned that even if she was able to go full term, the baby would be born sick, or worse. When she went into labor, she lost consciousness; her body was far too weak to handle the pain of the contractions. Throughout the winter, Peretz had taken it upon himself to bring her extra food after Mordechai became busy with pressing revolt issues and was not happy about the pregnancy to begin with. As soon as Anna understood that it was a given that regardless of what she said or did Leah was determined to go through with the birth, she came around and did everything possible to help Leah through the ordeal. But Anna's and Peretz's efforts to provide Leah extra rations were far from enough. For most of the house, the already living were the priority, particularly little Yehuda, who required solid food now. Leah was not only risking the life of another child but was putting the entire house in jeopardy.

It only took her thirty minutes of labor to pass out and all of the other housemates tried frantically to save her baby. Within minutes, it had become clear that if she did not awake soon, the baby would not make it, so they worked harder, desperately trying to find ways to get Leah through the pain. They brought in sheets from the rooms, went off to get warm water, which no longer ran through the flat's pipes, and yelled a lot. But Leah never regained consciousness and after over three hours of trying everything in their power, Leah and her unborn baby were dead.

Anna sat next to Leah for two hours until finally, Peretz forced her to let go of Leah's hand and let them take her out of the house.

It had become commonplace for bodies to be thrown into the street at night so that the funeral would be at the Judenrat's expense, but none of the housemates would agree to that. Like so many other issues that were discussed, argued, rationalized, and finally decided on either by vote or consensus, the burial of Leah was no different. In the end, following deliberations that went on deep into the night, with Leah's swollen body lying on the floor next to them, they decided they would bury her themselves. It would be a movement operation and be done at night. No one wanted to risk Nazi snipers ruining a good funeral precession. They knew the streets, the guard movements and parts of the cemetery that were obscured from Nazi pillboxes stationed in the area. Now all they needed was a shovel.

It was Moishe who came up with the shovel in the end. In a reckless move that could have ended in disaster for the entire house and possibly some of the movement leaders, he stole it from under a guards' tower in the middle of the night. The actual theft was one of the most fearless things anyone had seen. However, what was unknown to most of Moishe's roommates at the time – although Anna had some fears – was that Moishe was trying to get killed. Leah's death set off a switch in his brain. He refused to speak to anyone other than uttering one sentence as he returned to the house at one in the morning with the shovel in his hand, "Let's go now."

He led the charge to the cemetery. As they left the building, a group of eight, one dead, with Hanna staying behind to care for Yehuda, Moishe headed off without taking the necessary precautions that Peretz had so painstakingly reviewed before they left the house. After failing to get Moishe to cooperate, a decision was made to let him go to the cemetery on his own, so as not to jeopardize the lives of the rest of the group who would follow behind with the body. They were aware of the risk that Moishe posed to himself but were not willing to let that threat endanger them as well. Anna would have objected, but she knew that Moishe was no longer Moishe and the group was right in letting him go. He knew the safest way and she was sure that he would be smart – at least until he had a chance to bury the body.

After Moishe disappeared from view, they set out, stopping before passing each building or intersection. At one point they crawled down into a sewer that led to Okopowa Street, adjacent to the cemetery. When they arrived at the sewer exit, they saw that the manhole had recently been moved, and they knew that Moishe had made it safely.

Upon reaching the cemetery, they saw Moishe frantically digging. Next to him were two mounds of earth, one small and the other growing with every swing of his arms. He was no longer the brawny man who had controlled the busses in the street of Warsaw; he had lost most of his muscle mass, along with all of his body fat. But he was waving the shovel with the vigor of a man who had never missed a meal in his life.

"Why two holes?" Peretz asked him.

"We're burying the baby too," he said without missing a scoop.

"The baby is still inside. What do you want to do, cut it out?"

Moishe suddenly stopped digging, and holding his shovel like a rifle over his shoulder he walked around the mound of earth to face Peretz.

"Yes," he said sternly. "It's my baby and he deserves to be buried as an individual human being."

Peretz straightened his slumping back and met Moishe at eye level. Both were staring each other down, not speaking. It was Peretz who broke the silence.

"No. We are not cutting out a baby. You're not, I'm not, and no one else here is either."

Moishe was breathing heavily. Anna came up to him, took the shovel out of his hand and gave it to Ida. As Ida passed it on to Emil who continued digging, Anna turned Moishe toward her, took his face in her hands, and kissed him on the cheek.

He hugged her and began to weep.

"Is this what awaits us all?" he asked. "Is this where we'll all soon be? Why Leah? Why sweet Leah?"

Moishe and Anna remained standing together while Emil, Rachel and Peretz took turns digging Leah's grave. After several minutes, Anna felt Moishe's body suddenly become rigged. He stopped crying and grabbed her shoulders, staring into her eyes, which could hardly be seen in the darkness of the winter night. The moon was just a sliver and low in the sky, and the only other light was coming from off in the distance where the plots stopped and the houses on Geisa Street began. Moishe pushed Anna away and ran towards Emil who was taking his turn digging. He grabbed the shovel from his hand as Emil dumped the dirt out of the deepening grave. He turned the spade of the shovel around and quickly placed the blade on his jugular. Then he jumped into the hole with the handle of the shovel facing forward. Emil, who was still stunned from having the shovel snatched from him in mid-stride, saw what Moishe was trying to do. Instinctively, he dove at Moishe from within the hole and hit the handle of the shovel, keeping it from hitting the ground that would have inevitably forced the spade through Moishe's neck. Moishe fell face-first into the soft, muddy earth, with the shovel only scratching his cheek.

Immediately there was mayhem, but as they had trained themselves not to panic under pressure, no one yelled. The other six housemates all jumped into the hole, one grabbing the shovel and the rest grabbing Moishe who once again was crying.

Moishe's suicide attempt greatly disturbed Anna and from that moment on she watched over Moishe as she watched over Yehuda. However, Moishe's determination to join Leah and their child wherever they may be was stronger than Anna's ability to guard him. One week later, Moishe left the house, walked directly at one of the gates to the ghetto with a homemade spear in hand, and charged the gate. After the guards called him to stop, he intently drew a hail of gunfire as he thrusted the spear directly into the guard's chest.

Eleven

"This is the Voice of Israel from Jerusalem. The time is two o'clock. Here is the news from Liora Schoenfeld." The bus went silent with the beeps of the hourly news broadcast. It was a national addiction, and there could be nothing worse than not being able to hear the news every hour on the hour – and on most radio stations, on the half-hour as well. On this summer day, perhaps more than any other time outside of war, the country was glued to the news.

"…President Idi Amin continued his discussions with Foreign Ministry representatives, but no details of the talks have been disclosed. Prime Minister Rabin has warned Premier Amin that the responsibility of the remaining 100 hostages of Athens to Paris, Air France flight is his. Yesterday, the hijackers released all but the Israeli and Jewish passengers of the flight, as well as the crew, who refused to leave until all the hostages were released.

"The terrorists are still demanding the release of 53 prisoners held in jails in five countries. They threaten to blow up Air France flight 139 and all its passengers if the deadline of 11 AM, July 4 is not met.

"Prime Minister Rabin has once again reiterated that Israel will not negotiate with terrorists. …"

The passengers on the bus remained silent well after the news concluded, and Yaakov once again turned down the radio. For most of the week, the country had been in shock from the news of the hijacking, and later, reports of selection, where the Jews and non-Jews were separated, who would live and who would die, just like in the death camps.

"We should blow up Uganda after this," said Anna to Rami.

"There are rumors," said Rami, "that the army is planning a rescue."

"But it's too far. Uganda is in the middle of Africa. How will we get there? What will we do when we get there?"

"This is a country that sells arms to half of Africa," said Rami. "We can get there. The question is, what will we do once we land?"

"I know there are great strategists in the army," said Anna. "But I don't think that this kind of invasion is plausible. I mean, look at the distance, the risks. We are good, but no one is that good."

"Trust the IDF."

"Even the great Israel Defense Forces are not that great," she said. "I've seen what armies are capable of. They are all made up of human beings who die when you shoot them. Believe me, even the strongest army, the most ruthless and evil army in the world can be slaughtered."

Anna was not talking about Uganda any more – it was something deeper, stronger, and even more brutal than the Palestinian and German terrorists who were dividing the hostages into Jews and gentiles.

"Yes," said Rami. "We are all just skin and bones."

"I'm sorry," she said looking up at him. "I didn't mean you."

"I know. It's okay."

"Would you like a piece of fruit?"

Twelve

July 22, 1942

As the day broke on the 9th day of the Hebrew month of Av, Nahum and Miriam were planning on making a run to a local fur dealer who had some stock he wanted to be smuggled out of the ghetto. They could not understand why he had waited so long but agreed to assist, as they had developed strong contacts on the Aryan side of the walls with the Polish underground and Jews who had been able to hide their background and could help move the products easily. It never ceased to amaze them how during this time of chaos and suffering throughout Europe, someone somewhere was looking to buy a fur coat. The worst part of the operation was wearing the coat in the sewers in July. Winter smuggling was difficult because of the biting cold, but summer smuggling was no picnic either.

By the summer of 1942, the ghetto was one large, crowded death cage. At all hours of the day, hoards of bodies roamed the streets, many with emaciated hands reaching forward and small, squeaky voices asking for food or money. But there was little food, and money could not buy much. The masses bumped into each other as they filled the streets; bodies of the dead and dying lined the sidewalks. Peretz had scribbled a small sign and stuck it to the wall in the house:

Look straight ahead

When they finally asked him what he meant, he said he was trying to tell his housemates that "the living are walking upright. They are the ones we have to keep alive right now. Those already on the ground will not make it long enough to see the next winter. Don't look down at them. It will only increase despair – our biggest threat."

However, the summer of 1942 would prove that even many of the upright would never again feel a snowflake, and those who did would do so in a place far worse than the hell they had been experiencing in the ghetto. As difficult as it was to fathom, there was a place worse than the Warsaw Ghetto. The upright would leave the ghetto. The horizontal would get to die.

Miriam had agreed to meet Nahum next to the Jewish hospital at Stawki Street at noon. Nahum had set out early in the morning to meet with a jeweler who had requested they find him some copper for his trade; it was

95

difficult, almost impossible, to find good metals those days, and the movement had developed a reputation for being able to get almost anything in or out of the ghetto. That was until July 22, 1942.

Although the Judenrat and the Jewish Police already knew of the German plans for Große Umsiedlungsaktion, the Great Resettlement Action, the plan had yet to become common knowledge. Someone in Hashomer Hatzair intelligence thoroughly messed up that day because no one seemed to expect what was to occur; least of all, the ancillary household that was run by Anna and Peretz – neither had any information to share with Miriam and Nahum as they made their fateful arrangements at the hospital.

Most of the Jewish leadership, that is the non-movement leadership, was planning on spending the day at the various synagogues still functioning in the ghetto. The ninth day of the month of Av was a day of mourning for the Jewish People. So much sorrow had been bestowed upon them on that day in history that they should have expected something terrible to happen. Officially, the day of mourning was associated with the destruction of the first and second temples in Jerusalem – the first in 421 AD and the second in the year 70 CE – both on the same day in the Jewish calendar. However, the woes of the Jews on the ninth of Av, known in Hebrew as Tisha B'Av, were not going to stop there: The Bar Kochva revolt for independence in 132 was crushed; ten thousand Jews were slaughtered during the first crusade in 1095; the Jews of England were expelled in 1290; and in 1942, the inquisition in Spain and Portugal culminated with the decree of expulsion of the Jews from the Iberian Peninsula, all on the same date on the Jewish calendar. It was a bad day for the Jews, and this Tisha B'Av, in the Jewish year of 5702, or 1942, another historic tragedy was about to be added to the long and growing list.

After 10:30 in the morning, far too late to warn Nahum of the German's plans, notices had been posted and special orders were delivered to 6000 Jews with clear instructions: All Jews, regardless of age or sex, will be resettled, with the exception of those working for, and the wives and children of, members of German institutions or companies or the Judenrat, Jewish hospital personnel, Jewish Order Service members and Jews in Jewish hospitals on the day of resettlement. Each person would be allowed to bring up to 15 kilograms of belongings, plus any valuables. They would need to have provisions for three days and the operation would begin one hour from the moment of the decree. The Judenrat would be required to deliver 6000 people each day until told to stop. The Jews would assemble at the Jewish Hospital on Stawki Street at 11:00 AM, commencing July 22, 1942. The building would be evacuated immediately to utilize the wards for the operation.

It became the Judenrat's responsibility to accommodate the Nazi plans, and they also had to make sure that the Jews of the ghetto knew exactly what the punishments would be. These orders were posted as soon as the operation had begun:

Any Jew found trying to leave the ghetto at any time during the resettlement action will be shot.

Any Jew performing any form of opposition to the resettlement will be shot.

Any Jew who is not exempt from the resettlement operation and is found anywhere in Warsaw after the operation is complete will be shot.

If these orders are not carried out as stated, a corresponding number of Jews will be shot at random.

"They sure like having people shot," said Peretz upon seeing the orders.

The Judenrat was instructed to begin with refugee assembly institutions, prisons and old people's homes.

What Nahum did not know, as no one in the movement knew, was that he and Miriam could not have chosen a worse place to meet.

Just as Miriam was preparing to leave the house that morning, Ida came running in, slammed the door and tried to catch her breath.

"It's...It's starting..."

"What's starting?" asked Anna and Miriam in unison.

"The deportations to the camps...They've made a decree. At 11:00..." Ida sat down and held her head.

After a moment of rest, Ida told them what she had heard. The first 6000 would be from the weaker parts of the population, including children, but it looked like they weren't going to stop until there was no one left.

"You can't go," Anna said to Miriam.

"What about Nahum?"

"I don't know."

"Don't go out there," said Ida. "It's crazy now. But we won't be able to stay here for long either. Soon our names will be on the list. We have to get out of here."

"We're not leaving yet," said Anna. "Most of us aren't listed with the Judenrat, so you won't have to worry about being on a list. But this house won't be safe for long."

"I have to get Nahum," said Miriam. "He has no idea."

"He will soon," said Ida. "News travels fast and the Judenrat will waste no time creating their lists."

"Scum," said Miriam. "Those Judenrat, dirty scum. I hope they rot in hell. I hope they're the first to go."

"They're exempt," said Ida. "So are the Jewish Police."

"Those bastards!" said Miriam. "I knew we didn't kill enough of them. I have to go find Nahum."

"No one can leave here now," said Anna as little Yehuda climbed onto her back. "We'll wait for everyone to return, and tonight we'll discuss our options. I'm glad you made it back Ida. This is no time to be making runs."

"Who's here?" asked Ida.

"Emil and Tuvia are in the other room sleeping," said Miriam. "Rachel is upstairs visiting the Sprinsak family. I think two of their boys are very ill."

"Where's Peretz?"

"He should be back soon," said Miriam. "He went to the movement office."

"As soon as they all get back, we'll talk," said Anna, placing Yehuda on the floor. He had just learned to walk and was moving on to the running phase, although he did not nearly have the strength that Shimi had had. But thanks to the superhuman efforts of Mordechai and other movement members, he was getting fed, eating almost twice as much as the rest of his housemates.

"How long will Nahum wait for you?" asked Ida.

"I don't know," said Miriam. "We didn't say. I imagine he'll see what's going on down there and leave the area."

"He'll be back," said Ida.

But Nahum did not return that day, and as soon as Peretz came home and heard the news, he immediately left again to find out what he could.

Peretz left with Ida back to the movement office where it turned out some members had been monitoring the Aktion closely. One of the leaders had threatened a Judenrat member and had received a copy of the list that was given to the Germans. The movement was checking that none of their members ended up on the transport.

It was within these investigations that news of what had happened to Nahum reached them. It was Peretz who first received the information and within a short time of the commencement of the Aktion, Peretz and Ida returned home to tell the rest of the house of Nahum's fate.

"There was pure madness at the hospital, as you could imagine. We don't know how many were shot, but there may have been hundreds. In the end, the Germans got their 6000 and even a few more. We heard from one member who escaped the hospital – he had been working there when it was evacuated – that Nahum arrived into the madness and was immediately hauled to one of the back rooms of the hospital. He didn't try to resist, probably because he had no way out – except death. He tried to hide in the upper floors, but this just delayed his departure for a few hours. By the end of the evening, all the Jews who had been rounded up in the hospital were taken to the trains. It seems Nahum was among them and left on one of the night transits to either Majdanek or Treblinka."

"Treblinka?" said Anna, "That's the new camp we heard about."

"Yes," continued Peretz. "If he's there, we won't have a chance to contact him. We haven't established contacts with the prisoner yet. None have escaped. Too young a camp. If he's in Majdanek, we may be able to get information about him."

"How can they do that?" said Miriam. "Those Judenrat, criminals. How can they do that?"

"Don't worry," said Peretz, "they'll pay. We'll see to that."

"Assassinations?" asked Miriam.

"We've been discussing some serious actions to teach these people a lesson. They are Jewish Nazis. Simply sadistic Jewish Nazis. There has been so much betrayal that we no longer can sit quietly."

"Shouldn't it be," said Anna, "the Germans we're fighting? This could be counterproductive."

"You seem to be regressing, my dear," said Peretz. "Anna, I love you dearly, but you must understand how angry you make me every time I convince you of something, and then a week later you let your conscience get the best of you. Nahum is gone; we probably will never see him again, and we have to do something before we're next. Do you get it? We have to destroy the infrastructure of fear and deception that the Germans use to control us. Yes, starvation is an effective tool…"

"Effective tool? You make it sound like a strategic element. It's an effective tool to kill us. They control the food entering the ghetto, and despite our efforts, they do a damn good job at keeping us to a slice a bread a day – if we're lucky. And now look what's going on. The effective tool you're talking about will annihilate an entire people in this city. I don't think by helping them kill a few Jews we will do anything but make them laugh a little harder. Let's start shooting at some guards at night. That will shake them up. In a few months, there won't be anyone left here. I have a feeling that they will soon cut off the last of our rations, and we will only have what we can smuggle in. And from the looks of things, even that will be next to impossible. Peretz, we need to focus our energies on disrupting their machine, and killing a few Judenrat...and don't get me wrong, I agree they deserve to die...won't do it."

"You find a way to shoot guards without having the Germans come in the next day to execute ten people for every bullet we shot, and I'll be the first to open fire. We're not ready for that kind of activity. We have too much to lose. Right now we need to slow them down by removing their conspirators. And as far as I'm concerned, they stopped being a part of the Jewish community the minute they led the first family of Jews to their death. And it's not just the Judenrat that needs a good whipping. The Jewish Police, who killed eight of us in cold blood just a few months ago, must also be stopped."

But the next day, one of the Judenrat leaders surprised all of them. That afternoon, word came that the head of the Warsaw ghetto Judenrat, Adam Czerniaków, preferred to take his own life by swallowing a cyanide pill rather than give the Germans Jewish children. After failing to exempt orphan children from the Aktion lists, he chose to end his life. It was a sign that even the Judenrat was beginning to understand that the operation was not a resettlement operation, but an act of eradication.

In the house that night, a strange and controversial memorial service was held for the bold leader who refused to live with the knowledge that he was helping the Germans kill children. It would be a significant moment for Anna because she too began to feel that suicide was now her only alternative. However, she, like many others in the movement, was determined to take with her as many Germans as possible. She began talking to people about their options. Already, many in Hashomer Hatzair were talking about using the few weapons they had to slow down the deportations, but they feared the reprisals would cost them even more lives. Anna had other ideas. She wanted to make it look like the Germans were being shot from outside the ghetto, by the Polish underground.

While she was working on her new strategy, Peretz was moving ahead with his plans. He worked diligently with other movement leaders throughout the Great Resettlement Action to target Judenrat members who were not as brave as their ex-leader. There seemed to be a consensus among the movement's militant heads that this was their only course of action. The Germans could not have been so effective without some cooperation, and the Judenrat had been consistently providing it. Not all members of the Judenrat had cooperated with the Nazis. Some had used their position to quietly sabotage efforts to implement the deportation but usually failed miserably. These few noble men of Sodom gained the respect of the youth movements, while the others were about to feel their wrath. This group, many of whom had made the decision to join the Judenrat out of public responsibility to the community, became nothing more than Nazi puppets. Many Jewish leaders placed themselves in leadership roles outside the Judenrat, assisting in everything from welfare and education to underground political action. Needless to say, they were highly respected by the youth movements and often sought out for advice and assistance. The youth leaders themselves, because of their age, never had to face the dilemma of whether to join the Judenrat – they simply were never asked – and this gave them an advantage in being able to present an alternative to the leadership of the Judenrat. However, up until the mass deportations, no group, youth-led or otherwise, ever proposed a viable alternative entity to the Judenrat. The Judenrat itself was involved in helping set up a youth movement training kibbutz in the ghetto – although some Judenrat members were vocally against helping the youth movements. It was only after they were seen as Nazi conspirators that things began to get nasty.

By mid-August Peretz and his friends at the underground's headquarters were ready to begin implementation of their plans to assassinate Judenrat leaders who they felt were particularly aiding the Nazi cause. Their first target would be a man, Josef Levinski, whom no one really liked even before the war. He was a pompous, grouchy, irritating man with a voice far too piercing for his size. Most people were quite shocked the first time they would hear him speak, not only because of the trash that seemed to continuously stream from his mustached mouth, but because of the high-pitched, nauseating sounds reverberating around the room. He had been a businessman, a ruthless one at that, and had trampled many on his way to the top. Movement leaders had even gone so far as to accuse him of being solely responsible for anti-Semitism in Poland. Regardless of whether that accusation had any merit, he was an inspiration for the movement to produce his antithesis: a new Jew, a Jew that would no longer find pride in being the middleman, financing, taking loans and living off the interest, a Jew who would work the land, not only for a living but to better himself. The new Jew would build a country that the whole world could look up to and who would be "A Light unto the Nations."

But first, people like Levinski had to die. As an active leader in the Jewish community before the war, he was a perfect candidate for a leadership position within the Judenrat, and following the recent suicide, was a candidate to head the organization. However, his rash attitude and business history had made him plenty of enemies. There would be few willing to let him take any position of power in the community – except perhaps the Germans. He was perfect for them.

Although he was not appointed to head the Judenrat, he was doing enough damage from the side. The Hashomer Hatzair leaders figured that his death would not trigger a strong reaction from the community – not that anyone was in any kind of condition to react to anything at that point; he was simply an easy target. Being close to the food source, he was still quite heavy for his size. Prior to the war, Levinski was fat, very fat. Some thought it was an image thing, but it was more a result of having so much money and power that he never had to pick up anything. Even after three years where everyone around him was starving, he maintained a good deal of his pre-war girth, bringing Peretz to tell whoever would listen that "we could hit him in a dark alley, blind-folded and standing on our heads." His vigor granted him the opportunity to do the honors and assassinate Levinski.

But Peretz didn't kill him on that mid-August evening when the assassination attempt was made in front of Levinski's tiny house. The street was well lit, the weather was perfect and Levinski was right on time. Peretz did get off a shot, and it did hit the man as he strolled home from a long day sending Jews to their death. But it didn't hit him where Peretz had intended. In fact, it barely nicked the side of his fat arm. Peretz and his accomplice did not wait around to see the results of their mission, because, as it happened, Levinski was sure he was much more seriously injured than he turned out to be and fell to the ground upon getting nicked as if getting shot right in the heart, where Peretz was actually aiming. Peretz and his friends were long gone before any German guards or Jewish Police could arrive at the scene, but he left behind an embarrassment that would plague him for the rest of the year.

Earlier that evening, Peretz and another young man from headquarters, one of Mordechai's men, set out to ambush their victim. They knew where he would be because not only was he powerful, he was audacious, making him powerful and predictable, the result of a blemished upbringing, too many toys and simple foolishness. They could not understand how someone in his position could be so assured of his safety on the ghetto streets when night after night people were slaughtered and dumped to rot on the cold cobblestones. Did he not realize he was being talked about? That he was a target? He overestimated the German's ability to protect him, and he was not alone. Many felt that the Jewish Police and the Judenrat were impervious and did not need to fear unexpected death despite proof to the contrary. Germans had killed both Judenrat members and Jewish Police when they felt like it, and no one, no matter how pompous, was immune. The intelligent knew it and took the necessary precautions. The dumb got killed. Of course, prior to the shooting of Levinski, no one thought the bullets would come from a Jew. And the unintended consequence of that fateful night would be that from that moment forward, Judenrat members went home a lot earlier.

However, on that night, Levinski's life was spared. He was spared as the Jewish leaders spent the day preparing lists that would lead to the banishment of thousands to a fate no Jew, even during the worst pogroms where rape and pillage rained like manna from hell, could imagine. He was spared just because of a few freak occurrences taking place simultaneously.

It all began with a dirty hat. The man who accompanied Peretz on his operation, Avrum, was instructed to follow Levinski home that night, and it seemed that Levinski's hat was a bit dirty. Walking briskly, Levinski decided to bang the hat against his leg to clean it off. However, he seemed to have lost his concentration, because the hat slipped from his hand, was caught by the breeze and flew about twenty meters behind him right at Avrum's feet. Avrum tried his best to act like he should have been there, but no one outside of the protected few walked the streets after sundown, and Levinski was suspicious.

"What are you doing out at a time like this?" asked Levinski."

"Just going home, like you, I suppose," said Avrum. "Here's your hat."

"Thank you. Get off the streets."

"I will. Thanks for your concern."

"No concern. Get off the streets."

Peretz had taken a position at the next intersection. The neighborhood was quiet, except for a siren that could be heard far off in the Aryan part of town. There was a very light breeze, it was the one that grabbed the hat, but the trees hardly bothered to respond to it. Peretz prepared the pistol and waited behind a small bush. He had removed his scarf and tied it to his waist under his shirt. It was dark enough for him to stand – no one would have noticed his presence – but holding a gun, he thought it best to hide behind something and make sure his white scarf was well hidden under his shirt.

He had asked for this mission, he had wanted to do it. He had said, "I am destined to go down in history as one who fought back." Anna lost the argument with him this time, but he told her on several occasions that he respected her judgment and would first find a better way to express himself before firing the first shot. She didn't find that funny in the least and told him to go to hell. He said he would.

Now he was poised for his first kill. His pistol, a gift from the Polish Home Army, an underground resistance organization just beginning to rise

103

from the ashes of a destroyed nation, was held ready. He had been trained in theory but had never actually taken a single shot in his life. He, therefore, knew that he would have to wait until Levinski was passing only a few meters in front of him before opening fire. He also knew that he had only one shot, one chance to do what he knew was crucial to slowing down the German death machine.

Levinski finally turned and left Avrum with a dilemma. Should he slow his pace and remain a safe distance behind, possibly arousing suspicion, or should he pass Levinski and act as if he was really on his way home, taking into account the instructions of such an important man. Whatever he did, he had to still make sure that Levinski crossed the next street and was shot as planned. He opted to walk ahead of Levinski, who waddled along the road quite slowly. Passing him, he looked over at the bushes for Peretz. As he crossed the intersection and walked onto the street where Levinski was to be put to death, Levinski was only a few steps behind him. Avrum did his best to walk slowly to keep Levinski in the corner of his eye.

Levinski crossed the intersection and as he too entered his street, he stopped to scratch his knee. There was no way that he could possibly scratch his knee and continue walking at the same time; that would be a task demanding agility he had not had since he was a baby.

Avrum kept walking, and Peretz, who was bending out of sight, could not see the two approaching. As Avrum passed the spot where Peretz was to attack, Peretz attacked. He jumped out of the bushes causing crackling sounds that could have been interpreted as tiny bullets blasting. Thinking no one else should be there at that time of night, he aimed the gun at Avrum, as Avrum was supposed to be following him from behind. Avrum raised his hands, and Peretz saw that the man in front of him was far too thin to be Levinski, so he lowered his weapon. Levinski, who had finished with his itch, saw Avrum raise his hands and stopped cold in his tracks. Avrum pointed behind him, and Peretz took aim. Had it not been for the grey cat that came scampering out of the bushes between Peretz and Levinski, he may have hit his target. But the cat distracted him, and during that split second, Levinski stepped to the side. He was most likely trying to jump but his mass prevented him from taking any kind of flight. Peretz took a step in his direction and pulled the trigger. Levinski fell. Avrum grabbed Peretz's arm and they ran.

It wasn't until the next morning that word came about Levinski's injury.

"He's where?" said Peretz, quite shocked that he had failed.

"In the hospital. He'll be released later today. He was shot in the arm.

It's not serious at all," said Ida who had returned early that morning from doing some surveillance rounds.

"Did he see you?" asked Anna, who was still quite angry with Peretz for going through with it in the first place.

"I don't think so. He was too far away. That's why I missed. Avrum was in front of him. There was something with a hat and then he stopped in the street... I don't know what happened. It was so simple, and we messed it up."

"I think you messed it up long before arriving at his street," said Anna.

"What's that supposed to mean?" said Peretz. "Do you think it'll do any good to say I told you so now? Let it go. What's done is done. If I could do it again, I would."

"Listen to me, Peretz. This was stupid. You are trying to prove something that may give you some pride, but will not help keep people alive... ."

"Pride? Do you think I'm doing this for my own well being? Anna, I'm surprised at you."

"The Germans don't care about a few dead Jews," said Anna. "I hate Levinski as much as you, but this was wrong. Now, what are we going to do? You have to find out if he saw you. We know he saw Avrum, and he will have to go into hiding. I am going to try to get him out of the ghetto today."

"They sent him to the ditch," said Ida.

The ditch was an underground room that could be reached through the sewer entrance on Leszno Street near the ghetto walls and was a key meeting point for those entering and exiting the ghetto through the underground passageways. It was not a bad place to wait out a German operation, but to stay down there for more than a few hours would be hell. It was quite dark, although the light from the underground tunnels reflected off the concrete walls enough to be able to see silhouettes. Rats were running around – the types of silhouettes that you really did not enjoy seeing, although they tended to leave people alone, unless, of course, there was bread around. But the worst part of the sewer system was the stench. It was enough to drive you mad. Since this particular sewer system ran under the ghetto, the most densely populated urban prison in human history, dead bodies lined the streets and the rains washed their odors into the drains leading below the city. The reek was intoxicating – and not in a good way. They say that humans get used to bad smells, but not down there, not underneath the small plot of hell they called the Warsaw ghetto.

It was to this glorious spot that Avrum was banished, and Peretz began thinking that he too should join him. Ida had ideas on how they could escape the city and run to the forests where the partisans would be able to integrate them into their forces. But ever since the start of the Aktions, it was much more difficult to get males out of the Warsaw area. While smart, blonde girls could either do their Aryan act and if need be use their sexual charm to get past an eighteen-year-old German boy acting like a soldier, the men were always immediately asked to drop their pants if there was any doubt or suspicion. Even a hint or inkling that there may be the slightest possibility that Jewish blood ran close to his veins would be cause for the guard, or worse yet, SS officer, to say, "Drop 'em." And that would be the end. No covering up that surgical error. Circumcision was final and in occupied Poland it was fatal.

Ida, however, had a plan. During her travels outside of the walls, she had noticed that there was a section of Aryan Warsaw that was virtually unguarded. She never understood why, but she knew that if they could emerge from the sewers several blocks east of where they normally ascended, there was an easy route out to the forests. From there it was just a long walk out to where the partisans would meet them and take them under their combative wings.

Peretz was all for it but first wanted to wait and see if he had been seen.

Late that night, long after everyone had gone to sleep, there was a knock on the door. It was a messenger from Mordechai. It turned out that Levinski was so shaken up by the event that he either honestly had amnesia or had made a decision not to rat out more Jews. The tale that he told was one that only someone of Levinski's supercilious nature could think up. He said that it was a Polish bandit who had tried to hold up another Jew, Avrum, and Levinski, in an attempt to save him, got himself shot. A very heroic lie, but one that infuriated Peretz so much that he threatened to go back out there and get it right this time. Peretz was so angry that he entirely forgot that his life had just been saved. Of course, some thought that having the opportunity to escape Warsaw was a preferable alternative. But for Peretz, remaining and fighting was much better. His heroism was based on humility and not on dedication to a cause he honestly believed in.

Avrum was released from the sewers after 24 hours in the ditch, smelling much like the rats who eventually stopped ignoring him. After reviewing the events of the evening, it had occurred to Peretz that Avrum must have looked quite innocent to Levinski, and there really was no way he could have known that he was in on it; just a man walking home late at night and getting mugged. And Peretz was quite far from Levinski, probably looking much like a ghost in the dark night. They all decided to put the whole ordeal behind them, and Anna demanded that Peretz concentrate on more constructive things, like preparing for the inevitable – Aktions against their house.

While Peretz and Avrum were attempting to gun down the Judenrat members who had been doing their best to assist the Nazis, Anna was preparing a plan of action to enlist as many movement people as possible to prepare for resistance. One night, while holding a clandestine meeting with some of her roommates and children she had led before the war, she commenced her campaign.

"It is no coincidence," she began, "that our movement is taking on leadership roles in this community. We have never held the position that sitting on the fence and waiting for action can be anything but detrimental to our fate and that of the Jewish community, who now faces a threat so great that it will shape the lives of all Jews for the rest of eternity. We have a strong organizational, educational and ideological foundation that has been an integral part of our strength in this new reality. Our movement-grown leadership, along with a wide range of public services, organizational skills, strong values of responsibility for the movement as a collective entity and for the Jewish People as a whole, have all contributed to bringing us to this position of action. We, as young, energetic people, are free from the bonds of public expectations and normative behavior, unlike all those adult organizations that surround us. And that allows us to act along lines of what is right, what is good and what is necessary for our survival – not just our own personal, physical survival, but the survival of the movement and our people as a proud contributor to making the world a better place.

"We have adapted to this hellish reality well, contributed to the education, the morale and the physical needs of our community. Now it is time to make our final contribution: to fight before there is nothing to fight for. Thousands of our friends and family have been taken to camps, to become slaves, to serve German masters and to die. We are not going to follow in their footsteps. We will give the Germans cause to worry, cause to fear the Jews who would not give up. The Great Resettlement Aktion is slowly removing what little dignity we have in the ghetto. No more.

"It is time for us to leave this small apartment, as many of us are registered, and it is only a matter of time before they come knocking on our door. We must go into hiding, prepare munitions, evacuate the weak to safety and make sure the strong can stay and fight. Everyone here has a role to play, and I want us to start implementing the preparation plans that Mordechai has spoken about. He is the only person in the ghetto who can lead now. The Judenrat is dead, as are the mongrels from the Jewish Police. We are in charge now. We are going to fight."

Anna's words were heard outside of the walls of their apartment as one of the participants in the meeting decided, with Anna's permission, to write an article in the movement newsletter echoing Anna's call.

While the movement debated Mordechai's plans and Anna's demand for action, Anna was facing a much more personal crisis. She did not fool herself when she said that the weak must escape, understanding very well that the weakest among them was little Yehuda.

"Hanna, I have to ask you something," she said the next day. "You know what is going to happen here. I know that you are not one of the fighters among us…"

"I would do what is necessary," said Hanna, "but, no I do not want to fight."

"I wouldn't expect you to. But I need you to do something for me, something much more important than fighting."

"What is it?"

"I want you to escape to the forest, to the partisans, with little Yehuda."

"What about you? You can't leave him!"

Anna's eyes filled with tears. "It's what I have to do. As bad as it has been here, it will only get much worse once we start fighting. Tuvia agrees. He was apprehensive at first, but I of course, I am too. I know that he will be safer with you, with the partisans, who can take care of him and maybe find him a temporary home until this war is over. I will prepare a few things and make sure that you have a clear passage. Hanna, there is one more thing."

"What is it.?" Hanna reached out and took Anna's hand.

"I want you to try to get him to Palestine. If you don't want to go nor have a safe alternative, I will understand if you allow someone else to take him. But do me this favor. Yehuda was never circumcised. It was intentional since I feared that there would be a day when he would have to escape the ghetto. If he is caught, you can always claim he is your son and that you are both gentiles. But as soon as he is safe, as soon as he is in Eretz Yisrael, have him circumcised so he will not stand out in our Jewish homeland. Can you do that?"

"I have long ago adopted your love of Eretz Yisrael, Anna. Even though I was never a movement person, I have been around you long enough to understand its importance – especially now."

Anna broke down and held Hanna. Even though it would still be weeks before they parted, Anna knew that the fateful date would eventually arrive, and there was no guarantee that they would ever meet again.

While Anna was preparing to send her son off to the forests of Poland, a great debate began within the movement as to whether it was not a smart move for all of the movement members to do the same. The argument held that a 300 strong force that could be removed from the ghetto to fight the Germans in the forests would be a force to contend with, an army that could do serious damage to supply lines and divert German energies from the front to the inland areas. Anna had still not attended a single meeting in the movement office, and she was not going to change that policy now. She always felt it was too risky and a second, less official office needed to exist just in case the Germans, or the Jewish Police, ever came across it. She invited a number of junior leaders to her house and let them know what she thought about the idea.

"I know that you think that just because I am sending my son to the forests that it may be a good idea for more of us to join the partisans. You are wrong. There is no place in Poland that symbolizes better the struggle of Jewish life than Warsaw, and here we must stay until the last of us is driven out by force. This is our home, and it is imperative that the Germans understand that they will not be able to remove us from our home without a fight. I do not know what that fight will look like. I am still not convinced that it will have much military merit, but it will send a clear message and let us retain our dignity.

"Our movement has always been the vanguard of Zionist thinking, and I do not intend to let that change now. If Gordonia, Halutz or Macabbi Tzair want to leave, let them. Hashomer Hatzair must stay.

"Yes, I am sending Yehuda to the partisans, but he will not fight." There was a nervous chuckle from the room. "I do recommend that anyone who does not feel fit enough to stay and give to this cause join him. "You must all know that this will be the most difficult thing I will ever do in my life. I am not sure whether life in the forests as a fugitive will be any better than life in this miserable place. But I do know that when the fighting starts and Germans are killing Jews on sight, this will be no place for a baby."

Thirteen

January 17, 1943

Had Tuvia known that giving up rations for his son would almost kill him, he may have searched out an alternative. But by the time he realized that he was deathly ill it was too late, the damage had been done, his frail body would work no more. He had taken on a significant role in setting up camps within the dwindling ghetto, which now held only 60,000 of its once close to 450,000 Jews. As he lay almost motionless on the bed next to his sleeping child, the ghetto's silence startled him.

Anna, who was also a recipient of Tuvia's generosity, was still the healthiest of the group. She had tried to keep the rations coming to keep Yehuda strong, but she was oblivious to Tuvia's sacrifices. Jews in the ghetto were officially rationed 1,100 calories a day when the ghetto first closed. However, the deliberate Nazi policy was to cut that ration continuously, bringing on illness and starvation. The reality was that by mid-1941, each person in the ghetto was allotted a weekly amount of food that consisted of 14 ounces of bread, 4.5 ounces of meat products, 1.75 ounces of sugar, and 0.9 ounces of fat; this meant that each Jew in the Warsaw ghetto was getting only 350 calories a day from the German rations. If not for the smuggling efforts, most of the ghetto would not have even survived through 1942.

Tuvia and Anna had made it a point to make sure that Yehuda received at least 1000 calories a day, a feast by ghetto standards, and a nearly impossible task if not for the apparatus that Anna and the youth movements, with the help of the young women smugglers, had set up. But even with the extra smuggling, Tuvia felt that Yehuda needed more than what his mother's breasts could provide. So he added some of his rations to Yehuda's and Anna's. It eventually took its toll.

By this time, Anna was deeply involved in the movement's preparations to stun the Germans if they decided to restart the Aktions. Hanna was caring for Yehuda, and Ida had become so skilled at getting in and out of the ghetto that she once told Anna that it was easier for her to walk around the Aryan sector of Warsaw than to go down her own street.

They all had been encouraged by the return of one of their fellow Hashomer Hatzair members, Berl, who had escaped from the train to Treblinka during the previous summer. After weeks of roaming the Polish countryside, moving from Polish farm to Polish farm, he returned to the ghetto. Anna and her housemates were sure that Nahum would have been able to do the same. If it was possible to escape the death trains, then Nahum would do it.

A few weeks prior, Anna had been involved in writing the call to resistance by the Jewish Fighting Organization in the Warsaw ghetto. She contributed a few lines, but only now was reading the final version that had been distributed among the "Jewish Masses." It read like the Communist Manifesto, Anna thought, but after a second reading realized it wasn't up to Marx's level.

To the Jewish Masses in the Ghetto,

On January 22, 1943, six months will have passed since the deportations from Warsaw began. We all remember well the days of terror during which 300,000 of our brothers and sisters were cruelly put to death in the death camp of Treblinka. Six months have passed of life in constant fear of death, not knowing what the next day may bring. We have received information from all sides about the destruction of the Jews in the General government in Germany and in the occupied territories. As we listen to this bitter news, we wait for our own hour to come – every day and every moment. Today we must understand that the Nazi murderers have let us live only because they want to make use of our capacity to work to our last drop of blood and sweat – to our final breath. We are slaves; and when the slaves are no longer profitable, they are killed. Everyone among us must understand that, and every one among us must remember it always.

During the past few weeks, certain people have spread stories about letters that were said to have been received from Jews deported from Warsaw, who were said to be in labor camps near Minsk or Bobruisk. Jews in your masses, do not believe these tales. They are spread by Jews who are working for the Gestapo! The blood-stained murderers have a particular aim in doing this: to reassure the Jewish population so that the next deportation can be carried out without difficulty, with a minimum of force and without losses to the Germans. They want the Jews not to prepare hiding-places and not to resist. Jews, do not repeat these lying tales! Do not help the Nazi agents. The Gestapo's dastardly people will get their just desserts. Jews in your masses, the hour is near! You must be prepared to resist, not to give yourselves up like sheep to the slaughter. Not even one Jew must go to the trains! People who cannot resist actively must offer passive resistance – that is, by hiding. We have now received information from Lvov that the Jewish Police itself carried out the deportation of 3,000 Jews. Such things will not happen again in Warsaw. The killing of Leibski proves it. Now our slogan must be:

Let everyone be ready to die like a man!
January 1943

She now sat wondering if it would have any effect on the Jews of the ghetto. They had endured so much, they were exhausted and frightened, Death was so much easier than fighting. Would those few who had survived the last Aktion be willing to fight? Perhaps they would hide. That was easier than fighting. What would the Judenrat do with this? she asked herself.

The repercussions of the flubbed assassination attempt reached far and wide, and the movement chiefs, determined to redeem themselves, had that November successfully killed Leibski, a Judenrat leader involved in the great deportations of the summer. Amazingly, their policy had unexpected consequences when no less than three Judenrat members asked what they could do to assist in the movement's efforts to disrupt the Aktions. The first thing on the list was to remove all of the main players, including everyone living in three movement apartments, from any lists the Germans or Judenrat had. Since most of the lists had not been delivered to the German offices as of the August attempt on Levinski's life, the job was easily done. And from August on, the eight members of the house were no longer alive, according to the Judenrat; all killed off by starvation. The flat was empty, as was the building used for the Hashomer Hatzair offices. Had Peretz not been so embarrassed by his blunder, he probably would have come back to Anna with a nice "I told you so." But in the end, she was the first to admit the error in her judgment.

"Tuvia, what is it?" asked Ida who had come with a special ration of bread for Tuvia. "Have this."

"It's so quiet out there," he said.

"It snowed last night. You know how the snow silences the streets."

"I used to love to see the snow covering the streets."

"There are fewer bodies out there," she said, "it's kind of pretty again."

"I'm not going to make it am I?" he said, closing his eyes. Yehuda turned over and took a deep breath. "How's he doing?"

"You have a strong boy."

"Anna's genes."

"Tuvia, you'll be fine. I've seen worse."

"Yes, but they were already dead."

"You'll be fine. I'll see to it. Now eat this, and I'll melt you some fresh snow to drink."

As Ida began to leave, Tuvia grabbed her hand. She stopped and looked down at the frail man who had been dissolving before her very eyes.

"Thank you," he said.

Ida smiled and left the room. When she returned a few minutes later, Tuvia had fallen asleep. She was startled at first, thinking he may have passed away, but that would have surprised her since she had been honest when she said she had seen worse. Tuvia, as bad as he looked, could still come through if he received a small amount of extra rations. Anna had told Ida that it was most important that movement activists get all of the extra rations. Everyone else in the ghetto would most likely not survive the winter anyway; either they would be deported when the Aktions resumed, or they would die of disease or exposure – although there was now ample living space for the 60,000 who remained.

But Tuvia was just sleeping, and Ida left the water next to his bed for when he awoke.

While Anna planned her revolution, Ida took her job seriously, nursing Tuvia back to health with the muster of a mother and the hardiness of a warrior. But it was a daunting task, one that almost killed her several times. Her drive to bring Tuvia food brought her into close contact with Nazi patrols and even a few of the remaining Jewish Police – whom she simply threatened by mentioning Mordechai's name. But on more than one occasion, Ida's life was in jeopardy, and all for a piece of bread or a slice of cheese smuggled in to feed Tuvia.

Had the Germans known the extent of the smuggling by the Jewish movement girls they would have raised the ghetto and shot every female on site back then. But the movement women were now professionals; after all, they had been at it for years. Just as one exit was discovered and closed, another two were opened, and the traffic of women entering and exiting the ghetto kept thousands alive. For a few city blocks aromatically sealed, there were a lot of holes. Most were dug by these brave young women, driven by an ideology instilled in them by leaders like Anna, Mordechai and Ida. Self-confidence and Aryan features were the key to their successes outside the ghetto walls – that and fast thinking on their feet. Many times the correct answer with the right smile or sway of the head would save a young Jewish woman posing as a Pole on the forbidden-to-Jews trains during a surprise inspection. Ida herself had almost been caught returning to the ghetto with a handgun. Several SS officers boarded the train at one of the stations and began asking for documents. That in itself was not a problem for Ida; her documents were well forged and had often passed the tests of German and Polish officials. However, the guards were also checking handbags and luggage, and the contents of Ida's bag would have landed her in a German torture chamber, where any attempt to equivocate would, if she was lucky, promptly lead to receiving a bullet in the temple. Ida kept her wits and immediately saw a solution. She ran to the German train driver, hoping that there was at least one humane German left on the planet, and asked him to hold the bag. His hesitation was almost fatal to her since the German officers were approaching her car quickly. The conductor asked her what it was she was hiding. She smiled at him in a flattering fashion and said, "Counterfeit money for poor Poles in frontline villages." He smiled back at what he believed to be a generous Polish gentile and agreed. Her life was spared. On another occasion, Ida was surprised as she turned a corner and ran directly into a checkpoint. This time she was carrying maps and codes from the Jewish resistance and her only option seemed to be to run. But she didn't run, and when asked to open her bag and present her documents, she buckled over in apparent pain. When the officer asked her what was the matter, she said, "I am having my period and I have terrible cramps." But what she had actually done was slip the maps and codes into her undergarment while bending over. The officer was so embarrassed by her open disclosure that he never even checked her documents and let her go on her way.

That afternoon planes could be seen flying over the ghetto. They did not look like the low-winged German Messerschmitt fighters flown by the Luftwaffe that had been seen from the ghetto streets in the past. Rumors circulated that they were American planes, as someone thought they recognized the five-pointed star on the side of the aircraft. These sightings gave way to additional unsubstantiated reports that the Germans were faltering on the Eastern front and that it was only a matter of time until the Russians advanced back into Poland. The stories fueled additional vitality to the resistance efforts, and the movement worked harder than ever to gain access to weapons and ammunition needed to take on the enemy. They felt the Nazis would be so preoccupied with their war efforts that they would not be able to send reinforcements once they met with the Jewish guerilla resistance. Anna, of course, warned the movement leadership that they were underestimating the German desire to annihilate the Jews, and they would just as soon divert forces from critical battles in Russia than let the Jews have an easy victory in Warsaw. "Never underestimate the enemy," she told them.

For Anna, the day she had dreaded arrived with notice that the Germans were going to resume the Aktions. Eight thousand Jews were ordered to assemble in the courtyards of their apartment houses where their papers would be checked. She knew that it was time to send Yehuda away with Hanna, and the departure had to be that evening. Two other girls would be joining them. The four would leave via a sewer passage in the central ghetto.

They received explicit instructions from Ida, including maps, code names and addresses of people who would assist them to leave the Aryan part of the city and find the partisans.

Hanna was visibly nervous as Anna prepared a bag for Yehuda.

"I have something I would like you to keep with Yehuda at all times. It will be a way of him knowing who I was if we don't meet..." her voice trailed off as she began to cry. Ida and Hanna were crying as well as they all hugged until Anna released them to finish what she was saying. She removed from her pouch a silver oval locket with a brushed finish on a silver chain and placed it around Hanna's neck.

"When he is old enough not to choke on it, I want you to give it to him. Hanna reached down and looked at the locket. There was no picture inside, just an engraving in Polish:

From your loving mother
ANNA

"I will make sure that he has it," said Hanna. "But there is one thing that I am sure of, more than anything else, more than I am sure I will survive, I am sure that you will see Yehuda again. I am willing to bet on it."

Hanna and Anna used to joke about how Anna always won the bets they made. Whatever it was they bet on, Anna was always right and Hanna was always wrong. And they always bet for the same thing, blueberries and cream, served in bed for breakfast. Hanna had brought Anna that dish so many times that she would buy the ingredients as soon as the bet was made, knowing that Anna would once again earn her meal. But Anna always shared the bowl of berries. Hanna would always say, "Next time, I'll win."

"I will take that bet," said Anna. "Not because I do not believe that we will never meet again, but because I want you to finally win."

"I will, you'll see."

"I am looking forward to preparing the blueberries and cream."

"Don't talk about food," said Ida.

The three girls stood with tears streaming down their faces. Yehuda was asleep in his crib, and soon Anna would lift him out for the last time, wrap him in blankets and send him out of the ghetto through the underground passages that the movement had turned into their personal walkways. Anna had hoped that the Germans would wait until spring before starting the Aktion. She knew that sending Yehuda out into the devastating cold would make the journey even more dangerous for him, but she could not chance to leave him in the ghetto a day longer.

Anna went over to the bed, bent down and placed her arms under his limp body, rested her lips on his forehead and wept, her tears dripping down her cheeks and onto Yehuda's. After several seconds, when Ida and Hanna, both still crying themselves, came and put their hands around her, she sniffled, took a deep breath and lifted Yehuda out of the bed. She turned and walked over to Tuvia lying in the bed next to Yehuda's crib. He was still weak, very pale and fast asleep.

"It is time," she said to him, setting Yehuda down next to the frail man. That was enough movement to wake him. "It is time."

Tuvia opened his eyes and saw Anna's wet face. He grimaced, shut his eyes tight, and through his own tears, he said, "I can't. Please take him."

"Say goodbye," said Anna.

Tuvia turned his head toward Yehuda, kissed him and cried like a little boy who had lost his pet – like a father who was losing his child. Anna looked down at the enervated man and his strong son. There was no resemblance. Yehuda looked like Anna. Tuvia looked like a ghost – a crying ghost. Lifting him up out from under Tuvia's moan, Anna walked as slowly as she could to the front door. Ida opened it, and standing by the door, like angels waiting at the gates of heaven, were two young girls, each with a small pack and faces filled with hope. How could that be possible, thought Anna? In this moment of horror, in this place, where beasts rule and no good exists, where mothers bury their babies or send them off for someone else to protect, how, in the name of this god that does not exist, can their faces hold hope. They are just children, not more than sixteen, and they will now be responsible, hope and all, for guiding my baby to safety. Anna looked at them and forced a smile. Once her thoughts calmed, she began to see the girls for who they really were, gallantry personified, the true heroines of the Jewish People, a direct line from the four matriarchs, Sarah, Rachel, Rebecca and Leah, saviors from certain death. And they were Anna's prodigies. She had trained them, sent them on their missions to deliver messages, retrieve weapons and remove people to safety. And it was she who taught them that survival is in the mind. If she was wondering where their hope came from, it came from her.

"We know, Anna," said one of the girls. "This is the greatest treasure you have ever placed in our hands."

As Anna gave Yehuda another kiss, he stirred, and she held him tight until Hanna took him out of her hands as the two young girls picked up Yehuda's and Hanna's small bags.

Anna felt like her heart was being ripped from her chest as her baby boy was taken from her grasp. Walking out the door into the freezing chills of winter was her second child without the one person she could trust to ensure survival, herself. And like her first child, lost to the angels of death sent by men with Swastika's, she could do nothing to keep him by her side.

She was losing another son, and someone was going to pay for it.

117

On the following day, January 18, 1943, the Germans entered the ghetto to recommence the Aktions that would put an end to Jewish existence in the Polish capital. For the movement, it was a signal to open fire, and Anna, despite her state of mourning, wanted to be the one to do the shooting. Since the summer, a group of over 300 young men and women, some in their teens, were preparing to engage the Germans if they tried to send even one more Jew to the Death Camps. Despite the proof provided by numerous sources, many in the ghetto did not believe that the relocation meant death, and just the extra food rations promised by the Germans was enough to get them to volunteer to take the place of the movement members who had slipped on to Judenrat lists.

The leadership of Hashomer Hatzair, Dror, and Hehalutz had made elaborate plans that any field marshal would have been proud of. They were natural commanders and military strategists, although none had even studied a single battle in any war, ancient or modern, and none had ever held a weapon until the smuggled guns had been put into their hands. There was fear that in the moment of truth some of the young warriors would freeze and not be able to shoot on cue, but as for Mordechai, the only prerequisite for having a weapon was a verbal agreement that it would be used. Military training camps had been created and the movement leadership believed that they were as ready as they would ever be. For months they had prepared for what they thought would be the final set of deportations. They constructed underground bunkers that would house them for the duration of the battles. They prepared food, water and ammunition, and each man and woman, boy and girl, knew where they would be when the day came to assault the Germans in charge in the ghetto. For the most part, these bunkers would be used to hide out during the January Aktions, but they could also provide cover when the fighting commenced.

Anna had told her housemates sometime prior to the January Aktion renewal that this uprising, bringing young men and women to kill and be killed in the Warsaw Ghetto, was the response of youth with nothing left to lose.

"No other part of the population could have given their lives in the same manner. This is the response to the insult of our own helplessness, the helplessness of being led to slaughter. Martyrdom is the only respectful way to die. We are protecting our dignity, and if need be, we will give our lives for it."

"Not a very Jewish thing to do, is it?" said Emil.

"Not a Jewish thing to do?" said Peretz. "When was the last time you read the Bible? It is the most Jewish thing we can do."

"I thought it said, 'Thou shall not kill,' in the Bible," said Emil.

"No, read it again. It says, 'Thou shall not murder.' Big difference."

"Two-thousand years of tradition has changed a lot of that."

"Two-thousand years of being pushed around…"

Anna held out her hand to calm Peretz, who she could see was starting to get worked up. She knew Peretz well enough to know that this conversation would only upset him. Emil had not received the same movement education as he had. Like most of the Jews at the time, Emil could not fathom the perception that there had been a historical skew over the past two-thousand years that turned the biblical Jew, who the movement could look up to, into the traditional, diaspora, religious Jew, stuck in Talmudic study and removed from the land.

"It's not our fault," said Anna. "We weren't allowed to own land, work in half of the professions available. We were ostracized, persecuted and expelled, year after year. It wasn't entirely our fault. But that history is over. There is a new existence; a new Zionist push toward the normalization of the Jewish People. We will free ourselves from being loan sharks and businessmen, and we will return to the land. The Old Jew is antiquated and obsolete, a pre-Zionist figure to be ridiculed and isolated, the middle-man in a money-laundering scheme, the slave of the Capitalist system. The Germans are seeing to it that this Jew be exterminated, not only physically, but spiritually. In the conflict between the New Jew and the Old Jew, we only have one choice, to create the New Fighting Jew. We have to choose honor over life, arms over passivity, to regain our control over the means of production, and for that we need to fight."

"What are you talking about?" said Emil. "The Germans are about to kill every single one of us, and you're complaining about the means of production? Are you mad?"

"He won't get it," said Peretz to Anna. "He's just not one of us." Peretz was referring to Emil not being a movement person. He was now the only one left in the house that had not grown up in a youth movement.

"Do you think I'm an idiot," said Emil, "because I didn't sing the International on Friday nights instead of lighting Shabbat candles, and because I don't spout Marx every chance I get? I understand why we have to fight, but it has nothing to do with the proletariat cause, Imperialist expansions of world markets or human alienation. The Germans are going to kill us. That is the only reason we must fight back. Forget righting social and historical wrongs. I just want to survive."

"Then," said Peretz solemnly, "you're in the wrong place."

"What's that supposed to mean?" asked Emil.

"We won't survive. At least not the few hundred left in the wretched ghetto. We will fight, but we won't live to see the results of our actions. They will beat us because they are stronger, have no conscience and would prefer to carpet bomb Warsaw before letting one Jew get out of here alive."

"We are not fighting to win," said Anna to Emil, who had his head in his hands. "We are fighting to show that we can fight."

"I am fighting," said Emil, standing up, "because of what happened in Lublin, in Vilna, and here since last April. Most people wouldn't believe it until it happened to them. God, some didn't believe it after it happened to them. But I did. We all did. That's why we're here. That's why we're fighting."

Reports of the Lublin ghetto liquidation and mass murdering of the community had arrived almost a year earlier to the shock of Warsaw Jews. Most dismissed them as scare tactics or exaggerated inaccuracies. Many claimed they had received letters from the allegedly executed well after the dates they had said to have died. The stories were too ghastly to believe. It was thought that not even the Germans, Amalek reincarnated, could do such things. Then, on the 17th of April 1942, German SS hauled fifty Jewish social workers from their beds in the middle of the night and slaughtered them in the streets. The next day, ghetto Jews were frantically searching for reason, but there was none. The leadership figured it was a political move, or a warning, aimed at halting the illegal activities going on under the German's noses. But the youth movements knew better. They wrote in their newsletters and periodicals of German plans to exterminate the Jew like bugs. They told whoever would listen that there was a grand plan in action and that it would end only after the last Jew was dead. But no one listened, and their cries to take action were met with disbelief that would lead to the rather simple Aktion of the following summer.

"No," said Anna. "We are fighting for something much, much greater than that. We are fighting to cause the world to understand that we're not just trying to save our own skin. We are taking part in a revolution, a Jewish revolution, tearing down the old society and building a new one..."

"Here comes Marx again," said Emil. "Can't you let him go?"

"First of all, no, I can't. Second of all, he was right. I am only sorry that none of us will live to see that."

"Tell that to the Ukrainian peasants."

"Emil, since when does Soviet Russia reflect the writing of Marx? They'll get there, I believe, but they are sure headed in the wrong direction now. That's not what I'm talking about. If there is a nation that can really change the face of history, change its own destiny, create a truly free and egalitarian society, it is the Jews in Eretz Yisrael. And it will happen. You will see..."

"I thought you said I won't see."

"You'll see from heaven."

"Oh, that coming from the head of the Atheist's Workers Party," said Emil.

"Emil, you're missing the point. The new Jew is a working Jew, and the new Jew is a fighting Jew. That is what we are showing the world here. That is why we must resist and with a vengeance."

The plans focused on two modes of attack. The first was the hand-to-hand combat, with Mordechai in charge of the operation. It would take place on the way from the courtyards, where the Germans had ordered the Jews to gather to have their papers checked, to the Umschlagplatz, holding areas near deportation points. The youth movement members had studied the previous Aktions and knew that the Germans would be ill-prepared for an armed attack, particularly in the cold of the winter. With thick jackets, some confiscated from abandoned homes in the ghetto following the summer deportations, members would infiltrate the columns of Jews being hoarded to the trains, hiding handguns and grenades, and at a given moment strike.

In the summer of 1942 Aktions, the Germans had a simple procedure for gathering the Jewish tenants of any particular building. The German gendarmes and Ukrainian police would surround the building while the Jewish police would enter the courtyard and call all the inhabitants down, threatening to kill any who lagged behind. Once the last was gathered, the police conducted a house to house search, shooting on sight those who failed to obey the orders. When they were sure that the building was empty, they would march the cold and frightened masses, many only with what they had been wearing to bed, down the streets to the Umschlagplatz at the far end of the ghetto, where they would await the deportation trains.

This time, the Germans would be in for a surprise. Armed movement people would infiltrate the ranks being marched down the street and on a prearranged signal would remove their weapons and attack. Though it was clear days before the start of the January Aktions that the fighting would begin shortly, some of the battle groups were taken by surprise and unable to reach their weapons in time or make it to their posts.

The second resistance plan was led by the Dror movement and consisted of simple sniper fire from some of the apartment complexes on the corner of Zamenhofa and Mila Streets. Anna had originally planned to join them, but at the last minute, after Yehuda left and it was clear she was not in a lucid state of mind, she decided to join Mordechai, in what was a much more physical and daring operation.

"I think I want German blood on my hands," Anna had said to Ida after they held each other for over an hour the night before, both crying like babies. "If they come, I will kill as many as I can. I am going with Mordechai

121

tomorrow."

Tuvia made a feeble attempt to persuade her to stay put and join the weaker housemates in the bunker below their building. It had been a great engineering project that took months to complete, but the house bunker, although far from commodious, was one of the most elaborate in the city, hidden well with blockades of garbage, and a tunnel system that would allow them to move from building to building. There was great pride in the success of the bunker project, and they knew that it would not only save lives but would provide perfect cover for their attacks.

Anna was ready for anything by this time and felt that she would be making history. Her feelings of national pride and honor now far outweighed the sense of pain and loss that sending her son out of the ghetto had caused her. She was primed to fight, to give all that was in her, to take revenge and to show the world that there is a new dawning for the Jewish people, a new Jew that would fight no matter what.

At six in the morning on January 18, 1943, there was a knock on Anna's door. It was a message from Mordechai. They had received word from a source in the Jewish police that one of the buildings that would be evacuated was on Zamenhofa Street, and they were to assemble in the courtyard as if they lived there.

Anna quickly went to her room and placed a hand under Yehuda's empty bed. She tried not to look at the bed itself, for that just restored the pain in the pit of her stomach. She removed a pistol wrapped in a handkerchief and began checking to make sure it was loaded.

"Where did you learn how to use that?" came Tuvia's voice. She was startled by it, thinking that he had been asleep. He was still lying in bed, his health improving slowly. She stopped what she was doing and turned to look at him. Her hands dropped to her sides, one holding the gun loosely, the other the handkerchief. She had not thought about Tuvia since Yehuda had left. She had hardly talked to him. Now she was going to fight the Germans, possibly never return from the battle, and she had not thought for a moment that she needed to say goodbye to the father of her child. Her chest expanded as she took a deep breath, exhaling steam like waves of white water vapor condensing the cold air. She took two steps toward him, kneeled down and embraced his frail body.

She lifted herself up. "I'm going to join Mordechai. We are going to start the revolution."

"Don't," he said bluntly. "You're not thinking straight. You're not trained for this."

"This," she said, "may be our only chance. The Germans have come to liquidate the ghetto. This is the final stand."

"I am not ready to lose you."

She took hold of his hand. "You know, I don't know how I know this, but I'm not going to die. Not today. It's not my time. Maybe tomorrow, but not today."

"Since when do you have premonitions?"

"Since today."

"Why do I believe you?"

"Because I'm always right."

"Now, I'm really worried."

"Don't be. I'll be back, and when I return, we'll get you up and about. We'll need more fighters tomorrow."

She left the room, stopping at the door to look back at Tuvia. She thought she saw him wink at her, and she smiled.

As she walked toward the front door, Ida and Miriam were waiting there.

"We haven't been called yet," said Ida. "Peretz left."

"I know. He's gone to check on the ammunition. If you're called, be careful."

Miriam's eyes were glassy, and Anna reached out to touch her face. She grabbed Anna's hand and held it to her lips, as Ida wrapped her arms around both of them.

"You too," said Ida. "I love you."

"I told Tuvia, I'm going to be alright. This is just the beginning. There is a lot of fighting left. I have a lot of Germans to kill. This will just be the first batch."

Anna met two other movement members on the way to Zamenhofa Street and arrived at the quiet apartment building, where two other fighters were already waiting.

"Where's Mordechai?" asked Anna.

"He'll be here. I think he's making sure everyone can get to their weapons."

Anna took a deep breath and looked around the dark courtyard. Had she come here before the building was interned into the ghetto, she may have seen less laundry hanging from the windows, but other than that it would have looked much the same at this early hour. The brown stucco walls had patches of black mold that looked like dark shadows in the early morning haze. The sun had yet to rise, and the only light crept in through the entranceway. All the windows were dark, some of the apartments were now empty, some with unsuspecting people who would get the shock of being woken in a few hours by the yells of Jewish Police or SS guards telling them

123

they have one minute to take no more than 15 kilograms of luggage.

"He's not coming here," said a woman who ran into the courtyard out of breath. She could not have been older than sixteen, she had scraggly red hair that protruded from a worn scarf, her black coat several sizes too large for her, and her shoes looked like their previous owner had been a large man. "He'll meet the people just down the street as they're walking."

"Why?" asked one of the men waiting.

"Because," she said catching her breath, "he said it would be easier to get more fighters into the masses after the Germans collect a few hundred from more than one building. When we get to the intersection at Mila Street, we'll attack."

The group looked at each other, wondering what to do next. Rays of light were entering the courtyard from the breaking day, and they knew that they would not have to wait much longer. But should they wait there?

"Should we come with you?" asked Anna. Anna had seen the girl before. Her name was Bella and she had been at a summer event long ago. She had matured, but her body looked meek after years of malnourishment. Anna remembered her as a shy and reticent girl who seemed to prefer to be alone. She had wondered what attracted her to the movement but never had a full conversation with her. That introversion seemed gone now, and the young woman standing before her had an air of buoyancy and confidence about her.

"Hi Anna," she said, "I'm sorry about Shimi."

"Thank you. I didn't realize you knew him."

"I didn't really, but I heard. No, we should stay here. There should be a few of us coming from this building. I understand that there is an apartment on the third floor that is empty. We should wait there. Let's go."

Bella led the two men and Anna up the staircase to the third floor of the four-story building. The morning brought with it dampness, and the solid stairs seemed glossy and slick. She led them straight to the corner apartment, pushed open the unlocked door and stepped inside as if she had been living there for months.

The room was full of furniture. For a moment, Anna thought that there must still be someone living there. Chairs, books, lamps, rugs and paintings were all still in their place, but when she looked into the kitchen she understood what had happened. There was a smell of dust mixed with sour milk. Bella immediately went to open a window. The cold morning air drifted in, replacing the stale stench. It was best they could breathe, even if they would have to suffer the elements for the short time that they waited. In the bedroom, four beds lay unmade, sheets and blankets falling off to the ground as the breeze entered the room. On one of the beds was a doll with torn clothes and a comb still in its hair.

"This was Dr. Zeppinik's home," Bella said. "He was taken last summer."

"Who's Dr. Zeppinik?" said one of the men. "Should we know him?"

"He was a great surgeon," said Anna, walking around the main living room, lifting doilies and a book that seemed to have been awaiting the return of its reader. "I remember when he was taken."

"He was taken," said Bella, "from the hospital. There were rumors that he was shot before he even got to the transports but no one was ever able to confirm it. The next day, his family and two other families that were living here were taken in the afternoon and put on the next train to Treblinka. That's why this place looks like this."

The kitchen told the story of the hasty departure. Dirty dishes filled the sink; there was a pot on the stove with remains of what once may have been a potato boiling, and there was a stench of mold that had lined the kitchen table with a few pieces of decaying bread left out. The floor was oily and rat droppings could be seen in the corners.

"They're here!" yelled one of the men, who had been looking out the window. The group of four went over to see the commotion below. Four SS officers and several Ukrainian policemen had entered the courtyard and were banging on the doors. Within minutes, most of the remaining occupied homes were emptying, and the terrified tenants were filling the courtyard, many still in their nightclothes, shivering in the morning chill. There were fewer than they had expected, and the police went door to door to make sure no one was left behind.

"We should just shoot them from here," said one of the men.

"We don't know how many guards are outside. That wouldn't do anything."

"Let's go," said Anna.

As they opened the door, Bella looked over at Anna and smiled as if to assure her that it would be okay. But Anna understood that there was fear behind the gesture, and she placed her hand on Bella's shoulder, squeezing gently.

"We'll be okay," said Anna.

"Wanna bet?" replied Bella, and walked out.

The whimpering of an older woman caught Anna's ear as she exited the apartment and followed the two men down the staircase. The woman was holding a handkerchief to her mouth. Her husband held her arm as they slowly limped down the stairs. She was smart enough to take a coat, unlike some of the tenants, who seemed to believe that this was just a drill of some kind. The man had a small bag of belongings, but no suitcase. He had a stunned look on his face as if he knew exactly what was in store. As she got closer, Anna saw that the couple could not have been more than forty years old; but the ghetto had taken its toll on their appearance. She thought to herself, if I can save these two, then this will all be worth it.

Some of the people lining the courtyard had been ready for this and lugged huge pre-packed cases. One of the SS officers was yelling at one man, telling him that he would not be allowed to bring such a large bag. As the man pleaded with him, without a moment's thought, the officer removed his pistol and shot him in the head. He dropped onto his oversized luggage, topping it over and falling supine in the silence of the courtyard. The gunshot caused the elderly man who was now just one flight of stairs from the bottom to begin to whimper as well.

It astonished Anna that so many of the people in the courtyard looked as if they had no idea what was really going on. Why would anyone leave their home in their pajamas when they know what has happened to so many of the neighboring buildings? When one woman tried to return to her home, she was hit in the back by one of the soldiers and crumbled to the cold stones. It struck Anna that the youngest of the tenants looked no less than forty, which made the four young terrorists stand out. And there was not a child among them.

They quickly found their place among the older tenants huddled together and listened to the directions given first in German and then translated into Polish. One man quietly translated to his wife in Yiddish, while she stood shaking and wiping the tears from her face. Meanwhile, Ukrainian soldiers were kicking open doors looking for stranglers. On occasion, a gunshot rang out and a muffled scream could be heard from one of the tenants in the courtyard who realized that a loved one had just died.

When the command came to march, Anna could see two guards in front, two in back, and one on each side of the line that continued down the street. One and a half shots each, and they would all be dead. They only had to walk a few blocks, when they were joined by two other lines of Jews from other buildings, and with them, six more guards and several soldiers from each group. This happened one more time, and the whole group looked to be over three hundred Jews. Anna began to imagine what would happen when they opened fire. Will the guards just start randomly shooting? Will the terrified masses disperse in every direction? What would happen to them? How many would survive?

It would not take long for her to find out. As the second group was joining the lengthening line to the Umschlagplatz, Anna could see Mordechai and several others join them as if they had been stragglers from the first group. The guards did not notice, and soon they were part of the mass of sobbing exiles making their way through the soggy streets of the fading ghetto. Mila Street lay up ahead. As if the sight of the street triggered something in her brain, she began to smell baked bread. At first, she was sure that it was a hallucination, but soon there was a commotion in the crowd. During earlier Aktions, the Germans offered food to those who willingly showed up. This was a sign to many that they would be rewarded for their cooperation. But Ann knew better. This was no more than a ploy to create false hope, and sure enough, a few blocks later, the smell was gone, and the exiles went back to starving quietly. Quietly that is until they reach Mila street.

It started with a yell, a battle cry, and then two gunshots. The sounds reverberated off the buildings and sounded like an entire army was descending upon the unsuspecting columns. But it was just two shots at first, and with them, Mordechai had killed two guards with his first two bullets. The people around him began to scatter in every direction, holding their heads, as if that would be enough to stop the German bullets from penetrating their skulls and killing them on the spot. And then the madness came. The echo triggered more gunfire, from Jewish warriors, from startled guards and from trained SS officers seemingly ready for this kind of event, but just randomly shooting.

Anna, screaming like the true warrior that she was as she reached for her weapon, aimed directly at the guard next to her and fired. When she squeezed the trigger it took more power than she had anticipated, causing her to move the aim slightly left. She felt the kickback jolt her hand, and the weapon was suddenly warm against her frozen hand. The smoke from its barrel drifted over to her nose as everything around her slowed down. She felt almost as if she could watch the track of the bullet as it hit the young, blonde soldier in the arm and he flew backward, grabbing his shoulder and dropping his rifle. He had been startled by the commotion, possibly believing that ghetto duty was a walk in the park, definitely preferable to the catastrophic Russian front where the Germans were bogged down by obstinate Russians and their uncooperative winter. He now understood that this too was war and even these bugs they call Jews present a threat. He fell to his knees and was immediately kicked in the head by a young girl wearing army boots. There was nothing unexpected about that, except perhaps the way he fell to the ground, stopping for an instant to look up at Anna as if saying, but I'm just a kid, I didn't do anything wrong. Anna was surprised, not by his glance, nor by the manner he fell, but by her sudden, very short-lived sympathy for him. And it was short-lived because before she could understand why her feelings went out to a Nazi soldier, a bullet whizzed by her ear, causing her to turn around. There was another soldier, possibly a good friend of the one that was just fallen by Anna's bullet and a good kick to the temple, possibly just another boy, scared and panicked, and he was set to fire at Anna again. But for no discernible reason, with mayhem all around, some people dropping to their knees unable to cope with the alarm, others running back and forth across the busy street, seeing another gun and turning in the other direction, the soldier moved his rifle to the left and shot a man who was too distressed to fall or run. But then he fell. And Anna ran.

Anna moved out of the now deformed line of people and saw her comrades fighting. A surge of adrenalin caused her to feel her heart pumping in her neck. The girl who had kicked the soldier in the head and confiscated his weapon was now shooting his rifle in the direction of an SS officer. But before she could get off a clean shot, she was hit by a slug coming out of the SS officer's gun. Anna wanted to get behind something before opening fire again. She ran out from the center of the street and over to a stairwell that led down to the basement entrance of the boarded-up, street-front store. She squatted on the stairs and took aim. Looking over the raging battle, or what seemed like a raging battle to the inexperienced Anna, she saw what hand-to-hand combat was really about. She saw her comrades dropping to the ground as German snipers picked them off one by one, leaving the ratio of guards to resistors growing by the second. Anna found her target, a German soldier standing next to a poll on the far side of the street randomly firing at the crowd. He looked as if he had experience shooting at crowds, and she could almost make out a grin each time he hit his mark. She took careful aim, making sure her hand was steady against the railing, set her sights, kept both eyes open and slowly pulled the trigger. The soldier dropped to his knees and then onto his face. Anna did not wait to see if he moved after that. She was ready to shoot again.

However, she would not get the next shot off, as out of the corner of her eye she saw it; it seemed strange that a German soldier would be cocking his arm back to throw a rock in her direction, but the entire picture before her eyes was strange. She turned her head and realized that it was no rock; it was a grenade that was about to be sent in her direction. Instinctively, she jumped to her feet, all the while watching as the solid green projectile left the German's hand. She saw that it would bounce off the wall behind her stairwell and land smack at her feet. She dove out of the well, and since her concentration was on the soldier to her right, she didn't see the SS officer running across her path. She bumped him in the back. As he turned startled at the engagement, she grabbed his shoulders and threw him into the stairwell. She heard the click of the grenade hit the wall but never heard the sound of metal on concrete as it fell because it landed directly on the officer's leg. Anna would have enjoyed seeing the officer's face at that moment, any of the Jews in the ghetto would have enjoyed it, but she was too busy getting out of the way. As she rounded the side of the building, a safe distance from the shockwave and shrapnel, she heard the scream of the officer, followed by the explosion.

Anna looked down the street and saw three of her comrades running down one of the alleys. They were being shot at, but no one seemed to be chasing them. Up until that moment, she had felt no fear. The screams, the bullets and even the grenade seemed as if they should have been there all along. No surprises, she had been suspecting that kind of action from the moment she knew that she would be joining the attack. No fear, just wonder. Wonder at the way people solve their problems, at her courage and stupidity for putting herself in harm's way. For the first time, she wondered what she was doing there. Why didn't she just leave the ghetto and run with her son? Because she knew that was not in her nature. She was not the type to give up and leave a dying friend. This dying friend may just be a walled piece of earth, a place she never called home, but she still felt an over-inflated sense of responsibility. That was how she was brought up – not by her family, but by her movement. And now, after she saw her friends fall in the middle of the street, a lone few managing to escape the carnage and run for their lives down an alley that led in the direction of more death, she felt fear for the first time. Anna knew that it was best for her to drop out of sight as well since it looked like their work had been done. She turned the corner. As she glanced back over the disturbing vista, she saw another man shot to the ground. There were bodies throughout the street, and she knew that many of her friends had died that day. She turned and ran.

Fourteen

The bus rolled along the foothills towards the flatter terrain southeast of their destination. The two-lane road had neglected potholes still untamed by the Public Works Council, and when the bus hit one, the people in the back jumped. The smell of orchards occasionally drifted into the bus from open widows left ajar by the undisciplined – despite the air-conditioning blowing at full blast. For some, the cold air coming out of the round vents above each seat was too frigid. Many were wearing short pants and chose to close the vent in order to remain just a bit warmer. The warm outside air was a break from the chills of summer bus travel. The driver didn't even ask them to close the window after his first request. It wasn't worth the battle. A stocky man with dark skin and sweaty armpits lit a cigarette in the third row. The smoke drifted up to the main vent at the roof of the aisle and was distributed equally around the bus.

A fly flew from passenger to passenger, waved off in a swat and settled on the head of Anna. She didn't feel a thing as she turned toward Rami.

"I want you to know that I admire what you are doing for our country," said Anna to Rami.

Rami seemed to shift in his seat, the click of the metal gun hitting the side of the bench. "Thank you, but what is it exactly that I'm doing?"

"You're serving in permanent duty. Aren't you a Lieutenant? Those bars make you just like a Lieutenant. That means you signed on and chose to give more of your life to the IDF."

"Yes, but it's just a job to me."

"A job to give your life? Would you like an orange?" She reached into her bag and pulled out a sack of oranges.

"No thank you," he said. It had been the third time she had offered him and his third refusal. "It's a job until I find something better to do. I like being in the army right now. It suits me. I guess I have some natural leadership qualities and without the opportunities I've had in the army, I never would have known. I thought about leaving when my three years were up, but then I thought, why? I never would have been able to find a better job than this at this point in my life. It's a great job for a young person like me. What would I have done in civilian life?"

"Listen to me," she said, turning around in the stairwell, "no one fights as a job..."

"That's not true," he interrupted her. "Plenty of people are professional fighters."

"Not here. I fought a little in my day as well. It is not a job. You fight

131

when you need to survive. That is exactly what the IDF is all about. The Israel Defense Forces – the key word here is 'Defense.'"

"I thought the key word was 'Israel.'"

"It's not. We need you to give your time to our country while you are still young and strong because that is what's needed to survive. Nothing more. If it suits you to give that time, wonderful. I am proud of you regardless of your motives, but don't tell me that you only see it as a job. If you were serving coffee in some office I may agree, but you are holding that gun wherever you go and that is a sign that you are a fighter."

"You may be right."

"I know I'm right."

Rami laughed. "I won't argue with that."

She could see he was making fun of her so she cut the conversation and started with Yaakov again.

"You know you can say something, don't you?"

"What," said Yaakov, "do you want me to say?"

"Support me in my argument."

"But you won the argument. Why do you need my support?" Yaakov honked the horn at a car passing him on the right. It was a dangerous maneuver and he cursed as he hit the horn.

"You sound like a man I once knew. He never understood why I needed his support. Men never understand."

"That's quite a generalization," said Yaakov.

"It's true. You know I'm right."

"Actually, I have no idea what you're talking about."

"My point exactly," said Anna. "You just don't understand. All of you."

"Do you have something against men?"

Before Anna could answer, Rami entered with an irenic attempt to keep the conversation from getting out of hand. "I'm sure she had nothing against men."

"I have something against ignorant men."

"Where did that come from? I'm just trying to get us safely to Tel Aviv and all of a sudden I'm verbally assaulted by some lady," he said to the large mirror above his head as if talking to the entire bus seated behind him rather than to Anna. He then turned to Anna. "Are you calling me ignorant?"

"God forbid. I said nothing about you. You seem like a decent man. And you're Polish. That's already something. Some of the nicest men I ever met were Polish."

Rami laughed again.

"Why are you laughing," said Anna. "Do you think there is something wrong with being Polish?"

"I wouldn't know," said Rami. "My family is from Russia and Czechoslovakia."

"Well that's a strange combination," said Anna, shaking her head in disapproval.

"They met in the Hagana. They were stationed not far from here. They fought together at Latrun."

"Well then, you seem to have fighting in your blood. That even sounds romantic. I met my husband in the Warsaw ghetto – my second husband...I liked him better than the first," she smiled. "We did some fighting as well. It's a terrible place to have a relationship – the battlefield I mean."

A man and a woman sitting in the second row leaned over to look down at Anna. Then the woman turned to the man and whispered something in his ear. He nodded and looked back down at Anna.

"You fought in the Warsaw Ghetto? I understood that you were in the ghetto, but I hadn't realized that you actually fought," said Rami.

"I did. So where are we?" she said, turning back toward Yaakov and blatantly changing the subject.

"We're not far from Ramla. We won't be stopping, don't worry. You'll still reach your sister on time. Soon we'll be..."

"Tell me about it?" asked Rami before Yaakov could finish explaining. He was persistent in his questioning, despite Anna's disregard.

Anna turned back around and gave Rami a questioning stare. She liked telling her stories but some were just too painful. "Oh, you learned your history. I don't think you need to hear more from me. I told you one story already. It was sad enough. Why doesn't Yaakov here tell you? I'm sure he's heard wonderful stories from his kibbutz members. Many of them were also there and fought as well. Right, Yaakov? Some of them were with me there you know, but I don't personally know anyone on Yad Mordechai now."

"I don't want to hear second-hand stories. I want to hear from you, someone who was actually there, actually fighting. I can read things in books, or hear my commanding officers tell battle tales, but I've never met anyone who actually fought in the Warsaw Ghetto. I thought that most of the fighters died there."

Anna didn't answer right away. She was deep in thought and Rami saw that she was uncomfortable with his nagging.

"We did," she said. "We did."

Fifteen

January 18, 1943

News of the street combat spread around the ghetto quickly. It was possible to divide the reactions of the remaining ghetto Jews into two groups. The first group consisted of those having nothing to do with resistance. They were simply terrified and felt that it was just a matter of time until they met their death. Most of them had felt that way anyway but the events of the previous day had intensified their fears. They knew that the Germans would be less tolerant and more likely to just kill whoever stepped out of line – not that there had been much tolerance before. The second group was the fighters, the able resistance with guns hidden away ready to take on the German army in all its grandeur, fearful and cautious, but knowing they have nothing left to lose. They were also victorious, as far as they knew. Himmler's orders to take just 8000 Jews that January had not reached the fighter's ears. They had been sure that the only reason the Germans stopped the deportation was because of the armed defiance the young Jews put up. It was a moment of pride, Jewish fighters killing Nazi slime, and all in the famished streets of the ghetto.

However, their triumph was not without pain. Most of the movement members taking part in the Mila Street fighting were killed. Mordechai had run out of ammunition when trying to fire on a Ukrainian soldier who was aiming at one of his friends. He heard the click of his pistol, but nothing exited the gun. His friend fell in an instant, and then the barrel was aimed at Mordechai. But he managed to escape, almost the last of the fighters to vacate the scene.

Anna survived as well, taking refuge in the sewers until nightfall. Had she not spent so much time over the past year instructing other girls where to find the sewer entrances, she would never have found this one. Her housemates were sure she had been killed in the fighting, although her body was not seen among the dead. When she showed up that evening, smelling of rancid meat, the remaining six housemates hugged her for over ten minutes. They all cried and began telling stories of what they had heard of the events of the day.

"The Germans stopped the deportations," said Peretz. "It seems as soon as the fighting stopped a message went out to get out of the ghetto. They only got about 5000 of us. But they'll be back. You can be sure of that. And we'll be ready for them.

"Eliyahu and Margalit died," said Ida.

135

"I know, I saw her fall," said Anna. "I was standing not far from them. It was horrible. These two SS officers with two pistols each were turning and firing at anyone who wasn't on the ground. They had the look of wild animals in their eyes. I tried to take a shot at them but missed. They killed Margalit."

"Who's Margalit?" asked Miriam. "Was she ever here?"

"No," said Anna, glancing over at Peretz as if to ask permission to tell the story.

"It's okay," said Peretz. "I'm over it. I redeemed myself today." Peretz had not been fighting with Anna but instead had held up in an apartment building across the street from an SS office that was used to coordinate the transports. They had opened fire, killing two guards and scattering the rest to find safe haven elsewhere.

"Margalit and Eliyahu were involved in the Judenrat killings last November," said Anna.

"Oh," said Miriam. "They finished the job Peretz botched up."

Peretz gave Miriam a dirty look. She smiled at him.

"We did well today," said Peretz. "I think the Germans won't be bothering us for a while. They ran out of here with their tails between their legs."

"Where else was there fighting?" asked Anna.

"I understood that the only place there was a real fight was where you were. We just shot from the upper floors of the building. They got off a few shots back, but mostly just ran away. It was too easy."

"It wasn't too easy," said Anna. "They'll come back prepared next time, you can be sure. So we need to be ready. Have you heard what Mordechai is planning?"

"I heard," said Ida, "that he wants to develop the tunnels and boost the smuggling. The Polish resistance has pledged more weapons. We'll need a lot more than we have if we really want to make a stand."

Her words seemed to hit a nerve with everyone in the room. "Make a stand." That was the best they could hope for and now with so many killed in a simple surprise operation, they were all quite sure that in the big battle, the one that really mattered, their chances of survival were nil. But they all knew that wasn't why they would fight. Anna looked down at her hand. It was cut. She could not recall when that had happened. Possibly it was when she was hiding, or when she crawled into the sewer. Then she remembered. She had been nicked by a bullet. It was soon after Mordechai's call to break ranks and attack. The shooting began, and all hell broke loose. She was removing her weapon when her left hand, her non-shooting hand, was nicked. But the adrenaline and excitement kept her from feeling anything.

The bullet must have just scratched the wrist as she moved to shoot. She took a deep breath and checked both her hands to see if there were other unnoticed injuries. There were none. She brought her wrist up to her eyes to take a closer look.

"Let me see that," said Ida.

"It's nothing, I just got scratched."

"Strange scratch. That's from a bullet."

"Maybe, I really don't remember."

But she did. She now recalled that it was the bullet that hit the girl who kicked the soldier in the head. It was actually meant for her.

"I...," said Anna to the group, "I think we need to plan for some of us to escape. It won't be enough to stand up to the Germans here if there is no one to tell the story. I know all of you are willing to give your lives, but some of you must live to tell the world what happened in this place."

"What do you have in mind?" asked Peretz.

"We don't know what will happen when the fighting starts. Who knows? The Germans may just carpet bomb the entire ghetto from the air...."

"They won't do that," said Tuvia, who had come out of his room, walking slowly, but at least walking. "They need those planes and bombs to fight the Russians. You've heard what's happening to them there."

"Okay, but we really don't know what they will do. We need to make sure that whoever is fighting when it seems they have given their all, has an escape route. We need to make sure the sewer exits and tunnels are clear and safe. Most of us won't make it out, but someone has to tell the story, and the story has to be told to whoever will listen. That is the only way these events will have meaning."

"I think Mordechai has a plan for that," said Ida. "At least, he should."

"He may, but I want us to have one as well."

"I'm not leaving," said Peretz, "until the last of the Germans leaves Poland."

"Then you may end up buried here," said Tuvia.

"Thank you, Tuvia," said Miriam. "Very optimistic."

"I'm just realistic. We all know that there will be no way to actually beat the Germans. Even Mordechai has said that. I don't think there is any value in fighting just for honor. I agree that it is a good idea to plan our escape, but most of us won't get the chance to leave once the fighting starts. The Germans will destroy the ghetto the next time. Defense and salvation are diametrically opposed terms. Fight or flight. We need to choose just one, and fighting will just get us all killed. I don't really think that anything good will come out of either decision but if you want to get back at the Germans, then live."

Since his illness and Yehuda's departure, Tuvia had become a rather glum roommate. He often talked about death, for he had had a great deal of time to believe that his demise was imminent. He tended to start many a sentence with the words, "When I die." Anna had a difficult time rejuvenating his optimism and was worried that even if he did survive the winter, he would not be a positive influence and an even less effective fighter. For a fighter, more than anything else, one needs a will to live. Anna had watched as Tuvia's will to live drifted out of the room and into the stale ghetto air.

"Don't think I have any faith in escape," said Tuvia. "We know that the way to the partisans in the forests is no safer than sticking around here. But at least out there, you can breathe."

"What will you do once you're there?" said Peretz. "You know that there is no way you can escape completely."

"What about the passports from Latin America?" asked Emil, who was still in a state of malaise. Over the winter, Emil had been ill several times and each time he came out of it weaker. Now he had bronchitis and was coughing most of the time.

"You mean the Swiss connection to Paraguay?" asked Peretz. "I don't know anyone in Switzerland, and I don't have any way of getting my picture to them if I did."

"But there are options there," said Emil.

"Completely unrealistic," said Peretz.

"And fighting will save us?" asked Tuvia.

"Tuvia, you of all people know the value of armed resistance. No, we will not all survive, but we will also not be defeated passively. This is our chance to change the way the world sees the Jews. There is value in our resistance that cannot be measured in military successes. Tuvia, you can leave when you want, but I am staying to fight."

"There is no way," said Anna, "that we can save everyone. It is just not realistic. We, the members of Hashomer Hatzair, understand more than anyone else the value in the collective. We have to stick together here. That does not mean suicide. It means fighting together, as many of us as possible, and when we are at the end of our rope, we can jump together, out into the forest and fight some more with the partisans until we can get to Eretz Yisrael."

"If you want to think ahead," said Tuvia, "then we should prepare false documents for when we do escape."

This was a common discussion among the movement members

during the months after the January uprising. No one viewed one path as braver than the other. No one saw one answer safer than the other. Both were dangerous and destined to meet with the same result – death. But the discussion had a value in itself. It allowed the young men and women, who one way or another were about to give their lives, to maintain a feeling of choice. They had the freedom, the ultimate freedom, to decide how they would die. That for them was a great opportunity; perhaps all they had left after everything else was lost.

The next day, Mordechai's assessment of the first battles was spread around the fighting forces. Only five of the fifty battle groups were able to reach their weapons and fight. He also said that street fighting was too costly, and they were not well enough equipped to keep something like that up. He wanted to switch to partisan fighting. With the pistols and home-made explosives, they would be able to do much more damage.

It was clear by that point that they had changed the course of history. Anna was sitting with Ida when Peretz came into the room.

"Did you hear about what happened at the trains?"

"You mean the speech? I heard," said Anna. "It was brave."

"What speech?" asked Ida.

"One of the battle groups," said Peretz, "that had not reached their weapons was taken by the Germans and brought to the Umschlagplatz. About sixty people were waiting to enter the cars when Davidson turned to the group and with a short statement, spoken only in the forceful fashion he knows how, caused each and every one of them to refuse to enter the trains. It was a mass protest that ended in disaster. The bastard SS officer in charge wasted no time and personally shot all sixty."

"They gave their lives for the cause," said Ida. "It shows the power of resistance. A few weeks ago no one would have done that."

"The atmosphere here has changed," said Anna. "Everyone is feeling inspired, even though we lost so many dear comrades. We made the Germans run. We are the first to make them run. Our will can beat them, even if it is just for a moment. They were forced to change their plans. That's all that matters."

"Outside," said Ida, "they are talking about hundreds of Germans killed here."

"We know that's not true," said Peretz.

"But let them think that," said Anna. "It will inspire the Poles and the partisans to fight harder. We may even get more support the next time we ask."

And they did. It seemed that the fighting brought about a change in the attitude of the Polish Underground toward the Jewish fighters. They were taken seriously and no longer complained that sending guns to the ghetto was a waste of resources.

Over the next few weeks, the activity increased. The resistance organizations had taken the leadership role in the central ghetto. Since the violence of January, the Judenrat and Jewish Police had all but lost any control they had previously held. It was clear now who was in charge, and that was evident by the Judenrat providing serious funds for the purchase of weapons for the fighters. The months that past had seen the ghetto return to Jewish control. Fighters roamed the streets freely, mostly armed and ready for attack, many continued to go about their business, since the Germans were no longer terrorizing their lives. However, everyone knew that it was just a matter of time before that changed. Rumors had reached their ears that the SS was planning an offensive at the end of February but nothing materialized and the information, it turned out, had been fabricated by the SS itself.

These were tense but liberated days for the Jews of the movement. They bathed in their victory, which was still considered a victory, if just for morale purposes, as they now knew that the Germans never intended to completely liquidate the ghetto in January but just needed a few thousand workers. It made Anna's heart skip a beat each time that Ida would walk in the house with her pistol openly placed on her hip after returning from her business. Anna saw her as the ultimate Jewish warrior princess, ready to confront her foe in a skirmish, a melee, or an all-out war. Since Biblical times there had not been a Jewish woman so ready to engage in battle.

For those that felt escape was their best alternative, the Paraguayan passport option, which provided another in a series of false hopes, was dismissed as a non-option for the Warsaw Ghetto. It was too difficult and even if they could get the documents, they could only get a handful. This was ruled out by Hashomer Hatzair as it was opposed to the movement ideology, the kibbutz and the standard of mutual responsibility and opportunity. It was unheard of that only some of the members would be spared. They had to stick together as one unit. So they began preparing for war.

The bulk of the activity in preparation for the impending German invasion into the ghetto was creating passageways between the buildings. Many would connect attic to attic, while others created elaborate tunnel systems under the now vacant city.

By the beginning of April, over seven hundred young men and women were ready to fight. Most of the resistance organizations' members had weapons. Those who did not were busy preparing Molotov Cocktails and make-shift grenades.

By this time, there was cooperation between all of the political factions in the ghetto, or at least between the Zionists. Among the movements preparing to fight were Hashomer Hatzair, Halutz, Dror, and a few remaining members of Akiva. Most of the members of Gordonia had left the ghetto prior to the Aktions of the summer, which caused Peretz to go on a rant about how he always felt that Gordonia was a cheap excuse for a pioneer movement and that their contribution to the Zionist cause would be minimal at best. Even the Bund had agreed to join the fighting forces but had their own ideas of how things should work. This unity allowed Mordechai and other leaders to implement plans quite freely. Anna felt that had any of these groups decided to abandon the battle plan, they all would have suffered.

Although the Germans were not physically inside the ghetto while the Jewish resistance forces held control, they did not cease to make attempts to manipulate the Jews. Numerous propaganda tactics were used to convince the ghetto to cooperate with the Judenrat and work for the Germans in factories within Warsaw and the surroundings.

One Sunday morning, ten men from the Lublin concentration camp, a work camp according to them, were brought into the ghetto by the SS to encourage the Jews that wanted to live out the war under "fine working conditions" to join them in their factories. They were dressed in clean work attire and not the striped prisoner garbs that they would have normally worn. They had even been bathed and smelled of floral scents, looking more presentable than the Germans themselves. The movement saw right through the charade and Anna was put in charge of counter-propaganda.

"First, we have to drive them out of here," said Peretz.

"First," replied Anna, "we have to find out what they know about the outside." Anna did have an ulterior motive. These men had come from Lublin, the general direction that Hanna and Yehuda had traveled. She thought that maybe, just by chance, one of these men may have heard something about their whereabouts and successes to reach safety.

"You don't think that you can just talk to them, do you?" said Peretz. "They're not really acting as Jews, they're German puppets. They'll just tell you what you want to hear."

"But they are Jewish. If they know something, they will tell me. Then we can kick them out of here."

"It's a waste of time."

"We don't have anything to lose. If they don't know anything, then we continue with the plan. But if they do, we get the information before we stop this farce."

"You don't get it, do you? They are German spies. It is just as important for them to know what we want to know as it is for them to tell us what we want to hear."

"I am not going to disclose resistance secrets," she said.

"But you are. You are going to ask about a woman and a small child who escaped. You are telling them that they escaped."

"What, do you think the Germans don't know that we have escape routes? And besides, they escaped a while ago. There is no harm in trying to get information. It is rare that Jews from Lublin enter the ghetto, and our sources for outside information have been compromised of late. I will talk to them and I will be careful."

"Suit yourself," he said, shaking his head. "But don't say I didn't warn you."

The next morning was cold and snowy. Anna, Peretz, Ida and Miriam set out across the streets of the central ghetto to the building the Germans had placed these men. Aside from the three apartments they occupied on the first and second floors, the building was vacant, as well as the buildings on either side. As they reached the courtyard entrance, Miriam turned to Anna.

"Take this," she said and handed her a pistol. "We each have one."

Anna looked down at the weapon as if she was being handed a scorpion. Gently, she removed it from Miriam's pale and thin hand and placed it under her coat. "If we need these," she said, "then we're already dead."

They entered the courtyard and saw that one of the flats had frosted windows and there seemed to be a glow from the fireplace. They knocked on the door. A man with a long beard, who would have been mistaken as a rabbi had it not been for the war lengthening all men's beards and hair, opened the door. He signaled to enter the room, without saying a word. Inside sat five other men, who looked to be in their fifties and sixties, all bearded, all dressed the same, all sipping tea and all far too thin to be living the luxurious lives they had claimed the Jews of the Lublin camp were enjoying. Anna's first course of appraisal was to look at their hands. Many had cuts, bruises and calloused fingers. Although it did seem they had bathed, their fingernails were long and soiled and deep inside the crevices were traces of dirt. It took her less than ten seconds to confirm the movement's assessment of these men, and she was not going to let them continue the travesty for even one minute.

She nodded to Peretz and he began walking around the house, opening doors and peaking into each room. All of the occupants were sitting in the parlor and Peretz, who was now looking in the kitchen nodded back. All three of the girls removed their pistols and raised the guns, each holding the weapon with both hands, aiming directly at the heads of the three closest to them.

"Hey look," said Peretz, who was coming out of the kitchen area, "they're even feeding them."

"If I was a slave and being offered food," said Anna to the men, "I still wouldn't betray my people."

"We are not betraying anyone," said the man who had opened the door. He was the only one standing, slightly bent forward as if his cane had been taken from him. He had tired eyes and a soft voice."

"What are they holding over you?" asked Anna.

"What do you mean?"

"What do they have that you want? Why are you doing this? You don't want to help these pigs, do you?"

"I know you!" said Ida suddenly. "You were in the Judenrat in Lodz. I saw you at a meeting once."

Peretz moved into the room and held his pistol at his side. "So that explains it. You're all Judenrat. Now do you see?" he said looking at Anna.

"Yes. But I still want information. There were three Jews who left the ghetto a few months ago. Two women and a small boy. If you saw them or heard of them, you'd remember, since not many small boys have been running around."

"I know of them," said one of the men without hesitation. "Yes, a small boy with two women. Yes. I heard they were in the forests with the partisans."

"Where did you hear that?"

"From a man who was recently caught and brought to Lublin to work. He told me that the Warsaw Jews were able to get in and out of the ghetto and even a small boy did so."

"And he told you there was a small boy with two women from Warsaw?"

"Oh yes, that's what he said. They are safe, he said."

Anna took a deep breath. It was all she wanted to hear, and she lowered her pistol.

"Wait," said Ida. "How was he caught?"

"Who?" asked the man.

"The partisan who told you of the women and the boy. How was he caught?"

"How would I know that?"

"Because partisans are rarely caught and kept alive. It would have been the first thing he told you," she said with anger in her voice. She walked up to the man sitting in the chair; her pistol aimed at his face, she placed the barrel on his temple. "Now, how was he caught?"

"I don't know. I don't know. He didn't say."

143

"You're lying aren't you? You just made that up. Anna, you gave him too much information. It was easy to just make it up. You're lying aren't you?"

The man closed his eyes and prepared to be shot. Ida had a fierce look in her eyes as if even shooting him would not give her enough satisfaction.

"Last chance," she said and pressed the gun into his forehead.

"Okay, okay, I lied!" he said.

Ida lowered the gun. She knew better than to waste a precious bullet on an old Judenrat Jew who would probably die soon anyway. "Sorry, Anna."

Anna's face was sallow, and her mouth gaped slightly open. She had had a few short seconds of hope, of the belief that her Yehuda was alive in the forests, with the real fighters. For a moment she thought that perhaps it would have been better had she been left believing the lie, but then she came to her senses, or rather her senses came to her. The room became crystal clear and the men all looked frightened and weak. Suddenly, she felt sorry for them, for all of them except the man who lied to her. Gradually, as if she was not controlling her own hand, she lifted her pistol and aimed at the man sitting in the armchair. As sure as she was that her purpose in the ghetto was to die for the Jewish People, she knew that this man should go first. He had lied to her face about her son; he had fabricated a story to deceive all in the ghetto; and she knew that he, and all his measly friends, would, in a heartbeat, drag more Jews to their death, just as they had done when they worked in the Judenrat. As she began to apply pressure to the trigger, Miriam grabbed her arm.

"No, Anna," she said softly.

Anna took her eyes off her target and released the gun into Miriam's hand, while a tear streamed down her cheek.

"The best thing we can do right now is to ensure that these men fail in their mission. The Germans will take care of the rest."

"Listen here," said Ida in a vociferous voice. "You will leave by tonight or we will be back."

"If you hadn't noticed," said Peretz. "We are the new Judenrat in Warsaw, and the only thing we have in common with the old one is the word Juden."

As they walked back toward their home, Anna walked up to Peretz.

"Sorry I didn't trust you," she said.

"That's okay. You'll learn eventually that I am as accurate in my estimates as you are. We are both using the same map and it is often difficult to read it in the dark."

She placed her arm around him, and they walked back together in silence.

Later that night, after the men from Lublin did not leave on their own accord, a group of resistance fighters returned to their building and forced them out of the ghetto at gunpoint. Anna did not join them, as she feared that this time she would be lighter on the trigger.

Sixteen

"Let me tell you this," said Anna. "When we fought in the ghetto, we were young, highly motivated and obstinate. We thought we were right and the whole world was wrong. We blamed everyone for our troubles: Capitalism, the Judenrat, the Americans and of course the Nazis. They were all at fault as far as we were concerned. But we never blamed fate, and it may just be that fate had more to do with our death and our survival than we ever gave it credit.

"You see, we were heretics, non-believers, atheists, and no one could get it through our thick skulls that there could ever be any divine power ruling the world. We were ruling the world. And we were ruling the Warsaw ghetto for a while too. That's a story that nobody seems to want to tell. The ghetto was ours. For a few short months before the real fighting began, we owned the streets of the ghetto. We had our independence, which gave me my first taste of Jewish autonomy, even though we were locked inside a tiny area...."

"Just like Israel now," said Rami.

"I suppose. We too knew that beyond the walls there was nothing but danger. It was difficult for us to get used to the freedom we suddenly acquired. Having gained our sovereignty by armed struggle, we were proud – so proud of our accomplishment – but we weren't ready for it.

"I recall, during the first few weeks after the Germans left the gates, we knew they would not come into the ghetto – well, at least not into the central ghetto – but we were still spooked every time we saw someone walking down the street in our direction. Once, just a few days after the first street battles that won us our liberty, I was walking with my friend Ida in the evening. We knew the safest routes to take because the guards would shoot on sight at that time of night. We were only a few streets from our home when we saw two shadows off in the distance walking toward us from the intersection ahead. We could only see the tops of the shadows, but they looked just like soldiers marching. We ran down an alleyway, off the main street and into one of the sewers. As we opened the entrance, I looked back to see if we were being followed, and I was sure that one of the men who had reached our street was glaring right at us and pointing. We jumped into the tunnel, closing the passage behind us and waited. After a few minutes, no one came, so we figured the coast was clear. We opened the sewer exit slowly and emerged from underground. As my head came up from below, I heard the cocking of a pistol. I turned around very slowly. Two figures stood over us pointing guns at our heads. It was my roommate and one of his friends. They were both laughing."

"What did you say to them?" asked Rami.

"Nothing, but Ida went back down into the sewer and came up with a handful of crap and threw it on them."

"They actually cocked their weapon? That sounds dangerous."

"No, it wasn't loaded. But you can see that we were far from comprehending how we had attained control of the streets. That's how it was for a long time. Those were wonderful weeks. You hear many stories about life in the ghetto; the hunger, the illnesses, the random killings. It's all true, but for the movement people, those few short months were different. It really doesn't matter how bad off you are, as long as you maintain a glimmer of hope. And we had much more than a glimmer. Sometimes I think that Israel forgets that it holds control of its own destiny. It still lets its enemies set the agenda instead of making plans that will change the world. Back then, in the ghetto, we were making big plans, for the future of Warsaw Jewry and for the Jewish People."

"How could you be thinking of the Jewish People at a time like that?"

"You didn't think about the Jewish People when you were fighting in the last war? It didn't dawn on you while the Egyptians were firing on you…"

"The Syrians," corrected Rami. "I was serving in the Golan."

"The goys, okay? It didn't occur to you that you were giving your life for a cause much greater than yourself?"

"No, actually. I was thinking about my survival and that of my unit. I think that war, the Yom Kippur War, made me think that it's not worth it. We shouldn't have to pay this kind of price for statehood. I'm not alone. A lot of my unit left the country after the war."

"Well, that's just sad. It's sad for all of us. We did not fight in the ghetto for anything less than the future of the Jewish People. We were so proud to know that our fellow Jews were fighting in Palestine for a state. And we would have been proud of you for fighting the Syrians, even if you were not aware of the true reason. 'We shall do and we shall hear,' it says in the Bible."

"I don't understand."

"It is from Exodus. We shall first do what is asked of us, and only later will we grow to comprehend the meaning of our actions. You will soon understand why you were fighting in the Golan. It may take some time, but you will eventually know that it had nothing to do with your own survival – well maybe a little – but it mostly had to do with the will of your people to stop being persecuted."

"I thought you were from Hashomer Hatzair, an atheist. Now you're quoting the Bible?"

"I never said I was not educated. I read a lot. You can not reject something if you do not understand it."

"So you reject it?"

"No, not as a wonderful source of lore and the cultural backbone of our people. It is just not a book from heaven. Great stories and great philosophies for its time. Some of its passages are still relevant today. Like that one."

"Philosophy? I guess that makes some sense. But I hated learning the Bible in school."

"Schools tend to do that to good material, don't they? I worked in a school for a while... to make up for missing out on bringing up my boys." Anna looked up at the sky through the front window.

Rami started to speak but stopped before the first words could leave his mouth. Anna had once again gone into a trance. Her eyes were glassy as she stared ahead blankly.

Over a minute passed when she said, "I was too busy shooting people."

Seventeen

21 March 1943

Miriam came through the door like the Gestapo barging in to make an arrest.

"The metal factory workers at Melmann's have been detained," she said. "A few hundred of them are being held."

Over the past few weeks, the Germans had been trying to convince the Jews of the factory to leave the factory voluntarily. They had plans to get the machinery out of the ghetto and transferred to a more hospitable climate. They were not comfortable in the ghetto and it showed. They had attempted to bribe the Jews to leave, but only a handful did, leaving them little choice if they wanted to save some face.

Anna looked at Miriam, who was damp from perspiration despite the cold, cloudy day that greeted them. "We need to get them out. Can you get to Mila Street and call for help? We'll go in there right now."

Miriam left and Anna went into the back room where Emil and Peretz were playing cards. Peretz had stolen the deck of playing cards from a German guard post that they had attacked one evening. They killed two guards and the third was seriously injured. They stole their weapons, some food and the deck of cards and left the injured soldier to watch them trash the place. Peretz also stole the soldiers' shirts, coats and hats. He said he knew they would eventually come in handy. That operation taught the fighters that it was much easier to overtake a guard post than they had previously thought. Still, they found it not worth the risk and rarely did it again. But at least they knew they could.

Peretz looked up at Anna. "Going to kill someone?"

Anna told them what was happening, and within two minutes the three of them were out the door and ready to join the other cells that Miriam would involve. Anna placed a hand on Emil's shoulder. She thought of how far he had come since joining the house. Emil hardly made it through the winter. His illnesses came and went and only in mid-March did he finally rid himself of bronchitis. Anna thought that there was something stronger than just a simple will to live that brought him through it, and one night, when she was returning home, she saw what it was. Emil was standing under the full moon hugging someone. Anna could not make out who it was, but she eventually discovered that it was a sixteen-year-old Halutz activist who had been helping Emil with one of the bunkers.

"How come you seem to be enjoying these missions more and more,

Emil?" asked Anna.

"Because we're winning."

"Ah," said Peretz, "you have the bug. Once you start, you can't stop until you fall. Once a Nazi killer, always a Nazi killer."

"That's not what I meant," said Emil. "Why does everything have to be so simple for you, Peretz? Black and white. It's all black and white to you."

"Better than black and blue," said Peretz.

There was more than just love that had changed Emil over the winter. Anna had been holding study sessions, much like she had before the war. It was a movement meeting where they discussed social relations, society, economic structures, conceptions of history, Hegel, Mills, Engels and of course, Anna's favorite, Marx. Emil turned out to have a knack for conceptualizing social theory and had contributed greatly to the discussions, which were frequented mostly by movement teens looking for intellectual stimulation while they prepared for battle. Sometimes when Anna caught them attempting to view the ghetto conflict in historical, dialectic terms, she would always remind them that although the Nazis are no less human than the slave owners and Lords before them, they are the result of much more than what Marxist theory could explain. She tried to help them understand that you can't see the picture when you're inside the frame and only a retrospective historic understanding of their actions will be analyzable. Her intention was to remove the young minds from the ghetto. It was an escape attempt that relaxed all of them.

Anna looked proudly at Emil as if she had something to do with his transformation. He may have been the first to admit that she did. One night he even told her how much her work with them had driven him to overcome the illnesses that had plagued him throughout the winter. He wore his pistol in his hip pocket with pride, and she could see that he wanted everyone to know that he belonged to the ghetto fighters.

The plan was simple. There would be four groups of three, each armed with pistols. Two would break into the warehouse where the workers were held. All of the intelligence information they had gathered consisted of knowing their exact location inside the complex. Of course, they were banking on the Germans believing that no Jew, even those who had been blowing up factories and sniper shooting guards, would have the audacity to try an escape operation. They knew the warehouse since some movement members had worked there in the past. They also knew that the Germans never seemed to place more than two guards for every twenty Jews. They would use the element of surprise, barge into the warehouse and open fire on the guards. As a military plan, it was terribly flawed, but in the ghetto, it was the best they could hope for.

In the building next to the factory was an abandoned room where they assembled to review their plan. Anna was looking at the shabby group that had gathered to take on an operation that even trained militias rarely attempted. But she knew that their will was strong, and that gave them an advantage. She had no doubt they would succeed, but at what price.

During the prep meeting, one of the younger up and coming leaders, Morgenstern, who went by his last name even though it was long and cumbersome, took charge and explained the plan.

"There are only two exits to that warehouse. It's just one big room, and there is nowhere to hide. Anna, Sarah and Yaki, you will remain outside the main doors to make sure there are no other guards in the vicinity. I doubt there will be. I was looking in the side window before you came, and it looks like three of the guards are sitting at a side table playing cards, while the fourth is standing around looking bored."

For a boy who never had the chance to finish secondary school, Morgenstern was intelligent, astute and shrewd and had a great understanding of people. Peretz called him "Morge."

"He won't be bored for long, Morge," said Peretz.

"Peretz, I want you to take Emil and Zvia, she's the best shot we have." Morgenstern smiled, and Zvia blushed. Anna noticed. "I'll come in the back door with Miriam, Yitzhak and Ari. We need to spot the guards and shoot them before they understand what's going on. Peretz, I want you to come in only after you hear the first shots. They will have all their attention on us, so it should be easy for you to take out any of the men we miss."

"What about the workers?"

"They will be tied up somewhere. The guards are going to be too stunned that we're attacking in broad daylight. We have to take them out before they open fire on them. Aaron, you and Edek, stay here and keep watch. You should be able to hear what's going on. Take this," he said, removing a wooden whistle. "It's loud, we'll hear it if you blow it continuously. Watch and see if anyone is coming down the road. If you see anything, start blowing the whistle, we'll run out the back with as many of the workers as we can."

As they were waiting to move in, two guards appeared at the front doors. They had come from inside, but Morgenstern could not be sure that they were the men he had seen before. Regardless, with the guards posted at the front doors, it meant they needed a new plan.

As they entered the alley, Anna had seen a German motorbike with a sidecar parked to the north of the building. It was far enough away from the entrance that the guards would not know if it was taken. She quickly devised a plan.

"Peretz, those uniforms at home. Can you get them?"

"Sure. I have hats and coats." He had more than just hats and coats. Peretz had been collecting German attire for months. Every time he had a chance to remove something from a dead German, he did.

"Bring one soldier coat with boots and a hat and one full SS uniform." She knew he had all of that. She had helped him remove some of it. "We need to take the bike and have two of us ride up as if we're SS coming to check on the hostages. They won't fire on us, thinking we're German. Instead of the people in front entering when the first shots are heard, those of us in the back will wait for the gunshots."

Peretz took off to get the coats and Morgenstern and Emil got the bike. They walked it around the back of the building and on to the next street. When Peretz returned with their costumes, they got dressed, started the bike and sat inside.

"How do we look?" asked Emil.

"Hitler would be proud," said Peretz.

Within a few minutes, they had all taken their places according to Anna's and Morgenstern's new plan. Peretz and Zvia would wait in the alley beside the warehouse until the guards outside were shot. They could then enter the warehouse with Emil and Morgenstern, just after the back door was breached. Anna moved under the awning, now that Morgenstern had moved to the front.

Anna took a deep breath as she heard the motorbike approach. The sound echoed off the adjacent building and sounded as if it was coming from the opposite direction. Anna hoped she was hearing what she expected to hear and not another bike that happened to show up.

"When we get into the warehouse," said Anna, "stay low and watch your shots. They'll be entering across from us wearing German uniforms. They look very real. Don't shoot them."

Two shots rang out and there was silence.

"Go!" yelled Ari. Yitzhak kicked in the door. All four of the fighters entered the back door and opened fire immediately upon passing the threshold. The blasts echoed off the walls as did the stray bullets, and it sounded as if thirty shots had been fired. Two of the Germans still sitting at the table fell immediately, playing cards flying in every direction, as a third reached for his rifle.

Anna steadied her aim and fired one shot directly into the chest of the third soldier fiddling with his weapon. He fell forward onto the table, collapsing it with a crash. The room filled with additional popping sounds, as the front door burst open, and Emil charged into the warehouse, dressed as a German patrol guard, with his SS commander, Morgenstern, right behind.

Behind the front door, slightly hidden from Anna and her comrades' view, was a fourth guard. He had been standing watching over the hostages, who no one seemed to have noticed when the shooting began. His rifle was aimed at the four fighters who entered the back door when he saw the front doors open. As he began to apply pressure to the trigger of the weapon aimed at Miriam who stood across the room, Morgenstern yelled, "Halt!" The soldier was distracted long enough for Emil to bash him in the head with his pistol butt. As he fell, his gun fired. The bullet hit a light fixture above the hostages. Glass and metal rained down on the ten workers lying on the floor huddled together trying to make themselves as small as possible. They were tied together with one long rope.

There was silence in the building until Morgenstern yelled, "That's it. Let's get out of here," as Peretz and Zvia ran into the building hoping they would still have a chance to kill someone.

Everyone moved to untie the hostages, as Peretz approached one of the Germans and tore off his coat. "Someone help me here with their weapons," he said.

Miriam began gathering the pistols and rifles from the dead guards.

In less than two minutes the warehouse was stripped of anything the fighters could use, and they were filing out the back door with the ten stunned workers. The smell of gunpowder replaced the heavy smell of dust and grease, and traces of smoke drifted up over their heads.

"You were incredible," Morgenstern said to Anna and Miriam, who were the last three to walk toward the back exit.

"You," said Anna, "have a great future in military planning."

Just then there was a crisp blast from the far side of the warehouse. The guard Emil had hit came to and fired a pistol Peretz and Miriam did not notice hidden on his hip. Morgenstern stopped in his tracks and sank to his knees, leaning onto Miriam as he slouched down.

Miriam, trying to hold him up yelled, "Help!"

Zvia, who had been walking in front of the three and was one step from the doorway, turned on the balls of her feet, drew her pistol and fired, hitting the soldier directly in the face.

Peretz led the rest of the fighters back into the warehouse, weapons drawn and ready. "What happened?"

"We missed one," said Miriam. "He got Morgenstern." Yaki and Peretz grabbed their unconscious friend and dragged him out of the building. He was dead well before they reached safety, with the bullet penetrating his back and stopping his heart.

The workers dispersed as soon as they left the building, running as if there was a fire to escape. The fighters dragged their murdered comrade back to the organization's headquarters, where they left him in the hands of his housemates to make sure he had a proper burial.

Anna, Peretz, Emil and Miriam reached their home a short time later. Emil was the first to speak.

"I didn't shoot him," he said. "I should have shot him."

"You did what you needed to," said Anna.

"But I didn't kill him. I just knocked him out. I should have killed him."

"You couldn't have shot him, he was almost behind you. You didn't have the angle. He would have seen that you were aiming at him. He thought you were with him."

"I could have shot him once he was down."

"Then you would have been just like him, a cold-blooded murderer."

Emil looked up at Anna with a puzzled look. "How can you..." he stopped and shook his head.

"He was just a boy. Didn't you see? He was enlisted into Hitler's army and given a post. I don't want to kill them for the sake of killing them," she said. "I just want to kill the ones that are going to kill me."

"That's all of them," said Emil. "I should have killed him."

Anna realized that she wasn't going to convince Emil that he was not at fault for Morgenstern's death. There was little she could say. She placed a hand on his shoulder and squeezed hard. "You did fine," she said and walked to the back room where Tuvia and Ida were waiting for her.

"I heard you got them out," said Tuvia.

"We lost Morgenstern."

"Anna..." said Ida.

"What is it? What happened?" Anna asked, letting her arms drop to her sides and her shoulders droop.

"We're hearing things," said Ida.

Anna moved over the bed where Ida and Tuvia were sitting at its foot and sat down between them. Ida took her hand. Anna knew what this was about. She knew that eventually she would hear something about Hanna and Yehuda, and she was in constant fear that the news would be tragic.

"We heard that they were captured and brought to Treblinka," said Ida.

"Who told you?"

"There are some weak contacts we've established. I don't know whether to trust them. I'm not even sure they're talking about Hanna and Yehuda. There are thousands of mothers traveling alone with young

156

children."

"So why do you think it was them?"

"Only because they were caught in the woods north of here with a group of partisans. That was the general direction they must have gone."

"It's just a rumor then, isn't it?" said Anna, forcing a smile. "We need more information than that to draw conclusions."

"You're right," said Ida and hugged her.

"Even if it is true, at least they're alive."

Anna knew very well that had they reached Treblinka, Yehuda would no longer be alive. They were all well aware that the Germans killed the children and the elderly as soon as they arrived at the camps. Hanna, on the other hand, could possibly have been kept alive to work.

As much as Anna pretended that it was only a rumor, the news affected her. She had been the only person in the house to remain healthy the entire year. From the moment she heard that Yehuda and Hanna may have been taken to a camp, her strength weakened. By the following day, she was running a fever and had replaced Emil as the cougher of the house.

Tuvia was finally gaining his strength. He would have loved to have taken care of her but was far too busy making up for lost time and planning escape routes for the fighters once they ran out of ammunition. So once again, Ida was left to nurse Anna back to health, a task that she enjoyed more than anything else; for to be in Anna's company was the greatest part of living those days. Anna felt exactly the same.

Ida kept reminding her that without her help, the ghetto would be lost. Anna dismissed these flatteries as jokes and told Ida that it was she who the fighters needed the most. On and on they would go, praising each other, laughing about it, as Anna struggled to maintain a physical condition that would allow her to function in the house and in the community. The truth was that Ida was now the most important person in Anna's life. And Anna was the only one left that Ida truly loved, and they both knew it.

It took over two weeks for Anna to regain her health. On the first day that she left her bed, a second rumor about her son arrived, this time from an entirely different direction. It seems that Hanna and Yehuda had not made it to the partisans at all but were living with a family on a farm outside of Siedlce, just east of Warsaw. It was highly conceivable that once they left the walls, they were directed towards Polish farmers who had been assisting the underground and would be willing to take in these refugees. It would also have been possible for this information to easily be transferred to the ghetto via the Polish channels and be considered credible. The source in this case was a Jewish runner who had met the two girls who left with Hanna and Yehuda. The girls had stayed until Hanna and Yehuda were safe and then made their way south to attempt to reach Palestine. It was the greatest news Anna could have possibly heard. That night she decided it was time for a small celebration.

It was not all that difficult to acquire alcohol in the ghetto, but like any other food, it was scarce. Peretz had made it a point to take any alcoholic drinks he could find among German soldiers and he quickly realized that alcohol was a staple among the Germans guarding the ghetto. It seems the work was so gruesome and inhumane that only drunk could one comply with the vicious orders handed down by the SS. So along with his stash of uniforms, Peretz had several flasks of home-distilled drinks that were available at Anna's small party.

The seven roommates were all home, gathered together in the cool room. Over the winter, Rachel had attained better carpeting for the main room, although it was just laid over the old one. The room felt warmer and the inhabitants enjoyed spending time together. Many a night study sessions, ideological discussion and planning meetings were all taking place in this one room, where they had been living since the ghetto was closed. They had lost six of their comrades, including little Yehuda and Hanna, but the compassionate atmosphere of their tiny flat never waned. They were a family, and they had even vowed to call each other brother and sister from this point on. However, during all this time they had spent together, they never had reason to celebrate anything. Life in the ghetto provided few joys, no reason to jump up and down and no ecstasy. So when Anna, who was truly happy about what she had heard, called them all together to rejoice with Peretz's spirits, her glee brightened their faces as a small candle lights up a large room.

"L'chaim," said Emil, raising the small glass he was given.

"To Yehuda," said Ida.

"And Hanna," added Miriam.

"How much of this stuff do you have?" asked Tuvia.

"Enough," said Peretz. "I can't believe how much those Germans drink and are still able to run a war. It's no wonder we've had so much success."

"We've had successes because we're smarter than they are," said Rachel, who was having a very hard time downing her drink. Her whole face became contorted with each sip and she eventually gave it back to Peretz.

"We've also had some help," said Peretz, who was now lying on his back in the center of the room. He had been complaining of back pains after climbing a wall a few weeks earlier. Not one to pule, he had taken the aches in stride, only to find himself needing long periods of rest on hard, cold floors.

"What do you mean?" asked Emil.

"I mean the Polish underground. They've provided us plenty of weapons since January. We just received twenty more large guns and I don't know how many grenades. They've impressed me."

"If they've impressed you," said Ida, "then that says a lot.

"I've been thinking," said Miriam. "I want to get out of here and fight with the partisans. I think I could do a lot more good out there."

"Why not do both," said Tuvia.

"You mean to wait for the fighting to resume here and then flee? I don't know how easy that will be. I want to fight here, but I really think that I would make a better partisan than an urban fighter."

"Why's that?" asked Anna.

"Because I'll feel freer and that will make me a more efficient fighter. I can't explain it. When I was on my runs, I always felt like I was home, even when I was in the middle of some village I had never been to. I was able to see the German forces coming well before they arrived. It was strange, but I knew exactly where I was and where they'd be. I guess I have a great sense of smell."

"The Germans do smell," said Peretz.

"So you want to leave now?" asked Anna.

"What do you think? I know I can help here, but I also know I would be great out there."

There was silence as everyone contemplated Miriam's request. She could have easily just left if that was what she decided, but it was a group decision, and she would never go against the will of the group.

"Maybe," said Anna, "we need to devise a plan that would allow you and perhaps a few others as well, to get out of here after the fighting gets out of hand. We know that the Germans will eventually bring in mass forces. They will need to save face and would never let us get away with an ongoing resistance. Let's be ready for that inevitable moment when we have to choose to die or to run."

"Mordechai will never go for it," said Rachel. "He'd tell you that there is no choice. Running is not an option."

"Mordechai does not have to know everything we are doing. If surviving, getting our story out and assisting with the resistance outside of the walls is an option, then I want to plan for it."

This was the start of something they would begin referring to as Miriam's plan, although it was Anna who really formulated it. The plan was fairly simple. There would be anywhere from three to five groups of four or five, mostly women, who would have prearranged escape routes. These groups would always be within reach of the exits and would be able to leave the ghetto at a moment's notice. Each group would have one runner who would know the route to take in order to safely get the groups out to the Aryan side of Warsaw and then to the forests, where they would meet up with the partisan fighters. Only a handful of girls had firsthand information about the whereabouts of partisan locations, and each group would have one of these girls with them. None of the groups would take the same route out of the ghetto in order to ensure that at least one of them would make it. It seemed that the most important goal of the plan was to make sure that the Warsaw Ghetto story was told through the eyes of the fighters themselves. It was clear to them that had they left the story to be told by those who had been deported, the understanding of the motivation and ideology behind their actions would be misconstrued and their pride would be lost.

Rachel was the only one in the group who did not like the idea and made it a point to refrain from joining one of the groups. Anna told her that if at any time she desired, she could join their group, which consisted of Miriam as the leader, Anna, Ida and Rachel if she so desired. Anna made sure that despite her obstinacy, she knew where they would meet.

In the meantime, there was a lot of activity in the ghetto. On occasion, the Germans would round up a group of Jews and bring them to the Umschlagplatz to await deportation. Although this activity had been commonplace since the deportations began, it was now considered completely intolerable by the fighters. Less than 40,000 Jews were left in the ghetto, over a thousand of them were connected to one fighting organization or another, and they were not going to allow the rest to be taken to their deaths. They knew that the Germans needed to keep many of these Jews alive for slave labor. The Germans were using about half of the population in the ammunition factories, so as long as the German factories were functioning, the Jews of the ghetto would have the time needed to continue organizing. The fighters had a vested interest in Jewish workers continuing to do their job in the factories. Once they were gone, and the only Jews left in the ghetto were the fighters, it was reasonable that the Germans would begin to use excessive firepower.

So it was their mission to release these prisoners being rounded up and taken to the camps. They attacked the Umschlagplatz and instructed the Jews who were gathered there to run. In the past, they would have been met with hesitation or dispute, but now, with most of the Jews understanding their fate, though not all, they ran and ran fast. Since the guards were under attack, they never had the opportunity to fire upon the escaping masses and instead concentrated on restraining their attackers. The fighters were now good at what they did, and although they did have casualties, it was nothing compared to what happened to them in the streets during the January uprising. Their real motive was to continue to keep the Germans out of the ghetto and on edge when they entered it. They were taking back their streets – one Nazi at a time.

The fighters were aware that the Germans were feeling the tension in the ghetto. Their body language had changed, and there were no longer SS officers strutting down the streets unprotected. Even when they were determined to deport a group of Jews, they were extremely cautious. They no longer searched for Jews in the basements, which had now become the fighters' bunkers, and they would not intervene when commotion inside the ghetto called for police action. It was clear to the Jewish fighters that had they resisted long ago, Polish Jewry would still be alive. The Germans had been counting on the fear of the Jews to keep them cooperating.

It was this realization that also caused the fighters to turn their anger toward the remaining Judenrat members and other Jews who seemed to never terminate their assistance to the Germans. These were the people the fighters were blaming for the plight of the Jews. Had they had more guts, had they had more will to withstand German aggression, to fight fire with fire, the Jews of Poland would never have been removed from their beloved capital.

"I have had it with them," said Peretz, one night when they were making plans to assassinate one of the Jews hostile toward the fighters' plans. "They have gone too far this time. How can a Jew turn in another Jew?"

"How can a Jew assassinate another Jew," asked Emil.

"He gave the Nazis Haim's name. He told them when he would be going to the factory and that he was collecting gunpowder in the lining of his coat. The bastard told the Nazis everything. And for what? For a lousy loaf of bread. This is one man I will be happy to take off this planet."

The next morning Peretz returned from being out all night. He was met by Ida and Anna.

"One more mission accomplished," he said.

"You shot him?" asked Ida.

"I didn't, unfortunately. But he's dead. We decided to be creative. We captured him and brought him to the eastern guard post. We tied his hands and legs and put him in the middle of the street in front of the post. Then we hid behind the building and shot at one of the guards. The other one turned around and machine-gunned the bastard. I wonder how long it took them to realize that he was unarmed and tied up."

"Wouldn't it have been easier to just shoot him yourself?"

"And waste a bullet on him? No. This was a good plan. We killed a guard and that traitor with one bullet. A bit too complex for my liking, but it worked."

This was not the only case of the fighters turning their weapons on other Jews. It seemed that nothing upset the fighter leadership more than traitors. They terrorized a number of remaining leaders, driving some to suicide and others to flee into the Aryan side of the city, likely to be caught by the Nazis as a Jew out of the ghetto. It was difficult for those who did not know their way around and did not have contacts in the city to survive. The women could pretend to be Aryan, but the men could not and eventually, someone would require them to drop their pants.

Anna had been one of the few to question this policy, but deep down she knew that there was no choice. As a rule, she never wanted anyone in the ghetto to take part in immoral activities, feeling that their role was not to win at any cost. She was willing to do anything to stay alive and prevent more Jews from being deported, but it would be within the realm of her morality. Many, Peretz included, would have liked to see the ghetto cleansed of opposition to the resistance at almost any cost. However, Anna, whose only real concern was that they were moving too fast, was bringing up the issue more as an intellectual exercise than a policy discussion. She knew very well that for the resistance to continue to gain strength, they could not afford Nazi conspirators among them. In many cases, the young Jews recruited to the fighting organizations were supplied arms. It was imperative that they be loyal to the cause and any hint of compromise would be met with strict movement measures.

However, their biggest concern was not other Jews, but German attempts to relocate the factories out of the ghetto. Although the Germans had ceased all Aktions after January, they were very active with the factories on the outskirts of the ghetto.

One night, well past midnight, when the house was quiet and still and Anna had fallen asleep between Tuvia and Ida, there was a knock on the door. Hashomer Hatzair had its own coded knock that everyone in the movement knew and this was it. Peretz met the activists at the door and invited them in.

Anna, woken by the noise, left her warm bed and went into the main room.

"We need fighters," said one of the boys with red hair and a long, thin face. Anna had never seen him before, but the other boy was a movement veteran she had worked with before the war. He was just a small boy then, but she recognized him nonetheless. She had known his brother well, and she felt like she had gone back in time and was looking at the older sibling who had died during the first winter in the ghetto. He smiled at her when she entered the room. Anna nodded back.

"They're moving a transport from the metal works tonight. We have charges that need to be laid. We hear you have a specialist."

The specialist they were referring to was Rachel. Without anyone in the house knowing, Rachel had used her time to become a demolition expert. She had studied physics in school and had always taken an interest in explosions. Over the previous month, she had been training at one of the resistance camps where the movement leaders were training their own elite fighting groups. Rachel had been a part of those groups and had learned to rig explosives for just this purpose.

"We don't," said Anna. "You must be thinking of David. He doesn't live here."

"No," said the red-head boy. "We need Rachel."

Anna and Peretz looked at each other.

"I'm here," said Rachel's soft voice from behind them. "Let's go."

"I'm coming with you," said Peretz. If there was an opportunity for Peretz to blow something up, he wasn't going to miss it. No one objected since it seemed the boys were looking for back-up as well as their expert.

Anna also joined them, thinking it would be a good learning experience. With all of the activity going on, Anna had not taken part in many sabotage expeditions. As a leading player in the resistance, she felt it would be good for her to understand how these operations were conducted. Also joining them were Ida and Emil, who both had awoken startled; they ran to the front door to join the others racing to the railroad cars where the factory equipment had been loaded.

The operation itself was not very difficult for the fighters. Their experience had made them efficient and smooth. There was only one guard guarding the train loaded with factory equipment. Rachel worked her way under the train with the explosives, while the rest of the team watched that the guard did not approach as she laid the charges at the foot of each car. It only took a few minutes before everything was ready and Rachel gave the signal to retreat. She would detonate the charges, which would not only destroy the railroad cars but kill the guard as well. As if she had been conducting undertakings like this her whole life, Rachel set the fuse alight and ran to meet the group. The guard, who looked sleepy and bored, didn't even have time to turn around when the shrapnel from the bombs decapitated him and set the railcars ablaze.

While they were walking back, Anna approached Rachel, trying to understand why she was keeping her involvement in the demolition team a secret from the rest of them.

"I have not felt a part of the house for a while now," she said. "Peretz tends to ridicule me, you rarely give me support and the rest ignore me most of the time."

Anna did not respond. She felt ashamed that she had let one of their housemates feel this way. Rachel had been the last to join the house and it turns out never quite felt at home. Anna had known that she preferred to be with Mordechai and would have moved there had she felt it would advance the cause. But nevertheless she stayed and compensated by spending most of her time outside of the house in what turned out to be a training camp. But it hurt Anna to know that she did not feel comfortable enough to share her feelings with the group, and Anna took the lapse as hers personally. What had begun as simple sadness on Rachel's face, now looked to Anna as despair.

"Why are you so eager to fight?" Anna asked Rachel, knowing very well that she had answered that question the day she arrived, albeit a partial answer. Anna knew there was something deeper. Each one of the ghetto fighters had a personal vendetta against the Germans who had set out to efface their entire existence. Their homes, their families and their way of life had been destroyed. They were hungry, cold and ill. It was a natural will to want to kill this force that had caused such grief and suffering. But in addition, they all had something else on their minds when they made the decision to sacrifice their lives for the Jewish People. There was something personal, a craving for the righting of a wrong, the loss of a specific loved one, the kind of revenge that only a first-hand sufferer can know. Or perhaps they were proving themselves to someone dead or alive. Their parents were gone. Their peers were now their family. What made them give every drop of energy? What made them open fire on men aiming machine guns at them? What made them rummage in the sewers, walk the streets on the Aryan side, smuggle arms and steal ammunition, was greater than just vengeance. There was always, behind each and every fighter, a personal story and a deep need to belong to this elite fighting unit.

Rachel stopped walking and turned toward Anna. "I saw myself fall," she said softly. "I was not gunned down into a mass grave like my parents. I wasn't gassed at the camps like my teachers and my classmates. I was fighting. I had a weapon in my hand and I was a soldier for the Jewish army. It was a dream I had when the war just broke out. I awoke and knew that I would die in combat. That was it. Each one of us has seen her death. Each one of us wants to fulfill a dream. For me, they are one and the same."

"I haven't seen my death," said Anna.

"Then it is too far off in the future, isn't it?"

Eighteen

"Ay!" yelled Anna as the bus suddenly dropped into a pothole in the road. Her seat, being the bus floor, was taken from beneath her, leaving her dangling in the air until gravity returned her to the rubber with retribution. Anna felt her bottom contact the bus like two giant magnets crushing together.

"Sorry again," said the driver.

The scenery outside was now devoid of vegetation. Dry fields were off to the left, but the right-hand side, the side Anna could see through the glass on the front doors, was dusty and barren. Most of the land they were passing was preparing itself to be transformed into urban sprawl and whatever greenery there may have been was now destroyed by bulldozers and dump trucks in order to make room for apartment complexes, schools, shopping centers and government buildings.

"What are they building here?" she asked the driver.

"Just another town. I guess they're still expecting millions of Jews from around the world to come live here."

"Of course that's what they're expecting. We will be ten million strong by 1990. I hope to be alive to see it."

"We're hardly three million," he said. "Do you think that seven million people will move to this desert?"

"Of course I do. It's the only way we'll survive. Look what these terrorists are doing, hijacking an airplane like that. That's why I never fly, you know. Boats are much safer."

"Well, I don't think that we'll reach four million by 1990. I think that more people will leave before anyone comes."

"You are very pessimistic. It's not wise to be so pessimistic. It makes you sour. You should try being more confident in your convictions."

As the bus turned toward the north, the sun moved across Anna's face and she held her hand to her brow to block the rays. No clouds were in the sky. As far as Anna could remember, she hadn't seen a cloud since May. The next rain would fall in October, usually following the last days of Sukkot, with the first big rains not showing their power until mid-November. Anna preferred the rain to the sun. There was no escaping the Middle East heat in the summer, whereas the cold air reminded her of her childhood. However, the air on the Israeli coast never reached freezing and she always found that a coat would easily be ample coverage for the sting of winter. Her home in Poland had always been like that coat, protecting her from the biting weather that had taken so many of her friends and family during the war. She tried to remember the cold whenever the sun beat down on her head and she longed for a splash of cool water. She tried to recall how there was once a time when the sun was the greatest treat she could have. To awake on a winter day with temperatures causing her hair to acquire frost and her eyes to smart from exposure, and find that there was actually a sun out there in the sky, burning down and warming something somewhere. Only while one stood behind a glass window could the warmth be felt on those bitter winter days. Only while there were other alternative forms of heat, the sun not doing its duty, could the rays be appreciated.

Now, on the bus, the sun was just a nuisance and Anna wondered how that strange ball of burning hydrogen could transpire from friend to foe in such a short time.

Yaakov, noticing her struggle with the glare, lowered the shade over the windshield, helping to block the light in her eyes.

"Thank you. Much better," she said. "They destroy so much to build."

"What else are they going to do? How can they build a city without destroying the wilderness around it?"

"So this doesn't disturb you? Look how ugly it is."

"And the city built in its place will be even uglier, but we don't have a choice."

"We could build underground," she said. "It worked for me. Although we didn't have these big tools and things. We had to work in secret and build quietly. But we didn't destroy anything. We left that for the Germans."

"You know, growing up on Yad Mordechai, I have grown used to living with survivors. But none talk so much about their past. In fact, they do everything they can to avoid it. How come you talk so much about that horrible time?"

"Because, someday, when I least expect it, someone will be listening."

"And that someone will do what?"

"I don't know. But I know that I have always told people my story and have listened to hundreds of other stories in order to learn from them. Sometimes we don't understand our need to talk about things. I know that most of the people that I lived with in Poland, the few that survived, would better prefer to talk about their back pain or the wonderful medication they just received. No, I want to talk about things with meaning. There is nothing more substantial to me than that period – the darkest in Jewish and perhaps human history. If I don't talk about it, then who will, right? There are few of us who can talk about it. I am not ashamed, I am proud. And who knows, maybe something good – I mean really good – will come of it."

"Doesn't it seem self-righteous?"

"Self-righteous? To talk about my war? Are you crazy? Are you insane? I have been called many things in my life but never self-righteous, particularly for talking about my war."

"Look, I don't mean to offend you, but I don't have any reservations about talking about that stuff either. Nothing is sacred to me. I lost everyone in that war – and I never met them. But I don't think that bragging about it is helping anyone."

"Do you think I'm bragging?"

"Well, you talk about the courage, the battles, the building…"

"We built great bunkers! I'm proud of what we did. It's no wonder there are two kibbutzim with museums about the ghetto. This is something to be uplifted by, not something to hide. We should all be talking about it all the time.… And we built great things under those cursed streets, great things!"

Nineteen

30 March 1943

By late-March, having been given almost two months to coordinate their efforts, the fighting organizations were ready for battle. Since mid-January, a sort of interregnum from Nazi rule had allowed the Jews in the ghetto to reorganize and prepare for the inevitable battles to come. The January Aktion had been the perfect test run, and like any good military training facility, the ghetto fighters implemented necessary changes from the lessons they learned. Now, there were twenty-two fighting groups, twelve of which were pioneer movement groups. Four of those groups belonged to Hashomer Hatzair and Anna's house made up half of one of those groups. The fighting groups were split up between three sections of the city. Anna's group was assigned to the central ghetto, where it was assumed that most of the activity would be taking place. Her group was one of nine in the area and Mordechai was the commanding officer.

It was unclear when the next Aktion would begin, but they would not be taken by surprise. All of the fighting groups were ready for combat at all times. There were far more active fighters than there were arms, so many of the unarmed members of the resistance were busy digging tunnels and setting traps for the Germans. Mines were set on the routes the Germans were likely to take when they entered the ghetto and outposts were built on the upper floors of the building.

"I don't think we could have asked for a better group of bunker builders," said Anna. "Look at these guys. They're the best engineers, the best building minds we have."

"Did you have any doubt?" said Tuvia.

"Yes, as a matter of fact, I did. When I heard the original plan, I never thought we would be able to pull it off like that."

For months the Jews of the ghetto had been working on plans. As the workers worked and the fighters fought, the average Jew in the ghetto continued to struggle with survival, battling the elements, the hunger and thoughts of the future. Each one tried to find a way out for when the Aktions would return. No one had illusions that the Germans wouldn't be back to get them. So options were needed. Building the bunkers was the activity that gained the most support out of all the fighters were doing. Those Jews with Polish contacts, Aryan looks and some means of finance attempted to get false documents for when they escaped. However, most did not have that option and thoughts of "after" were just as troublesome as their current reality.

"Each night," said Anna," when I hear the sound of hammers and chisels underground, I feel a chill down my spine. It's a wonderful sound. We are finally creating again. Creation has been missing from all of our lives for a long, long time. Most of the time, I feel that we deal much more in destruction than anything else. It's wonderful to create. Just wonderful."

"You never cease to amaze me," said Tuvia. "We're creating hiding places and escape routes. The things that make you tick..."

"Tuvia, these are the things that make all of us tick," she said.

"Don't you think it's amazing? Some of these bunkers go down three floors. We've managed to connect them to electric lines and water veins. We have a whole city down there. The Germans will be shooting us up here when most of the activity will be down there. We've found the craziest ways to find all we need and it's working."

"We still won't last more than two days against them," he said.

"What happened to you? You lost a part of you. You were never that pessimistic."

"We're going to die, Anna. How can I not be pessimistic?"

"What happened?"

A tear trickled down Tuvia's face. "I lost my family. I lost my son."

Tuvia had never mentioned Yehuda leaving, and after he became ill, Anna never felt it was the right time to talk about it. There was an unspoken agreement between them not to mention it at all. Only during the small party that Anna held after hearing the positive news, did Tuvia even acknowledge that Yehuda was alive. It had seemed to Anna that since he left, Tuvia just let him go.

Anna moved closer to Tuvia, who was sitting on one of the chairs at the kitchen table. She took his hand.

"Listen to me my love," she said. "Yehuda is okay. I know it. I know we'll see him again. I can't tell you how I know. It's just a feeling, but I do. You have to trust that feeling. Can you?"

"No, Anna, I can't. Neither of us believes in premonitions, omens or signs. They're right up there with believing in a god that doesn't exist. I can hope, but I can't believe. Do you understand? Yehuda may be alive now, but I will never see him, because I will never leave this place. It's my last stop, Anna. There's nowhere else to go."

"You may be the worst casualty we have had," she said and left him sitting at the table.

"You know I'm right," he yelled after her as she moved to the bedroom.

Anna stopped and turned around, her eyes were glassy and her mouth sour. "I know I loved you when you had hope."

Tuvia stared at her and she wiped her cheeks with a strong brush of her fingers. There was a great deal Anna could tolerate. She was strong enough to lead men and women into battle, to send young girls to smuggle weapons and to kill Nazis, but she was not ready to continue a relationship with a man who could not dream. It wasn't as if their relationship had been that healthy since Yehuda left. Anna tended to spend much more intimate time with Ida than with Tuvia, and all of them seemed better off with that arrangement. Nonetheless, Tuvia was still the father of her child and she, up until that moment, was not planning on breaking off the relationship. During the few months since the January uprising, Anna had seen many people around her change. But they had mostly changed for the better. Shop owners and bakers had given the fighters goods and baked them bread, community leaders had praised them and one woman even stopped Anna in the street and gave her a hug after recognizing her. Community leaders understood the need to create an atmosphere of inspiration and the young people of the ghetto were doing that. They were giving each other a reason to get out of bed in the morning, a reason to live and reason to hope. Tuvia was the only one of the housemates who reached a level of despair. So many in the ghetto had lost their will to live and Anna had met scores of them. She was always able to recognize the moment when it was likely they would no longer be able to return to the living. Some committed suicide, others let themselves die of starvation, but most just turned into zombies, drifting along the streets of Warsaw like the leaves that blew at their feet. They were exhausting to watch. Anna needed all of her strength now, and for the first time, she saw in Tuvia's eyes that he was gone. She knew he wouldn't kill himself, and the house was supplied with enough food to keep him from starving, but he could do something stupid. He was not the person that she had known, and she did not want to be around him.

Ida stuck her head out of the bedroom and saw Anna standing in front of her holding her head. She placed her arm around her, walked her into the room and shut the door behind her. That night, and every night from then on, Tuvia slept in the main room.

Anna's rift with Tuvia caused tension in the house at a time when unity was paramount. There was little more important than the task of preparation, and Anna understood that. Tuvia became more and more distant, because, if the housemates had to side with one of them, Anna would always be the favorite. It was during this period that Anna wrote her first letter to Yehuda.

Dearest Yehuda,
It has been the coldest winter of my days. The air would not only

chill my bones but without your warmth, I allowed it to chill my soul.
There is no reason for these words to be put on paper. There is just a
longing to speak to you. You would not understand my ramblings today,
but you will read these words when the roads are cleared and passage
home, in an ascent as we would call it, to a new world of love and freedom,
will allow us to be together. Evil forces have taken over our people, my
dear. I can only hope that you will retain little of that in your heart, that
you will not know these things that have replaced good with terror, passion
with fear and light with dark. Even your father, a man of conviction, of
love and of understanding, has been compromised by the witches of despair.
I beg of you to forgive him, for he did what he did out of mercy and pain.
My dear Yehuda, know this…

But Ann never finished her first letter. She had meant to tell her son
of the undying love that both his parents had for him, but those words were
never written. As she held the pen in her hand and as her thoughts drifted
far from the ghetto to wherever her son had been lying, she fell asleep. And
when she awoke she could not recall why she was writing the letter in the
first place. She folded up the note and placed it in between the pages of a
book on her shelf. She did not even look at the book, not finding any kind of
symbolism in placing a letter to her missing son in any specific author's care.

She had recalled her request to forgive Tuvia and fought the will to
believe she was talking to herself. There is no forgiving despair in the ghetto;
for the ghetto was unforgiving. At least not while they prepare to fight, she
tried to reason. Tuvia would have to change if she was ever to exonerate
him. So why would she ask Yehuda to do so?

Once again, Anna traded pain with activity, vigorous, hasty, congested
activity. She had set out to be the organizing echo, a back-up plan for all the
fighter's endeavors, to make sure that whatever was going to happen would
happen the way Mordechai and his fighters wished. And when all was
coming to an end, when there were no more bullets to shoot, or
optimistically, no more Germans to kill, they would make their escape and
perhaps, for she could still dream, they would be able to make their way to
Eretz Yisrael. However, she was much more concerned about going to
Jerusalem of the Heavens. They all were. Few could state clearly their true
feelings regarding their chances to survive. That was not ever part of their
discussions. Maybe no one wanted to be disappointed when they found
themselves dead. Maybe they just were smart enough to know that
everything they were doing was purely symbolic. It didn't matter. They were
working full-heartedly, and Anna was the one pushing her comrades to give
a little more.

Anna was also busy denouncing the Judenrat, or what was left of it. Few listened to their ramblings and their position in the ghetto leadership had faded as they had become insignificant. On the other hand, the fighters were overrated and Anna knew it. She often encountered people with the impression that the January uprising had completely deterred the Germans from emptying the ghetto.

"All we did was postpone the inevitable," she said again and again. But it was difficult to erase hope with facts and Anna did not like her role as a realist.

The ghetto was quieter than normal these days. Still, corpses were showing up on the streets; however, it was much easier to care for the dying since January. but there was an overall feeling that the ghetto was in its final days. The Germans failed in their attempts to eject the Jews by transferring the factories, and everyone was aware that they would not sit quietly for long.

18 April 1943

That morning, Anna was washing some shirts when the door burst open and Miriam barged in. She had just returned from outside the walls and was breathing heavily as Anna quickly brought her some water.

"There's movement out there," she said. "I haven't seen anything like it since last summer. There are military units, they've doubled the guards at the gates, and the Poles are saying there will be another Aktion soon. I guess they were just waiting for it to warm up."

"We need to check the bunkers and distribute the ammunition," said Anna, as her heart rate increased and she felt a tingling in her spine.

"Yisrael and Berl are already on it. I just wanted you to know. I think you can stop washing your shirts now."

"Right," she said, looking down at her soapy hands. "I suppose I won't need these much."

Anna took a deep breath. The previous weeks had been rough, but satisfying. The bunkers had been prepared, with electricity, water, food and radios put into the main spaces. Anna had been very active in the preparation, making sure that her girls were bringing in any missing supplies that Mordechai felt they needed. She was also coordinating the money transfers. Most of the Jews in the ghetto with any available funds were helping however they could. Anna would get their money to the runners who would in turn bring the cash to the Poles delivering the provisions to the smugglers. For every two successful transactions, there was one failure and in one case, one of the runners was killed on her way back to the ghetto with several tins of jam. Despite the many frustrations, the bunkers were filling up and the fighters were ready.

Anna left her apartment for what would be the last time that afternoon. She went down her street and over to headquarters on Mila Street, where scores of youth were running in and out, getting their orders and moving to the next stop. Some were carrying weapons, others toted bags of food or Molotov Cocktails. Before entering the building, Anna stopped to watch the mayhem. What struck her first was that she recognized no one. This was already a multi-organizational operation, and although she had been active from the onset, she was shocked by the response the young ghetto inhabitants had with their chance to fight. The second thing she noticed was that no one seemed scared. They were about to take on the largest and strongest army in Europe, perhaps in the world, and no signs of fear were seen on their faces. In fact, it looked more like a sporting event than war preparation. Teenagers were running back and forth, yelling short and precise directions at each other, each carrying just what they needed to bring to their posts. For every man and woman who entered the building, another exited, as if to maintain balance.

Finally, Anna entered and walked to one of the main rooms next to Mordechai's office.

"Yan-Varshaw," whispered a young girl who could not have been more than thirteen. She was looking up at Anna as if asking for permission to do something, but it was actually her job to make sure the fighters knew the new password.

"Thank you," said Anna and turned to look for Mordechai.

"He's out," said a young man with a black beret. He went to check the roof passages. He'll be here later."

Anna walked into the next room. There were five men stacking sandbags on the window sill. Through the slit that remained open, Anna could see that men and women were emptying the heavy furniture from the apartments in the complex and using it to block the front gate. Already, there was an overturned wagon making passage difficult. Anna could not have been more impressed by the sheer amount of energy that was coming out of headquarters.

As she turned around, she finally saw a familiar face.

"Ida! It's good to see you. Are you on your way to our bunker?"

"Just came from there. Peretz, Miriam and Tuvia are already there. I think Emil is getting more fuel for the MC's and I haven't seen Rachel all day."

"She's outside the walls. Should be back soon. I think she went to

174

make sure the Poles know what's going on in here. We'll need their help."

"She shouldn't be out there. They have dogs looking for Jews. How could she be running around now?"

"I didn't give the order. It came directly from Mordechai. She's under his command now. It must have been important."

Anna had seen Rachel drift away from the house and into Mordechai's den. As the explosive expert she was, she had a role to play in central command. That was why her absence was so disconcerting. Anna was trying to sound like it made sense to her that Rachel would be the one to carry an important message out of the ghetto, but it did not make sense to her, and she was concerned.

"She's needed here, Anna. I'm sure she has some charges to lay."

"Perhaps. She'll be back."

Mordechai entered the building surrounded by some of his closest friends, who had become regional commanders for the operation. As they entered the room, the fighters all seemed to take a collective breath as Mordechai and his comrades were a very impressive group of men and women.

Anna met him halfway across the room and without asking the question, he answered.

"She's got something to do," he said.

"What?" asked Anna, unable to leave it at that.

"She's laying explosives outside the walls. We need them to think that the Poles are attacking as well."

"You mean they're not?"

"I can't be sure. I'm not taking any chances."

"That's a dangerous mission for her."

"Is there anything here that's not dangerous?" he said and smiled.

"Who's with her?"

"There are eight of them. They'll be back by nightfall. Don't worry. I wouldn't let anything happen to her. How's your bunker?"

"I don't know. Haven't been there."

"It's fine," said Ida. "We just need some fuel and we're set."

"Mordechai," said Anna. "If I don't see…"

"Don't," said Mordechai, placing his hand on her mouth. It smelled like gunpowder and soap. "It's going to be a long battle. We'll probably even have some time for some of your study sessions. A little discussion on liberty may do us all some good."

They embraced and Ida led Anna out the door and back into the street.

Anna's bunker was just three blocks south of headquarters and had two tunnels in close range leading out of the ghetto. The plan was that if one of the tunnels was blocked, they would use the second, even though it was thought to have been less stable. Inside, each fighter received a pack with undergarments, food and bandages. When Anna entered the bunker, Emil was sitting on a bench on the far side of the room looking at his pack.

"When I looked at these bandages," he said, "it hit me that we're going to war."

"Worried?" asked Anna.

Emil smiled.

"Me too. Let's just stick together. Did you get the fuel?"

"Yes. I think we have enough bombs to raze the ghetto ourselves."

"Good. We'll need every last one of them. Has anyone checked the weapons?"

"I don't know? Ask Ida, She was here before. I've been running around smelling like a torch."

Ida had gone over to the area designated as the kitchen. She was preparing something to eat and telling a few of the others what she had seen outside the walls. She also asked them if they had all packed their belongings and were ready for the long haul. There was an air of excitement, but everyone was overtly tense. One of the girls, who looked to be about sixteen years old, was biting her nails as she tried to read a book. But she could not concentrate on the book, looking up every few seconds at the people running in and out of their new underground home.

"Ida," said Anna, "is everything out of our house."

"I don't know, I wasn't the last to leave. Isn't Tuvia sticking around there? What about Miriam? What were her plans?"

"No, I think they're gone. Miriam should be here soon and Tuvia is with Peretz."

"I'm going back to the house a bit later. Anything I should bring?"

Anna thought for a minute. She had not thought about a long stay in the bunker, but she was becoming aware of the reality that would keep her from home for quite a while. She had little in the house that she needed – perhaps a change of clothes and a few books. But most of what she would have wanted had left the ghetto long ago. She had transferred a suitcase to the bunker with most of the food from the apartment several days earlier. There was a scare when a German division was spotted by the scouts closing in on the ghetto. It turned out to be a false alarm, but the fighters took it to be a sign that they need to quicken their preparation and most of them send bags to the bunkers.

"I left a small bag in my room next to my bed. Could you please bring that?"

"Sure," said Ida.

There was little in the bag that Anna really needed, except one trinket that had more sentimental value than anything else she had ever owned. It was a gift from her grandmother, almost fifteen years prior, when Anna was just a child. Her grandmother from her mother's side was ill with a degenerative disease and Anna spent countless hours watching her wither away in her fluffy bed. It was difficult for the adults around her to see the removal of life from a once vibrant woman who had always controlled every room she walked into. But for Anna, it was like a game. She would test her grandmother to see what she remembered, what she could still pronounce, and what stories she would retell that day as if it was the first time Anna would hear them. There was something lucky in the way her mind and body deteriorated in unison, like a horse running away, the sound of the hoofs and the sight of the rider fading together. While she was bedridden, she would tell the same stories over and over, and for Anna, this was wondrous because her voice was as excited the tenth time as it was the first. Her hands would make the exact same gestures each occasion, and Anna would mock her, knowing exactly what was coming. By the end of the second month of her illness, Anna had memorized the first thirty years of her grandmother's life.

Helena Abramsson was born in the thriving business town of Vitebsk, where her father was a pious rabbi and her mother, other than being the rabbi's wife, was a seamstress. It was said that Helena was a descendant of the first Jews to come to Vitebsk. Her ancestors had acquired great wealth through a Swedish Count, who secretly was a Jew and donated magnificent amounts of money to Jewish causes after being taught Torah from the father of the first Jewish family to move to Vitebsk. The names Nachum and Tevel, the father and son who helped the Count learn his roots, were well known in Vitebsk, and Helena was very proud of her bloodline, although she would see little of Vitebsk as an adult.

As life would have it, Helena was matched with another rabbi's son, who was on his way to Minsk to study. As Vitebsk was one of the largest business centers of the Jews during the 1800s, Minsk was a center of learning. So reluctantly and under very specific conditions, Helena agreed to leave her beloved town and move under Russian rule. She was only thirteen years old – old enough for her parents to release her into a young man's custody, but far too young to leave the nest.

Her first two years in Minsk were the worst of her life. She would cry herself to sleep nightly, and when her husband came to fulfill the commandment "Be fruitful and multiply," Helena held back the tears so as to not insult the young man. The conditions that Helena had set, not that she really had any choice in the matter, as her father would most likely have sent her away regardless, were that she be the one to name her first child and that she be allowed to return to Vibebsk to visit her parents after her first son was born. Not seeing anything unreasonable with those requests, both her father and her husband agreed to the terms, and Helena was forevermore Helena Sebezsh.

However, Helena could not bear children as quickly as her husband had hoped, as she was a late bloomer, only receiving her first period well after age fifteen. After two years, her husband became impatient. He had been consulting the rabbis for months when finally they called upon Helena to concede that she was not capable of bearing children because she willed it so. Helena was appalled at the accusation, stating her agreement to be able to return to see her parents following the birth and that there was nothing she willed more than to bring children into this world. Deep down she began to question the rabbinical council's state of mind, understanding full well that there was no way to will a conception. Her husband, ready to request a divorce and believing the rabbis' claim that Helena had full control over her uterus, gave Helena an ultimatum. Helena now did not know what to wish for. She was well aware that whether or not she had a child, she would be able to return to her parents; either she would be visiting, or moving back. The thought of remaining barren was comforting, as it would release Helena from an obligation forced upon her by her parents, who had rejected her by sending her so far away, and by her husband, who seemed to care more about the next generation than this one.

Several months and many, many horrible nights of attempting to conceive later, Helena became pregnant. She was going to be able to provide her husband with a child. These were the only months of her marriage that were happy. Her husband treated her with respect and they spent hours upon hours discussing the scholarly achievement their son would attain. Why it did not occur to either of them that this child may turn out, by a stroke of ill-luck, as far as her husband was concerned, to be female, was beyond comprehension.

When Helena gave birth, her husband was not in town. It was a difficult labor and she almost lost her life in the process. If not for the skills of two of the city's favored midwives, she would not have survived at all. When her husband came home to find his wife holding a baby, he dropped to his knees and cried. He whimpered a few prayers and thanked his god for the fortune bestowed upon him. For what seemed like an eternity to Helena, he kneeled on the floor crying and praying, never looking at either Helena or the child. Finally, he stood, eyes shut as if looking at the baby would blind him. Moments later she told him the news. "It is a girl," she said and his tears of joy turned to rage in an instant.

Had he been a violent man, who knows what he could have done to them. But instead, his actions were far more painful to Helena than any physical torture he could have instilled. His face became beet red, all expression vanished, he turned around, walked out the door and never returned.

Anna's mother was brought up as an only child and her grandfather's actions were the reason Anna had no aunts or uncles on her mother's side. Helena was never able to remarry since she was not given her Get, the Jewish divorce that only the husband can provide; and she did not return to Vitebsk since she had neither the funds for the travel nor the support of her family. They blamed her for everything, even attempting to cite biblical precedent for having a daughter in spite, although Helena never heard nor found the passages backing the claim. She was a sixteen-year-old mother of a girl in a town where studying Torah, allowed for boys only, was the only means of advancement – that and marrying a scholar.

Helena wanted to provide her daughter every opportunity possible but knew that the restrictions of the conservative community in Minsk would only keep her child from growing into the strong woman she wished her to become. She was lucky to be taken in by the family of one of the midwives, as they had no children of their own and were happy to care for Helena and her daughter. It was here that Helena learned what loving family support really meant. The midwife and her husband treated Helena and her daughter like they were princesses.

When she turned eighteen – after two years in the home of the pious family that took her and her baby daughter in despite the sign of Kane on her forehead – she was offered a job as a nanny in Warsaw. A wealthy, young Jewish businessman from the big city was passing through Minsk and had been invited to stay for the Sabbath at the home where Helena had been living. He was a pleasant man, who looked more Slavic than Jewish, both in his features and his mannerisms. He had decided that Yeshiva study was not for him and he preferred to travel in order to promote his business ventures. He was well versed in world affairs and well mannered in trivial conversation. Helena enjoyed his company so much that she almost never left his side for the entire weekend, except to tend to her baby. As he watched her care for the child, he realized that she would be the perfect person to look after his own children, as their mother was unable to care for them alone, being stricken with Polio after her last birth. He offered to take her to Warsaw, provide a small cottage next to their estate and in return she would tend to the children, adding her own daughter to the four already in the house.

Helena knew that this was an opportunity to break free of the chains her husband had placed upon her in Minsk. Unable to marry, she did not see any other prospects in her future. Even so, to leave the family that had given her so much felt like a betrayal. But the midwife, who had grown to love Helena as a daughter, was very clear in her words, "There is no better way than the one that fate provides. We did not invite Yitzhak for Shabbat to hear about the ills of the Tsar. We brought him here for you. It is time for you to move on." Helena knew that she was speaking out of love and not just trying to get rid of her. So after a short deliberation with the wonderful family that had cared for her, she accepted the offer, parting ways with them and with Minsk.

As she was packing her belongings, the midwife came into her room and closed the door.

"These were given to me by my grandmother, who received them from hers." She was holding a small velvet bag in her hand and from inside she removed two silver chains. Each chain had a gold ring attached. The band was blank, with no inscription and no markings.

"These rings were made for a wedding that never took place. My great, great grandmother was to marry when as the ceremony was to begin, she looked her future husband in the eyes and asked, 'Will I be gold to you?' He turned to her and said, 'You will be my wife.' With that, she replied, 'I will be gold or I will be nothing.' She grabbed the rings and ran. She ran for two weeks until she found refuge, starving and cold, in a neighboring village. There she fell in love and married my great, great grandfather. She did not use the rings for her wedding, for they symbolized to her a freedom she could not find in marriage. She decided that she would pass the rings down from daughter to daughter. For generations, mothers and their daughters would each wear the rings, symbolizing the connection prominent in Judaism, where the bloodline runs through the women and not the men. Ever since, when a daughter of the family leaves the house, they receive the rings, to bestow upon their daughters.

"I have no children of my own. You are my daughter and you will carry on this wonderful tradition."

As the tears trickled down Helena's face, she took the rings and embraced the woman who had saved her life more than once.

She was happy to be returning to Poland, as the Russian rulers had been most ruthless to the Jews. Pogroms were rampant, although Helena herself was never directly affected by them. She knew that it was just a matter of time. However, Warsaw was not the warm place she had hoped to find, and even with her association with the wealthy family who cared for her every need, she was lonely, unsatisfied and consistently sexually threatened by Yitzhak, whose charm and allure had worn off rather quickly. For six long years, Helena brought up five children and one disabled woman. She cooked, cleaned, taught the girls to read while the boys went to school and fended off advances by the strapping businessman, who had had ulterior motives for bringing Helena into his home. Only once did he actually succeed in getting close enough to her to kiss her and that was when he came into her room while she slept. She smashed a small lamp over his head, causing minor cuts to the both of them, but he never tried that again. Nonetheless, neither did he cease to touch her as she passed him and made numerous remarks about how he would have enjoyed spending the nights together.

Helena was twenty-four years old when Yitzhak suddenly died of Influenza. He had contracted the disease on his travels and neglected to get care for it. He died and left his wife and children more property and wealth than they would ever need; and Helena became the de facto head of the household.

It was not until her daughter, Anna's mother, was married at the age of twenty-two, much later than tradition would have it, that Helena left the estate to move in with her new family.

Since Helena's daughter never actually left her care, Helena never had the opportunity to pass on the rings. So as she lay dying, knowing she would not have another opportunity, she gave Anna the rings and told of her tales. In retrospect, Anna realized that her grandmother had been much more coherent than she had seemed. Perhaps she was even faking the mental deterioration and her repetition was just a way of making sure that this verbal lesson be successfully transferred to the next generation.

Anna would not have trusted anyone but Ida with the task of retrieving the bag from their apartment. She knew that it would arrive safely, regardless of the dangers Ida would face on the way. Ida was funny that way. She always carried out instructions and requests like a Musketeer would to protect his king and queen. And when those instructions came from Anna, they were from a queen.

Sure enough, Ida returned a few hours later with the small bag containing several books, some old letters and a small velvet receptacle containing the only true object of value left in the ghetto for Anna.

Twenty

"Where's my purse?" Anna yelled suddenly. "My purse! My purse is gone!"

The entire front of the bus jumped from their seats and began looking for the purse. It was as if someone had just said there was a bomb on board and the first one to find it gets a prize. Everyone was up and about in the thin aisle looking up and down, under seats, in the overhead rack, while Anna, still seated in the stairwell, held her cheeks and turned her head back and forth.

"Is that it?" asked the man in the third row.

"No, that's mine," said the lady in row two.

"Oh," said Anna, "here it is. I guess I placed it in the grocery bag by mistake." The passengers let out a collective sigh and sat down. "Why are you laughing?"

"Because," said Rami, "that was hysterical."

"Of course I was hysterical. It was my purse."

"I didn't say you were hysterical. I said the scene was hysterical."

"So tragedy is funny to you, is it? I hope you never face tragedy in your small world."

"My small world? What are you talking about? What's this about anyway?"

"I'm sorry, but you were acting a bit cheeky there, don't you think? I was worried I had lost something of value to me and, well…you wouldn't really understand these things. You know, I have lost the most valuable parts of my life and I would like you to respect that."

"I sincerely apologize," said Rami. "You are right. I had no right to laugh."

"Well that's okay," said Anna, "you're still young and have much to learn about life."

"Can I ask you something – from one fighter to another?"

"You're trying to flatter me now, aren't you?"

"I…I just was wondering…and tell me if this question is out of place…but I was wondering if you ever killed a Nazi."

Anna looked straight into Rami's eyes and Rami could not help but look away. She seemed angry, there was a stillness to her, but her eyes squinted and her brows coupled inward. For a long moment, she maintained her stare as if locking onto Rami's face before firing a deadly shot. Rami looked scared awaiting the answer to her question. It seemed he was not the only one awaiting the answer and was definitely not the only one to look

183

frightened. Finally, she spoke.

"I did," she said. "I killed more than one. And this may be hard for you to understand, but I am ashamed of each life I took."

"Yes," said Rami, "that is very hard to understand. I have killed Syrians and probably Iraqis who joined them, but I never felt remorse. They were coming to kill me. I had to shoot first."

"Yes, that is true in my case as well; but after every young German man fell to the ground, I felt like I had taken something from another mother. That, I'm afraid, is something that only a mother can understand."

"No," said Rami. "I can understand. I just can't empathize."

"Well, that's important too. I did not feel vengeance when I shot the invading Germans coming to take the last of my dignity and the lives of my friends. I did not feel hate, nor abhorrence or anything negative against them. I just felt their mother's pain. The feeling did not come right away. Too much adrenaline, I suppose. No, the feelings my action generated came much later, sometimes at night in my dreams and sometimes only after months or years of thinking about those dreadful moments. Knowing that I would die had I not pulled the trigger was no consolation. They were human beings, German human beings, I a Jew, but what we both had in common was humanity, even if they were assisting in the crimes against it.

"You must try to feel for the people you kill, no matter how evil, or dangerous, or spiteful they may be. You do not have to like them, or befriend them, or even trust them, but you must feel for their mother's loss."

As the bus traveled on, Anna sat in silence, occasionally looking up at Rami, almost as if to see if he had recovered from her words. She placed her arms behind her to jack herself up. The bus bumped as it rolled over the rough pavement. Anna had become accustomed to the small shocks that rattled her soft bones. One of the passengers in the back had peeled an orange and the smell drifted up through the vents and to the front of the bus. Anna took a deep breath as if it was a scent she had longed to smell for ages. It was more than just the strong citrus qualities that tingled her nostrils, there was a feeling that came with it.

Anna looked up at the driver. He was nervously rolling his hands over the large steering wheel. His deep breaths indicated to Anna that he was in distress.

"What is it?" asked Anna.

"If I died," said the driver, "there would be no mother's loss."

Twenty-One

19 April 1943

"Run, now! Tell Mordechai!" The lookout gave his friend a slap on the back to send him on his way and went back to peering through his binoculars at the Germans as they unloaded their trucks. Running down off the balcony that overlooked the central ghetto square which was filling up with German soldiers quickly, the young man took the flight of stairs like it was a ramp and sprang out the door into the street, making a sharp left as he hit the pavement. The sun had yet to rise that day and there was almost no reason for it to do so, as it would surely become a very black day. All the boy could hear was the clicking of his shoes on the street and his own breath, cool in his lungs and noisier than he felt it should be.

He ran just a few short blocks to headquarters and entered the blockaded courtyard, yelling the password as he moved the wood panels keeping intruders out. From the street, the building looked deserted but that could not have been farther from the truth. No one had slept that night and the underground leadership was preparing for the invasion like any army in any country would. The boy entered the offices of Mordechai and his men and told them that the Germans had entered the ghetto and had gone straight to the central square.

"We heard the trucks," said one of the young fighters.

"What are they doing?" asked another.

"They've unloaded tables and benches and set up telephones. It looks like that will be their new registration point."

"What kind of hardware do they have?" asked a red-haired man.

"So far, there were groups of soldiers and motorcyclists and they brought in at least two machineguns. There were some light tanks and what looked like an ambulance."

"They're here to fight," said the redhead.

"They're mostly infantry with some Ukrainians," added the boy. "There may be more outside of the gate. We couldn't see, the ambulances were blocking our view."

"Don't worry. They're still underestimating us," said the first to speak.

The boy was told to return to his post and let them know if there are any significant changes. Within minutes of the boy's departure, word went out through a spectacular chain of contacts to all of the other bunkers that the Germans have entered the ghetto armed and ready for an attack but are well undermanned.

Anna had left headquarters and joined up with two other fighting forces to await the arrival of the Germans. They would be the first to greet them, hidden out on the tops of lower buildings near the entrance to the ghetto. As the first light began to remove the night's blanket, Anna could see a line of soldiers merrily marching into the ghetto. They were walking in unison, rather disciplined in their steps and some were talking among themselves as if they were taking a morning stroll in their hometowns. They were decked out in their shiny boots and perfectly ironed uniforms. Anna thought, who had time to iron a uniform during war?

"They look so young," said Ida who was watching their progress through a pair of German binoculars that Peretz had stolen.

"They are," said Anna. "We're even too old to court them."

"We're too Jewish as well."

"Zacharia is giving the signal."

The girls were two of over twenty fighters who were to be the first to take on this set of unsuspecting Nazis. Command had rated this particular mission low-risk, as they knew that it would come as such a surprise to the Germans that they would more likely run than fight.

"So comrades, come rally," one of the boys standing next to Anna began singing, "And the last fight let us face. The Internationale unites the human race."

"The last fight?" said Anna. "This will not be the last fight. I can guarantee you that."

Just then there was a whistle followed by two explosions. That was the signal to begin bombarding the Germans who had reached Anna's station. They quickly hurled several hand grenades and Molotov Cocktails onto the heads of the German boys, who were so taken aback that not even a single one of them could find his weapon in those first moments. Anna quickly realized that many of these soldiers had most likely just been recruited, as the Germans must have thought that no special training would be needed to evacuate a few unruly Jews.

The same soldiers who had happily pranced into the ghetto were now torn pieces of flesh, blown apart by Jewish bombs and guns. The soldiers unlucky enough to be at the front of the column were hit the worst. They had frozen in their tracks, as they were met with the firepower they could not have imagined was in the hands of the Jews of the ghetto. The soldiers in the back began to fight when the Jewish fighters left their hiding places and attacked with their full force. Slowly, the street began to fill with German blood as one by one the snipers' grenades and pistols took them out.

Anna, after launching her arsenal off the balcony, ran down with her comrades to the street to finish the job. As she exited the building to join the

186

fighting, she realized that somehow, there were more Jewish fighters than Germans. It was a different feeling than her first battle. Most of the Germans were injured or fleeing and the few that stuck around to take on the Jews were outnumbered two to one. A Nazi arm lay in Anna's path as she ran out of the courtyard and into battle. She kicked it accidentally and almost fired a shot at it, thinking it had a live body attached. In front of her was a chaotic scene of bodies dead or dying; Germans trying to escape or take cover in the nearby shops; and Jewish fighters shooting, yelling and running toward the retreating soldiers.

As it looked like the battle would be over almost as soon as it began, additional fire came from the back half of the German column. The Jews ran from the middle of the street and took cover while other fighters rained grenades and homemade bombs on the Germans' heads.

Anna saw Rachel on one of the balconies taking careful aim at an officer, who seemed to be one of the few standing his ground in the middle of the street. He only had a pistol and was randomly shooting in the direction of the smoke hovering over the bloody street. Her shot hit him square in the back and his body curled, both shoulders clamping toward each other backward as he fell. Rachel then turned and aimed at a second soldier who seemed to be having trouble with his weapon. He was flustered and panicked, no more than eighteen years old and had most likely never seen combat, trying to dislodge part of the mechanism that would allow him to continue to shoot. But before he could, her slug hit his face and his head jerked sideways, spraying blood and tissue in an arc around his body. Anna was not thinking about her victims this time, but about Rachel's marksmanship. She understood why she wanted to fight so dearly. She was a natural and had little trouble pulling the trigger and letting a bullet land where it was meant to. The soldier fell limp over his damaged gun.

Anna had placed herself between two buildings, well protected and able to easily view the enemy. She knew she only had a few bullets left and once those were disposed of, she would have to retreat and return to her bunker. There was half a block and scores of dead Germans between her and the line of Nazis still firing their weapons. She took careful aim when she let herself shoot, which was rare, telling herself that each bullet she used would save a Jewish life.

As time went on, the shots coming from that direction decreased, until finally, they stopped altogether. Anna's pistol had been fired only twice since she took her position at the side of the building, and she had no clue as to the accuracy of her attempts. There was a comfort in that. It had been difficult for her to see the faces of those she killed. She thought that if she had to be a fighter, she would have preferred to be a pilot, dropping bombs from high overhead, never knowing the gore caused by her actions; because here in these streets, during these first battles, she was already thinking about the funerals that would be held for these soldiers. After all, they too were warriors.

The battle on Anna's street went on for almost two hours, ending with a complete German retreat. The road was littered with soldier's bodies, some blown apart by the grenades, others dead from perfectly executed sniper fire to the chest. After the quiet returned to the ghetto streets, Anna and some of the other fighters left their havens and surveyed the carnage.

"We did this?" said one of the young girls who had been dropping homemade bombs off the rooftops.

"Never thought we were so good at killing, did you?" said Anna

"I never thought I'd be proud of it," she said.

It would be several hours later before the Germans returned with enhanced forces. By then the young fighters would be safely back in their underground bunkers, awaiting their next skirmish. During those first battles, the Jewish fighters suffered no losses, a perfect score in one of the greatest ambushes of the war, while the Germans were not only run out of the ghetto but left countless bodies behind as they fled.

There were several other attacks that day at other entrance points, with similar results. By nightfall, the Germans had left the ghetto entirely, but continued to rain bombs down on the empty streets from outside the walls. These arbitrary missiles prevented the fighters from moving freely during the hiatus, but they were still able to communicate between themselves, and they compared notes on the various confrontations.

Anna was determined to fully understand what had transpired that day. She was trying to gather much more information than she needed to know, believing that if she was well enough informed, she could assist with strategy as well as operation. However, there was not much strategy left to design, and she would soon understand that the main strategic objective was just survival.

There was a festive atmosphere that night in the bunker. Anna instructed everyone to get a few hours of sleep, as it was thought the Germans would once again be returning before dawn, and this time it would be a much more trying battle. By the way that they were bombarding the ghetto, it was clear that they had no intention of salvaging a thing, neither life nor property, and all would eventually be destroyed until the fighting ceased. However, there was far too much excitement among the young warriors and each had a story of heroics and valor to tell.

"Jewish Fighters," said Peretz when he finally returned to the bunker after taking part in the successful battle, "you have now all been baptized, as our Chritian friends would say. You will be forever eternalized as the Ghetto Fighters of Warsaw: men and women of strength and courage, who, in their first war, turned back the Nazi pigs. You should be proud, as I am honored to fight with you."

"Shut up," said Tuvia and everyone laughed.

Rachel did not return to the bunker that night, which caused Anna to speculate that she had moved into the bunker with Mordechai. She had threatened to do so long before, but Anna had insisted she stay with them. She was telling people that she needed Rachel's expertise, as a sharp-shooter and demolition expert, but her real motive was to be able to get her out of the ghetto when the inevitable end arrived. For that she needed her close by and accessible.

Late that night, when the bombing and artillery fire stopped, a boy came to their bunker and told Anna that Rachel had a message. The original plan for the following morning was to have Anna's group wait at the Brush-Maker's Gate for the German's to enter. The messenger, a sixteen-year-old freckle-faced boy with a large gash on his cheek told them that there had been a change in plans. They would have a little surprise in store for the Germans if they decided to enter at the gate. Instead of the entire group, they would only need two snipers and no one else.

Morning arrived and Anna was stunned to see she had slept until after nine, as had most of the others in the bunker. Her sleep was full and dreamless. The bunkers were supplied with mattresses on the floor, some with sheets others without. Anna and her previous roommates had all made sure to bring their bedding, as it was clear they would not be back in their apartment for a long time, if ever. Each time Anna entered the bunker, the smell of dust and closed quarters overcame her, but it only took a few minutes before the sense numbed and the odor seemed to vanish. There was hardly enough light to read, so Anna's books lay unopened those first few days, collecting more of the dust that would add to the stench. But for a bunker, it was clean. Tuvia said that had a lot to do with there being women in the room.

Two of the men from the second group volunteered to be the snipers at the gate. Anna decided on her own accord that she too would join them, thinking it couldn't hurt to have backup. The rest of the group was reassigned to a different gate, where they were instructed to open fire as soon as the Germans tried to enter.

Anna and her two comrades left the bunker a little after ten in the morning. No one had come to tell them that the Germans were on the move, so there was no reason for them to leave any earlier. In fact, the Germans did not try to reenter the ghetto that morning, as it would not be until the afternoon when they would return with their enhanced forces. Anna and her friends took positions outside of the Brush-Maker's Gate in one of the attics. Holes had been cut in the walls to allow them to view the gate. The three sat for almost five hours waiting for some movement. The only thing they had to look at during that time was Rachel, running to the street and checking something dug under the cobblestones. She would leave from one of the shops, run to the middle of the square on the ghetto side of the gate, look at what looked like a hole in the ground, and return. She did this three times in the first two hours that Anna waited.

At three in the afternoon, Anna could hear trucks and the clicks of soldiers' boots on the far side of the gate. Within a few minutes, they were approaching the entrance. There were at least 300 of them, walking in unison, guns drawn and ready. As the first group crossed the line that marked the entrance to the ghetto, a line blocked off for three years allowing only certified people to cross, Anna asked one of the snipers if he was told when to open fire.

"They said we'd know," he replied, and sure enough he was right.

As the first fifty soldiers crossed into the ghetto and reached the hole that Rachel had been examining earlier, the mine under the road went off. The blast shook the walls of the surrounding buildings, as bodies left the ground and crashed back on top of each other. The Germans behind the front line scrambled for cover, most retreating from the ghetto, screaming and running, like frightened children escaping an imagined monster. Several lay dead in the street, as the smoke lingered over them. All movement was met by additional fire from the rooftops and attics and soon the Germans were gone.

Anna could not believe what she had seen. For all her involvement in the planning of the uprising, she never realized the magnitude of the weaponry the fighters had at their disposal. Her mouth hung open as she watched the soldiers blown apart by the mine, and she knew then that those would not be the last of the Nazis to die in the ghetto. It was the second time in two days that Anna had witnessed a bloodbath rarely seen by civilians. It was also the second time the Jews would stanch the German entry into their home. She thought that being a civilian was taking on a very different meaning these days.

Within minutes of the blast, the surviving Germans had disappeared, and the dead remained silently sprawled at the entrance of the gates. Anna, still dazed by the events of the day, exited the small room overlooking the square, down the stairs and out into the street, where she saw Rachel walking back into the ghetto towards headquarters.

"Rachel!" yelled Anna, as she turned a corner and out of direct eyesight of the Brush-Makers Gate.

Rachel turned around and smiled. Her poignant eyes still had difficulty expressing the satisfaction she must have felt from a mission accomplished. Her blonde hair was tied back behind her and she was holding something that looked like a grenade.

"What's that?" asked Anna.

"A grenade," she said. "Didn't need it this time."

"You will."

"Coming back to headquarters?"

"Yes," said Anna. Anna wanted to ask her how she pulled off that amazing feat but decided that it was a trivial question that need not be asked. She knew that Rachel's demolition talents were far superior to Anna's understanding of them, so she just put her arm around her and told her that she was impressed.

"It's my calling," said Rachel. "I will do this until the day I die."

"Can you see a grandmother setting off bombs?" said Anna, still hoping to convince Rachel to leave the ghetto with her when the outcome is clear.

"Anna, we both know I will never be a grandmother."

Anna didn't want to know that, but she did. She had tried countless times to envision Rachel pushing a stroller on a farm in Eretz Yisrael, surrounded by orchards and tall grass. But it was never Rachel's face she could conjure up in her mind. There were others Anna could easily see in that position; others who could be grandmothers in Eretz Yisrael, whose happier faces were clearly visible in Anna's faint imagination. But she never saw Rachel's sad face in her mind's eye.

The fighters walked together to headquarters and reported the events at Brush-Makers Gate. There was once again excitement as Rachel described the explosion and Anna added a description of the scene from her vantage point, including the aftermath.

A few hours later, after Anna had left her post, returned to the bunker with Rachel to give the report and back to the post where she was to stanch the enemy once more, the Germans tried their luck again. This time they were extremely cautious, aware that the vertiginous Jews were hostile, dangerous and well-armed. Anna could see through her binoculars the fear in the eyes of the young German boys being sent in along the far wall of the ghetto. They remained close to the shops, knowing that at any moment they could be attacked. And sure enough, as they approached the middle of the street, the fighters in the surrounding buildings, Anna among them, opened fire.

As if the Germans had entered the ghetto just to trigger an attack, as the fire fell upon them, they ran. Some jumped into the shops on the street, others returned to the gate; however, most of the young boys who entered the ghetto that afternoon, like the many before them, simply dropped dead in the street. Those lucky enough to reach the exit would surely be sent back in at a later time. Most never meet another Jew again.

A third attempt by the Nazi forces to enter the Brush-Maker's Gate that evening was far more guarded and far more violent. The Germans debouched with armored personnel carriers and attacked with forethought. The fire raining down on the armored cars could not slow their progress and they were able to reach the far side of the square. From there, they entered the second building where the Jewish fighters were shooting from the attic. Anna watched through her binoculars as several German soldiers made it up the flight of stairs and into the attic where later she would hear that hand-to-hand combat took the lives of two of the Jewish fighters and seven Nazis. Most of the Jews in the building managed to escape before the soldiers attacked.

However, the Germans were unable, or perhaps unwilling – it remained unclear to Anna why – to reach the other buildings, including the one where Anna awaited her fate. Following the entry to the first building, the Germans ceased their attacks and the factory manager, Mr. Liss, entered the gate with several SS officers waving a white flag. They called out to negotiate a cease-fire and after allowing them to cross the line into the ghetto, the fighters responded by opening fire once again, killing the officers and wounding Mr. Liss, who hobbled off with a Jewish bullet in his leg. Anna was watching as the SS officers fell and Mr. Liss, who she had met once at the factory, ran off injured. The circumstances of their meeting escaped her at the moment. All she could recall was that he was rude to her and to everyone else around him. He felt superior, she thought, and there was nothing that any of the measly, rancid, half-dead ghetto Jews could offer him. Now, she chuckled as she watched him stagger away, then she caught herself and thought that laughing at the poor man was inappropriate – but it wasn't; Mr. Liss deserved the bullet.

The loft where Anna had set up her lookout was dark and damp with light entering from a slit in the boarded window on the street side. The room was empty, except for a few scattered boxes and the weapons and provisions Anna and her friends had brought up. There were three floors below Anna, all vacated in haste when the summer Aktions took place. Some of the apartments had canned food left behind, which was quickly brought to the bunkers in the center of the ghetto. She had now spent close to thirty hours in her little attic and was beginning to feel claustrophobic. The room was definitely smaller now than it had been when she entered it. The ceiling was lower and the air denser. With the Germans successfully entering the building down the street, Anna knew that it was just a matter of time before she too would have to escape the oncoming threat. But at least she would be freed of the fear that soon the room would be no bigger than a coffin.

By nightfall, the gate was quiet. Anna decided to return to her bunker and get a good night's sleep. Her comrades in the attic had agreed to keep watch during the night, but before she could leave, Ida showed up with a message from headquarters. There was a fear that Germans would be entering the Brush-Makers gate with enhanced forces, and there was little chance of standing ground there. The two men were to return to headquarters for instructions regarding their relocation and Anna and Ida were to remain in the attic until morning.

After the men left, Ida sat down on the dusty wood floor next to Anna. The smell of filth in the coffin-like room was mixed with a scent that neither of the girls could recognize but reminded both of lilies. Anna looked out the slit in the side of the building to see if she could make out anything that resembled plant life, but her eyes only saw shadows, grey and black, with orange streaks from the lights outside of the ghetto walls sneaking in and disrupting the unity of the gloom. Ida was looking down at her own hands as if preparing to wash them. Anna turned to look at her, but before her face could complete the circle, Ida spoke.

"We're to run at the first sight of trouble," said Ida with a smile.

"Not going to happen," said Anna, looking back out the window. "We'll walk slowly. How are things at headquarters? Is Mordechai calm as usual?"

"I haven't seen him. But Rachel is full of fire these days – literally and figuratively. She has planted more explosives than I have ever seen. It's crazy. She loves it. But I'm worried about Miriam. She's not having an easy time with this fighting business. She wants to contribute, but I can see that it's starting to get to her."

"She's a tough girl. Don't worry about her. What's with Tuvia?"

"Another basket case," said Ida. He tried to wash the floor of the bunker, but he forgot there wasn't any water in the pipes. He talked in his sleep last night. Said something about being wrong about the Russians. Don't know what that was all about."

"When I first met him – before we entered the ghetto – he told me that he thought the Russians were worse to the Jews than the Germans. I guess he's getting it now."

Ida stretched her arms above her head and yawned. "Emil didn't come back last night. He has someone. Do you know her?"

"I heard something. He doesn't talk much about it."

193

"Well, he talked to me. She's sixteen. D'vorah, I think. He's in love – and during the uprising. He said that he knows he's going to die and to die in love is proof there is no god. You've had an influence on him."

"Emil said that?"

"I've been watching him change since the winter. You know, if there is someone who deserves to survive this hell it's Emil...and you."

"I don't know who will survive, but I do know that love has a power that makes people do things." Anna glared up toward the boarded ceiling, her eyes unfocused as her stare hit nothing in particular. She was thinking about love. She had had the strongest feelings imaginable for another human being and she had stood by, almost as if out of her own body, as those feelings drifted out into the atmosphere like dust disappearing off a dirt road. That's all it is, she thought – particles of dirt floating in front of her eyes and rising through the air and into nothing. She had been so caught up in the eddies of the uprising, that her love hadn't entered her mind for months. Her mother had once told her there was no such thing as lasting love. "Love doesn't last," she had said, "it either grows or it dies – like all living things." Anna felt that her loves had been dying, just like everything else around her. It was no surprise she couldn't make out any vegetation outside – it had all died. But then she looked over at Ida and realized that there was at least one love that had grown to staggering proportions, she reached out and took Ida's hand, pulled her close to her and hugged her.

"What is it, Anna?"

"There is much here that I cannot explain."

"No one can explain death," said Ida.

"No, not the death, the life," Anna pushed Ida upright as she held her arms. "We have grown to become monsters...who love life. How can we love life so much and kill so easily."

"That's not what you wanted to say," said Ida.

Anna looked down and let out a chuckle. She'd been caught. That was not what she wanted to say. She wanted to say something so much more meaningful, so much more significant and so much more eternal that she was scared. So Ida said it for her.

"I love you, Anna. We have become monsters because we have become one entity, one organism that can no longer be separated without dying."

"We will both live, or we will both die," said Anna.

Ida took Anna's head and kissed her cheek. The lone tear, all that Anna would allow herself to shed, slid onto Ida's upper lip and around her mouth. Anna placed her left arm around Ida and squeezed.

Then the wall exploded.

Twenty-Two

Anna looked up at the driver and then back down again. If you died, she thought, there would be no mother's loss? "No mother's loss," she said aloud. She looked up at the driver once again. For the first time since she was a small child, Anna was speechless. There had been many times when she did not speak, but it was always out of choice. Anna's mother had often asked her politely to pipe-down. She talked about everything at every moment, mostly asking questions until her inquiries irked her conversation partner into total despair.

When she was six, her aunt took her to a play. It was a Polish adaptation of Shakespeare's Much Ado About Nothing. Anna was intrigued but understood much of nothing. Even the Polish had been translated to sound old, and Anna never stopped asking questions. "What did she say? Who's that man? Why is she crying? Was there a wedding? Did someone die?" And on and on she went, gathering sneers and hushes from the people sitting around them. After the play, Anna would continue to ask questions and make comments on the story that she didn't understand, on the costumes she didn't like and on the seat that was too low for her to see comfortably over the woman sitting in front of her with the high hairdo. Anna's aunt would never take her to a play again.

That wasn't the only kind of talking she did; she was a grand orator as well, lecturing at every opportunity. At age thirteen, when she had begun reading the literature her movement counselors recommended (they already recognized her potential), she would spit back what she read at her poor parents. They never knew how to respond. After all, it was Socialist rhetoric of the worst kind – regurgitated by a teenager who doesn't fully understand the concepts, but thinks she does. The truth was, however, that Anna did understand – far better than anyone gave her credit. She at least understood far better than her parents. However, most viewed her urge to carry on as nothing less than endearing.

This time, on the bus sitting below the driver with no mother, Anna wanted to say something, but no words came to her. Anna knew that there were many more orphans than women like her – who had lost their children. Maybe it was better for a child not to worry about his mother's loss. Maybe that was the best way to be a fighter. But it occurred to Anna that most children don't think about that. They don't want to live just to prevent their mother's from mourning; they just want to live.

Yaakov, perhaps sensing Anna's dismay, turned to her and said, "You lost your son. I lost my mother. We're a match."

"Do you think about your mother?" she asked.

"I do, all the time, even though I can hardly remember her. All I recall is that she was very quiet and very sad. It's not actually an image that I have of her, but a feeling – a sad feeling. I don't have much of a memory of her. But I guess I miss her…I mean not knowing her at all."

"I hardly knew my sons too."

"Did they both die in the camps?"

"No, actually neither did. My first son died at home, of illness. And my second was smuggled out of the ghetto. I had hoped he would survive, and for a long time, I knew nothing of his fate. But later, I got word of his passing. He was just a baby when I let him go. How could I have thought differently?"

Again no one spoke and the hum of the bus engine and the bumps and cracks of the chassis were all that could be heard. It was Anna who eventually spoke again.

Twenty-Three

20 April 1943

As part of the wall protecting Anna and Ida from a fall to the pavement blew up into them, Anna felt a stab in her upper arm. The arm had been on Ida's shoulder and around her back, and had it not been there, the shrapnel that pierced her left triceps muscle would have hit Ida in the neck. As it was, the rest of the wall, along with a few other shards released from the small missile that destroyed their tiny room, mostly fell on Ida, but apart from the one small piece of sharp metal, there was nothing that penetrated either of them.

Still hugging, the girls had fallen into the room and onto their sides; they were covered with debris from the destroyed outer face of the building. The missile had hit the floor beam at the lower edge of the wall looking out toward the courtyard and had taken out a good chunk of the wall up to around belt level. Had it hit a few centimeters higher, they would both have been killed. And had Anna not hugged Ida at that very instant, Ida's jugular vein would have been perforated by the projectile that cut deep into Anna's arm. The girls remained embraced and waited for the next blast. Anna was thinking that she had been wrong about her future. She was to die here and now, if she hadn't already, and they would never share an incarnadine sunset on the shores of the Mediterranean Sea as she had dreamed. For a split second, that eternal fraction of an instant when she thought they were dead, Anna was happy. She was happy because she was holding Ida and if they were to die in the ghetto, they were dying together. She waited for the next bomb to enter their now exposed hideout and finish them off.

"Anna!" yelled Ida. "Oh no. Anna!" Anna was not moving and it took Ida very little time to notice the blood dripping onto the floor. With a hole the size of the two of them at the bottom of the wall, light from beyond the boundaries of the ghetto flowed into the room. Since Ida seemed to be intact, it must have been Anna who was hit and Anna wasn't moving.

But Anna was just waiting to die. For the first time since the beginning of the war – the first time in her life – she was waiting to die. She would later wonder why she had given up on life during that moment, as it was a new feeling for her. After all she had gone through, all she had lost, why give up now? It would haunt her for a long time until one day she would remember that for the first few minutes after the blast, she couldn't hear anything.

"Anna! Get up, Anna. Oh, Anna!"

Ida was shaking Anna who was lying next to her, both covered with dust and wall parts.

"Are you okay?" asked Anna finally.

"You're bleeding!"

Anna could hardly hear Ida but felt her shaking. "My arm. My arm hurts."

Anna's arm was still draped over Ida and since Anna's elbow was higher than her shoulder, the blood had made its way around her upper arm to her biceps and was dripping to the ground. Ida removed Anna's arm from around her, turned toward the light shining nicely from the destroyed wall and looked at it. A perfect red circle, like a poker puncture, was oozing drops of crimson from Anna's arm. Ida looked at it and looked at Anna. "It could be worse," she said.

"There's something in there," said Anna. "I can feel it. It's burning."

Ida took the corner of her shirt and dabbed the wound; Anna cringed. Through the blood pooling in the tiny hole, Ida could see a reflective object embedded in her arm and flush with the skin. It was impossible to know how deep it went.

"I can get it out," said Ida. "But it will hurt."

Anna's hearing was coming back and with it her will to be whole again. The moment of passivity and resignation was over. "It hurts now," said Anna. "Get it out. Get it out!"

Ida reached into a pocket in her coat and pulled out a piece of wood the size of a kitchen knife. The wood had engravings on it. They formed a landscape of a lake and mountains on one side and snake on the other.

"What's that?" asked the gasping Anna.

"It's my good luck charm. I carved it a few months ago and have had it ever since. I always knew it would come in handy someday." Anna wondered how she had never seen it. She also wondered what Ida planned to do with it.

"Bite on it," said Ida. She shoved the piece of wood into Anna's mouth. They were sitting up now, Anna holding Ida's leg with her free hand, while the other wounded-arm hand lay limp against Ida's stomach. Ida reached down to her belt and pulled out a letter opener. Anna looked at the long piece of metal and knew that this tool, created for opening pieces of mail from loved ones, was being used as a weapon. It was Ida's knife and it had already been christened with German blood. Now Ida was going to use it to remove a stubborn piece of German shrapnel that was burning a hole in Anna's left arm.

"Hold still," she said to Anna.

Anna bit down hard on the wood. She could feel her teeth forever marking the piece of art with her dental imprint. She also squeezed Ida's leg with her free hand.

Ida dabbed the wound again with her shirt; then she took the silver letter-opener-turned-knife-turned-scalpel and solicitously centered it in the wound. She said something about the light being good to Anna, but Anna could not hear a thing. As the point of the letter opener pressed against the small circular piece of metal, Anna screamed into the wood. Ida used the opener to pry the shard high enough to grab it with her dirty fingernails. As she pried, more blood filled the hole and Anna screamed more. She slowly dug out the metal until the top of it was a centimeter above the skin line. It was still unclear how deep it went, but Ida now put down the opener and took her index finger and thumb, pinched the silver piece of metal, and without hesitation, yanked it out.

Anna shrieked again into the now damp wood and cried, breathing shallowly as she wept.

"It's out," said Ida. "It's beautiful."

Ida was holding the metal that had been stuck inside Anna and turned it in the light. It was the size of half her pinky and was shaped like the cylinder at the end of a fountain pen – but pointed on both ends. Once Anna would clean it, she would turn it into a necklace and give it to Ida as a memento of when they saved each other's lives. Anna was sure that had Ida not been able to remove the fountain pen with her letter opener, the ensuing infection would have killed her. Ida knew that had Anna's arm not been there, she would have had her throat cut by the beautiful piece of German shrapnel and no letter opener would have been able to save her.

It wasn't that the two needed an additional experience to seal their bond, it was just the type of tutelary experience that had been missing.

When Anna finally removed the wood from her mouth, it had stuck to her teeth. Her bite was so strong that the landscape no longer looked serene and the snake had been cut it half by her teeth marks. A dentist would have surely concluded that Anna had a beautiful bite.

Ida tore a small piece of cloth from her already blood-stained shirt and tied the wound closed. As soon as the exquisite piece of shrapnel had been removed, the bleeding stopped. Anna really had felt burning deep in her arm; the hot shrapnel had singed the blood vessels and stopped the bleeding. It would also serve the purpose of sterilizing the wound and preventing the very infection that Anna requested to avoid by removing it. All in all, it was a successful operation.

It took the two young women, one wounded and one now with surgical experience, several more minutes to realize that they should leave the building. Although no other missiles were fired at them that night – or at any other building for that matter – they had no way of knowing what the Germans had in store. And Anna was in no shape to stand guard.

With Anna's arm dangling at her side and Ida's arm now draped around Anna, the two fighters slowly walked back toward headquarters. They knew that someone else would have to stand guard at the Brush-Makers Gate tonight. They wondered if anyone else was in the vicinity and if they knew about the lone attack on their post. As they walked through the vacant streets from post to headquarters, Anna thought about the end and shared her thoughts with Ida.

"It's going to be over soon," she said in a whisper.

"What's going to be over?" asked Ida just as quietly.

"The ghetto, our place in the ghetto, the war for us, perhaps our lives. It's all going to be over, and as dreadful as it has been, there was always a sense of purpose here. Will our future hold purpose, Ida?"

But Ida did not get a chance to answer. For Anna, it had been a rhetorical question – one that she knew could only be answered in the positive. That was how Anna was. There was no life without purpose. Perhaps the purpose would not be as noteworthy as preventing the Nazis from carrying out their extermination plans, but there would be purpose. She knew that, and she did want to hear what Ida thought on the matter, but that was not to be.

"Halt!" yelled a voice from the darkness around the corner of the building in front of them. Anna giggled. Had the light been better, Anna would have seen the appalling look that Ida gave her; it was an inappropriate response to the circumstances. A German may have been about to shoot them and Anna was giggling.

"Halt," said the voice again.

"Go back to bed, Jurek," said Anna.

A dark figure appeared from behind the corner of the building and the girls could see the silhouette of a boy half their size.

"How did you know it was me?"

"You have to work on that deep voice of yours. What are you doing here anyway?" asked Anna, still amused by the child's attempt to sound adult. Jurek was fifteen years old, but his voice seemed to remain young. In fact, his whole body stayed small – most likely due to malnutrition. He just stopped growing the day he entered the ghetto. He wore a gray coat several sizes too big and a beret that fit him surprisingly well.

"I was asked to stand guard here. How did I do?"

"Very well," said Ida. "I was convinced – even a bit scared."

"Anna wasn't convinced," he said disappointed.

"Has there been any activity around here?" asked Anna, ignoring the comment and attempting to restore his self-esteem by asking him a professional question.

"What happened to you?" asked the boy, now ignoring her question.

"She got hit by a mortar attack that destroyed our post," said Ida. Anna nodded.

"Does it hurt?"

"A little. I'll be fine in the morning."

"I'm afraid of being shot," he said, confiding in the two women.

Anna knew Jurek from headquarters. His parents passed away in the harsh conditions of winter early in 1942. When the food they had saved for their children ran out, Jurek took his younger eight-year-old brother to beg on the streets. He found his way to Mila Street and sat on the sidewalk a few buildings from headquarters. Everyone knew him because he would always wish people happy holidays, regardless of the time of year. During the summer of 1942, his brother died right there on the street. Jurek had fallen asleep and his brother passed away with his head on Jurek's lap.

He stopped wishing people happy holidays after that – even during the holidays.

One of the fighters, who stopped to ask him why he no longer greeted everyone, decided to bring him to headquarters. He was excited about helping the Jewish resistance, but when the guns were given out, he refused to take one. He said he could do better as a runner, but everyone understood that he was just too frightened to hold a firearm. Jurek became the headquarters' messenger. He was fast, smart and careful, but refused to be armed.

So when Anna noticed the pistol in his hand, she wondered what was going on. She nodded in the direction of his waist.

"I was almost caught the other day. I guess I missed the turn and ended up next to a Nazi patrol off the east side. They shot at me, but I ran and got away. When I returned to headquarters, I asked for a gun. But I don't know how to use it."

"And they asked you to guard this street?"

"Well, not really. I decided to do it myself. I'm not guarding against Nazis. They don't come here anymore."

"So what are you guarding against?"

"I can't tell you, but you're lucky I didn't shoot you."

"It wasn't luck," said Ida. "You don't know how to use that thing, remember."

"But I would use it if I had to," he said.

"I'm sure you would," said Ida. "Would you walk us back to headquarters?"

"Sure," he said, slipping his gun back into his belt. Anna patted Jurek's shoulder with her good arm. She assumed that he was just testing himself with the new gun and guarding against something top secret was the best way to do it. He was happy to find them and talked the whole way back about the events of the day from his perspective.

As they reached headquarters, Ida said to him, "I'll have to teach you how to use that thing, okay?"

He hugged her and wished her a happy holiday. It was, after all, Passover.

Ida and Anna entered the building that was still bustling with activity. They worked their way into one of the back rooms and called in Lejb. He was their doctor. Actually, he had only finished two years of medical school when the war broke out, but he seemed to know enough to be able to help with most of the first aid issues that were common among the fighters. Lejb removed the makeshift bandage and looked at Anna's wound.

The room was brighter than it had been during Ida's surgery, and they all could see that the round hole was now black – a good color for a hole in the arm. The light was available due to one of the most daring operations of the early uprising. The Germans had cut off water, electricity and gas to the entire ghetto, so the fighters, as with everything else they needed, had to smuggle in power. An electric line was stolen from one of the abandoned factories and connected to the building on Mila 18. The fighters then used the sewers to bring the line to the edge of the ghetto and steal electricity from the very lights that were shining on the walls of their cage. The Germans never knew that the line existed at all, and the fighters were even able to see their wounds at night.

Lejb was very impressed by Ida's work and immediately asked her if she wanted to assist him in other medical operations in the future. She kindly refused, stating that had it been anyone else, she would not have succeeded.

"Definitely punctured the triceps brachii. Hum? I wonder," he said, "if it reached the long head. It's quite deep. The lateral head is cut, that's for sure." Lejb enjoyed muscles. Many felt it may have been the only thing he learned in medical school.

Lejb's final assessment was that the wound would heal well, but she'd have a recognizable scar for the rest of her life.

"Good," said Anna. "I need something to remember this place by."

Anna and Ida slept at headquarters that night, not returning to the bunker until the following morning. In addition to Anna's medical checkup and Ida's evaluation as a surgeon, they had been witness to one of the greatest successes of the first three days of battle: the capture of two German machine guns and several other weapons. The leadership of the revolt thought that this would effectively prolong their resistance for at least an additional week.

However, they had underestimated the Nazi cruelty. On the third day of the uprising, Anna, Ida and Miriam were awaiting instructions in the bunker when Jurek arrived panting and out of breath.

"They're…they're burning everything!"

"What are you talking about, Jurek?" said Miriam, standing up and instinctively dressing in ammunition.

"The Brush Makers Gate and everything around it is burning. They started firebombing the outside and are working their way around the block. It's all on fire. We have people trapped there. They can't get back to the center. They're all just burning."

The Germans had decided that instead of facing the Jewish thugs with their extensive firepower, they would avoid all contact and simply burn them out. Along with the flames came gas pellets and mortar shells, but the flames were enough to push the fighters out of the exterior regions where they had made such courageous stands.

"What do we do?" asked Ida, looking straight at Anna. "Rachel's there. Should we go?"

"Rachel's not there," she said quietly. "Emil is there."

"We have to see if they're okay!" said Miriam. "I'm going."

"No!" said Anna. "We have to leave now. It's over! We have to leave!" There was fire in Anna's eyes and with it, water. Her jaw was trembling as she spoke and her voice loud and coarse. She was having a difficult time accepting the fact that they must leave the ghetto. Her ambivalence would keep them in Warsaw for another few days and all of them, at one point or another, would come dangerously close to losing their lives during that time. Had she, at that moment, been certain about her conviction to depart that night, they would have been gone by morning. But Anna understood Miriam's sentiments more than Miriam would ever know – she too could not fathom abandoning the ghetto while the fighting continued.

"We have to find Emil!" yelled Miriam.

Anna stood up, held Miriam's shoulders and peered into her eyes. Miriam was shaking, but was doing her best to keep her composure – she had once told Anna that crying was not something she ever did in public. "We," said Anna slowly, enunciating each word to show her determination, "have done all we can. We must leave the ghetto now."

Miriam looked up at Anna. Their wet faces showed their deep despair – although, for Miriam, only her eyes were allowed to cry; the rest of her stayed composed. They all knew this moment would come. They all were aware that eventually, they would have to depart in haste. But as the moment arrived, they realized the gravity of their situation. They knew that many of the fighters would never run. They would prefer to die in burning buildings. But Anna had decided long ago that her life would continue after the uprising. She had convinced many that after they had made their stand and could no longer have an impact on the German advancements, they would retreat and set up their fight elsewhere.

"I first must go and see what is happening," said Miriam in a calmer voice. "We can leave after that."

Anna nodded in approval, and the three women followed Jurek back to Mila Street.

The walk from their bunker to headquarters was no more than a few blocks, but the streets now felt hostile again. The German aura was back and they ran instead of walked. The sky was full of smoke and they could hear the constant gunfire coming from the Brush Makers area. Unlike during many of the other German operations during the war, they could hear no screaming. The cries of victims were commonplace in the ghetto, but this time, all that could be heard was rumbling, gunshots, an occasional mortar shot and a faint crackling coming from the burning buildings. Anna was wondering what they were shooting at. And who was shooting? That gunfire may have been resistance fighters attempting to stop the firebombing.

Jurek was faster than the girls and he was off running ahead of them when a blast knocked Anna into Ida and they both found themselves facedown on the cobblestone road. The Germans were raining mortar shells into the center of the ghetto and one had hit dangerously close to them.

Anna lifted her head and looked over at Ida. She had her eyes closed and her chin on the cool rocks. Slowly, Ida too lifted her torso and picked herself up.

"We have to get out of the street!" yelled Miriam.

Anna grabbed hold of Ida's hand with her good arm and helped her to her feet. Anna's first thought was that all three of them were okay.

"Over here!" yelled Miriam again. She was standing in the doorway of what was once a bakery; of course, that was a lifetime ago, before the war and before the Nazi invaders ejected the Polish family running the place. It was never known what became of them or any of the other unfortunate Poles who happened to have lived in what became the Jewish Quarter of Warsaw. Since only Jews were occupying the ghetto streets, the bakery had become a home to far more families than would ever feel comfortable together. All of them had been deported to the camps, and much like the Poles whose family business was left behind, no one had any idea what fate met the ex-occupants of the room the girls now stood before.

It was while standing in the doorway, waiting for another bomb to detonate in front of them that Anna saw Jurek still lying on the damp road, his small body in the oversized coat looked like a pile of laundry left for the poor.

Anna did not hesitate to run toward Jurek. However, without realizing, she had yelled out his name before her legs started moving and Miriam, fearing that Anna would do exactly what she intended to do, grabbed Anna's injured triceps to hold her back.

Anna never screamed. She was just not a screamer. Even when Ida removed the smoldering shrapnel from her left arm, Anna's scream was more of a loud grunt – and the wood ornament muffled it significantly. As a child, many of her girlfriends would scream in jest, pretending to be terrified of one thing or another, but not Anna. However, when Miriam's thumb touched Anna's hole in her arm, she screamed. She screamed so loud that Ida jumped and Miriam let go of her arm. Now, instead of running out to check on Jurek, she was buckled over in pain, grabbing her arm with her good hand. Ida too had noticed Jurek, her focus on him was enhanced by Anna's shriek. Ida looked at Miriam and simply said, "Don't touch her arm." Then she ran into the street.

By the time Ida reached Jurek, Anna had straightened herself up, she and Miriam were watching Ida kneeling over the boy. Miriam was keeping her hands away from Anna, which prevented her from being in place when Anna darted out to Ida and Jurek. Miriam then followed, whispering to herself, "Damn them."

Anna and Miriam reached Jurek and saw, as Ida had, that he was dead. Ida had tried to turn him onto his back, but as she lifted his light torso, she saw that there was little left of his face and his chest had a giant hole in it, so she left him face down. The mortar shell had exploded right in front of him. He never saw it coming and never had a chance to dive away from it.

The next sound the women would hear would be another whistle and another explosion. As the whistle sounded and the missile began its descent toward the three warriors kneeling in the center of the street, unprotected and defenseless, Miriam yelled, "Get back!"

Neither Anna nor Ida understand what she meant and therefore no one but Miriam moved. Miriam had anticipated the landing spot of the missile and was trying to get them all to move toward their previous safety spot. She jumped at Ida and Anna and pushed them backward, over Jurek's dead body and onto the ground behind him. The missile landed about ten meters ahead of them and off to the side of the road near the adjacent building. The blast caused part of the building's facade to break off and splatter on the concrete sidewalk. The slight breeze in the air was what had saved their lives. The wind had taken the missile a few meters farther than it would have on a calm day, and the blast was blocked by the building's pillar. Only a few small pieces of shrapnel reached the center of the road. One entered Jurek, whose lifeless body blocked the metal shard from hitting one of the girls. (c)

All three jumped to their feet as soon as the debris from the explosion stopped falling around them and ran to the side of the road. Jurek would have to wait out the night alone in the middle of the street. Anna looked over at him and hoped her own lost boy, Yehuda, wherever he was, would be as brave as Jurek had been. She thought to herself how strange it was that she thought about Yehuda at a time like that. But for Anna, Jurek was another one of her lost boys; another death not to be bemoaned – at least not now.

Anna's gaze was still fixated on Jurek when Ida and Miriam looked at each other and said simultaneously, "Let's go."

It seemed the only safe route would be through the tunnel systems they had prepared. It would take them longer, but at least they would be out of range of the random German attacks. All three knew the systems very well. There was an entrance not far down the street, and they decided to stay close to the buildings until reaching it. Once inside, it would be a short walk to headquarters.

As they entered the tunnel, Ida turned to Anna and said, "He was a brave boy, Anna."

Anna tightened her lips, nodded her head and said, "He gave his life purpose."

Once inside the Mila Street headquarters, Anna followed Miriam to the back rooms where most of the people in the know were working. There were few people around that morning; most had left to see what information they could gather of the burning ghetto. But Peretz was there, and he was sitting with his head in his hands.

"We lost some good people," he said to the three without raising his head. "Janush, Miki, David..."

"Kreiger?" asked Ida.

"No, Bloom. He was trying to take out some of the Germans when he got hit by the flame shooter. What a way to go. I watched...couldn't do anything...he ran around on fire. Mania, Kuba, god knows who else."

"What about Emil?" asked Ida.

"Emil?" Peretz raised his head for the first time. "He was there?"

"Yes, he was on watch," said Ida. "You don't know what happened to him? Let's go ask Mordechai."

"You'll never get to Mordechai now. He's far too busy."

It seemed to Anna that Peretz was almost falling asleep as he talked. She had never seen him so glum. Even during the worst moments of the hard winter's privation, Peretz had an internal fire that kept all wondering what glorious thing he would do next. But now there was little life in him; he had given up," Anna thought.

"Your leg!" said Miriam, bending down and looking under the table he was leaning on.

"I got hit," he said casually.

When Anna leaned down to look as well, she saw that his pants were torn, and his leg looked like it had been hashed up by a mixer. She knew at that moment that the hypnagogic Peretz had not lost hope, he had lost blood.

"Get Lejb!" called Anna. "Get Lejb!"

Ida, the now experienced surgeon, leaned down to take a look as well. Miriam went to call Lejb. Anna was pulling him out from behind the desk and laying him on the floor as Ida examined his leg.

Within seconds, Lejb was in the room yelling at Peretz. "Do you think you are superhuman? Why didn't you call me? You can die from this!"

"I'm fine," said Peretz. "It doesn't even hurt anymore."

"He's in shock," said Lejb. "We need to sew this up. I'll be right back." As he began to leave the room he turned to Ida and said, "You'll be able to operate with me after all," and smiled.

"This was not what I bargained for," said Ida. "Two in one day."

Lejb returned with the few tools he had at his disposal. Everything was in a satchel that may have been used as a book bag before the war. He removed a small box and opened it in front of Ida, handing her the lid. She had already been made his assistant. She rolled her eyes. He took out a small bottle of a clear substance, a spool of thread and a needle.

"That looks like a sewing kit," said Miriam.

"You're not going to sew me, are you?" asked Peretz, still in a bit of a daze. "Just be kind."

Lejb then removed another bottle and a syringe. "You're lucky. I just got some of this stuff. You won't feel a thing."

"Where did you get that?" asked Ida.

"Some of the fighters found it in an abandoned German outpost. It was in a first aid kit. We've already used the rest of the stuff we found."

"What is it?" asked Ida. If she was going to be a surgical assistant, she may as well know what she'd be helping to administer.

"Cocaine, novocaine, who knows. But it works," he said.

Lejb tore open the rest of Peretz's pant leg and exposed the full extent of the mutilation. There was a slice along the outside of his calf, from top to bottom, but it did not look like a clean-cut, but rather as if someone had chopped at it with a fork. Lejb found an undamaged area to the side of the laceration and injected Peretz with the German local anesthesia.

"I thought you said I wouldn't feel a thing!" said Peretz. The shot seemed to have woken him up a bit.

"Do you feel this?" Lejb was poking the good side of his leg with the needle he was about to use to sew up the wound.

"Feel what?"

"Ida, I need you to hold this part of his leg. I'll begin the stitching. Make sure it stays tight and doesn't move."

Ida grabbed his leg from under the knee with one hand and pinched the cut together with the other. Lejb thread the needle and dipped it in the clear liquid antiseptic in the bottle. He then dabbed a small piece of gauze with a tiny amount of liquid and wiped clean the areas on both sides of the cut.

"It will be a miracle if this doesn't get infected," said Lejb.

"Don't worry," said Peretz. "I don't plan on living long enough for that to kill me."

"That's the attitude," said Miriam, who was standing off to the side with Anna.

"Well, maybe," said Lejb, "but had I not come now, you would have died a lot sooner."

"This injury won't kill me," said Peretz.

He was almost right about that.

"I'm done," said Lejb and Ida let go of the leg.

"Am Yisrael Chai!" said Peretz. It had only been since the beginning of the fighting in January that Peretz had taken to praising any positive event with "Am Yisrael Chai," the People of Israel live. It was strange to all of them to hear him say it at first, but soon they got used to it and some of the other fighters would say it as well.

"Now rest that leg," said Lejb.

"Right," said Peretz and everyone, except Lejb laughed. Whatever happened over the next few days, one thing they could all be sure of was that Peretz would not rest his leg – or any other part of his body. After Lejb left and Peretz was comfortably sitting up against the wall – the pain killers had not yet worn off – Anna told him of their plans.

"We're leaving tonight," she said. "There's no reason to stay any longer. The entire ghetto will be razed in a matter of days."

"There are two kinds of people," said Peretz, "those who fight to fight and those who fight to live. I have become one who fights to fight and we have about three more days to do it."

"We may have more than that," said Miriam. "I think we're abandoning the cause too early." Miriam, who had changed her mind and now wanted to stay, was toeing the line of the leftist fighting organizations. The rightist fighters in the ghetto, well before the fighting even began, had created plans for evacuations of their fighters when all seemed lost; but the left-wing fighters, Hashomer Hatzair leadership included, felt that providing an "easy" out would only encourage fighters to leave prematurely. Anna had never officially weighed in on that subject but did come out in favor of having plans ready for implementation. Of course, she would have not liked to have been labeled as someone with a right-wing perspective.

"Too early for what?" asked Peretz. "Everything we do now is just a bonus. We have fulfilled our dream; the Jews are fighters. We have accomplished our goals; the resistance was a success. Did you think we could beat the Nazi military machine completely? That wasn't the point…"

"I know that," said Miriam. "I just think we can still do more damage. We can cause them to divert more energy toward us and maybe give the Russians or Americans a chance to advance faster. We still have a lot to contribute."

"We can contribute much more in the forests," said Anna, despite the optics of being bunched together with the right-wing groups for having an evacuation plan in place. "You were the one that said that! You were the one who encouraged us to make the escape plan to begin with. I know things have changed since you said that you wanted to fight in the forests with the partisans, but you've made a complete turnabout."

Miriam looked at Anna contemptuously. "I just want to fight."

"I don't want to stop fighting. I just want to stop fighting in here. It's over for us, Miriam. As hard as it is for me to admit that – it's over. We need to move on."

"I agree," said Peretz. "The only thing left to do here is fight to fight. Some of us will do that. Others, like all of you, must fight to live. There's another thing you should all know about. It's the Polish Underground.

"Has anyone met with them recently?" asked Ida.

Peretz didn't answer right away; instead, he adjusted himself against the wall, took a deep breath and then spoke.

"Let me tell you about my meeting," he said.

"Wait," said Anna, "you left the ghetto? When? How?"

"It doesn't matter. We met in a dark part of town…I mean really dark. The electricity had been out for months – some bombed-out building – lightning doesn't strike twice and all…. The lights were out; it was perfectly

209

safe. Easiest thing I ever did. Getting there, I mean. The meeting was not so easy."

"I told you it's easy to get in and out," said Ida. She'd done it tens of times.

"I met with one of the senior commanders of the Polish underground fighters," said Peretz. He was a guy named Karanski, who had been in constant touch with the Polish government in exile. I was there with Fat Bundy." Fat Bundy was the nickname given to one of the Bund leaders whose real name was Gideon Schalemberg. He was one of the oldest activists involved in the uprising, and his grey temples, deep voice and tall stature provided an air of candor when he walked into a room. Despite his name, he was not fat. No one could recall why that nickname had been given to him, but it stuck.

"How did he fare outside the walls," asked Ida, seemingly puzzled that Fat Bundy even went outside the ghetto.

"He surprised me considerably," said Peretz. "It was as if I was roaming Warsaw with a Polish nobleman. He transformed himself completely into a distinguished gentleman. When we talked to Karanski, Fat Bundy painted a bleak picture of our situation for the Polish man – even I was depressed by it. He talked about how the future of Polish Jewry is over and how Poland, as a country, will always exist, but without any Jews. He gave a heart wrenching description of the ghetto streets, complete with personal stories of women and children dying in front of him. I think we frightened Karanski. But whatever it was we said got his attention. I tried to explain to him that we were not just being turned into slaves, but we were being exterminated. His questioning look made me think I hadn't made myself clear, so I started with the stories we have been receiving from the camps. Both Fat Bundy and I made it clear that no one – neither the Poles nor the allies – could save us now; Polish Jewry was doomed. What we asked from him was two-fold: First, to assist us to make a last stand. We wanted them to help us with our attempt to postpone the inevitable and hinder the Nazi plans; and second, to tell the world the truth. We also asked him to petition the Allies to mercilessly bomb Germany, but we knew his influence was limited. Our feeling was that if the Allies knew what is really going on, they would help; they would bomb Germany and would do all they could to at least save a few of the lives being lost. Everything we told him about the German death camps was news to him. He asked for details and numbers. We told him that to know exactly who had been killed one simply needs to look at the German deportation records from the ghetto. Everyone taken from there was killed. He couldn't believe what he was hearing, but by the end of our conversation, he had been convinced. I can be very convincing –

Fat Bundy too. I could only see his silhouette in the dark room, but when I gave him some numbers, it seemed to me that he was about to faint. The Germans had murdered over one and half million Jews, I told him. And more were dying every day.

"I offered to show him the ghetto – this meeting was during the hiatus – but Fat Bundy didn't like the idea. He was right; it was far too dangerous to bring a Polish Underground leader here. But Karanski surprised me; he told us that he had already visited the ghetto the previous November. He then described for us what we see every day: corpses lying in the streets, thrown from windows by Jews too poor to pay for a burial; naked women and children sitting on every sidewalk; the smell of decay and death. He told us all this. He said he saw people barely alive at every turn. I told him that all those people are now dead.

"What came of the meeting was a commitment by him to assist all Jews who make it out of the ghetto. There is a list of names and addresses that we were finalizing when the fighting began. We had not been able to confirm all of the names he gave us; he himself wasn't even sure of all of them – but it is all we have. Take the list, it is in the other room. I trust him and what he told us. We have already been able to take advantage of his assistance. Now you can as well."

It was at that moment that Anna fully understood that this would be the last time any of them would ever see Peretz again. From the onset of the resistance movement, it was clear that some of the fighters would never stop fighting until they died. It was also clear that some would only fight until they knew that death was their next operation – then they would move on. All were willing to die in the ghetto, but some would fight to live first. She had always known that her part in the uprising would be to fight until she could no longer contribute and then leave the ghetto walls to tell the tale. It was clear to her that the story of the ghetto fighters would not be a fleeting moment in Jewish history, but a significant step toward building confidence and creating a viable Jewish existence in the future. That was Anna. She had insight into the significance of history in the making. That's how she knew she would never see Peretz again once they left that room. Her eyes filled with tears and Ida was the first to notice.

"Anna?" said Ida.

She wiped the tears with her good hand and forced a smile.

"Maybe I should stay," said Miriam.

"Maybe you shouldn't," said Anna and Peretz together.

Anna moved closer to Peretz and touched his shoulder. He was so thin now. He had always been underweight, but the ghetto had left his body wasted and emaciated.

Peretz looked up into Anna's tear-filled eyes. "God be with you," he said sarcastically.

Anna smiled. Peretz knew that God was not someone Anna would take with her on her journey. She leaned over and hugged him. He squeezed her tightly and she was surprised at his strength. For her, there was little to squeeze.

Ida followed Anna in bidding farewell to Peretz. She gave him a gentle kiss on both cheeks, much more like a formal greeting than a fatal farewell among friends. Miriam approached him last and as they were embracing, she said, "Maybe I should stay." And he whispered back, "Maybe you shouldn't." Miriam allowed one lone tear to run down her face.

The following week, just two days after Anna, Ida and Miriam had left Warsaw, Peretz went out with three other fighters to the edge of the central ghetto. Most of the area around the center of the ghetto had been burned out and Germans were continuously bombarding the ghetto with whatever firepower they could spare from the front. Peretz felt that the fighters needed to get as close to the Germans as possible and take out as many of them as they could with their dwindling arsenal. Peretz and his fighters positioned themselves high in one of the buildings overlooking a German outpost used to supply the cannons shooting into the ghetto. Peretz made two tactical errors that day. The first would cost the lives of two of his comrades. The second would cost him his own life – bad leg and all.

The first mistake that Peretz made would have caused Anna to chew him out in a fashion that only she could manage – had he remained alive. He had underestimated the German forces they were watching. Peretz had told his comrades that the machine guns below the building could not be placed at an angle that would warrant any threat to the Jewish snipers. What Peretz failed to consider was that the Germans never placed only one set of forces at any given location and their backup guns, which were not cannons but machineguns, would have no trouble at all cutting down the threat from above.

Peretz and his friends began firing at the Germans from their nested spot. The plan had been to kill the gunners and then retreat through the empty building to the tunnel below. That was Peretz's second error. There was no tunnel below – at least not directly below their building; they would have to cross the street to reach the nearest entrance.

The first two bullets that left Peretz's gun hit the first gunner, dropping him to the ground. Immediately, his comrades opened fire on the Germans as well; however, their aim had much to be desired and their bullets just ricocheted off the cannon itself. Peretz fired another two rounds and hit the second gunner. The fighters thought that there was only one more gunner to go, but since they had not taken into account the machine gun on the far side of the outpost, they could not have known that they were seconds away from becoming targets themselves.

As they all reloaded, the German guns began firing. Peretz and his friends were well out of the line of fire of the cannons, which as predicted by Peretz, never got off a shot, but the machine gun had no trouble hitting the men on top of the building – except Peretz. He had been saved by his friends, who were the only obstacles between Peretz and the 7. 92mm bullets exiting the Maschinengewehr 34 at a rate of 800 rounds per minute – not that the Germans needed a full minute to kill Peretz's friends.

Understanding his miscalculation, Peretz fled down the stairs through the courtyard and out into the street, leaving behind his two dead comrades. He had been sure that the entrance to the nearest tunnel was directly under his building, but well before reaching the street, he realized that he had been off by one building and one street. He ran out of the courtyard, believing that the Germans were only on the far side of the building, well out of reach.

It would have seemed to anyone watching, as it did to one girl, twenty-year-old, Lenka Gutenplan, that Peretz fell well before the sound of the very same machine gun, the 800 rounds per minute Maschinengewehr 34, could be heard at all. Lenka was watching as Peretz was first shot in the leg – his bad leg – and fell to the ground. She was not surprised that he was shot, as she had seen from the moment he left the courtyard that he was limping terribly and the Maschinengewehr 34, with two gunners and an SS officer had just been waiting for someone to attempt to cross the street. The only thing that surprised Lenka that day was that Peretz didn't die instantly. She saw as he bravely tried to drag himself across the street – one leg dead and the other, along with his hands, struggled against the slippery cobblestones toward the far side of the road. She watched in pain, although she had never met Peretz, as dust pellets seem to bounce off his leg again and again. The only part of Peretz's body that was hit at first was his bad leg – and only below the knee. Remarkably, Peretz made it to the far side of the road. As he approached the building, he stood up. Lenka could not believe that he was standing, and she was astonished to see that he was aiming his tiny pistol at the Maschinengewehr 34. And what really made her jaw drop was that he hit one of the gunners! The second gunner stopped firing for a second to watch his sidekick fall and took over the firing – without the support of someone to hold the 75-round continuous belt-feed. But the half belt left was more than enough to finish off Peretz. As he stood, he tried to fire again, but this time the 7.92mm bullets first hit his gun, then his hand, then his arm and finally, his chest.

As he fell, the guns went silent. Lenka heard a yell coming from his direction, but after that many entry wounds, she could not understand how he could have had the strength to muster up any vocals. What she thought she heard was, "Am Yisrael Chai!"

Twenty-Four

"I cried when I left the ghetto, you know. It had been hell and we struggled to survive…. We even killed each other to survive."

"What do you mean?" asked Rami.

"There was terrible infighting among the Jewish factions. The fighters were divided into two main groups: the ZOB and the ZWB. One was right-wing and one was left. 'A house divided cannot stand,' we would say. But no one listened. The two groups each had their own agenda and it was very difficult to agree on anything other than that the Nazis were evil. Anything beyond that was reason to argue."

"Two Jews, three opinions. It's like our political situation today."

"Not really. Today we have so many parties that you don't know who to vote for. Fifteen parties in the Knesset today. Back then, although we were many movements: Hashomer Hatzair, Dror, Gordonia, Betar, Bnei Akiva, we were split into two camps. It was easier back then because the ideologies were clear. Here…"

"The ideologies are clear," said Rami. "If you vote Labor, you know what you're getting."

"Do you?" Yaakov intervened. "Look how many Knesset members have left the Labor coalition since the last election. It seems every day another Knesset member switches parties. It's like a professional football team – trading players every week. I voted for one group of people and I now have another. The Labor party today is made up of a few smaller parties and you never know who is going to have control on any given day."

"I don't know about that," said Rami, "but you know that Herut is right-wing and Labor is left."

"You're misusing the terms," said Anna. "Right and Left-wing refer to the economic stance of the parties. In Israel, everyone mistakenly refers to the Right and the Left in regards to their position on the Arab-Israeli conflict, although in the case of the Labor party, you can clearly see they are a left-wing party in the true sense of the word."

"Mapam is the only real left-wing party," said Yaakov. Mapam, the United Workers Party, was affiliated with Hashomer Hatzair and the National Kibbutz Movement, of which Kibbutz Yad Mordechai was a member. "So you see, they are a part of the Labor coalition, the Ma'arach and I have no idea how to relate to them. Is Labor really left, or is Raffi the leading party in the coalition?"

"Shimon Peres is Raffi, right?" asked Rami.

"Right," said Yaakov. "And Yitzhak Rabin is Mapai. I wish I could still trust him."

"Why can't you trust him?" asked Rami.

"You should know this," said Anna, not letting Yaakov answer. "Rabin is the only person in government today who can bring peace to the region. If Peres had his way, we would maintain the conflict forever. That's the Raffi way. He's continuing the Ben-Gurion policy. Did you know that Ben-Gurion could have signed a peace agreement with Egypt in 1956? Egypt was ready, but he was afraid that the country needed a unifying enemy."

"Where did you hear that nonsense?" said Yaakov.

"It's true, and look what happened. We have been in two wars with Egypt since. Who knows, if that Fascist Begin ever gets his way, we'll be fighting another war very soon."

"Begin will never gain power in this country," said Rami.

"Never underestimate the enemy," said Anna.

"I agree with Rami," said Yaakov. "We will never see a Herut government. Labor has 51 mandates, that's almost half…"

"Forty-nine," corrected Anna. "He's lost two since the elections. No matter. All I know is that only Rabin will bring peace. Only Rabin."

"Let's see how well Rabin gets through this crisis," said Yaakov. "Then we'll know what kind of chances he has in the next election."

"Anna," asked Rami, "what did you mean when you said that you were killing each other in the ghetto."

"There was terrible fighting between the factions – even a few political murders. Each side was sure that their way was the right way and they were willing to kill for it."

"Even the side that believes that 'Man must prove his truth?'"

"Yes, even us. Dogmatic attitudes are not restricted to fascists. Both the left and the right are willing to kill for their convictions. Don't think it can't happen here either."

"What do you mean?" asked Rami. "You think there could be political murders in Israel? Maybe nationalistic murders – Arabs killing Jews and such. But there could never be a political assassination in Israel."

"There already has been. Who do you think killed Arlosoroff?"

"That was ages ago. In the twenties. Things were different then. Even what you are talking about is a unique situation. In mainstream Israeli politics, the worst thing you'll have is verbal violence."

"The Knesset is full of that already," said Yaakov.

"It happened in the past, and it can happen again, "said Anna. "Maybe in twenty years, but it can happen, and we should all be aware that we are no different than any other people in the world. We can be just as violent and as indifferent. We can kill and we can save lives. We just have to decide. You know, Theodore Herzl, when he dreamed of a Jewish homeland, said that it will have doctors and lawyers and teachers and factory workers; but he also said that it will have murders and thieves and swindlers – I'm paraphrasing of course. He meant that this country will be like any other country in the world. A normal place."

"But now," said Rami, "It's the only place in the world where Jews are being killed just because they are Jews. Is that what he had in mind as well?"

"Herzl did not know what the future held. After all, he was just a reporter with a vision – a vision of anti-Semitism in Europe and what the future held for European Jewry. He did predict a catastrophe in Europe and he did foresee that there would be a state, but he could not have known what the nature of that state would be. It is now up to us to make the country a respectable place to live, a good place to bring up children – and that includes making peace with our neighbors. That is what we always wanted and someday, our neighbors may want it as well. For now, we just have to keep fighting, don't we?" She looked over at Rami and smiled.

"I suppose," he said.

"And as for this being the only place where Jews are killed for being Jews – that statement is true only because the existence of the State of Israel has provided a haven for persecution. I saw firsthand what can happen to a people without a homeland. It may be true that Jews are only dying here, but the Germans have shown us the alternative, and the fact that Jews are not being killed because they are Jews elsewhere is the greatest accomplishment of the Zionist movement. We are here now to ensure that that never changes."

Anna had a way of ending conversations with inarguable statements. Rami seemed to be struggling to come up with a response, but Anna had made a strong point that even an officer in the IDF couldn't contest.

"Now what was I talking about?"

"Politics," said Yaakov.

"No," said Anna. "I was telling you that I cried when I left the ghetto."

Twenty-Five

21 April 1943

Reports of the fires continued to reach the bunker where Anna, Ida, and Miriam were spending the evening planning their escape. A few hours had passed since they bid farewell to Peretz, but they had not been able to come up with the right plan to get out. Of course, the real reason that they did not leave the smoldering ghetto that night – nor the next four nights – was Anna's ambivalence about leaving. Miriam took advantage of Anna's indecision and kept them busy. There had already been two groups of fighters who had escaped the burning ghetto. Anna had tried to get information about the routes they had taken but no one seemed to know the details. It was clear that the Germans had blocked several of the exits, and the fires had blocked many of the rest.

"The north sewer on Franciszkanska will do," said Miriam while staring at a handwritten map of the ghetto. The sewers had all been plotted along with the tunnels inside the ghetto. Miriam did not need the map. She knew exactly where each entrance and exit was and could have easily guided them in the dead of night – which was exactly what she was to do. But it never hurt to take a look at the map.

"Where did you get that?" asked Ida, glaring at Miriam's map. "I thought there weren't any plans of escape. Didn't Antek say there were no plans for escape?"

"This is a map for smuggling, not escape. But it works just as well. Besides, I think that Antek understands that we can't stay here forever."

"Isn't that entrance under the rubble?" asked Anna.

"No, the building next to it is gone, but it's off the courtyard and most of the building surrounding the yard is still intact. It's perfect."

"Anna!" yelled Ida suddenly. "You're bleeding!" No one had noticed, including Anna, that her arm was not the only injury Anna had incurred when the lookout wall blasted in on the two guards. Ida raced over to Anna, who was sitting on her bed, folding a shirt, and lifted her pant leg. The cloth was soaked in crimson dampness, and when Ida looked at Anna's ankle, she gasped.

"I don't feel anything," said Anna. "Nothing." She looked down over her own knee and saw that there was a gash from just above her ankle to the topside of her heel. I could have been a continuation of the wound on Peretz's leg, had the two legs been one. Lejb, who always enjoyed demonstrating the little knowledge he did acquire in his few years of medical school, would have told them that the laceration began at the Fibula, continued through the Lateral Malleolus and ended at the top of the Superior Peroneal Retinaculum. No one would have been impressed but his smile would express his self-pride. After all, muscles were his specialty, and he would never miss a chance to talk about them. "There are over 100 muscles in your foot alone." It seems three of Anna's had been cut.

"How could you not feel this?" asked Ida.

"Adrenaline," said Miriam, without taking her eyes off the map.

"I'm not getting it sewn," she said. Tie something around it. I'm not going back to Lejb."

The wound had stopped bleeding now, although, by the looks of her pant leg, it had bled quite a lot. It would have most likely needed several stitches under normal circumstances, but these were far from normal circumstances.

Ida went back to her mattress and took a shirt that she had placed in the pile of clothes she would not be taking with her. Most of their items would be left to burn in the bunker after their departure. They each would only take a small sack and all the clothing they would take would be worn. It was not warm yet, so they were able to take whatever they needed on their person. Ida tore the shirt into strips and used two to tie Anna's ankle.

"Now I feel it," she said. Since the wound would never be sewn, it would also heal with the most gruesome of scars. High socks would cover most of the scar, but for the rest of her life, whenever Anna would wear a dress, inevitably someone would be caught staring at the ragged white line that went from her Fibula through the Lateral Malleolus and to the top of the Superior Peroneal Retinaculum.

"Stand up," said Ida.

"Why?"

"Because I want to make sure I'm not taking an invalid with me to the forest."

Anna stood and rolled her eyes. She gracefully walked across the room, without showing any kind of obstruction.

"Fine," said Ida. "You'll be fine."

"Thanks, Doc," said Anna.

"Yep. You'll go through the north sewer," said Miriam.

"You?" said Anna and Ida together.

"I'm still not sure I'm joining you, remember?"

"Oh, you're joining us," said Anna.

"I can't carry Anna alone," said Ida. Anna gave her a dirty look.

Miriam had set down the map and was now braiding her long hair. The three sections of the braids were identical in width, and it never mattered how hastily she would work, or whether or not she had a mirror – which she did not – the braid always turned out perfect. She sat down on the side of the bed.

"I have done so much here," she said. "This is my place. This is where I need to be right now. What good will I do out there? I know these streets, these tunnels, these people. I know I still have a lot to contribute. I know the fighting will not end tomorrow. We will hold out a great deal longer than anyone ever expected. But if I leave, I will always feel I abandoned my comrades in their most dire time of need. And I'll be…" Miriam stopped braiding her hair and sat perfectly still, staring aimlessly at nothing.

"What?" asked Anna. "You'll be what?"

She looked up at Ida and Anna. "I'll be scared again," she said quietly.

Anna remembered her story about getting caught with Tuvia and being raped by the Russian soldiers. There is something about being caged up in the ghetto, she thought; you have no freedom to lose. Miriam was afraid to have independence to roam because it could so easily be taken from her. Her previous moments of wandering the Polish wilderness were laden with suspicions, dread, and trepidation – all of which came true in a Russian truck. As horrifying as the ghetto had been, it had been a place of support and few surprises for Miriam – particularly during the months leading up to the revolt. In the ghetto, Miriam may have felt more secure and protected than anywhere else in her life. The constant fear that freedom held in Nazi-occupied Poland was not something that she was looking forward to. Anna knew that the only way Miriam would join them was if she was convinced that the ghetto would no longer be the same place she had felt so secure. For that would be the only way that Anna herself would leave the ghetto. She too was scared; after all, Anna had not left Warsaw since the beginning of the war.

Miriam had held multiple positions during the uprising. The fighters had divided the ghetto into several areas with little contact between them. Her primary task had been to be the liaison between the Többens and Schultz sector and the central ghetto. She was one of a scarce few who spent most of her day roaming the streets, the tunnels, and the bunkers, passing messages and continuously risking her life. But Miriam never seemed to feel threatened doing her job.

"Miriam," said Anna, "the ghetto you knew is gone – and perhaps that is a good thing. After all, this was hell on earth."

"Not for me. Hell on earth was my home, that Russian truck and those camps that we may all end up in if we get caught."

"The ghetto was hell for you too…"

"But I was doing something! I was doing something!" she held her head in her hands and rocked back and forth like a Hasidic man praying.

Anna watched her rocking herself and wondered if anyone had ever rocked her.

"I'm not ready to stop fighting." This time she spoke calmly, in a manner that said, I will go with you despite my inner wishes.

"Then don't stop," said Anna. "Help us get out of here and join the partisans in the forests. They need us now more than ever."

Miriam said nothing, but her hand slowly moved to the end of her bed where the map had been set and she lifted it. Slowly, as if she did not want to hear the crinkling of the paper, she brought the map into her lap and looked down at it. "We'll take the northern tunnel."

It turned out that Miriam had been correct to predict that the ghetto fighting would continue for longer than anyone else expected – particularly the Germans. Anna had been wrong about their exit that night. The turn of events that kept Anna and her friends in the ghetto longer than intended began with an ostensible German declaration giving the ghetto fighters five days to voluntarily give themselves up. Miriam used the declaration to convince Anna that they still had time and would be able to assist in enhancing and strengthening the outposts that remained – particularly in the Többens area, where Miriam had been active in the past.

Both the Brush Makers Gate block and the central ghetto were seriously damaged by fire and mortars. Most of the fighters had left the central ghetto and had relocated to safer bunkers under the rubble in the southern part of the central ghetto. The Germans had set fire to building after building, causing some to be trapped and burned along with their homes. Others managed to escape the flames and run directly into German arms.

Among these unfortunate fighters were Emil and his ghetto love, D'vorah. One evening, after a day where an estimated two hundred fighters had been captured, incinerated or executed, Anna, Miriam and Ida went to an adjacent bunker to see if they needed anything. There were seven fighters in the bunker, most from the Halutz movement. When the girls arrived, the Halutz fighters reported to them what they had each seen during the day. Many had witnessed the mass executions of captured fighters, and others had themselves barely escaped the flames of collapsing buildings. One young man in his late teens told of how his sister had died that day. Tears streamed down his face as he relived what he had seen. He told them that his sister and her boyfriend had been on lookout in one of the buildings off the central ghetto. He too had been there but left the loft they were in just as German flamethrowers attacked the building. He ran across the street. The

Germans were too busy aiming the flames to notice his exit, and soon the building was on fire. It took less than two minutes before his sister, D'vorah, and her boyfriend came running out of the burning building gasping for air and choking on the thick smoke, only to be gunned down by SS officers waiting for just such an exit.

Of course, Miriam did not need to ask, but she did. "Was it Emil?"

The boy just sniffled and nodded affirmatively.

As much as all of the young fighters knew that as soon as the Germans began fighting back, whether it be with Maschinengewehr 34s or gas-powered flame throwers, most of them would die, nothing prepared them for what they were to experience in the ghetto during the uprising. No one would ever be ready to hear of a friend or sister or lover dying. No one was immune. Anna, Ida and Miriam hugged each other, and Ida and Anna wept along with the boy who had lost his sister; this time, Miriam did not let the tears come.

So the fires raged and the stench was everywhere, and everyone knew that soon the entire ghetto would be gone. But the German declaration for voluntary evacuation gave the fighters time to regroup and re-plan. They were able to take into account the new Nazi tactic of firebombing and their response would be no less brutal.

Along the walls of the Többens and Schultz plants, the fighters were able to cause such disorder that the SS men themselves showed signs of fear when they entered the area. Miriam had convinced Anna and Ida to join her on one of the most successful operations of those five days. It was never actually called an operation – it was more of an opportunity. Anna's compliance with Miriam's plea to remain a little longer in the ghetto came with one condition: that the three of them stick together at all times. When Anna made her demand, Ida smiled wider than she had since the beginning of the war, and Miriam hugged Anna as if it was the one thing she desired to hear since entering the ghetto.

The three were patrolling the block when Ida, who seemed to be the most perceptive and the quickest of the three, grabbed Miriam by the collar of her coat and Anna by the belt and dragged them to the ground. It was a clear sign that someone was coming, but instead of seeing German guards marching toward them, a truck was making its way into the forbidden area under Ida's watchful eye. Less than half a block from their location was a basement apartment with a secret compartment. Stored there since late January were explosives and power charges. The girls ran to the building that housed the loaded basement. Five stairs led to the basement entrance and the door was open. Inside, only the light curving around the small stairwell and in through the crack in the open door reached the far walls of the small one-room slick. Had they not known that the wood panel on the far floor was a hatch to a box sunk into the ground, they would have looked for the explosives for hours. Miriam ran directly toward the hatch and grabbed the latch for Ida to unlock. The hidden weapons were scattered on one side of the dusty bin, and they each grabbed what they could from the hole dug into the ground.

Anna left the building first, followed by Ida and Miriam. She turned left toward the wall, behind which the German convoy was parked.

"No!" said Miriam, as they reached the street. "Right up there." She pointed to the building across the street and to the right. Miriam knew the area better than anyone. Although it seemed to Anna that they would have been closer to the truck had they turned left and went up to the roof of the next building, she was not going to argue with Miriam during an operation.

But it was Ida who saved their lives that day. Miriam led the way into the next building. Anna was directly behind her with one hand on her back as they walked up the staircase. As Ida entered the stairwell, she glanced to the side and saw the guards. Two Germans had seen the girls crossing the street and were running toward them. Ida didn't take the time to yell ahead to Miriam and Anna, but stopped, aimed and fired two shots. The first hit the guard on the right in the stomach. He fell. The second shot hit the second guard square in the nose, virtually exploding his head. He fell. Ida waited to see if there were reinforcements behind them. But there weren't. Anna never saw the dead guards until they would leave the roof of the building and return to safety. Then, as they would run past the dead bodies, all she would see was two dead children, and she would think about their mothers. Ida just saw two dead Germans, and Miriam saw two dead enemies.

After Ida waited to make sure there were no more guards, she followed Anna and Miriam to the roof of the building. The SS truck had just finished unloading a crate of some kind, and the sixty men in the back were waiting for the driver to return to his cabin and continue on their way. It took Miriam less than thirty seconds to set and toss the four-pound charges off the roof and directly into the bed of the truck. The explosion was so strong that pieces of German flesh could be seen hitting the third floor of the building across the street from the doomed vehicle. The girls did not wait to see how many of the SS men were killed. Had they, they would have seen that there were fifty-five fatalities as a result of their spontaneous operation. Fifty-five mothers had just lost their sons.

Ida knew they deserved it. Anna wasn't sure. Miriam was elated.

Had they not been so successful making fifty-five German mothers grieve, they may have never made it out of the area alive. Had Ida not killed the two guards, they would have met them as they left the building. But there were now fifty-seven fewer Germans combing the Többens and Schultz area, and Miriam felt just a bit safer.

They retreated toward Mila Street just as four Bund fighters came to see what all the commotion was about.

That wasn't the last time they would come close to losing their lives during those final days in the ghetto. The next time, they would be spared by a little luck and a seasoned sniper who would save them.

The mines that Rachel had set were useless now that the Germans had cut off the electricity. They just sat under the roads, no current to detonate them since they had been using charges that were attached to the grid. Without power, the mines remained dormant, unable to fulfill their designated purpose. Someone at headquarters came up with the idea of shooting at them when they needed them to go off, so of course, Ida and Miriam, who knew the Többens area well enough, volunteered for the job. Ida's sharp-shooting skills, and now her operating skills, had become well known in the ghetto.

For the first time, it became clear to Anna that her insistence to stick together was a detriment. Ida needed to be on the rooftop alone. Anna and Miriam didn't need to be there at all, but if they were to be in the area, it could not be in the same building as Ida; after she shot at the mines, she would need to escape as quickly and as quietly as possible. Two more bodies running down the stairs would not be of help. So Anna decided that she and Miriam would cover her from a distance. They took positions on a balcony on the fifth floor of the building across from Ida's post. They had a perfect view of the street ahead, although they could not see the targets that Ida would be shooting.

The plan had been to open fire on the mines, which had been marked by Rachel with black stones directly east of each mine. The stones were undetectable by anyone not looking for them – another Rachel brainchild. The firing would commence as soon as the German convey passed the gate. Unlike in the Brush Makers block, the east Leszno Street entrance was harder to ambush. Leszno Street sliced directly through the heart of the old ghetto; everything outside the central ghetto, the Többens and Schultz plants, the Brush Makers factories and what was termed the small ghetto far to the south, had long been cut off and liquidated. Scores of fighters lost their lives when everyone south of Smocza and Geisa Street was deported or killed. Once that part of the ghetto was gone, Leszno Street was no longer in the middle of the ghetto. The Többens and Schultz walls were now the southernmost point of the ghetto, and to reach Lenzo Street you had to cross no man's land.

The first flaw in the improvident plan to shoot the mines was that no one bothered to consult with Rachel. The mines were well marked and easy to find – if you knew where to look – but would not explode when shot at. Rachel could have told them that. Each mine had cobblestones covering them, and the bullets would simply ricochet off of the stones without hitting the mine itself. Rachel would have told them that even without the cobblestones the mines most likely would not have detonated by a bullet anyway. But Ida didn't know that – neither did anyone else at headquarters, although one fifteen-year-old boy did manage to blurt out during the discussion that it was a crazy idea. However, he was far from confident enough in the company of all the "older" fighters (average age 21) to defend his statement. Ida was setting herself up to be the target.

Of course, luck would also have a major role in saving Ida's life. Firstly, the same guy who came up with the idea of shooting at the mines to detonate them ordered three snipers to be on hand "just in case." His motives were far from noble – he was not planning on simply protecting Ida; his main intention was to provide backup for the detonation; "just in case" meant just in case Ida missed. The same fifteen-year-old boy had said, "That's nuts," when he heard the vote of no confidence in Ida. Ida would later remember the boy and wish she would have said something to him after that meeting. He was captured and executed against a wall along with eighteen other fighters the next day.

Secondly, Ida could not have picked a better convoy to try to blow up. Actually, to call it a convoy would have been a dishonor to any respectable convoy – this one was made up of only two trucks – both were empty, except for a driver and one soldier in each. It turned out to be quite an operation just to disable two personnel carriers, devoid of personnel. But it was also what saved Ida's life.

Ida had taken her position above the mines and prepared to open fire as soon as the first convoy passed over a predetermined line in the middle of the street. The streets were empty, and as far as Ida knew, only Anna and Miriam were somewhere in one of the adjacent buildings. There was a stench of smoke in the air that seemed to be stronger at the top of the building. Ida could see the smoke rising from all around the ghetto, and from her perspective, it didn't seem like very much wasn't burning. The fires had been raging for several days. Each morning the Germans had chosen another block to set on fire, and the casualties were rising faster than any of the fighters ever could have imagined. Most of the Jews in the ghetto had retreated to the underground bunkers only to appear at night to set traps and attack when they could. It was already clear even to Miriam that this may be their last operation and if they didn't get caught, they would have to leave the ghetto immediately.

As the first convoy came rumbling down the road just outside the ghetto walls, Ida prepared her aim. She knew exactly what she wanted to hit and was even ready to reload and shoot again. Any more than two shots would have been considered a failure. The first convoy that came into sight did not turn into the ghetto. It continued along Dluga Street and turned away from the ghetto entrance. Since her view was partially blocked by a building just on the edge of the ghetto, at first she thought the convoy would enter across from her building. But when she heard the engines but saw nothing, she realized that it had turned. She released her grip on the rifle and waited. The second convoy was the small one that entered the ghetto. It too came down Dluga Street, but instead of turning south, continued toward Leszno Street and through the ghetto entrance.

Ida watched as the trucks approached the line that would indicate the moment when she should open fire on the stones marking the mines. The trucks changed gears after they passed the gate, and the rumble of the engines went from loud to soft and back to loud again. Ida took aim. She held the weapon like a professional. It would have been hard to believe that this girl had never even seen a gun before 1943, let alone fire one In four short months, Ida had gone from novice to marksman and was the envy of many of the male fighters, who, had they been Poles, would have been drafted and fought a different three weeks in September 1939, when the Germans cut through the Polish army like a knife through butter.

Ida's first experience firing a gun happened two weeks before the January Aktions. A small group of fighters had taken three pistols and were going to practice loading and shooting. Ida joined them at the last minute, and when the commander, a young boy with long bangs, round glasses, and sad lips, said that each of them could take one shot, Ida was excited. Her first and only shot that day was at a chalk-drawn target about fifty yards down an alley that had been abandoned since the previous summer. They had decided that early morning was the best time to make gunshot noises since the German patrols guarding the outside of the ghetto walls were scarce – in early January the patrols inside the walls were well regulated and predictable. Ida hit her target square in the center to the surprise of all her comrades. Some were embarrassed by their own showing, and no one, not even the experienced, long-banged, sad-lipped instructor came close to the accuracy of Ida's lone bullet. Her marksmanship only improved once the opportunities to shoot real people began in mid-January. By the start of the April Aktions, everyone knew that Ida was the best shot in Warsaw. She was even called "the Little Lyudmila," after Lyudmila Pavlichenko, the remarkable Russian sniper who became well known among the ghetto fighters. Pavlichenko fought for the Red Army in Odesa, Moldavia, and Sevastopol, but her work reached the fighters through various channels. "We mowed down the Hitlerites like ripe grain," she had said. Even though she suffered shell shock, multiple wounds, and the Germans tried to bribe her with chocolate and rank, she never wavered. The Germans even threatened to tear her into 309 pieces, her number of confirmed kills. She found the threat amusing since it meant her accomplishments were well known.

Now Ida had to emulate Lyudmila and hit the smallest target she had ever attempted to shoot. Even if it had been possible to detonate the mines with a bullet, the accuracy demanded of Ida, as facile as shooting a weapon had come to her, was incalculable. The diameter of the mine was less than half the size of a German torso, and the distance was twice as far as any other ambush. In retrospect, it would have been a much more effective trap had Ida just aimed for the driver of the truck. But how was she to know that the truck was empty? She pulled the trigger. The bullet left the barrel and with it escaped a pop that rebounded off the building across from Ida's post and reverberated in the street. It sounded like several shots. In addition to the sound of the pin firing the bullet, the bullet itself made a sound hitting the cobblestones under which lay the mine. The bullet did what Rachel would have told them that it would do – had they asked her – it ricocheted off the street and into the building. Ida had hit the exact stone she was aiming for – but there was no detonation. She quickly loaded and set herself in position again. However, the soldiers had stopped the truck upon hearing the sounds of what seemed like a barrage of bullets, echoes and ricochets and without hesitation came out firing in Ida's direction.

Ida fired again, but just as she began to squeeze the trigger, a bullet from one of the German occupants of the truck hit her gun. Had that same officer been able to get off another shot, Ida would have surely been hit. However, the Jewish snipers, upon seeing that Ida "missed" had begun firing at the Germans – and not at the mine as they had been instructed. One by one, the Germans fell, until two abandoned trucks lay driverless in the middle of the street, and four dead Germans with loaded guns lay beside the vehicles.

There was no explosion. Ida escaped unharmed.

On April 28th the final sign given to Anna, Ida and Miriam came when the Nazis decided it was time to destroy the Többens and Schultz factories and all the buildings around it. They set fire to the blocks in the area, and the place where Miriam had felt the safest was gone. Her mission was complete, and now they could leave the ghetto.

Almost watching Ida lose her life was too much for even Miriam, and they all knew that there would be little left of the ghetto in a few days. Escape after that would be impossible. When Ida met Anna and Miriam in the bunker following the flubbed operation, Miriam was the one to tell Ida that they would be leaving that night.

"Eliezer is organizing a mass escape," Miriam said to Ida when she returned. Eliezer had been the commander of the Többens and Schultz units and was highly respected by Miriam. "We're not going with them."

"Why not?" asked Ida, although they all knew the answer. Leaving the ghetto in the sewer with forty people as opposed to three was vastly more dangerous. Miriam, who had tried to convince Eliezer to break the fighters into smaller groups, was convinced that it would be safer if they went alone. She knew there would be additional groups leaving the trenches as well, and she hoped they would all be able to meet up on the Aryan side and travel together to the partisans in the forest.

"I want to make it," she said. "Besides, they are leaving from the Leszno Street entrance, we want to go north through the central ghetto." For the girls to attempt crossing the liquidated part of the ghetto south of the main ghetto and north of the smoldering Többens and Schultz block would be suicide. Even if they wanted to join the group of forty, they would have to cross a dangerous sector at a speed that would put them at risk of being spotted far too easily. Miriam was sure of her plan, and Ida and Anna had confidence in Miriam.

Anna had been going over the list of names Peretz had given them and in the twenty minutes between their arrival in the bunker and Ida's return, had established a viable plan of escape. It began in the sewers and ended in the forests where Jewish intelligence units had suggested they would find the partisans.

The few hours they were to wait in the bunker were perhaps the longest of the war for Anna. They all felt guilty about leaving. Anna would have liked to ask Peretz a few questions about the Polish contacts on the lists but knew that there was no way of contacting him. They each lay silent awaiting darkness when they would be able to leave to the sewer entrance and out to freedom.

As the longest day of Anna's life came to a close, the girls prepared to leave the bunker and make their way toward the hidden passage entrance on Lubeckie Street. The problem with Lubeckie Street was its proximity to the Umschlagplatz, where many of the German divisions tended to concentrate. Just a day earlier, there was an attempt to send one of the Dror movement fighters out through that exit, but she was caught before reaching the tunnel and executed by two Polish soldiers at the command of the SS officer on duty. Anna was determined not to make the same mistake, and the only way to ensure their success was to create a distraction close enough to attract any Germans in the area, but far enough to allow them clear passage to the tunnel.

For that, Anna called on Tuvia. Early in the uprising, after trying to wash the floor of the bunker without water, Tuvia joined a band of fighters stationed on the west side of the central ghetto. He left Anna's bunker in a state that made Anna think that he would never return. She still felt that he was on the verge of injuring himself, but she let herself think that since her prophecy had not come to pass by the second week of the uprising, perhaps she had been wrong. When Anna needed someone to assist with a distraction – after ruling out Rachel, who would have been Anna's first choice – she thought about Tuvia and the Dror fighters. They were stationed close enough to Lubeckie Street and knew their way around. She had sent a message to Tuvia simply saying, "Leaving. Need cover at 23. K and M. Love, Anna." Tuvia would know exactly what she meant. Twenty three was a time, not a street number, K was Lubeckie Street, and M was Mila Street. Although much of the surrounding area was burning, from the information they had received, this intersection was safe. A message in Tuvia's hand had been sent back saying, "24."

"He needs an extra hour," Anna said to Ida and Miriam. "Or else he knows something that we don't." This was the second stage of the uprising. During the first stage, most of the battles were in the streets. The Jews attacked, the Germans responded. The second stage of the revolt was more defensive for the Jews. The Germans were actively searching for the Jewish bunkers and attacking, but they felt very insecure whenever they entered a bunker, as many were either booby-trapped or filled with fighters ready to pounce. On occasion, the resistance would leave their hiding spots and attack designated targets – but rarely during the day. Anna assumed correctly that Tuvia and his fighters would be on such a mission and would not be able to reach K and M in time. It was fine with Anna. What was one more hour of waiting?

At the snail pace that the girls would be moving toward the north-west part of the central ghetto, they would require at least an hour to reach the tunnel. At exactly 23:00 hours, the three fighters bid farewell to their bunker; each had put on enough clothing to get them through the cool nights that still lay ahead and had grabbed the small sack of essential items they had prepared. Before leaving the bunker, Anna checked to make sure her two chains and rings from her grandmother were in the bag. She removed the small receptacle and placed it in her pocket.

As soon as they stuck their heads out of the bunker, the sound of clicking German heals could be heard coming from the next street over. Anna wondered why they wore such noisy shoes. They retreated back into the bunker and waited. Their second attempt out of their underground home was successful. No sounds could be heard, and they easily reached the next building over. At each building, they would stop, hide in a dark spot, and move forward when they were sure no guards or troops were in the vicinity; they relied mainly on their ears and a sixth sense to know when it was safe to progress. It was a painstakingly slow process, but they all knew that there was no other way out of the ghetto.

By the time the girls were within sight of the building housing the underground passageway out of the ghetto, they could feel German activity all around them. Now all they could do was to wait for Tuvia's distraction to buy them time to make a run for the entrance. It was almost 200 meters from Lubeckie and Mila to the tunnel entrance. The entrance was far enough up the road from Mila Street that anything that happened around the corner would keep all the guards in the area occupied and diverted. But as they waited, Anna had a dreadful thought that she shared with her friends.

"What if Tuvia didn't understand where we were going? What if he sets something off exactly at the intersection?"

"He knows better," said Ida. Where else would we be going?"

"She's right," said Miriam. "The only exit from the ghetto is here. You told him we're leaving..."

As Miriam was speaking, Ida placed a hand over her mouth. There was movement from behind them. The girls froze as they heard running coming from the west on Niska Street. Lubeckie Street ran from north to south, meeting Mila Street one block south of Niska. The girls had passed Mila and entered from Niska to the west side of Lubeckie. The footsteps were coming from where they had been. Anna immediately knew that it was not the sound of Germans. Their boots clicked on the cobblestones. Before any of them could move to look down the street, a thin figure stood before them in the street.

"Tuvia!" whispered Anna.

Tuvia ran into the stairwell that led to a lower floor entrance of the building where the girls were hiding. There was enough light emanating from the end of the street that Anna could see Tuvia's eyes. This was not the same man who had been washing floors without water. He had a crazed look in his eyes like he was a wild beast stalking its prey. His head jerked from side to side and he was continuously looking all around, even though from the stairwell below the street level he could only see the other girls.

As if he had been talking with them for hours he spoke – never looking any of them in the eye. "And my men should be lighting the fuse any second now. I'll lead you out."

"Tuvia?" asked Anna, grabbing his shoulders and trying to get him to look at her. "Tuvia, what's going on? I didn't need you to come."

"You do. You do. You really do. It is imperative that you do as I tell you," he said, jerking his head from side to side. Something was seriously wrong with him, yet at the same time, he seemed confident in his plan. Anna was concerned but had no choice other than to follow his lead.

Within one minute of Tuvia's arrival, an explosion was heard coming from the southeast.

"Go!" yelled Tuvia and ran up the stairs. The girls quickly followed and before Anna realized it they were standing on Lubeckie Street in front of a boarded-up entrance to a courtyard inside which was the building with the tunnel entrance. Just a small hole the size of Anna's hips had been smashed open, allowing the fugitives to enter the courtyard. Luckily, Miriam and Ida were now much thinner than Anna. First Ida slipped through; then Miriam followed, and finally Anna.

Miriam and Ida ran directly toward the back end of the courtyard where the sewer entrance was located. This entrance was actually a makeshift tunnel dug by the fighters that led to the main sewer entrance. They quickly removed the camouflage covering – a piece of sheet metal with some garbage thrown over it – and began opening the hatch that led below the building. Anna, after squeezing through the hole, was watching Tuvia, who had not entered the courtyard but was still standing outside the boarded barricade.

"Come on!" said Anna.

Tuvia stuck his hand into the hole – he was holding a gun – and waved it as if clearing a spider web then backed out.

"Tuvia! Come in here!"

Tuvia then stuck his head in the hole again and said, "Leave now. You said you'd listen to me."

Anna had never said that but realized it was no use trying to drag him in. He had no intention of leaving the ghetto with them that day, and it seemed he knew what he was doing. Anna heard three gunshots coming from Tuvia's weapon.

Anna ran to Miriam and Ida who were already halfway down the tunnel entrance. She took three steps into the tunnel and saw that Tuvia had begun crawling through the hole; although, unlike the girls, he had gone feet first. Anna froze as she watched him standing with both feet inside the courtyard, and his upper torso, hidden by the boards, outside the wall facing the street. Anna could hear more gunshots, and she knew that they were coming from German guns. She took two more steps down into the tunnel when she again heard multiple shots. She looked back and saw Tuvia's body had gone limp – his feet inside, his thin waist hung over the bottom of the hole, and the rest of his body on the outside. With the Germans yelling and trying to pull Tuvia out of the way, Anna realized what he had done. His plan all along was to block the entrance to the courtyard to provide the girls ample time to escape. By the time the Germans got the body out, the girls had long left the ghetto, and the soldiers never even knew that they had been there. She then knew that she had been right about Tuvia's state of mind. Only a deranged human being could do something like that, or perhaps only a true selfless hero.

She was crying as she ran out of the Jewish Quarter of Warsaw to freedom.

Twenty-Six

"The two hardest things I ever had to do in my life were to let my child go and to leave the ghetto myself," said Anna to the driver after regaining the ability to talk. "Ironic, really."

Yaakov kept his eyes on the road and listened to Anna, occasionally glancing down at her. She was looking up at him as she spoke.

"First I let my child go. I mistakenly thought he would be safer outside the ghastly ghetto walls. I trusted that he would be protected by my close friend. She tried, I know she did. I also know that she lived every second of every day since failing to protect him thinking about what she could have done differently. I forgave her long ago, but she could never forgive herself. It gave her cancer, you know. She fought that as well. Before the ghetto, she was a happy person. Almost oblivious to what was going on around her – before the ghetto. But once we were caged inside the ghetto walls, the spark of life left her. She still sang every once in a while, but she was so miserable. I let her go too – with my son. I knew she would try to protect him. I knew she would."

"What happened? If you don't mind me asking," said Yaakov.

Anna didn't answer. She was looking up at Yaakov but was looking right through him. Her mind was back in the ghetto. Back in the moment that she decided to let Hanna take Yehuda out, and the hope, the undying hope, that they would both survive and make their way across the Mediterranean Sea to the shores of Eretz Yisrael.

Yaakov understood and didn't ask again. A moment passed and she began to speak.

"The second hardest moment for me was leaving the ghetto myself. How ironic, no? The most repulsive, sordid, inhuman place on earth and I didn't want to leave. But I knew that had we stayed we would have died. It wouldn't be good for anyone. I didn't know that my child was dead yet – actually, at the time he was still alive, but I didn't know that either."

She had spoken in a way that caused an additional gasp from the couple in the seat behind her. Instead of continuing with the story, she turned to the couple.

"I have to continue living. I long for my children every day. I wonder what they would have been like growing up. Every time I see a small boy, I think that this could have been Shimi or Yehuda. But I accept their passing. It is part of life. They say that a mother should never have to bury her children...I guess I never buried mine. They were just lost...sent away, never to be seen."

Anna turned and faced Yaakov again, leaving the couple stunned and

235

speechless. Rami, who had not missed a word coming out of Anna's mouth since they left Jerusalem, was just shaking his head.

"Where was I? Yes, I was leaving the ghetto with my friends. Oh, thank goodness for Ida and Miriam. Miriam didn't want to leave either, you know. She wanted to fight in the ghetto. I wanted to fight as well, but out of the ghetto. I don't recall if Ida wanted to fight. She just wanted to live – that I can tell you. No one wanted to live more than Ida. She never told me how she felt about leaving the ghetto. I guess as long as she was leaving with me she was okay about it. I guess. She liked me you know. We were very close, but she liked me as…well…."

Twenty-Seven

30 April 1943

The sewer system in the city was simply an underground one way street with obstacles as clear as fecal matter and as alarming as gas pellets that the Germans would throw down to kill all living things trying to escape. The main tunnels were two meters wide, and the girls were able to stand with the tops of their heads almost touching the dark brick ceiling. Miriam had joked that Golda Feinbaum, the wife of one of the rabbis in the ghetto, would not have been able to walk upright in the sewers if her life depended on it. Throughout her one year in the ghetto, Golda had maintained a hairdo that stood almost thirty centimeters above her head. No one could understand where and how she could have had her hair done in the ghetto, but she was always seen with that tower. She had been killed by a stray bullet while returning from synagogue with her husband. They also joked that Fat Bundy would have had no trouble in the main sewers, but would have never been able to negotiate the width of the one-meter high offshoots. These tunnels demanded constant bending over or crawling through the muck that had accumulated there. For anyone who had not received an updated map of the trenches, the sewer system, with all its twists and turns, could have been fatal. Many had entered but never found a safe way out; they eventually perished in the filth of Warsaw's communal lavatory.

Ida knew better than anyone that to stay underground for more than necessary was just as dangerous as walking the streets of the ghetto. During the first days of the uprising, hundreds attempted to escape through the sewers, only to be driven out by Nazi fires set at strategic locations within the tunnels. Later, the Germans threw toxic gas candles, grenades and explosive charges into the sewers when they heard movement. Ida and Miriam both knew the trenches well enough to understand that they had to be expeditious and silent – there was a distinct advantage to being only three people; the larger groups were easily heard. This was their world, and they both knew that every extra minute that they spent in the sewer was an extra minute closer to a gruesome death. Miriam planned to reach the Aryan side of the walls, take the first open exit out of the darkness, and reach the first Polish underground contact on Peretz's list. Many of the sewer exits on the Aryan side had either been welded closed or were manned by Polish guards. Polish and Jewish underground units had dug tunnels and alternative exits that the Germans had yet to discover. It was through one of these exits that the girls would attempt to reach the west side of Warsaw.

Less than fifteen minutes after entering the trenches, the girls heard movement and the sloshing of water around a bend in the main sewer line. At first, Anna thought the Germans had opened the dam again, which would have flooded the sewer and drowned them in minutes. But she remembered that the Jewish underground had bombed the dam, and even if that had been an option for the Nazis, the water would have come from behind them, as they were walking with the flow. She then realized that there was someone in the sewer walking toward them, against the current and back into the ghetto.

"Simcha!" said Miriam. She had noticed his distinct features reflecting the dim candlelight.

"Miriam?" replied the voice.

The figure approached the girls and they saw that he was carrying only a lit candle in one hand and a flashlight, off at the time, in the other, and a pistol was stuck into his black belt at his waist. As he reached the girls, he gave them a once over and shook his head. "Look at you three," he said.

"You're going the wrong way? How long have you been down here?" said Miriam.

"I'm returning to the ghetto to convince Mordecai to get out with as many fighters as possible. It's his last chance."

"He won't leave," said Anna. "I tried to convince him as well. He won't leave until he's dead."

"You'll never make it this way," said Ida. This is a dead-end. The entrance we used has been compromised. Go back and try a southern route."

"I have to try and get to the central ghetto. There's an entrance on Mila Street."

"Why are you here alone," asked Miriam. "You don't know these tunnels well enough."

"I had a Polish guide, but the Germans threw a grenade at us back there. He ran away saying I should just stay the course. I was going to pay him, but he won't get anything now."

"Well," said Miriam, "I suggest you turn back. This way is straight into the Germans' hands."

"I'll try one more entrance, and if that doesn't work, I'll come back with a better guide."

"I should help you," said Miriam. "You'll never make it on your own."

"If you three can make it this far on your own, then so can I."

"Don't flatter yourself," said Anna. "We have two of the best navigators in the city. We'll be fine." She turned and faced Miriam. "You're not going back with him. He needs more than what you can offer. We're out of the ghetto, and I need you with us now."

"She's right," said Simcha. "I'll be fine. You need to get these women out of here."

Miriam shook her head but did not object.

"I'll see you in Tel Aviv," he said.

"Be safe," said Miriam.

"You too. Don't turn right at the next crossing. There's a German control point. Get as far west as you can tonight."

"I know," said Miriam. "I've done this before."

"I forgot that you weren't just a fighter," he said.

They all hugged and Simcha went on his way upstream, sloshing the water that was beating his thighs.

They would not make it to the far west side of the city that evening. They had exited after a sharp right turn into a small one-meter high tunnel with sewage up to their knees. Bending over as they walked, their noses almost seemed to touch the putrid water. They had tied scarves around their mouths, but it was too little to keep the stench from driving them mad. Miriam knew one of the only manholes that was neither closed nor guarded. As they finally exited, they each lay on the street gasping for the fresh air. That night they slept in a park, under a tree, in the open, like free people. They knew the risk but used the logic that what Jew would dare sleep out in the open.

This was Anna's first time out of the ghetto since November 1940. As morning broke and they awoke from their first night of freedom, Anna surveyed her surroundings. She knew where she was, but it was not the Warsaw she remembered – and certainly not the Warsaw she had lived in. The streets were empty, there were boarded up shops, and at the end of the block she could see bombed out buildings – a result of the early Luftwaffe bombing of Warsaw in September 1939. Just beyond the rubble, there was a thicket that struck her as beautiful. Most of all, her senses were aroused by the smells of fresh air. The stench that was the ghetto was gone, and she breathed deeply, closing her eyes and parting her lips as she did so. She took a few steps around the park and looked down the bare streets. Where were all the people? she thought. The glow from a sun that must have been stuck behind the thick layer of clouds provided a feeling that someone was turning the lights out on the world. But for Anna, the feeling of freedom overtook her, and as she looked at the street, and then down at the grass under her feet, tears filled her eyes. She was standing on fresh grass for the first time in years. Grass couldn't grow in the ghetto – it was too toxic a place.

"We're out," said Ida who had come up from behind her, placing a hand on her shoulder. "We're done with the ghetto. Look at the trees Anna. Just look at the trees. We haven't seen trees for so long."

Anna turned around and placed both arms around Ida and held tight.

She was so grateful to have her there at that moment and so indebted to her for all she had given to the people in the house. It had begun to sink in that ghetto life was behind them. Although she was well aware that the dangers were still very much a part of their reality, she was free to choose where and when to go. They would still face numerous challenges, but again, she was thankful that Ida was with her – after all, she was the best shot in all of Warsaw.

That morning the girls began their search for the contacts on the list Peretz had given them. Miriam, who didn't seem to trust the list as much as Peretz had, was coming up with her own alternatives if the contacts proved to be too risky or perhaps even dead. In any case, it was agreed that Ida would be the first to approach any of the contacts, as she had the best chance of passing as an Aryan looking for work if trouble were to arise.

The first address on the list belonged to a Polish factory owner who had been active in the underground and, according to Peretz, had been very sympathetic to the Jewish uprising in the ghetto. They found the address easily, but when they arrived, it seemed that the building had been firebombed. The next name on the list was on the far side of town so they decided that they would leave it for later. The third contact just had an address and a note attached that said to knock on the front door after six in the evening and ask for Frankel.

Between walking from address to address, the girls spent most of the day sitting in a back alley next to the park eating the remnants of food they had. By late afternoon, they were planning the rest of their day, hoping they could find more food before sundown. They figured that it would take about thirty minutes to reach Frankel's street, and until they had to leave, they would be safest staying put in the vacant alley, well hidden from Polish Police and German soldiers – although they had seen neither all day. By evening, they were hungry again and had hoped that Frankel would be able to supply them with food as well as passage out of Warsaw.

While Ida went to Frankel's front door, Anna and Miriam hid on the side of the building, pistols ready for action. "You can never be too careful," Anna had said to them before approaching the house. They heard Ida knock and someone inside ask who it was. She said in perfect, accent-free Polish that she was looking for Frankel and the door opened. From the side of the building, Anna and Miriam could see the plumb, round-faced women who stood before Ida. She was wearing an apron and her face was damp as if she had been crying for some time.

"Frankel is gone," said the woman, looking in both directions beyond Ida to see if anyone was watching.

"We were told to come here to find him," said Ida, not realizing she had used the first-person plural.

"We? Who's with you?"

Anna had heard that Frankel was not there, and by the sound of the woman's voice, she seemed scared at hearing that Ida was not alone. Anna decided to leave the side of the building and approach the front door. She took Miriam's hand and walked up behind Ida.

"We are," said Anna. "We need help."

The stout woman with forearms larger than Ida's thighs waved them into the house, and quickly closed the door behind her. She pointed to a room off to the left of the entrance. Anna had almost forgotten what a normal living space looked like. It was clear that this family was well to do and had not skimped during the three years of Nazi occupation, for they seemed to still have all of their furniture – and it was quite an array of items. The room they entered had a red tint from the thick velvet curtains and emulated maroon designs on the flat woven Savonnerie carpets that covered the floor. In the far corner, there was a pair of walnut French Louis XV style elbow armchairs, and on the right, were two Victorian mahogany chairs next to a nineteenth-century antique desk. In the center of the left wall was a Georgian oak antique bureau bookcase. Anna immediately tried to glance at the books behind the glass but was unable to read the titles from her angle.

"Where is Frankel?" asked Ida.

The woman gave a light, quick smirk, wiped her eyes with the back of her hand, and said, "There is no Frankel. I knew I could let you in if you used that code. But what I meant by Frankel is gone is that I don't think I can help you. My men have been captured by the Gestapo and I don't have a safe house any longer. There was another group like you here a few days ago and I sent them to the film factory..."

"The film factory?" asked Anna.

"Yes, it is just outside of the industrial area, and in the attic, there are about twenty of you."

Anna squinted and cocked her head when she heard her say "twenty of you." How did she know who they were? And weren't they on the same side as she was fighting the Germans.

"I can give you directions, but you will have to get there yourselves. It's very dangerous now. Wait until later and leave."

"We want to get to the forests," said Miriam. It occurred to Anna that they were placing a great deal of trust in this woman. What if she was an informant? Perhaps this Frankel fellow had been compromised and she was willing to trade us for him. Anna wondered if they had been saying too much by volunteering information about their destination. But the woman's answer was calming.

"You three? The forest? What, to fight? You barely look like you can walk. Come in and eat. I will tell you about the latest underground activities and what your options are. You will have to leave tonight, for I fear that my men may be tortured and tell the Nazis my whereabouts. I was just cutting some onions for soup. That's why I'm crying." The woman waddled over to the next room. She had auburn hair that had been dyed sometime in the past. Under the handkerchief covering her head, gray roots could be seen along the scalp line.

Just the mention of food calmed their nerves and the meal to follow was the most spectacular they had eaten in years. While serving hot boiled potatoes and onions in thick gravy, broiled whole chickens and smoked meat (the girls feared that it was ham, but were too ravished to ask or care), the woman introduced herself as Wanda as she placed bowls of hot soup in front of each of the girls.

"I am a Polish Catholic who does not believe that the Jews killed Christ," she included. "I have been assisting the underground since the war broke out. I have lots of money. My husband, Frankel, died of heart failure in 1933 – January 30, 1933, to be exact, the day Hitler came to power. Do you have a weapon?"

The girls looked at each other as if wondering whether to disclose the fact that they were armed and then nodded affirmatively.

"Well, I probably bought it for you. The Jewish uprising has helped the Polish cause to no end. By attracting Nazi attention, we have been able to strengthen our ranks in the city. There will be a Polish uprising as well I hope, with the help of the Red Army we can push those bastards back outside the city limits."

"Pardon me asking," said Miriam, "but do you live alone?" There was no one in the house other than the lady, and the amount of food she had given them was a sign that she had been cooking for someone.

"Yes, I'm alone now. My daughters are both married."

"So," asked Miriam, "who was all this food for?"

"You," she said and smiled for the first time. No one asked the obvious question, but she volunteered the answer anyway. "I did not know you were coming. But over the past few weeks, between the Jewish fighters escaping the ghetto and the Polish underground coming by for money, I have had a lot of mouths to feed. There is always food here for the needy – as long as the needy are willing to help kill a Nazi or two."

The girls smiled nervously as they filled their empty stomachs with Wanda's cuisine. Ida and Miriam, in their smuggling tours outside of the ghetto, had each experienced meals like this, but for Anna, it was a first. The food in the ghetto had been sufficient since the January uprising, but it was usually hastily prepared and lacking all flavor – spices were a luxury that was difficult to come by.

"The truth is," said Wanda, "that I was hoping to have a little celebration today, but the Nazi pigs ruined it by capturing some of my best men."

"What's the occ…" Anna stopped herself in mid-sentence, looked over at Ida and Miriam and smiled. "It's May Day! How could we have forgotten."

"Oh my," said Ida.

Miriam just shook her head smiling at the embarrassment. May Day had been one of the most spectacular holidays in Hashomer Hatzair. Before their departure, there had been talk of May Day operations in the ghetto. If the fighters were able to hold on until the first of May, they would have a contest to see how many Germans they could kill on that day. What the girls did not know was that the action had already taken place, and it was a great success. That night, under the most horrifying conditions, where the Jews of Warsaw had made their last stand, their last battle, they gathered in the bunkers and the ghetto fighters of Warsaw sang The Internationale with more feeling and vigor than it had ever been sung. The words, which speak of reshaping mankind and the final battle of good over evil, rang out through the walls of the ghetto and throughout the Jewish world. Socialist fighters – Jewish socialist fighters – were singing their anthem and doing all they could to preserve human dignity in a crumbling world. Somewhere in the back of her mind, Anna realized that she had missed that experience.

"Then we should celebrate," said Anna.

"I'm terribly sorry," said Wanda. "I must respect the men who fell to the enemy today, but I believe that tonight when you reach the warehouse, you will have a little party with some of the other Polish fighters. Communists know how to celebrate on May Day."

The sound of utensils clicking and girls chatting came to an abrupt end when there was a loud knock at the door. It was more of a bang than a knock and the girls froze. So did Wanda, only she was looking at the ceiling as if an answer to who it was would come from God above.

After a very long three seconds, Wanda smiled. "It's your lucky night. We have visitors."

The girls were motionless, each holding their forks and knives dead still as not to make a sound.

"Oh, don't worry," she said. "It's not the Gestapo. They don't knock anymore. Listen." She pointed one finger in the air as if the sound they were

243

to hear was coming from the light fixture above the table. There was only silence. Then, as if ordered, a bird chirped three times.

"It's night," said Anna. "Birds don't chirp at night."

"Right," said Wanda. "It's your lucky night. We have visitors." She got up from the table and wobbled out of the dining room toward the front door.

Ida was the only one to return to eating after Wanda stepped out of the room. Both Miriam and Anna strained to listen to the voices from the entry hall.

There was silence again after they heard the door shut, the lock turn and Wanda shuffle across the floor.

"It's your lucky day," said Wanda as she entered the dining room. "That was Joziak. I thought he had been captured today. He and a comrade of his, I forget his name, but he can be trusted, will come and get you in one hour. They will take you to an abandoned warehouse outside of Warsaw. You will spend the night there. Tomorrow, weather permitting, you will be taken to Lomianki forests. You should be able to make contact with the partisans you are looking for there. But we'll have to get you all a change of clothes. You look wretched. Okay? Now finish eating."

The girls looked at each other. All three had expressed one form of skepticism or another regarding the list that Peretz had received from the Polish representative, but it turned out to have supplied at least one perfect contact – as long as this woman was not plotting to turn them in and grab a hefty reward in the process. But the girls would not allow themselves to think that way. They had no choice but to trust Wanda, for she was all they had at the moment, and her food was delicious.

When there was a knock on the door again, exactly one hour to the minute following the previous knock, the girls were ready to go.

"May I give you a hug, Wanda?" asked Anna as they all stood at the open door.

"I would not have let you go without one."

Anna placed her petit, poor excuse for a bag on the floor and wrapped her arms around Wanda. Wanda almost swallowed her up, with her bulky arms and round body engulfing every part of Anna. Anna felt a warmth that she hadn't experienced since she was a little girl as her body was pulled into Wanda's pillow-like torso. No one since her mother had hugged her like that. With all Wanda's size and mass, the hug was gentle, as if not to break the fragile little child that Anna was to her.

"You are brave and glorious girls," said Wanda as she released Anna. "I always knew that the Jews were not what those Fascists said about them, but I never imagined people with such courage. Be well, my children."

Anna thought about what a magnificent woman was standing before her. Obviously rich and in no need to help anyone, she was risking her life daily to promote the cause she believed in.

Ida and Miriam followed Anna in hugging Wanda, and as they left the threshold of the magnificent home, Anna was sure that she saw a tear run down Wanda's stout cheek. Anna turned around and whispered goodbye. Wanda wiggled her fingers in the air and smiled as she waved.

The girls were being led by two men in worn black coats with obvious bulges in them. Miriam was the first to ask what they were packing.

"We are well equipped," said the tall, thin man with shoes that looked two sizes too large. He had an awkward walk as if his leg had been injured – or perhaps he was just compensating for the oversized shoes.

"I'm Miriam, and this is Ida and Anna." They had been walking in silence for two blocks since leaving the house.

"I'm Henryk and this is Joziak. We're Gwardia Ludowa."

"Your Communists," said Anna. She turned to Ida and Miriam. "The Gwardia Ludowa has been a great help to the Jewish underground."

"Yes," said Joziak. "We're Communists."

"We're Socialists," said Anna.

"Good enough," said Joziak and laughed.

"Have you been working with the Red Army?" asked Ida.

"Yes, when we can," said Joziak. "It's hard to get word to them, but I have a feeling they'll be back here soon enough."

"And what, may I ask, is that feeling based on?" asked Ida.

Joziak looked over at Henryk as if asking permission to answer the question. Joziak had large eyes and wore his wool cap low over his forehead. His coat was far too small on him and the weapon looked like a third upper appendage under his left arm. It was clear that his weapon was a rifle, and not a pistol, although, by the looks of the bulge in his hip, he seemed to have one of those as well.

"The Germans have made a tactical error," said Joziak. "They are spread too thin, and if they keep moving into Russia, the Soviets will just wait for the cold to kill them."

"That's where we come in," interrupted Henryk. "We have to make it as difficult as possible for them to get supplies to their forces in the front."

"We're taking you," continued Joziak, "to the place where you can do the most damage."

"The Lomianki forests?" asked Anna.

"No, that's just a stop. From there you will have to make your way to the Wyszkow forests in the northeast – not far from Lodz. We have a division there that had already incorporated some of the Jews who have escaped the ghettos. Some from Warsaw as well."

"We need to get to Lodz?"

"Not right away," he said. "Tonight we'll sleep just out of the city and tomorrow will drive to the forest. First, you'll be able to help around here." Lomianki was only a few hours northwest of Warsaw, but if they were going to walk it would have taken several days. The roads were well guarded and they would have only been able to travel at night.

"I understand you have documents," said Henryk.

"Yes," said Ida. "They are from the best forgers in Poland."

"You two will have no problem," said Henryk pointing over to Ida and Miriam who were walking to his right, "but she may be questioned. How's your Catholic knowledge?"

"I don't know many prayers," said Anna, "but I have some information."

He pulled a deco flapper cloche hat that looked like it had come from a pre-war dancing saloon out of the knapsack he was carrying. The horsehair woven, beige ribbed hat looked unworn. "Take this."

Anna looked at the hat as if she had been given a new weapon to use on her enemies. Without hesitation, she placed the hat on her head and tucked in the brown hair that stuck out of the back. Miriam and Ida began to laugh, and Anna, who had never worn anything of the type, blushed – although no one was able to see her rouge cheeks due to the dim lighting.

"Going to dance for us?" asked Ida, putting her arm around Anna.

"You look Aryan already," said Henryk. "We're here."

The men stopped in front of a boarded-up building on the corner of two disturbingly empty streets. It looked as if the area had once been a bustling commerce center, but was now just a façade of boarded and closed buildings. Down to the left of them, the street ended in a pile of rubble that had once been the five-story building whose absence had left a conspicuously large gap between the buildings on the street.

Henryk pulled out an iron rod from his coat.

"Where was he hiding that?" asked Miriam.

"I wonder what else he has down there?" said Ida.

Joziak gave Henryk a hand removing the boards covering the entrance to the building in front of them, and behind the temporary wooden paneling, easily removed with the help of the crowbar, stood a black truck with a large V on the bonnet. It was a Volvo LV76, with an open bed in the back and room for three in the front. The vehicle was shabby and damaged, with scratches and dents all around its body. For a car that was eight years old, it had been through a great deal. The Swedish cars, although accustomed to tough winters, were not as strong as the German or French vehicles. Later versions of this same truck had enhanced chassis components, stronger axles and suspension and double mounted rear wheels. Mechanically, this car was known to be quite reliable due primarily to its simplicity.

Anna knew nothing about cars but wasted no time expressing her concern about their new mode of transportation. "This thing will get us out of the city?"

"Don't judge. This is our best friend. We've had no trouble with it, and it's even been shot at by German snipers," said Henryk.

"But they missed," added Joziak.

"Where will we sit?" asked Miriam, now walking in toward the car and looking inside the open window.

"In back," said Henryk. "We'll cover you with tarps. You'll be fine."

The men went around to the back of the room where the car had been hidden. There was hardly enough space to pass the black automobile and reach the can of gasoline that sat on the ground in the corner. Inside, it was rather dark, the only light coming from a street lamp across the road and Henryk's flashlight. The men opened the can and poured the entire contents of gasoline into the truck. Joziak entered the driver's seat and sat behind the wheel. The sound of the ignition switch clicking and the engine turning over without igniting the fuel broke the relative silence in the bleak neighborhood. The truck did not start on the first attempt, but on the second, the grinding of the gears and the chuck-chuck-chuck of the Swedish engine was finally heard. Within seconds, the room had filled with black exhaust and Joziak rolled the truck out into the street to avoid carbon monoxide poisoning. Henryk pulled the tarp off of the truck bed and signaled to the girls to get in. Anna and Ida climbed in over the back bumper, but as Miriam moved to join them, Henryk grabbed her arm and said, "You come in front."

Miriam looked into the bed of the truck at her friends, and Anna nodded approvingly. She walked to the passenger side and entered the cabin, sandwiched between the two Polish communists. Anna was happy to be alone with Ida, although she doubted the roar of the engine and the wind would allow them much opportunity to talk. They were sitting with their backs to the cabin, looking rearward as they left Warsaw behind them. Anna wondered if she would ever be back.

"This has been too easy," yelled Ida above the chatter and clinking of the beat-up truck.

"You said it yourself. We're out of the ghetto. I don't for a minute believe that it will remain easy, but we will reach the forests – I am sure of that."

Ida kissed Anna on the cheek and laid her head on her shoulder. The wind blew Ida's hair across her face, while the tight-fitting hat held Anna's in place.

Soon after the truck left the neighborhood, Ida and Anna fell asleep not far from where they had picked up the old truck. They were awoken by the silence that met them when the engine finally stopped churning and the metal bed of the truck finally stopped bouncing and banging against their bottoms. Soon the doors swung open, and Anna noticed that she had both her arms tightly around Ida. The wind had chilled them as the thin green tarp was not enough to keep them warm. Ida awoke when the door slammed shut again, and Miriam stuck her head over the side of the truck bed and smiled.

"Have a nice ride?" she asked.

"Were they gentlemen?" retorted Anna.

"Quite. They even had some interesting stories about making weapons. Rachel would have enjoyed them."

"Hello, Comrades!" bellowed a voice from the doorway to the warehouse. The building in front of them was three stories high and had no windows until halfway up the second floor. The metal caging bolted onto the outside of each of the windows seemed to be a precaution against break-ins but looked more like something preventing escape from within. The two-door doorway was midway between the sides of the building and was flanked by two heavy metal cargo doors. The man so excited to see them was waving his arms frantically around while barreling down the four concrete stairs that led to the threshold entrance.

"Who's that?" asked Ida.

Joziak smiled and faced the girls, "That's Abrasha. He's absolutely wacko. Should be institutionalized."

"He must be," said Miriam, "he's a Jew hanging out with this lot."

"I guess that would make us crazy, wouldn't it?" said Joziak. "Hanging out with a Jew can be quite dangerous to your health."

"Hello, hello, hello," he said. "It's a perfect pleasure to see you. Please let me look at the stupendous fighters of the ghetto lands, forgotten by God himself." The man walked right up to Miriam and gave her a huge hug. She never let her arms leave her side as he twisted her around in a dance. Then, grabbing her shoulders and holding her at arm's length in front of him, looking her over from head to toe, he yelled, "You are divine. So divine!"

"Yes," said Joziak, "He's crazy, but he's the greatest navigator I've ever met."

Anna and Ida looked at each other and then at the wild image of the man who had attacked Miriam. He spoke fluent Polish but had a strange accent that they could not place.

"Let me introduce myself," he continued, releasing Miriam and placing both hands inside the bed of the truck trying to grab hold of any part of either Ida's or Anna's body. He finally found Anna's wrist and held it tight with both hands. "My name is Abrasha Kleinman. I am originally from a small village near Lodz that I am sure you have never heard of, so I will spare you the details. I have been a highly successful liaison between the partisans in the Wyszkow forests and ghetto Lodz. I have smuggled more weapons into Lodz than anyone else, and now I have come here to bring the Wyszkow partisans some well-needed reinforcements…you. I am your ticket in, and without me, you will find yourselves alone in the forest fighting not only the Germans but the even less sympathetic elements led by Mother." They all gave him a puzzled look. "That's Mother Nature, my gorgeous new friends."

Abrasha Kleinman looked like an emaciated version of a Polish businessman. He wore an old pinstriped suit that seemed to have grown out of him – he was far too thin to fill its shape. His brown hair was unruly, long in front and pushed to one side. He continuously moved his bangs off his forehead. He had long sharp features, from his pointy nose to his twig-like fingers, and his height made him look even ganglier than he really was. Like so many others the girls were used to seeing, he seemed to have lost a great deal of weight over the past few years of serving the cause.

"Let's get you out of this nasty mode of transportation," said the gauche man to Anna and Ida who were still in the back of the truck. "I'm sure you're famished. We have stew and brew inside, and we'll have plenty of time to talk about life on the roads while you enjoy our makeshift May Day festivities. I have many wonderful adventures to share."

Ida whispered to Anna, "This is going to be a long journey."

"He's cute. Humor him," said Anna.

"Come now," said Abrasha. "There's much party left, and we are quite short on women to dance with." Miriam rolled her eyes.

Anna, Ida and Miriam were brought into the warehouse where they would be spending the next twenty-four hours before heading out to the forests the next evening. The large room had been used as storage for a paper mill and it still had several reams of paper scattered around the side. The Polish underground had been using it as a safe house due to its remote location, far from any main roads or residential areas. The rest of the industrial area had been abandoned since the early part of the war. Most of the factories had been moved into a more suitable location, which for the Germans meant closer to railroad lines.

The room had been stocked with two long wooden tables, several chairs and crates, used both for additional seating and storage of supplies.

Along the far walls were mattresses covered with bedding, and alongside each bed was a small bag.

"Welcome to your new home. Let me introduce you to the men," said Abrasha. Five men had been playing cards at the long wooden table, and as soon as Abrasha and the girls entered the room, they stood, as if their reward had just arrived. Two other men had been lying on their mattresses reading books. They too stood and began walking toward the guests. "My good people, this is…"

"Anna," said Anna.

"Ida," said Ida.

"Miriam," said Miriam.

"Right, and these are the glorious fighters of the Gwardia Ludowa – except me of course. I'm Jewish," he said quietly while blocking his lips from the fighters' view. "They don't accept Jews in the Gwardia Ludowa."

Almost in unison, the men said hello.

With Joziak and Henryk, there were nine men and three women who would be spending the next few days together. The ghetto women were used to spending cramped quarters with men, but not with men they had never met and could not easily trust. Yes, these were fighters, but they were Polish – except for Abrasha, who was nuts – and that made for a tense evening.

But the men did their best to accommodate the tired ghetto fighters and quickly arranged a corner for them to lie down. There was no music at this party, so Abrasha's threat to have them dance with the men was idle – so they thought. The girls placed their small packs next to the three mattresses and blankets that had been put into the far corner of the factory and returned to the center of the room where the cards were being dealt and the Polish beer was being poured.

None of the three had had a drink of beer since entering the ghetto. Miriam confessed that prior to the war she used to enjoy a lager from time to time, but rarely had the chance. Ida said she had never tasted beer – just wine and whatever it was the Peretz had given them. The men wasted no time rinsing a few glasses in a small sink near the entrance to the room and giving Anna, Ida and Miriam each a glass of beer.

"Where did you get this?" asked Anna.

"Oh, we've been saving it for tonight," said a man with a receding hairline, who looked to be in his forties, but was most likely just aged from the war. "This is the last of it. But there are still several breweries working in Poland. The Germans need their beer. They are German factories because Polish beer isn't good enough for them."

"I must admit," said Abrasha, "I had rarely indulged in alcoholic poison until I met up with this bunch of drunks. They have opened my eyes to the joys of the brew. I remember when I was trying to return to Lodz after a remarkable little trek…"

"We don't want to hear it now, Abrasha," said a small man with a pudgy nose and a bright red shirt.

"Ah, yes, yes. Not now, no," said Abrasha. "Let us hear of the uprising in the ghetto. What stories have you for us?"

Anna looked down at the table as to avert eye contact with any of the men. They were all staring now, awaiting the report that Anna did not feel like giving. It was Miriam who rescued her.

"What is it you want to hear? A lot has happened there. It's quite horrendous."

"How are the fighters fairing?" asked the balding man.

Miriam went on to tell the men what had been happening in the ghetto since the 18th of April. She told of the heroics of the women who gave their lives to smuggle in weapons; she told them how the bunkers were built; and she told them how the Germans were firebombing the buildings one by one. She left little to the imagination, describing burning bodies replacing starving ones on the streets of the ghetto, obfuscating only those details that she assumed these men could never comprehend. She even told them how the Gestapo had executed a woman and her young daughter in front of her father who was accused of being a ghetto fighter. The Polish fighters, who had surely received some information from the ghetto, were stunned beyond the ability to speak. Ida was sitting at the end of the table crying.

Abrasha was the first to utter a word after Miriam finished telling of their escape from the ghetto and the guilt they felt leaving their comrades to die the most gruesome of deaths.

"This is why we are fighting the Nazi slime. This is why we must maintain our strength and keep hitting them again and again until we are victorious. Today is a day to celebrate the workers' cause. We must drink to those courageous fighters who are right now giving their lives just to save face." He raised his glass, but no one followed.

Anna was still looking down at the table. Miriam's report was difficult to hear and brought back the feeling that they had abandoned their friends at such a critical time. All she could think about was what were her comrades doing now? How was Mordecai fairing? Had Simcha convinced him to leave the ghetto? Or had he even reached the ghetto? Where were Peretz and Rachel? She pictured Rachel running through the rubble, pistol in one hand, grenade in the other, finding charges that had not exploded and fixing them. Then her thoughts turned to Tuvia, her beloved Tuvia, who had given his life to save hers. Miriam had left out his sacrifice while recalling the story of their escape.

One of the men suddenly stood and placed his hands to his side and began singing:

> Arise, ye workers from your slumber,
> Arise, ye prisoners of want.

He was singing the Internationale, and slowly, one by one the nine men and three women in the room stood with him and joined in the song.

> *For reason in revolt now thunders,*
> *And at last ends the age of cant!*
> *Away with all your superstitions,*
> *Servile masses, arise, arise!*
> *We'll change henceforth the old*
> *tradition,*
> *And spurn the dust to win the prize!*
>
> *So comrades, come rally,*
> *And the last fight let us face.*
> *The Internationale,*
> *Unites the human race.*
>
> *So comrades, come rally,*
> *And the last fight let us face.*
> *The Internationale,*
> *Unites the human race.*

Anna could see that some of the men were weeping quietly. Their shoulders twitched, their mouths curled back and tears ran down their weary faces. Anna began to sing louder, now believing that these men could be trusted. By the time they reached the second stanza, their voices were so loud and powerful, and the echo in the warehouse was so great, that it felt like they were an army of hundreds. The words took on new meaning as they sang of the battles they'd had and the battles to come:

> *No more deluded by reaction,*
> *On tyrants only we'll make war!*
> *The soldiers too will take strike*
> *action,*
> *They'll break ranks and fight no*
> *more!*
> *And if those cannibals keep trying,*
> *To sacrifice us to their pride,*
> *They soon shall hear the bullets*
> *flying,*
>
> *We'll shoot the generals on our own*
> *side.*
>
> *So comrades, come rally,*
> *And the last fight let us face.*
> *The Internationale,*
> *Unites the human race.*
>
> *So comrades, come rally,*
> *And the last fight let us face.*
> *The Internationale,*
> *Unites the human race.*

Twenty-Eight

Yaakov looked into the large rear-view that enabled him to see every passenger on the bus – except Anna who was at his feet humming the Internationale. Two men were arguing in the back of the bus.

"Should I go see what the fuss is?" asked Rami.

"No, don't bother," said Yaakov. "Neither of them seem armed."

"You don't have to be armed to cause harm," said Anna without looking up from her seat in the stairwell and returning to her humming. After a short pause, she said, "Did I ever tell you about the time we…"

"Did you ever tell me? We've only known each other for an hour. How could you have ever told me anything?"

"I guess I feel like we've known each other forever. I feel close to you. Isn't that all right? Can't I feel close to you?" Anna stared at him.

"Yes, you can feel close to me," he said mockingly. "And you've probably told me whatever it was you wanted to tell me since you haven't stopped talking since you sat down."

"I beg your pardon," she said. "This conversation has been for both our benefits. You've asked me more than your share of questions, and if I'm not mistaken, you've taken quite an interest in my answers. So hush up. My students never talk to me like that."

"Your students? So you're a teacher? You haven't mentioned that."

"Yes I did. Just a few minutes ago. You're not even listening! Of course I'm a teacher. Well I was for a while. What else could I do? I have a lot of knowledge and love telling people about it."

"Yes, I know."

Anna glared at him.

"Okay, go ahead and tell me whatever it was you were going to say before."

"Never mind."

"Now you're insulted?" said Yaakov.

"No, You couldn't possibly insult me. When I start feeling insulted I just consider the source."

"And what's that supposed to mean? If you're trying to insult me…"

"If I wanted to insult you, I wouldn't have to try very hard. You are a very sensitive person."

"How do you know that?"

"I'm rather intuitive," she said. Rami was once again leaning forward in his seat trying to listen in on the conversation. "And I too am a very sensitive person. I know when people take things harder than they need to."

"Well, I would never insult you either," he said. "I do respect everything that you've been through. I myself remember very little, and what I do remember is a bit blurred."

"What do you remember?" she asked, then continued humming.

"Firstly, if you want to hear my answer, stop humming the Internationale."

"I didn't realize that you recognized it. I'm impressed, Yaakov."

"We sing it every May Day in the mossad."

"The mossad, you mean your school. I always found it odd that the Hashomer Hatzair kibbutzim called their schools mossad, an institution. Were you institutionalized?"

"Very funny."

"I'm sorry, go ahead, tell me what you remember."

Yaakov paused. "Forget it, I don't remember anything really."

"Come off it. You have to remember something."

"Not really. I remember the boat trip here. The first time I saw the shores of this country," he said, "I was looking at them from underneath a tarp. The boat was crowded and people were getting sick. I didn't understand what was going on. There were other children on the boat, but I didn't talk to them. I don't think I could talk to them. I only spoke Polish and they were from all over Europe. Now, years later, I understand that it was illegal immigration, and we were trying to avoid the British. But back then, as a small child, it was a game. They just put us on rafts in the middle of the night, and in the morning we were at a youth village. It was terrifying. Before that, I don't remember much at all. I know I was with a family somewhere. I remember a little girl with huge blue eyes and ponytails. I remember she used to hug me all the time. I remember feeling safe with her."

"Why did you need to feel safe?"

"Because I had seen my family get..." Yaakov stopped as he looked into the rearview mirror and noticed that the entire front half of the bus was listening in on their conversation. "They used to make buses louder," he said aloud.

"What's that?" asked Anna. "What about loud buses?"

"Nothing. Let's forget it. Can I just have some quiet now?"

"Suit yourself. You're the one who keeps talking all the time." Yaakov gave her a dirty look and Rami laughed.

"Yes, well, there are things I'm not going to talk about if it's okay with you."

"And if it's not okay with me?"

"Even if it's not okay with you."

Twenty-Nine

3 May 1943

When Anna jumped off the back of the truck, she was immediately surrounded by three children who looked up at her like she had just landed from the moon.

"Are you from Warsaw," said a girl who came up to Anna's chest. She was wearing a flowered skirt and had surely been well fed over the past few months. None of the children looked underfed by any means. "I was from Warsaw," continued the girl, "but now I live in the family camp."

A smaller girl with huge blue eyes and a ribbon in her golden hair smiled up at Anna. "I saw the moon last night," she said. "It looked big. Did you see the moon?"

Anna had seen the moon. They began driving at ten in the evening and the moon was low in the sky and orange. Anna recalled how her father had told her, sometime between the Great War and the Nazi war, that an orange moon means that there is a war going on somewhere. When she was a child, Anna was sure that there was always a war going on somewhere. Later, she would use Marxist deduction to comprehend why the moon was orange so often. "I did see the moon," said Anna. "It was beautiful."

"It was orange," said the girl with the big eyes. "That means there is a war going on somewhere."

Anna gasped.

"What's your name?" asked Ida, who had also jumped out of the truck.

"I'm Miriam," said the girl in the flowered dress. She was holding the hand of the girl with the blue eyes, she raised her arms and added, "This is Sarah and that's Ruth."

"Well," said Ida, "I'm Ida and this is Anna. See that girl over there. Her name is Miriam too. She'll be happy to hear that there is another Miriam here. It will make her feel at home." The little Miriam smiled and showed her missing front teeth.

Little Miriam and big Miriam would turn out to be good company for each during the few short weeks that the girls would spend in the Lomianki forest, their first stop on the way to their subsequent destination, the Wyszkow forests. There was something, Anna thought, in sharing a name that brought people closer. Anna never saw Miriam as the type who enjoyed children, but that was because other than Yehuda who was just a small baby, Anna never saw Miriam around children.

Anna felt her heart race as she looked at the small girls gazing up at her. Two things amazed Anna as she glanced around her new home in the middle of the Polish forest: First, the number of children – or just the fact that there were children; and second, that everyone was armed, except the children; some carrying 7.65 German Mausers, other Czech or Belgian pistols, and she even saw an American Colt. Then there were the guns that she didn't recognize, weapons that had not found their way into the ghetto: There were rifles from the Red Army, as well as a Machine Gun that had been captured in a raid on a traveling German unit – Anna recognized that since it had been pointed at her on several occasions. If there were children in the camp, perhaps there was one particular child. The thought would never leave her mind, and she knew that the first question she would ask every person she met in the camp would be, "Have you seen a woman name Hanna with a boy named Yehuda?"

Their ride had taken over ten hours, not because of the distance – the Lomianki forests were just outside of Warsaw – but due to the need to take treacherous back roads and stop every few kilometers to make sure there were no approaching German or Polish patrols. They had traveled through the Polish countryside, passing agrestic landscapes and rustic farms. At one time, Anna could smell what she imagined was bread baking as they drove past one of the old Polish farms. They finally arrived at dawn, with Ida swearing that she would not get back into that "rolling torture machine" again unless it was taking her to Palestine.

The Family Camp in the forest was one of three enclaves in a region full of partisans – both Polish and Jewish – who had gathered with the sole commonality of irritating the Nazis (they would have enjoyed destroying the Nazis outright, but they disagreed over goals and visions). Family camps existed primarily as a refuge for European Jews, whereas the partisan units were created to disrupt the Germans. These congeries of fighters were from such varied backgrounds that had they not had a mutual enemy they would have most likely killed each other (and eventually they did). It was a felicitous reward for the girls to be able to spend these few weeks here, as they deserved to be far from the horrors of the ghetto. The calm of the forest was noticeably apparent on the well-fed faces of the children in their flowery, but filthy, garments. Anna thought that this would be the perfect place to lick their wounds, both emotional and physical, before moving on to more battles. However, the docile atmosphere abruptly changed when a young man found Anna and ask her before she had a chance to ask him if she knew a woman named Hanna.

"Hanna! What do you know?" she said, snatching his hand from his stomach where it had been waiting to be moved somewhere.

"She's on the other side of the camp."

The speed in which Anna pulled the young man's arm and ran in the direction he had signaled not only startled him but everyone within a twenty-meter radius of them. She needed him to lead her, but she was moving too fast; he was yelling directions while being dragged.

"What happened?" yelled Ida.

"It's Hanna!" she shrieked as she was moving away from their camp.

Ida looked down at Miriam lying on her back on her mattress, dropped the blanket she was folding and ran after Anna. Miriam tried to get up but tripped over the very blanket that Ida had dropped in her path and in doing so, slammed her knee against a rock. Not to be left behind, she picked herself up and limped off after them.

Had Anna been looking around, she would have noticed how large and well-stocked the camp was: there were tents and campfires, piles of wood and stacks of boxes that contained food and other needed supplies. Had Anna paid any attention to the hinterland she would have noticed a radio transmitter with two men listening in on an Allied conversation, she would have seen the girl milking a cow and four Jewish fighters cleaning their guns. And, had she been at all attentive to her surroundings on her way to Hanna, she would have noticed the four women cleaning bullets and singing songs of Eretz Yisrael. But she saw none of that. In her mind, Anna didn't even see Hanna; she was looking for Yehuda. So when she finally reached the part of the camp where the person to which she had entrusted the well-being of her son was sitting and talking to two men Anna didn't know, she stopped cold at the sight of Hanna.

The Hanna sitting on the log didn't recognize who had been running toward her at first, although she had noticed them coming from far off. When Anna finally saw who was sitting in front of her, she let the man's arm drop to his side, as did both of her arms. Her shoulders drooped, and she looked back at the man she had been dragging through the forest. She shook her head and said, "I never asked you what she looked like."

Hanna got up slowly as soon as she realized that Anna was staring at her. "Anna? Anna Kapalevitz from Hashomer? I heard you were here! How wonderful to see you."

Anna tried to conjure up all her remaining energy to act even remotely excited to see this Hanna. Yes, it was a Hanna, but not her Hanna, and more importantly, not her Yehuda. Hanna Klein had been a co-counselor with Anna in the summer programs on the kibbutzim in the forests. She, unlike Anna's Hanna, had dark hair and brown eyes – not with the ability to change colors like Hanna's. This Hanna was plump, both in features and in figure, and it was clear to Anna that she had not lost one kilo the entire war. Lucky her. How did she avoid the ghetto? Anna thought.

257

Ida and Miriam eventually caught up with her and consoled her, to Hanna's dismay, in finding the wrong Hanna. They all exchanged formalities with Hanna, who was still very excited to see a familiar face, all the while Anna was dying to leave that part of the forest and return with Ida and Miriam. Anna walked back through the bustling forest holding hands with Ida and Miriam. This time, while walking slowly, she began to notice her surroundings. She could hear Yiddish, Polish with a distinctly Aryan inflection, and even what she thought was Russian. She noticed the many campfires with tripods and huge metal pots smoldering over them. She even stopped to admire the document copier, the type that had been used to put out the underground papers in the ghetto. As she approached her section of the forest, she saw the long table, like in their summer camps, where they were to eat their meals and later discuss strategy, divide responsibilities and sing songs through the night. Anna noticed everything, but since she was still nursing her disappointment, she had a hard time getting enthused by it. Later, when she would relax from finding the wrong Hanna, she would start to understand that she was in a new world. This was the type of place she could learn to love. And she would never stop asking people if they knew a Hanna, a blonde Hanna.

When they returned to their part of the woods, little Miriam and her two friends were waiting for them. At first, they wanted to know why Anna had run off like that. They saw the whole episode, and it intrigued them.

"I thought an old friend was there," she told the little girls while running her fingers through Sarah's hair.

"What's your friend's name?" asked Ruth.

"Hanna," she said.

"And Hanna wasn't there?" asked Miriam.

"There was a Hanna there, but it wasn't my Hanna."

"Is your Hanna pretty," asked Ruth.

"Yes, I suppose she's pretty."

"As pretty as Miriam?" asked little Miriam, smiling at big Miriam.

"No one is as pretty as Miriam," said Anna.

"I think you're pretty too," said Sarah.

That evening, big Miriam let little Miriam braid her hair. Little Miriam's locks were too short to braid, and as she slowly placed one thick strand of hair over the other, she told big Miriam how she was never going to cut her hair again. Big Miriam's hair was not nearly as full as it had been before the war. Malnutrition had taken its toll, and although her hair was still down to the small of her back, the resulting braid was about half its original width. Of course, that did not keep little Miriam from enjoying her work on big Miriam's mane. And big Miriam enjoyed having someone run their fingers through her hair. She sat with her eyes shut as the little girl with no front teeth slowly weaved the braid with resolve and dedication to the task.

The camps were mixed with Poles and Jews, and although the families were all Jewish, the partisans protecting them were well integrated. Anna found that strange at first, although she admitted to Ida that she liked the idea that socialists from different movements and nationalities could share such an experience. But as Henryk would tell them, these unions were not without conflict, and most of the camp's occupants, both Jews and Poles, were not socialists. Many of the Poles in the camps had grown up in anti-Semitic homes and were not as open as their partners in the forest were led to believe. Their inveterate prejudice became apparent on occasion, and as hard as they tried, they could not dissimulate their true feelings. Since they were there to serve the Polish cause of ridding their homeland of the German invaders, they kept their mouths shut and went about their duties, for the most part ignoring the fact that they were sharing food and weapons with Jews. But on occasion, when something tiny would get under their skin, they would throw out an anti-Semitic remark that would lead to an ensuing verbal brawl – usually between the instigator and his commanding officer, as if rank had any weight whatsoever among them.

That first evening, when the children had all fallen asleep and the fires were burning low as not to attract attention – although it was clear to Anna that had the Germans been looking for them, it would have taken nothing to find this lot – Abrasha called Ida and Anna over to the dining table, which consisted of three long boards of wood on tripod legs surrounded by wooden benches and tree stumps to sit on. Big Miriam had fallen asleep next to little Miriam a few tents over – that's how close they were becoming.

"It is time to break free of the doldrums of forest laundering," said Abrasha. "The camp next to us is planning a raid tonight and we want to know if you want in." Each family camp was dependent on a partisan camp for protection. Many of the fighters that the women had seen were actually from the adjacent partisan camp.

Anna and Ida looked at each other. They were there, among other things – such as saving their skin – to help fight, so why not join the raid. Ida's marksmanship would be greatly appreciated, and another hand to assist was always beneficial. But Anna was tired and felt that it was too early for them to start this kind of activity.

"I think we need another day or so," said Anna. "We just got here. I need a good night's sleep. What do you think, Ida?"

Ida didn't direct her answer to Abrasha but whispered to Anna, "I want to go, but I'm not going without you."

"What's the mission?" asked Anna, still unsure of whether it was a good idea.

"Here now are the brave men and women that will be leading the great deputation. My valiant comrades," he said, turning to the people standing an arms length behind him. "This is Anna and Ida. They may be of use to you."

Three men and one woman moved to sit around the table with Abrasha, Ida and Anna. The men all wore what looked like old Polish military uniforms, while the woman was dressed in black pants and khaki vest over a flannel shirt. They all were carrying rifles.

"Misha," said the first man to sit at the table.

"Hans," said the second.

"Levi," said the third, quite inaudibly.

"Tova," said the only girl in the group.

"Now that we are all good friends," said Abrasha, "Anna here was inquiring as to the nature of the operation."

"We're going to blow up telephone lines," said Misha, whose frail appearance made Anna think he was not quite up for walking, let alone a mission. Judging by the fact that none of the others even made a move to speak, Anna assumed that Misha was in charge, so she directed her questions to him.

"How would we be involved?" she inquired.

"I don't know. What can you do?"

"They sew," said Abrasha sarcastically. "What the hell do you think they do? They are experienced ghetto fighters. They were instrumental in setting up and pulling off the January uprising, as well as the one that is still burning bright in the ghetto. These are fighters!"

"Thank you, Abrasha, but it's a legitimate question. I am a sniper," said Ida, turning to Misha. "But this doesn't look like the kind of job where my expertise would be useful. And we just got here. I think we need some time to adjust…and rest."

Hans, who looked more German than any of them, whispered something to the dark-haired Misha.

Misha nodded and looked back at Ida. "Yes, that's what we thought. We'll keep you in mind for the next operation. Meanwhile, maybe get onto the guard duty list. We need more guards here. The camp is growing and night can be dangerous."

The four got up from the table, turned around and left without as much as a nod.

"What was that?" asked Ida.

"Well," said Abrasha, "had I known that you were not up for the task, I wouldn't have called them over. I sincerely apologize. You will let me know when you are ready to fight again, will you?" And he rose to leave. The disappointment in his voice perturbed Anna, and she was not going to let it go. Not today.

"Wait," said Anna. "You asked them over here well before you ever asked us what our plans were."

"Your plans, I so erroneously presumed, were to fight the Nazis at the first opportunity. This was it. Now I do apologize, and I don't hold it against you even for a moment. I know you will join us in all the glorious battles that await these troops, but for now, just accept my apology and let me be on my way. For you mustn't interpret my rude departure as anything other than a desperate need by a desperate man to relieve himself – and not a moment too soon. Fare thee well tonight. We will continue this transaction of thought in the morn." He trotted off toward the woods.

"If he had to go so badly, why did he babble on like that," said Ida.

"Verbal diarrhea," said Anna. And for a moment they laughed.

But their jubilation was short-lived and the subject of the evening activities was far from over; as soon as Miriam returned the next morning from her sleep with little Miriam and heard what had transpired, she made it known to the two of them what a mistake they had made. Of course, long before Miriam had had her say, Anna's conscience had its say. Anna could not sleep that night, thinking about how they had passed up an important opportunity to fit in. They had been asked to help the cause; so what if they were tired. Anna was up a good portion of the night distraught with herself. I should have been there. I should have gone on that raid. There was no good excuse to "wait for a better raid," as she had told Ida afterward. Now what will they think of us, and how will we regain the trust of those fighters – as glum as they were?

"Has this pastoral forest made you lose your mind?" said Miriam. "You passed up an opportunity to join a raid? Are you insane? Damn it! Why didn't you call me? Why didn't you come to get me? You knew I would have gone. This is why we're here. This is why I left the ghetto. I knew I shouldn't have gotten so close to that..."

"Stop. You may be right about the raid, but don't blame it on little Miriam," said Anna. "She's just a little girl who needs you right now. Don't blame her."

"Fine, you're right about Miriam, but I didn't come here to be a babysitter. I came here to fight. I came here to push the damn Nazis out of my country..."

"Your former country," corrected Anna.

"Well, as long as I don't have a new one, this is still my country. Damn you. You knew I would have gone. That's it, isn't it? You knew I

261

would have gone and that's why you didn't call me. Damn you."

"You're right, Miriam," said Ida. "I did know you would have gone, and I wanted to go as well. But…"

"I had a feeling about this job, Miriam," said Anna. "It wasn't right for us."

It was two hours later when Anna would discover what that feeling was. The group that had gone to blow up the phone lines had taken horses from the camp. They rode two on a horse through the countryside to a spot over thirty kilometers away from the camp. As they set up the charges, a farmer spotted them. He wasted no time opening fire on them and attracting a Polish police patrol, who in turn contacted a German guard unit not far from the farm. Within a few minutes, they had been surrounded by German and Polish patrols. The gunfight that would ensue killed two of the eight within seconds, Misha and Tova were the first to fall. The others fought on for another twenty minutes but were no match for the firepower of the German and Polish troops. All eight of the delegation were killed, but not before one of them, after being shot in the leg, managed to blow up the phone line, and a group of German soldiers who had come to see the remains of their enemy. The only partisan survivor was a scout who had been hiding in the adjacent forest. He had also been holding the horses while the eight fighters moved out to sabotage the telephone lines. He was the one who returned with the details of the brave deaths of the fighters at the hands of the Nazis and the Poles. The camp was in mourning.

The next operation to set forth from the camp would be to the farm of the Pole who had opened fire on the group. His house and barn would be burned to the ground. It was simply an act of revenge with no military benefit. When Anna heard about the act of revenge she called Abrasha to ask for an explanation as to what it was that they were doing in the forest.

"I can make up lascivious stories for your measly benefit, but I won't," said Abrasha. "This is what this war is all about. We are here to instill pain on the enemy – whoever that may be."

"But revenge for revenge's sake? That's not what we're about," said Anna.

"Who died and gave you the right to talk about what we're about?"

"Millions died!" said Anna. "And thousands more are dying every day. Our mission should be clear – to destroy the Nazis' killing machine, not to pillage some farmer who was just protecting his land – regardless of the consequences of his actions. It's the actions of blood-thirsty animals – just like them."

"That farmer is responsible for the deaths of eight of our men and women. If he was on our side, he would not have shot at them. Correct, this wasn't the exemplar of operations, perhaps it was even extraneous, but it was justified, my dear, and I don't appreciate your insinuating that we are as barbaric as the Barbarians."

"If the shoe fits," mumbled Anna.

"Pardon me?" said Abrasha.

Anna realized that it was futile to argue with Abrasha. And Abrasha must have felt the same way.

"How I am in desperate need of a good lager. How about you?"

"I'm fine," said Anna. They both had moved on to the next topic – Abrasha to drink and Anna to the matter she had been waiting to discuss with Abrasha since the night before. "Abrasha? I know it doesn't matter much now, but how did Misha and his friends react to our rejection."

"My dear, Anna. Don't for a moment think that anyone thought any less of you for postponing your reentry into battle. There will be ample time for that. Here in Lomianki, you shouldn't have to fight at all. It's a family camp. Save yourselves for what's needed. Most of these people aren't willing to travel as far as you will. Here we're thorns in the Nazi heals, but up there, we're a real threat."

"In any case, if you have any justifiable military operation, we want in."

"I told you, the farm was just..." he paused and smiled. "Well, that's splendid. I'll pass on the word. Now for that lager. How come we seem to have everything but a good drink around here?"

"Because it's not a necessity," said Anna.

"Speak for yourself," and Abrasha was off.

15 May 1943

If Anna had tormented herself during the night for not accepting the mission, Ida did so for days following the news of the group's slaughter. She felt that she, as the great markswoman she was, could have prevented the massacre. Had there been an opportunity to redeem themselves during those two weeks, perhaps Ida would have resolved her guilt. However, no opportunities were presented in the camp – either that or they were being left out due to their uncooperative attitude the first time around. Either way, Miriam had tamed her anger, but Ida could not calm her conscience, and for over fourteen days she moped around as if someone much closer to her than the eight fighters had just died.

"Let's take a walk," said Anna to Ida after Ida had told her how upset

263

she still was about the killings.

The two began strolling around the camp like a couple on a Sabbath walk, this time taking in the sights of small groups gathered around fires or stockpiles of food and weapons. The forest was alive with the sounds of scurrying people. They could hear their footsteps crackling against the few dead leaves that had gathered on the ground. Men were cutting wood and the chopping echoed through the trees. The scent of smoldering campfire smoke besieged them as they walked, forcing them to hasten their pace to reach a patch of the woods where they could once again only sense the whiffs of pine. Anna could not believe how well supplied the partisans were. It was far from the scanty image of the ghetto fighters' meager supplies – although she had considered the amounts of food at the fighters' disposal sufficient enough, if not bountiful, at the time.

"Abrasha told me that they recently found an abandoned storehouse full of food and virtually brought all its contents into the forest," said Ida.

"Now that's an operation," said Anna.

The camp had been well-stocked, even compared to other partisan camps. The location of this particular camp could not have been better: it was close enough to towns to acquire food and supplies (although when unarmed Jewish partisans attempted to buy goods they were generally chased off with axes, but when they came armed, they were given food for free), and the camp was remote enough, hidden deep inside the forest, to prevent the Germans from ever finding them. The Germans feared the forest. Anna thought it had something to do with the Brothers Grimm stories that were such an integral part of German culture. They inherently feared forests because as children they were taught that the wicked witch was waiting for them around every tree. Needless to say, scary stories about witches in forests were not told around the campfires when the children were present. They were satisfied with the thought that the Germans were told these stories as children and thus hesitated any time a mission into the ominous, ill-omened Polish forests was called for. At least, that's what Anna thought.

Much of the food was also provided by the Polish farmers – either willingly or unwillingly. If the relationship between the farmer and the partisans was positive – meaning the farmer provided support and supplies – then there was little need for harassment. But if the farmer did not cooperate, mild threats were usually all that was needed to persuade them to comply. The burning of the farmer's house was not an isolated event, although most of the partisans preferred to simply steal food, warm clothing and other needed supplies (such as the cow they had been milking all summer). But those extreme measures were rare. Usually, just showing up with a few armed men was enough of a punishment for the farmers. The storehouses, like the farmers, could be friendly or they could be death traps. If there was a fear that the Germans had visited the building, there was always the chance that it had been mined. Many partisans lost their lives attempting to rummage through ex-Nazi storage houses that were simply dynamite bins with trimmings.

As Ida and Anna walked through the camp, they noticed groups of people baking, sewing and chopping wood. Wood would be stored in pits dug deep to keep the logs dry for the long winter. Gathering and burying wood was a full-time job, and these lumberjacks could be recognized by their splintered and calloused hands. This summer, they were preparing for a mild winter. It was simply a statistical probability that the winter of 1943 would be "better" than the winter of 1942. The winter of 1942-3 had been the worst in Europe for over 100 years. Anna hadn't realized that, thinking that it just seemed worse because of the ghetto conditions. For the partisans, the horrendous winter was both a blessing and a curse. Foul weather and thick blankets of snow kept the Germans from advancing, added significantly to their fear of the forest and kept them away from the partisan shelters. The sheets of white for as far as the eye could see also helped the partisans recognize approaching troops – for they had the upper hand when it came to surprise in the wilderness. They had also mastered the art of walking backward since their footprints in the snow would have given away their location to any German tracking patrols.

Soon Anna and Ida passed an area that seemed to be quarantined off by a makeshift fence made of sticks stacked waist-high. They walked over to the wall and looked beyond. Seven people were lying in pine-needle beds, covered with blankets. The whole area had a large military tarp over the top, and each of the seven was being attended to by another woman.

"Do you know anyone here?" asked a woman who approached them from the inside.

"No," said Anna. "What is this?"

"It's our hospital. Well, we are only able to make these people as comfortable as possible before they die."

"What do they have," asked Ida, unable to take her eyes off the scene before her.

"This is the least number of patients we've had in a long time. Last night two died. These three over here have typhoid, and those four were wounded. I don't believe any of them will survive. But I just try to make them comfortable. So you don't know anyone?"

"No, we don't…wait," said Anna. "Who's that?" She pointed to the bed farthest away from where they were standing. In it lay a girl with deep-set eyes that were half shut. Her head was tilted toward Anna as if she was trying to get a better look at them.

"Her name is Paula. She doesn't talk much. She arrived yesterday. Henryk brought her with a group of them. She escaped from the ghetto."

"Can we talk to her?" asked Anna.

"You can try. As I said, she doesn't say much."

"What happened to her?" asked Ida.

"She was shot and inhaled some gas. Somehow she managed to escape with a bullet in her abdomen. She's bleeding internally. I'd be surprised if she makes it through the night."

Anna had recognized Paula by her thick, dark eyebrows. She had smooth skin and a baby face, but her bold eyes gave her a mature look. She was only seventeen when the uprising broke out, and she had spent most of it in the bunker on Mila Street, Anna recalled. Ida had known her better, as she had spent much more time at headquarters.

"Hi baby," said Ida, grabbing her hand. Anna went around to the far side of the bed and kneeled next to her.

"Ida," said Paula and smiled gently.

"You got out," said Ida.

"I'm not going to make it," she said, as a tear trickled out of her right eye and onto the bed.

"You'll make it," Anna lied. "You'll be fine."

Paula just turned her head toward Anna and forced another smile.

"What's going on back there?" asked Ida.

"It's over. They're all dead."

The words hit Anna and Ida like a winter ice storm. Anna could feel the blood rush from her face and she held Paula's hand tighter as not to collapse on to her.

"They found headquarters," continued Paula. "They had been searching for days, but we had camouflaged it well. Then, finally, they found it. Ida, it was horrible. We were all inside when we heard the officers giving orders. One of the fighters who knew German said that they had found us. I was so scared. It was the first time I was scared. The dogs were barking – we could hear them from below."

Paula paused as the tears continued streaming down her face. "The night before, I was stationed at one of the entrances to the bunker. All I heard was one fighter after another saying 'Jan,' the password to get in, and we'd reply 'Warsaw.' There were three hundred people in the bunker when they found us. Three hundred," she said, almost pleading.

The bunker that served as headquarters for the ghetto fighters at Mila 18 was their second headquarters. The first, at Mila 29, had been liquidated on April 23. Mordecai and all of the fighters inside escaped through the underground passages after the Germans started pumping gas into the bunker. The new bunker, one of the largest in the ghetto, had not been build in a cellar, but under the rubble of a large apartment building that had been destroyed by Luftwaffe bombings at the beginning of the war. The entrances had been well covered – initially to help hide the thieves and smugglers who had originally built it. There were five entrances to the bunker – the main one from the courtyard – concealed behind a pile of bricks and planks that looked like they had fallen from the tops of the building when it was bombed, as well as four other entrances leading to the adjacent streets and sewage pipes. The main entrance was built like a fortress with tunnels wide enough for only one person leading from the entrances to the main rooms of the bunker. Some of the rooms had been dug more than five meters deep and in the center was a large, very well-stocked storage room. The smugglers who had built the bunker for the thieves of the Jewish underworld had supplied it with generators for continuous electricity supply and running water for as long as the ghetto had running water. As the bunker had been designed for no more than eighty people, with three hundred it must have been unbearable.

"You know," she said smiling again, "we had such a great May Day celebration. We sang all night. The Communists were singing in Russian, and we were singing in Hebrew. I think we heard the Internationale in five languages. We weren't thinking about the death and destruction around us. We were singing and we were happy again. I wasn't thinking about my brother who had died a week earlier. I forgot about the Germans looking for us overhead. Everyone was just singing."

Anna began to cry when Paula mentioned the May Day festivals, and Ida reached across Paula's dying body and placed her hand on Anna's shoulder. Anna imagined what it would have been like in the ghetto, and somehow she was still sorry she had to miss it.

Paula's smile suddenly left her face as she continued, "The scouts had stopped making their runs and getting Mordecai the information he needed. That night, we knew that we would be found the next day. We just knew it."

"Did Mordecai consider escape?" asked Anna.

"It wasn't part of his plan. A few days earlier Simcha had come and tried to convince him to leave to the Aryan side. But Mordecai wouldn't hear of it."

"What happened to Simcha?" asked Ida. "We saw him in the tunnels returning to the ghetto."

"I talked to him when he came back. He was in shock but said he felt at home among the rubble. Can you imagine feeling at home in that place?"

"Yes," said Ida. "I can."

"Well, I couldn't. He was shocked to see all the buildings destroyed. He hadn't realized what a mess the Germans had made of the place. He said, 'You leave them alone here for a few days and look at what they do with the place.' He made me laugh. All I know was that he spoke with Mordecai, but Mordecai wouldn't talk about escape. Simcha left and said he'd be back later. The next time we met was the day we were rescued from the ghetto. Simcha helped us find passage through the Aryan quarter. He was a mess. He had returned to the ghetto. He told me he had to take a Polish guide through the sewer at gunpoint. He said that there were hundreds of Jews in the sewers – many dead. He was very upset because he had only reached the ghetto that day – 'One damn day too late,' he said. He thought that he could have saved Mordecai and hundreds more. I doubt that. Mordecai wasn't ready to leave even at the end. Someone, I doubt it was Mordecai, did send some men to see if an escape plan was possible, but they thought that the Polish underground would have to be prepared, and they said that they were sure we wouldn't survive outside the ghetto. We sent people to contact the underground, but they never returned. I guess they were caught."

"Maybe some of them made it," said Ida.

"Maybe," said Paula. No one slept that night. Three hundred people. There were children, some religious people who were praying. No one slept. The food was gone. Since we couldn't get in and out anymore, the food was finished. You know, the fighters hadn't been hungry in a while. The chompes were in a rage – they had never been hungry." The chompes were the underworld leaders who ran the smuggling operations. With their hands close to the food source, they were always well supplied. "We had been training for the possibility of being found for days. But nothing prepared us for that moment when we heard the ultimatum. An SS officer was yelling that whoever came out would be spared, and everyone else would be shot. It seems everyone looked at Mordecai at that point. He just shook his head and told us the plan. We would stay and fight, and as soon as the Germans broke in we'd try to break out through the more remote exits. Just the chompes surrendered. They left the bunker with a lot of people. But the fighters stayed. You know our dedication to Mordecai. No one could go against his will. I'd been fighting with him for months. I couldn't let him down – and I was more frightened of surrendering than getting killed in battle. God, was I scared."

Anna was looking down at this small child, just seventeen years old and had lived ten lives. She did not deserve to die after all that.

"Then they started drilling. Some of us had heard the drilling before in other bunkers. They were about to pump in gas. I got hit on the head by a piece of plaster that fell from the ceiling while they were drilling. The gas started in and I think they also threw in some kind of grenade. We ran toward the far room, closing the door to keep the gas out, but we knew we needed a better plan than that. I don't remember who said it first, but someone began talking about suicide and not letting the Germans have the satisfaction of killing or capturing us. I think Mordecai liked that idea. It was a nobler escape. But I..." Paula swallowed hard as if there was acute pain she needed to fight off. She closed her eyes.

"Paula?" asked Ida.

"I'm fine," she said. "I was going to say that the only thing I could think about was that I wanted to turn eighteen. My birthday is September 9 and I just wanted to live until then. There was a woman, she was older. I don't think she was a fighter, but she had stayed anyway. She kept saying, 'Put me out of my misery. Put me out of my misery. Kill me. Kill me.' Her son took his gun, loaded it, and right before our eyes shot his mother and then himself. That was when I decided to leave. It was horrible. Some people couldn't kill themselves, so they asked friends to do it. Some took cyanide – they just dropped without a sound." Paula paused before saying the one thing that Anna knew would eventually be uttered. "Ida, your friend Rachel died there. She didn't hesitate. As soon as the shooting began, she shot herself."

Anna felt the blood leave her head and bent over closer to Paula, as a pain she had experienced far too often over the past few years engulfed her. Anna let out a faint cry and started weeping. Ida was soon to follow and all three of them were crying.

After a moment's pause, Paula continued. "A few of us started searching for an exit that the Germans hadn't blocked. They seemed to have found all of the exits. I don't know how. They must have tortured someone. We were choking from the gas. We put wet handkerchiefs around our faces, but it was still hard to breathe. Finally, we found a tunnel that the Germans hadn't plugged and waited there until it was over. A few hours later, we were found by one of the groups that had left to talk to the Polish underground about our escape. They were too late for most, but they saved us. They got us out the next day and brought us through the sewers. That's when I saw Simcha again. He led us back to the Aryan side. I could hardly breathe from the gas and my stomach.... Simcha brought us to a point where we had to wait all night before he brought a Polish truck to take us here. Some people that were with us died that night – they were fighters who just couldn't wait to breathe again. They died from inhaling the gas. We kept sending notes out of the sewer for them to open it, but notes kept coming back saying that we had to wait, that the Germans were all over the neighborhood. Thirty of us got out and arrived here, but there were more than that with us in the trench.

Simcha went back to get them. He hadn't realized that they had been left behind. That's the last time I saw him."

"He was here?" asked Anna.

"Yes, but he's not back yet."

The three sat in silence as they each thought about the people who had died and how the uprising had ended. Then Ida asked, "How were you shot?"

"Stupid accident," she said. "One of the fighters shot himself and the bullet went right through him and hit me in the stomach. Very resourceful. Two with one shot."

"Did they get the bullet out?" asked Anna.

"No, it's still in there."

Anna looked at Ida the surgeon.

"No! No, Anna!" said Ida. "There is a huge difference between a stomach and an arm. There are vital organs in there. No, Anna!"

"You see," said Anna, "you even knew where the vital organs are. What's wrong? You heard the woman before. What do you have to lose?"

"What are you talking about?" asked Paula.

"Anna is having delusions of grandeur…about me."

Anna rolled up her sleeve and showed Paula Ida's work. "She saved my life."

"That's an arm, Anna!" said Ida.

"She wants you to operate on me?" asked Paula.

"I'm not a doctor, and I'm not going to operate on anyone," said Ida defiantly.

"What did that woman say?" said Paula looking over at the woman who had been talking to them as they looked in on the beds.

Ida gave Anna a ruthless squint.

"You may not have a better chance than Ida," said Anna.

Paula turned to Anna, "But there are doctors here. And if they say they can't operate, what makes you think that she can?"

"The doctors won't operate because they don't have anesthetics. But what they don't know is that you can handle pain – you're a fighter."

"You've lost it," said Ida. "Let's just say that she can stand the pain. Shouldn't we just call one of the doctors to do the operation?"

"The doctors won't do it. You will."

"No I won't!" said Ida.

"Stop!" said Paula. "It's not just the bullet. The gas did something too. I overheard them talking. They can't do anything for me and neither can you. Ida's right, Anna. If I was meant to die, let it be here, and let it be now. I'm much better off than had I been captured by the Nazis. They would have made certain I had a terrifying death. Here I am free. And there is nothing more satisfying than dying freely."

Paula died early that evening with Ida and Anna by her side. They had left for a few hours to tell the story of the fall of the ghetto headquarters to Miriam, who they saw break down for the first time. Miriam let herself cry like never before. She had always made it a point to limit her tears to one or two – at least that was how Anna saw it – but this time, particularly when she heard about Rachel, she cried, hiding her face in her hands, while Anna, Ida and little Miriam consoled her.

Anna and Ida returned to Paula after leaving Miriam in the good hands of little Miriam, who immediately returned to playing with her new toy, Miriam's hair, unable to truly comprehend the torment big Miriam was feeling. As they talked to Paula, telling her their stories and experiences in the ghetto they had all abandoned, she slowly faded. Occasionally, she would seem to fall asleep and then awake as if startled by a loud noise. Anna and Ida just kept talking since each time they would pause, believing that Paula had fallen back asleep, she would demand, now hardly moving her lips, for them to continue. But as evening fell, she lost consciousness and finally, her heart stopped. For a second, Anna thought she saw the life of little Paula exit her damaged body and sail out through the trees.

Anna and Ida asked two men from the camp to help them bury her right away. There was no reason to postpone. It wasn't as if they had to wait for guests to arrive for the funeral. In fact, out of all the people Anna and Ida had seen die, this was the first proper burial they were able to attend since Leah's nocturnal escapade. The two men dug the ditch, and Anna and Ida set the body inside. Her weight betrayed the malnutrition her body had endured during those critical years in the ghetto.

They had called Miriam to join them for the funeral. They needed to stay together in mourning as well as in battle. Little Miriam wanted to come along, but despite her pleas, big Miriam explained that there are many things that little girls cannot do until they are older. As she spoke, it occurred to Anna that little Miriam was only a few years younger than Paula.

The burial of Paula was more than just a service for a brave young girl. It was a symbolic funeral for all the young fighters who had died in the ghetto. After they set the body in the ditch in the forest, one of the men who had come to help dig removed a candle and matches from his pocket. He lit the candle and handed to Ida, who seemed to have been crying the hardest of the three – Miriam had allowed only a small number of tears for Paula; even if this was a symbolic funeral, she hadn't known her very well, at least not as well as Anna and Ida now felt they had. She had cried herself out over

Rachel the night before.

"This world didn't deserve you," said Anna, and placed the candle on the mound of dirt covering the seventeen-year-old ghetto fighter.

Thirty

"Why do you wear short pants?" asked Anna. "I mean, it's not dignified. You are a dignified man and your attire should reflect that."

"Well," said Yaakov, "it's the company attire. In the summer, it's warm, so we wear comfortable clothing."

"But this bus is freezing in the summer. The air-conditioning is far too strong."

"You are complaining of cold?"

"I'm not complaining, I'm making a statement."

"You remind me of someone."

"Yeah? Who?"

"My…"

Yaakov slammed on the brakes as a small pickup truck flew out of an orchard on the side of the road and turned left in front of the bus. His knuckles turned white, as he gripped the large wheel and steered the bus to the right, missing the tail of the truck my centimeters.

"Are you trying to kill me!" said Anna, who had flown forward into the wall in front of her. "Many people have tried to kill me and most of them are dead now. What's wrong with you?"

"I'm sorry, that idiot cut us off."

"Oh, now it's us. You're the driver. I wasn't cut off. I can't see anything. But I assure you that had I been able to see something, I would have been able to warn you before you almost killed me."

"Sorry," he said.

"Were you about to tell me how I remind you of your daughter again?"

"How did you know that?"

"You said I remind you of someone, and before you told me that your daughter was like me."

"You have an uncanny memory."

"You don't know the half of it," said Anna.

"Well, yes. You do have a similar way of…"

"Way of what?"

"Way of…" Yaakov laughed.

"Are you going to tell me?"

"You have a similar way of not shutting up."

"That's so nice of you to say," said Anna.

"Well, you also have a lot of interesting things to say. I have to admit that."

"Thank you. But my tongue can be rather sharp as well."

"I know that," said Yaakov. "I saw you in the kiosk. That was something."

"I've done worse."

Anna was giggling to herself as one particular memory entered her mind.

"What is it?"

"I once almost made a Polish militiaman pee in his pants."

Thirty-One

It would have been Paula's birthday on the day that Anna, Miriam and Ida set out on what was their first mission as partisans in the forest. Anna remembered, and while they ate breakfast that morning, Anna silently wished the would-be eighteen-year-old a happy birthday.

Just over a week after Paula's death, the three began their journey northeast to the Wyszkow forest. Led by Abrasha, Henryk and Joziak, they set out in the same old truck that had taken them out of Warsaw – the one Ida had sworn she would not enter unless it was taking her to the Promised Land. They were joined on the trip by three other ex-ghetto fighters who had escaped Warsaw early in the April uprising and one additional member of the Gwardia Ludowa. This time they all took turns sitting in the back of the truck, where a new tarp had been placed. The trip itself could have been extremely dangerous, but the Gwardia Ludowa men had done their homework and found a series of routes through Poland where the Germans hadn't left signs of occupation.

Wyszkow sat on the Bug River, a tributary of the River Vistula, and their excursion took them through numerous side roads to avoid the German patrols. They had arrived late at night and in the morning were shocked to see the size of the establishment in the woods. The camp in this forest was a great deal larger than the Lomianki camp. By this time, the Red Army had made contact with the partisans and was assisting in a far more active manner – particularly in the east. Some of that assistance reached the Polish forests via connections through the Gwardia Ludowa. Therefore, the camp was full of supplies that the girls had yet to see anywhere in the resistance movement – impressive weapons and explosives that they only could have dreamed to have had in the ghetto.

Late one night, after a few weeks of doing little but sitting by the campfire and assisting with menial chores, the girls were talking with the two men who had traveled with them from Lomianki.

"Do you know the story of the Jews of Wyszkow?" asked one of the men who had traveled with the girls to their new camp. No one did – in fact, most of them had no idea where Wyszkow was before arriving in the area. "Exactly four years ago today – on September 9," the man continued, "the Germans occupied the village. Wyszkow had always been a Jewish town. At the beginning of the war, there were about five thousand Jews out of a total population of twelve thousand. There was a time when the Jews made up almost seventy percent of the population. When the Germans came, most of the Jews escaped to the forest – this very forest we're in now. I was one of the few who went west. Most of the people continued east to Bialystok or deeper into Russia. The day the Germans came into the town, they hoarded a bunch of Jews into one of the houses and set it on fire. I don't know how many died. They also shot those they found in the street. They took the men out of the houses and shot them in the market square. They let women and children go. Remember, this was 1939 – the Germans had just entered Poland. If only we had known then what we know now. They just slaughtered any Jews they found, burned their houses and raped the women. For days they chased the Jews and killed them. Those that didn't run the first day were killed – over one thousand in four days. The Jews of Wyszkow have known their share of pogroms, but nothing like this. By September 13, not a single Jew remained in the town that had Jews since the seventeenth century. Mordecai was born there."

"You knew Mordecai?" asked Miriam.

"Yes. I knew him well – from Wyszkow. We were in Betar together."

"I forgot about that black spot on Mordecai's past," said Ida.

"He was a bully – Betar made sense for him. We left Betar together and joined Hashomer Hatzair."

"I always wanted to ask Mordecai about that," said Miriam. "How can someone jump from the fascist Betar to the Socialist Hashomer Hatzair? I don't get it."

"We were young," said the fighter. "It wasn't such a long leap. Besides, we did it for the girls."

Anna, Ida and Miriam all gaped at the young man.

"Yep, we switched to Hashomer Hatzair because the girls were much cuter – hell, look at you three. There's all the proof you need. But I have to admit that once we were there, we found all the right reasons to be proud of our place in such a tremendous movement."

That was how Miriam fell for Benjamin. The more he talked about the girls of Hashomer Hatzair, the more Miriam became enthralled. By the end of that week, the two were spending a great deal of time together. They would talk half the night and be found next to the fire, still chatting, as the morning light began peeping through the slits in the trees. Their relationship clearly would have developed into something romantic had it had the chance, but events in the Wyszkow forest would never allow things to develop. Benjamin believed that romantic relationships distracted from the goal of their presence in the forest. Miriam outwardly agreed, but Anna knew that deep down she was ready for something more with Benjamin. However, she would never dare come out publicly – and anything said to Benjamin would seem public to her – in favor of romantic relationships in the forest. Of course, with the dynamics of life among the partisans, even that would eventually change for Miriam but would have nothing to do with Benjamin. Miriam was the first of the three to be asked on a mission – most probably because of her relationship with Benjamin. Unlike in the ghetto where women were viewed as equal – at least within the youth movements – in the forest, many of the men did not feel that female fighters could cut it in the field. In the great scheme of things, they had a role to play for the partisans, but only as long as their work consisted of tampering with items that did not explode. However, Miriam's battle experience gave her credit among the fighters she had seen more action than most of them combined. The ghetto fighting was viewed as heroic, even by the anti-Semitic Gwardia Ludowa. And now, having a special companion who turned out not only to be a fighter but a commander as well, she was given special treatment. Her first mission was a simple one – at least it was safer than some of the later missions – and all that was required of her was to stand guard with a rifle while Benjamin and four others placed explosives on a train track in the Wegrow forest outside of Sokolka, a small village with many sympathetic farmers.

The group set out late at night and arrived at the tracks just before dawn. They worked quickly and easily managed to set the mines on the track without incident. Then they waited for the train to arrive and set off the blast just as the second car reached the casing. The train derailed, and the cheers of the partisans looking on from the trees around the tracks could be heard throughout the forest. This was one of the forbidden forests for the Germans. Other than the tracks themselves, there was nothing of interest for the Germans in the area, which was what made it so safe for the partisans. Even the blast itself would not have been heard by more than a few of the villagers who would never have suspected partisan military activity amid the dense woodland.

Although Miriam had joined them, she had done nothing at all. The blast had been a satisfying spectacle, and she raved about the derailment for days. But it was far from enough for the experienced fighter; she wanted more opportunities to harass the Nazis.

This was a time when the truth about the Gwardia Ludowa was coming to light. They were anti-Semitic, and most wanted little to do with the Jews who were fighting with them in the forest. Most viewed the Jews' presence as a necessary sacrifice, but it was one thing to tolerate Jewish fighters and another to tolerate female Jewish fighters. One People's Guard member was overheard yelling that all he wanted to do was to "bag the Jewish bitches." His friends, who laughed hysterically at the time, some nodding in approval, later attempted to apologize using the excuse that he was filthy drunk – which of course he was. It was clear to all of the Jewish partisans, particularly to Anna, that this relationship would not last long. Little did they know that once the Gwardia Ludowa was incorporated into the newly established Armia Ludowa, the People's Army, later that year, the tenuous relationship between the battle groups would deteriorate completely.

So the partisan women, who made up almost a quarter of the camp, were mostly responsible for cooking, cleaning and tending to the sick and wounded; and most of the women in the camp were happy with that role. But not Miriam and not Ida and after several weeks in the forest with these men, not Anna either. When one of the Polish men approached Anna one day and started harassing her about their formal request to join in the raids, she finally had an opportunity to give him a piece of her mind.

"So you want to fight?" said the hung-over Pole. Anna could see that he was nursing a headache, and after hearing the hostility in the tone of his voice, she planned on using his medical state against him. "You can't fight, my little Jewess. Why do you want to fight anyway? You wouldn't live out here for long. Why do you want to fight if you are surely going to die?"

Anna turned to the wobbly man who stood a head taller than she and said, "For those who seek life, we are not the address." That had become the motto of the Jewish partisans, and although Anna did not agree with it, it seemed a fitting statement here. But it was just a preamble to the full outburst that would come as soon as the man tried to place his hand around the small of her neck and pull her toward him to kiss her.

"Come close and do what you were put here to do," said the man.

"You wretched piece of scum," said Anna firmly as she easily hit his arm off her shoulder. He was taken aback at her strength, and she continued. "You call yourself a damn soldier? You are nothing more than a filthy, stinking drunk with no…"

"I won't take that from a woman! I won't take that from a Jew!"

"Shut up you lowlife pervert," she said poking him with one finger in the chest. He was moving away from her, clearly frightened by her determination and aggression. She was now raising her voice, and her harangue had caused a small crowd to gather around them. No one intervened. No one needed to. "You'll listen to me now. I've just about had it with all of your 'Jews don't do this, women don't do that' bullshit. Does your pea-sized brain have any concept of what we've been through? The greatest fighters in this camp are my two friends. No one shoots better than they do, and I'm willing to bet your life on it, you lame piece of dirt. Why don't we see if they can put a hole in your head from 100 meters while you're fast asleep on your side of the camp. Would you like to see that? Until then, you get this into your thick skull: the Jews in this camp are here to fight fascist Nazis not moronic Poles like yourself. If you haven't noticed, you belong to a communist militia. Do you know what that means? Do you? I didn't think so, because you look far too stupid to understand Marxist concepts such as freedom and equality. Did you know that Marx was a Jew? Did you know that Trotsky was a Jew? Now I don't want to see your grimy hands and putrid breath within twenty meters of a Jewish girl again. Because if I do, I will send my beautiful friends over to your bed. But they won't be there to satisfy your animal instinct – since I'm sure you are a horrible lover on top of everything else – they will be there to cut your dick off. Do you understand me, you walking phallic piece of crap?"

The crowd surrounding the now beet red Polish militiaman and Anna could have been split into two groups: those smiling and those gaping. Those smiling were the first to start the round of applause – and Miriam was the first to start whistling. The militiaman, who was visibly ill from the episode, and the handover, turned and walked away from the half-circle that had formed and back to his side of the woods. He was followed by three comrades who had belonged to the gaping half of the onlookers, now shaking their heads in dismay.

It was not long after the incident, generally known in the camp as "the Jewess explosion," that Anna, Ida and Miriam were at long last asked to join a mission. The word of Ida's skills had spread thanks to Anna's eruption, and all were eager to see her in action. This time they would need to use all their learned skills to assist in one of the more dangerous raids that the group had encountered. Their first mission consisted of ambushing a German truck and stealing whatever weapons were found inside. The key to success, as they were told by Benjamin the Jewish commander, who was younger than the three girls, but whose strong looks, chiseled chin and long, wavy hair seemed to be all that was necessary to win esteem, was to pick the right German convoy: too big and they would be outnumbered; too small and there would be nothing to steal. Scouts had been sent to see what approaching vehicles could be spotted, and on a sunny late-summer afternoon, the group participating in the raid was called together for a planning session.

The young Jewish commander, who called himself Yuri, although Abrasha insisted that his real name was Berl, pulled out a map of the area and set it on the table. "We have word from the other GL groups that a small convoy consisting of three vehicles will pass through this point," he said.

"His name is Berl," Abrasha whispered to Anna. "He just thinks that Yuri is a stronger name and that it impresses the Polish crowd. Pompous twit."

"We will attack from this forest," Yuri continued, "with snipers stationed here, here and here."

He went on to explain what each of the ten fighters would be doing in the raid, and finally, almost as if it was an afterthought, he turned to Anna and her friend. "I need you – Ida is it? – Ida, to be behind one of these trees. If you are as good a shot as they say you are you will have no trouble taking out the drivers of the three vehicles, which will start the ambush. Mikolaj will be doing the same from this side. You," he said pointing to Miriam, "will join Adam, Yaki, and Tomasz in this cluster over here. And you, Anna, will stay with my group. We'll attack from behind. Hopefully, by the time we get there, Ida and Mikolaj will have taken out most of the soldiers."

"Are you going to try to hit them with a mortar shell before we go in?" asked Miriam. All eyes turned to her as if she had just asked if she could get undressed in front of them.

"Mortar?" said Yuri. "Wouldn't that be self-defeating? We are not only interested in killing the few German soldiers that may be there, although that will be the fun part, but we want what they are carrying. That is far more important, so we wouldn't want to damage anything in the vehicles. Besides, we'll need the cars to return to camp, no?"

Miriam stared Yuri down, as he looked at her expecting an answer to his rhetorical question.

"Okay then. We'll be leaving tonight at eleven. We have a long walk ahead of us, so get some rest."

As the girls returned to their section of the camp, they noticed a man walking toward them. He was favoring his left leg and wearing a brown coat with tears in the sleeves. Had he not been limping, Miriam certainly would have noticed his height and distinct mannerisms; but his limp caused him to bend forward, making him look old and weak. As he closed the gap between them, Anna's first thought was that it couldn't be who she thought it was. Miriam was the first to run toward him. She sprang forward, passed a few piles of sticks and leaped directly into Nahum's outstretched arms.

Anna and Ida soon joined Miriam in hugging Nahum, and as usual, Anna and Ida began to cry. There would be plenty of time to hear the stories, for now, they were content to stand there and hold each other for a few moments.

Of course, the timing of Nahum's appearance was problematic at the least. The girls were expected to rest for their upcoming mission, and now, after all that time waiting, the last thing they wanted to do was leave the camp and join a mission that one or all of whom may never return from; not while Nahum was there. By his limp, it was clear that he was not capable of joining them for the ambush – even if Yuri/Berl would allow it – and they would be forced to leave him at camp.

After several minutes of embracing and weeping, the four sat down on logs next to one of the fires and heard Nahum's adventures.

"The whole time," he began while holding Miriam's hands, "the only thing I could think about was, 'I hope Miriam didn't come here.' I was stuck in the back of that hospital with hundreds of terrified people – children and women and sick people from all over the ghetto. People were crying and screaming and looking for family, and all I thought was I hope you didn't come to meet me. I kept looking for you in the crowds and was happy I hadn't seen you. But there were thousands of people, and up until now I wasn't sure if you had been taken or not."

"I didn't go. They wouldn't let me," said Miriam with tears in her eyes, but not letting herself cry. "I wanted to come to get you, but they wouldn't let me."

"That's a good thing. You wouldn't have found me and would have been taken yourself. It's a good thing. Eventually, I saw Nimi, from Dror – remember him, the kid with oversized eyes we used to call 'Owl'? It was nice to see another movement person. We immediately began thinking about how we could escape. But the Germans were one step ahead of us. At first, we thought we'd try and jump out of the window at the hospital, but there were guards everywhere. Then we thought that when they transferred us to the Umschlagplatz, we'd make a run for it, but they had snipers everywhere. When we got to the Umschlag it was insanity. I've never seen so much fear in people's eyes; the Germans had dogs that I saw attack several people; and the officers were just shooting children and women who didn't do exactly as they said. The whole area was lined with soldiers and dogs. There was no way we were going to escape. But there was no way we were going to the camps either. I knew that I would either die or get away. There was no other alternative. I had a knife, and at first, I thought I was going to stab a guard and take his weapon. But I looked around at all the children, and I knew that if I tried that, they would just start shooting people. Even without my action, the SS officers were firing at everyone. There must have been a hundred dead bodies at the foot of the trains. After I showed him my knife, Nimi and I decided that we would get on the train, but in one of the cars at the back. It was difficult, but we tried to make our way as far back as possible. We ended up getting pushed onto a car that was about five from the end. That turned out to be the best place to do what we did. I don't want to tell you what it was like inside those cars. We were only there for a few hours. The rest of the people were there for days. Even after a few hours, the stench was unbearable. As soon as we got on the train, we started looking for more young people to help us. That's when I met Gittel. She was sixteen, but looked even younger. I guess she overheard us. She said she wanted to help do whatever we were going to do. She said her mother and brother died during the winter and her father was shot that day, 'I have nothing else to lose,' she said. I'll never forget her face when she said that. 'I have nothing else to lose.'"

Nahum shook his head and looked down at Miriam's hands in his lap. "The three of us looked around the cattle car to see if there were any loose boards or anything we could pry open. Nimi found that one of the bars on the grating that was once a window was loose and he thought that with my knife we could pry open the rest of it. It was strange, but as soon as we began working on the bars, some of the people in the cars started yelling at us, 'They're going to kill us all! Stop that! They'll shoot you and me!' Gittel was great. She screamed back, 'Don't you get it? We're already dead! Shut up and let us work.'"

"She'd make a great fighter," said Ida.

"Well...Anyway," he continued, "we pried the bars and surprisingly we were able to remove them quite easily. It seems that something had damaged them and they must not have been inspected. But it was a small window, and we had to climb up to get out of it. By that time the sun was setting, and we decided to wait until it was dark and when the train made a left turn. We just hoped that it would eventually make a left turn since the window was on the right side of the train. We figured the guards in the back and front wouldn't be able to see us. Night came, and we stood under the window waiting for the train to turn. It seemed like hours before we finally felt the train lean left and the wheels screech. Nimi decided he would go first. I had to go last because I was tall enough to lift myself and Nimi and Gittel would need me to lift them. I lifted Nimi to the window and he pulled himself out. I was trying to help him get his whole body out of the window before he jumped, but he just jumped. His shoe got caught as he fell and for a second he hung off the side of the car by his foot and then fell. I knew he must have been hurt, but I had no idea what the extent was. Then it was Gittel's turn. She went right up and was out the window before I knew it. Then I climbed up and two men grabbed my legs and gave me a push. We were lucky it was a long left turn. I got half-way out and thought I was going to fall as Nimi had, but I made sure I was able to jump onto my feet. I still don't know how I did it, but I landed on my feet and broke my leg. That's the limp. Nimi wasn't so lucky. I crawled back and saw Gittel running toward me. She had some scratches but was fine. She helped me up and together we went to find Nimi. He was dead. He must have landed on his head and then his legs fell under the train. His foot was severed at the knee. He was dead. Gittel was amazing. She took me and we looked for a place to hide. There was nothing around where we had jumped, and I hadn't thought about what I was going to do after I got out of the train. Without Gittel, I would have died there. She practically carried me into the woods and the next day she went off and came back with bread. She said there was a farm there, and she had made friends with a little girl who got her the bread. I told her that was risky, but she just shrugged.

"We stayed in the woods for two days. My leg was not getting better, but I knew I could walk if I used Gittel as a crutch. We decided to go to the farm and see if they would take us in. I knew that was a dangerous move, but we had no choice. I couldn't move and that little girl wouldn't keep stealing bread from her family for long. There was only a woman there. Her husband had died before the war, and her two sons had both been killed during the German invasion. She and her ten-year-old daughter ran their small farm. We told them we would work for food and boarding. She laughed. She said it didn't look like I could even walk. Gittel said she'd work for the both of us.

"For over two months we helped where we could. Until one day, the woman came and told us that she was running out of money. There was something in the manner that she spoke that made me think she was considering turning us in for a reward. Autumn had begun, and the last thing we wanted was to be stranded in the cold, but Gittel and I agreed to leave that night. We just left in the middle of the night, didn't say goodbye, nothing. Gittel left the girl an embroidered heart she had made, but that was it. I was able to walk by then, so we decided to head for the forest and look for the partisans. Bad idea. We almost died that first month. We would dig pits and sleep in them to keep warm, but it was freezing already. We stole food and clothing; Gittel was good at that too. And then we were caught – well Gittel was. I escaped."

"What happened to her?" asked Miriam.

"She was shot in the back by Polish police coming back from looking for food. Remember our argument about there being good Poles? There aren't any. The bastards just shot her in the back and left her in the woods. They shot her like a hunter makes his kill. After the police left the area, late that night, I went back to her body. I picked her up and brought her into the woods. She was so cold. I placed her in the pit we had slept in. She had been so warm for so long. She was so cold. I think I sat there crying until morning. Then I covered her with dirt and leaves and moved around the countryside alone.

"After Gittel died, I didn't care what happened to me. I didn't eat for a few days. She was always the one who went into the villages to get food. But then I saw something that shocked me out of my trance. An old man was lying on a road outside of...I can't remember the name of the village. I decided to see if he needed help. I had been hanging around there hoping to find some food. I asked him if he needed anything, and he said, 'I have been lying here since this morning. No one has even asked of my well being. Bless you.' I helped him up and, I don't know why, but I told him I was a Jew. He said, 'So was I.'"

"Was?" the girls asked in unison.

"Yes. He said he had been orphaned and converted to Catholicism as a young child. He only recently discovered that he was a Jew, but the Germans hadn't. At first, I had thought I finally found a 'good Pole,' but I was wrong. He was a good Jew. I hadn't had a chance to help anyone since the ghetto – I mean, Gittel helped me more than I helped her – and there was something nice about helping him. I was suddenly jolted out of my depression and I wanted to live. He took me in, and on the second day that I was with him, I told him about Gittel and her death. You know what he said? He said, 'Gittel was your sacrifice to the gods. She came to you from heaven and returned there when you needed to move on.' At the end of the winter, he told me about this place. I don't know how he knew about it, but he did. I stayed with him until two weeks ago when he passed away. That's why I came here."

"I'm sorry about Gittel," said Miriam.

"You would have all loved her," he said. "I did."

The girls then told Nahum all that had happened in the ghetto, about their escape and what happened to the rest of the fighters. He asked questions, but they tried to be brief knowing that later that night they would be joining the operation and needed to rest.

Anna couldn't sleep much during those few hours before the operation, although at one point she did seem to doze off. Nahum had volunteered to wake them when they needed to leave. He had slept in their part of the camp that night.

"It'll be good to take some target practice on the Nazis again," said Ida, as they were walking to meet Yuri and the rest of the unit.

"This isn't practice," said Anna.

"Listen," said Miriam, "if anything happens..."

"Don't!" said Anna, and placed her hand over Miriam's mouth.

"I just wanted to say that I love you both."

"Don't," said Anna again. "This is a piece of cake for us."

"And tell Nahum that I'm sorry for leaving him...twice...I mean, at the hospital, and now. Just tell him."

"Would you stop that!" said Ida. "You're being a fool. It's not like you. What's wrong with you? Stop now."

"Fine," said Miriam. "I want strawberries."

"Miriam! Shut up," said Ida. "Wait for the spring. You're acting so strange."

"I think I'm happy. Look, Nahum came back. We're going on a mission..."

"Then why were you talking about dying?" asked Ida.

"Because...."

"Because," said Anna, "you're afraid of being happy. You have something to lose now. It's been a long time since you've had something to lose."

"I've always had something to lose. I'm not like Gittel. I could always have lost you two. Have I said I love you today?"

"Shut up," said Anna and Ida together.

The unit of ten men and the three women walked most of the night and arrived at the ambush point at dawn. Anna was impressed with the preparation, as the site looked exactly as she had imagined it from the briefing. There was a clear line of trees that led into the thick forest, looking at that time of day as a black wall lining a field. The field was beginning to show its colors as the sun's energy was lightening the clouds overhead. The field had been harvested recently, and only the tracks of the tractors and trucks that had hauled the crops yielded from the soil remained. No farmhouse was in sight, and Anna assumed that the farm was behind the next bend and was out of view from the forest perimeter. On the edge of the field, about thirty meters from the wall of trees was a two-lane road that cut around the forest rim and back out toward the north. The spot had been chosen because of an abandoned shack located on the side of the road. No one seemed to know what the shack had been used for, but for them, it would simply mean additional cover. It would be from behind the shack that the partisans would commence their ground attack, following the initial gunshots by Ida and Mikolaj. Upon arriving at the clearing, the fighters took their position and began the most difficult part of the entire operation – waiting.

They had estimated that the convoy of three German vehicles would arrive close to 9:00 in the morning. It was already 7:45 by the time they had taken position and signaled Yuri that they were ready. Almost three hours passed before Anna began to doubt their intelligence reports.

"Are you sure they're coming?" Anna asked Yuri while they waited behind two trees that had grown together. They would be the first to see the convoy as they were situated at the start of the bend that would bring the road up to the shack.

"They're coming," he said, "…unless someone else got to them first." And as he finished his sentence, the gentle rumble could be heard coming from the forest directly in front of them. It took Anna a second to realize that the sound was not being generated from the forest but was bouncing off the tree line and coming from the road. Within two minutes, the first of the vehicles could be seen.

"One," said Yuri while looking through his binoculars. "Two. Three…. Damn it! There are four vehicles. Damn it! One is a personnel carrier. There could be twenty men in there."

"Yuri," said one of the men squatting next to them, "do we call it off?"

Yuri didn't reply but kept looking at the approaching convoy. It was now close to two hundred meters from the point of attack. If he didn't call it off right now, the snipers would soon open fire. He removed his binoculars from his eyes and looked over at Anna who was lying on her stomach with her gun facing the convoy.

"Is she really that good of a shot?" he asked her.

"None better."

"Then we'll go with it, but if men start coming out of that carrier I want her to keep shooting no matter how many of our men are fighting down there. Go tell her."

Anna got up and ran back into the forest where her movements wouldn't be seen from the road. She reached Ida and told her the new plan.

"I have more than enough bullets for twenty men," she said. "All I'll need is twenty-one. I may want to shoot one of them twice."

Anna stood up to return to Yuri when Ida grabbed her sleeve.

"Be careful," said Ida.

"I'm always careful."

Two shots rang out just as the first car, a jeep carrying only two officers, reached the designated point just past the shack. The four fighters, including Miriam, who had stationed themselves behind the dilapidated hovel, moved slowly around to the back as the convoy proceeded past them. One shot was from Ida's gun and the other from Mikolaj's. They both hit the driver and he slumped over the wheel. The second officer tried to reach for his gun, but Ida was far too quick for the SS man. All four vehicles came to an abrupt stop, and out of the back of the personnel carrier came three soldiers – only three. As they came out, shots rang out from the forest. While Ida and Mikolaj were busy taking out the drivers of the next three vehicles, Yuri's band at the edge of the forest began shooting at the soldiers. Two of them dropped to the ground immediately; the last, however, managed to get off a round in the direction of Yuri's group.

"Everyone okay?" shouted Yuri. Anna immediately thought how unprofessional it was to start yelling from the woods during a shootout, but none of these fighters had ever really been trained for what they were doing. No one had been hit, and the volley of fire that was returned toward the lone soldier was overkill. He was hit by at least five bullets and fell to the ground with his other fallen comrades.

All of the fighters had been instructed to stop shooting as soon as they no longer saw movement among the Germans in the road. There were eleven dead Nazis on the pavement: four drivers, four passengers and three soldiers, and no one else on the road seemed to be moving.

Yuri waved his gun in the air, and the four partisans who had been waiting behind the shack slowly made their way toward the stalled convoy. The engines of all three vehicles were still running. Only the jeep, whose forward progress had taken it toward the side of the road after the death of the driver was no longer in line. As the fighters approached from behind, another shot rang out, and all four of them dropped to the ground as there was nowhere to take cover. However, the shot had come from Ida, and one of the dropped German soldiers gasped as he was hit again. He had been taking aim at the approaching unit and had Ida not killed him all four would have been shot.

Coming up from behind, Miriam and the three men split into two groups, each taking opposite sides of the trucks. Anna was watching carefully as they passed the last truck – the personnel carrier. One of the men looked inside. He waved that all was clear. They then approached the second car. The driver and the passenger, an SS officer, were both slumped forward up against the front of the vehicle – the driver with his hand on his weapon still in its holster.

As it became clear that all of the Nazis were dead, the rest of the partisans came down from the forest and began rummaging through the trucks. One of the men suggested putting everything into one of the smaller cars and driving it back to camp, but they all knew that the idea was not feasible. At one point, the Germans would begin searching for the convoy, and it was too likely they would be seen on the roads.

The number of weapons and ammunition that was found on the trucks was enough to justify the operation. Each fighter returned to camp with three or four weapons and a box of ammunition. They also removed uniforms from the soldiers and officers, leaving them naked on the road. Yuri was most excited about finding a box of cigarettes and enthusiastically distributed them to his men – none of the women smoked.

Thirty-Two

Anna had been squirming around on the floor of the bus for some time while Rami watched her.

"Anna, take this," said Rami. He handed her his coat. "Sit on it, you'll be more comfortable."

"Now you remember to give it to me? Where were you when the bus was barreling down the bumpy hill and my fanny was slapping the floor hard enough to crack wood?"

"I was offering you my seat before. You refused, remember. Just take it."

Anna took the olive green jacket and folded it up. "These bars are going to cut my tush," she said. She placed the folded jacket under herself.

"Better?"

"I'm higher now, at least. I can even see the tops of the trees out the front window. What a delight. If I could have seen this before it may have been a pleasant journey."

"Well it's been a pleasant journey for me," said Rami.

"That's nice to hear. You are a pleasant soldier."

"Am I a pleasant driver?" asked Yaakov.

"When you want to be," said Anna. "I can see your potential."

She could also see something else. For just a second, a split second as the light reflected off a passing car's windshield, Anna could see something in Yaakov that she had not seen before. Her new angle made his face look longer, and he reminded her of Tuvia. They had similar chins and lips – at least from below. The flashback of Tuvia giving his life so they could escape came rushing back to Anna and she shook her head.

Then she recalled a conversation she had had with Tuvia while she was pregnant. They had discussed whether they should have been more careful before conceiving Yehuda. "A mother can never regret having her child," she thought, "no matter what the circumstances." Tuvia nodded in agreement

"Unless something happens to you, nothing can take away the pride I have of sharing parenthood with you," he said.

Anna wondered what it was that made her recall that exact moment. There were so many moments when giving birth could have changed so many lives.

289

Thirty-Three

3 November 1943

"I think I'm pregnant," said Miriam.

"How do you know?" asked Anna.

"I haven't had a period in weeks."

"I haven't had a period since Yehuda was born."

"Neither have I," said Ida, walking up from gathering wood in the forest.

"Maybe you've been pregnant for two years," said Miriam. "I need to get an abortion."

"Are you sure you're pregnant?" asked Anna, knowing well enough that if Miriam said she was pregnant, she was. In the ghetto and in the forests, poor diet and malnutrition had caused most women to suffer from Amenorrhea, keeping them from having periods. But Miriam was not most women. It helped that she loved leafy vegetables, when she could get them, which happened to have vitamin A that helped with that condition.

"I don't guess at things like that," she said. "The doctors can do it. I want you to come with me," she said to both of them. There was no question in any of the girl's minds that an abortion was the only solution to Miriam's pregnancy. "And don't tell Nahum." But neither Anna nor Ida wanted to be involved in keeping the procedure from Nahum.

"No," said Anna. "You have to tell him. He has to know because he has to help you through this. I'll help you with anything you need, but you have to tell Nahum."

"I can't," said Miriam. "You tell him... No, don't. I mean... I don't know. I want strawberries."

"Strawberry season is over," said Anna pragmatically.

"If I get you strawberries, will you tell him?" asked Ida.

"Yes! Where do you have strawberries?"

"Will you tell him?"

"Yes! I said. My kingdom for a strawberry."

Ida disappeared only to return ten minutes later with a handful of grapes. "They're small but incredible."

"Where did you get these?" asked Miriam, staring at the grapes like they were poison. "They're not strawberries."

"Oh yes they are," she said. "If you want them to be strawberries, they are strawberries."

Miriam laughed and ate them with the vigor of a woman fulfilling her

291

greatest fantasies.

That night, Anna and Ida watched Nahum's body language as Miriam told him about her pregnancy.

"It seems to be going well," said Ida.

"He's still holding her hand," said Anna.

"His forehead is all wrinkled-up."

"I don't know what that means," said Anna.

"Never mind. Do you think that Miriam would have made a good mother?" asked Ida.

Anna looked at her and took her hand. "I think that all of us would make good mothers."

"Well," said Ida, "As far as my motherhood is concerned, I don't think that's going to happen, unless you can get me pregnant. Do you want to get me pregnant?"

"Wish I could, my dear. I wish I could because I'm quite tired of getting pregnant myself. Here comes Miriam."

"That was more frightening than the Brushmaker's Gate," said Miriam. "But he took it well. He said that it would be nice to have children someday, but there was no reason to start now. We have a job to do, and this will only get in the way."

"Is that what he said, or what you said?" asked Anna.

"It's what he said, but what I was thinking. Let's get this done."

The next morning the girls took Miriam to one of the newer doctors in the camp. It was very rare for girls to get pregnant in the partisan forests, but when it happened, and it did, the doctors were all qualified to perform the abortions. Even though some were Catholics, they knew they were saving the mother and that had the baby been born in those conditions his chances of survival were nil. The Jewish doctors never thought twice about it, since saving the mother's life was a priority under Jewish law.

As Miriam rested on the straw bed covered on a sheet that was as sterile as could be expected under the circumstances, she turned to Ida and Anna and smiled. "This wasn't what I wanted, you know."

Anna shook her head and squeezed Miriam's hand. Ida kissed her on the forehead.

"We were together only once. Really, once – only once. I didn't think this would happen. I want to have a child someday," said Miriam. "Someday, when I'm not blowing things up.

Physically, Miriam's abortion went smoothly, and aside from a few days of rest in the area designated for dying patients, she missed little in the camp. However, her emotional recuperation took quite a bit longer – not at all assisted by days of proximity to those poor souls spending the last few hours of their lives attempting to fight pain. Miriam too was in great discomfort following the operation, but nothing compared to the man who had burns over fifty percent of his body after a botched attempt to blow up a bridge. He died during the evening of the second day Miriam spent there, and she told Anna, if anything like that ever happens to her, shoot her right away.

If Miriam had seemed impassive before the procedure, she was utterly lethargic after it. She never shed a tear, as was in her nature, but neither did she laugh or smile for days. Nahum tried his best to encourage her, but she blamed him for the whole ordeal. Their relationship, as Benjamin had suggested, had distracted her from the singular purpose of being in the forest (not that she or anyone else had a better place to be). She resented Nahum for his role in getting her pregnant and forcing her to give up a child that she someday would want, but she would get over her resentment when the next opportunity to kill Nazis arose.

Meanwhile, winter would soon be upon them and with it the task of building zemlyankas – underground huts that the fighters had learned to build from the Russians. The summer was over, and the camp would be able to remain in its current location for the winter, as the Germans were not only afraid to enter the forest for fear of witchcraft, they also were learning the hard way that the allies' secret weapon was none other than Mother Nature herself. The winter of 1943-44 would not only bog down the German advance into Russia but would allow the partisans in occupied Poland to strengthen their forces and eventually assist in pushing the Germans out of Eastern Europe altogether.

But that was still some time in the future, and the partisans of the Wyszkow camp had planning for the winter on their minds. The building of the zemlyankas was the first of a series of tasks at hand. Anna suggested that the girls move their sleeping area and build their zemlyanka closer to the center of the camp. Her logic was, the more they were seen and felt, the more they will be asked to join in future operations. But it was Ida who picked the location. She had noticed that one particular spot in the forest rose slightly – perhaps half a meter – and continued to flatten out forming a mini plateau among the trees. She said that even after they dig the pit that would eventually become their home for the winter, they would be able to view their surroundings as they would be slightly above everyone else. It made perfect sense, only that Ida had never spent a winter in the Polish forest before, and the amount of snow that would be falling would inevitably even out the field and bury their zemlyanka so deep that only a periscope would allow for any form of viewing their surroundings.

By the time they had finished building their new home, Miriam was back to complete health, although still somewhat subdued. They had been asked to permanently join a raid and demolition squad that was to leave on a mission just ten days after Miriam had lost her baby.

"You are crazy!" said Miriam in response to Ida's suggestion that she stay behind and rest a few more days. "All I could think about was getting out there again and helping with the missions. You're mad if you think that I'm spending one more day in this place – without reward, I mean."

This time, the group departing for the operation was considerably larger than the previous unit. It consisted of twenty-four men and six women. The group was divided into three subunits, each with its own commander. Anna was assigned commander of her unit after Ida suggested her to one of the Polish commanders saying, "Anna is our man."

One of the women joining the operation was new to the camp, and Anna had yet to meet her. Anna had been taken aside the night before the mission to be given a detailed briefing. There stood a young fighter from the ghetto who had escaped and had been hiding out with a Polish family in Warsaw.

"My name is Lenka, Lenka Gutenplan. I know you, Anna."

"How do you know me?"

"I was on many lookouts in the ghetto. I'm from Dror. I don't think we've ever met, but I know you. You're famous."

"When did you leave the ghetto?"

"I left alone after most of my friends died in May. I don't even know the date I left – the beginning of May. I was on a lookout when I saw the Germans accidentally blow a hole in the wall off Konwiktorska Street – it was because of this crazy operation I was watching. I guess a stray mortar blew a hole in the wall. Afterward, I noted the spot and left the next night. I crawled out of the hole and went to my old neighbor's house. They were still there and they took me in."

"We left before you, I guess."

"I know," said Lenka. "Your escape was a bit traumatic for some of the group. It was as if…well, it was hard. The whole thing was hard."

"I'm sorry," said Anna. It was not what she wanted to hear. If her early departure was even in the slightest demoralizing, it was not what she had intended. What would Miriam say about that? she thought. "What kind of activity was there after we left?"

"Just crazy stuff. You know, a sniper here, a grenade there, just crazy. There was that one mission that resulted in the blown hole in the wall. These three guys went out on the roof of one of the buildings on Konwiktorska Street and started shooting at the machinegun units outside of the wall. Two were hit right away, but the third guy – I'll never forget him, he had a white scarf – ran out into the street – well he didn't really run, he more like waddled – he hurt his leg, I suppose. He didn't make it very far, but he did manage to kill another Nazi before being gunned down yelling. I thought he called out, 'Am Yisrael Chai,' but I'm not sure."

"He did," said Anna with tears streaming down her cheeks. "His name was Peretz. He was my friend and housemate."

This task," said a man named Boria who was dressed in a Red Army coat and worn black trousers but looked more like a subaltern peasant than a commander, "is quite complex and demands timing, accuracy, high-power explosives and coordination between several subunits. We are trying to disrupt the railway lines that pass through the area in three spots. The first spot will be here." He pointed to a black line on the map he had set down on the forest floor. "We have observed that a cargo train arrives at this spot every other day at 10:15 in the morning. The first cut in these lines will be conducted to derail that train. Two units will be assigned this spot. Unit one will cut the lines and retreat into the forest behind the tracks. Unit two will be the sniper unit," he looked directly at Anna. "Unit three will continue along the tracks for five kilometers, cutting the lines every one hundred meters. It will take those pigs months to restore the tracks, and supplies to the front line will be stalled once again."

Boria went ahead and detailed the operation. Cutting the rail lines would not be a major problem for the partisans, as they had been cutting lines since early 1941. However, the line that was to be cut this time would have to be camouflaged so the conductor would not see the slice in the track until it was too late. The partisans would dig out enough dirt under the tracks so that when the train reached the sliced track, it would split the rail in two and cause the train to derail. At that point, the two units, consisting of a total of eighteen fighters – fifteen men and the three women from the Warsaw ghetto – would attack the train and steal whatever supplies they needed.

The night they were to leave for the raid, dusk fell on the camp with a light that made Anna think that something horrible would happen during the operation. She did not know why. While watching the sun fall behind the thick forest, darkness spawned fire after fire to return the lost light; she felt a feeling of despair. She had never considered premonition one of her traits, but the feeling in the pit of her stomach forced her to discuss with Ida an action she had been considering for quite some time.

"I want to hide the rings," she said.

"What rings?" asked Ida.

"The rings from my grandmother; you know the wedding bands."

"Right. What do you want to do?"

"I want to bury them – hide them – here in the forest. I have been taking too much of a chance leaving them here each day – even in our little zemlyanka. They could be stolen, and they are the only items of value I have."

Ida and Anna took a flashlight and walked just outside of the camp to a small clearing. As they walked through the camp, they ran into one of the men who had been present at the briefing.

"Have you come to visit me?" he said. "Good idea to get your thrills before such a dangerous operation, no?"

"No!" said Anna. "Move away."

"What is it? We are partners in this scheme. We must get to know each other, no?"

"No. Now back off and let us pass."

The man who had not removed his hands from his pockets had apparently never heard about Anna's oratory capabilities and her ability to verbally castrate poor souls. He would have experienced it right then and there if not for Ida's attempt to distract the man instead of confronting him. It was too late at night for them to make another scene. There was no need to reinforce the point that Anna was not to be taken for granted.

"Do you have some drinks?" asked Ida.

"I...I can get some...in an instant. Right over there, please come join me?"

"No, no," said Ida. "Go get the drinks and we'll have some here."

It was too dark for Ida to see Anna's look, but had it been daylight, she would have seen the rage of a lion mixed with the shock of its prey. As soon as the man left toward his zemlyanka, they darted into the thicket. In the end, Anna was impressed, and they laughed all the way into the forest.

An old tractor had been left off to the side of a dirt road, and a large pine tree was tipped slightly to the south, pointing exactly in the direction of the hole they dug for the rings. Ida figured that it would be an easy place to find if they ever needed to return to the spot to retrieve them.

As Anna placed the small bag with the rings inside the hole they had dug, she said, "A girl escaped the bondage of life with a man who refused to cherish her. These rings are her freedom, and they are ours as well. Promise me, Ida, that if anything ever happens to me you will come to get these rings and pass them on to your daughters. Promise me."

Ida held Anna's cheeks and placed her lips on Anna's trembling mouth. "I promise," she said.

Anna was wrong about something terrible happening to her that night, but she was right about something terrible happening. Two unrelated events would occur that night, and Anna would be lucky to survive both.

The first happened two hours after the three units left the camp at midnight and walked toward the tracks they planned to sabotage. The fire that Ida had built at the foot of the plateau just outside the newly built zemlyanka had been left to burn. Early that day, Anna had been mending one of her garments and had left a ball of twine outside the entrance to the zemlyanka on the hill over the fire. The end of the ball had been tied to a stick to keep it from unraveling. When another fighter ran by the girls' zemlyanka he nudged the ball just enough to cause it to roll down the slight grade of the hill Ida had so carefully picked out for their home and directly into the fire. The twine caught in an instant, and the fire found ample fuel on its way up the embankment and onto the zemlyanka. It took the alert women of the camp only a few minutes to awake and notice the hut burning, but by the time they managed to put it out, all its contents had burned.

The second event to verify Anna's sick feeling in her stomach happened on the way to the tracks. To keep a low profile while on the move, the groups split into their three units. Anna's unit consisted of Ida, Miriam, Mikolaj and four other men, each carrying their own rifle and ammunition as well as either a steel saw, wooden crates or explosives. The plan was to meet up with the other two groups about one kilometer south of the point where they would derail the approaching train. Anna had instructed Miriam and one of the men to walk ahead of the group to navigate the terrain. Luckily, the night sky was clear and a half-moon provided sufficient light to see landmarks throughout the forest and among the clearings they passed.

Anna should have been aware of the danger – her stomach once again began churning as if she had just eaten a rotten piece of fruit. However, she, like the rest of the group, was taken by surprise when the word, "Halt!" came bellowing from beyond the line of trees off to their right. The forest stood still and silent as all six of them dropped to the ground. Anna immediately began to wonder what had happened to Miriam and Mikolaj. Had they been spotted, or worse yet, had they been captured. Anna instructed her team to hold fire until she understood what exactly was calling them to halt in the middle of nowhere.

She grabbed Ida's lapel and pulled her close. "Fall back and set yourself in position." As Ida slowly backed herself away from the group, a gunshot rang out and Anna got her first glimpse of the man who had first called out to them and then opened fire. He was wearing an SS uniform and his belt buckle was still undone. He had not been aiming in Anna's direction. She quickly deduced that he had stopped to relieve himself in the woods when he saw the partisans, wasting no time to open fire – possibly believing that the threat was even supernatural.

297

Before Anna could give any kind of command, another shot came from directly behind her, from Ida, and the SS officer, standing over fifty meters ahead, buckled over, falling head first onto the very urine he had previously spilled onto the forest floor. There was some yelling from behind the trees and two more shots were heard. They too were not shooting in Anna's direction but at Mikolaj and Miriam. Mikolaj was hit and Miriam fired back.

Once again, it was Ida who took out the two men who had come running out from behind the trees where the SS officer had decided to relieve himself. The first fell almost directly on top of the fallen officer, and the second was shot in the back as he attempted to run out of the terrifying forest that had taken his two comrades.

There was silence until Miriam screamed, "He's hit!"

The six fighters split into two groups. Anna, Ida and one of the larger men who had been nicknamed Elf, ran to the injured Mikolaj, while the three others ran to the SS officer and his two unlucky travel companions.

There was nothing to do for Mikolaj, who had been struck in the right temple. He was dead before he even hit the ground.

"You Bastards!" yelled Miriam, who was realizing that the bullet could have hit her. She began running toward the three dead bodies, causing Ida to pursue her toward the line of trees that hid a road that Anna should have been aware of. In her defense, she would note that the map failed to show a dirt road that close to the forest line, and the only road they should have passed on the way to the tracks was over two hundred meters to the west. When they reached the vehicle, they realized what had occurred with the SS officer, his driver and passenger – they were lost. Two maps lay sprawled out on the front seat and one more on the hood of the vehicle. And the dirt road was a farm path used to reach the fields on the edge of the forest – fields that had not been plowed since the start of the war.

When Miriam reached the SS officer, she began beating him using the butt of her rifle as a cudgel, all the while yelling, "You Bastard! You Bastard! You Bastard!" She hit him so hard that his skull cracked, and blood splattered over his spotless uniform.

Ida grabbed Miriam with both arms around her body and pulled her off the dead and now deformed officer. Miriam's wrath was no longer effective punishment, and the officer was having a bad enough day as it was.

While Ida was subduing Miriam, whose outburst, Anna knew, had more to do with her recent abortion than with the death of Mikolaj, two of the men entered the jeep and were driving it into the forest. Once they passed the trees and ran over some fallen logs, breaking the axle in the process, the other two men, seemingly unscathed by their friend Mikolaj's death, began looking for treasures. There were two sets of binoculars, maps, water cans and more weapons in addition to the guns each of the men had been carrying. There was also a packed meal – half-eaten – that the men immediately began devouring.

"Would you leave that!" scolded Anna. "We have a mission and we just lost one of our top shooters."

"He was not one of us," said one of the men, and he bit into a sandwich, causing pieces of meat to fall onto his scraggly beard. "It's okay. I won't hold a grudge from last night. I won't tell. It's me, Sasha, remember. I won't tell."

Anna walked up to him with a look of rage. Without speaking, she took the sandwich out of his hand and smashed it into his face. All of these men had heard of Anna's outburst earlier that summer – all but this one. As Anna looked him in the eye, with a little more light than during the previous encounter, she recognized that he was the same man who had confronted her and Ida the night before. Most of the men were afraid of her – which was exactly why she was given command of the group. Soon he would be as well.

"I don't care if you mourn the loss of our unit, you idiot," she said in a manner that kept him from responding, "and I don't give a damn whether you liked him or not. But don't you ever disrespect a fallen fighter. We are one man short, on top of everything else, and you two will carry his body so he can receive a proper burial. Got it? And as for all this junk, leave it!"

The man with the now very dirty face jumped.

One of the men was still sitting inside the car, and he slowly began exiting the vehicle.

"We should hide the good stuff, no?" asked the third man hesitantly, who had been watching his comrade being humiliated by Anna.

"It will all be here when we come back," responded Anna. "Just take the binoculars."

The two men who had been assigned the task of carrying Mikolaj seemed to be cursing under their breath as they lifted him off the forest floor where he had fallen. Ida had her arm around Miriam, as they watched Mikolaj lifted onto the shoulders of the larger of the two men.

"We should bury him now," said Miriam. The man holding Mikolaj nodded in agreement.

"We don't have time," said Anna.

"We do. We were ahead of schedule as it was. We could dig a grave in no time. Let's bury him now."

Anna noticed that Miriam's eyes were tearing. She knew she wouldn't cry, but it had been far too emotional for Anna to ignore her plea. Miriam's

299

inexorable demeanor was no match for Anna's authority. Now she was faced with deciding between what she felt was best for the operation and what she felt was best for her friend. She chose Miriam.

Miriam had been correct about the time it took to bury Mikolaj. The two men who had been spared the long walk with a dead man on their back were now digging furiously. They finished digging a two-meter long, one-meter deep hole in the soft forest dirt so quickly that even Anna was impressed. One of them unexpectedly said a quick prayer over the grave.

Anna was thinking about Peretz.

She had attended another funeral.

Thirty-Four

"I remember one day," said Anna while looking straight ahead at the bus console, "when my sisters and I – I call them my sisters since they're my family – were returning from an operation in the forests of Poland that it first occurred to me that my son may be dead."

Rami was leaning over the rail between his seat and the stairwell trying to listen to Anna who was now speaking softer than usual.

Over the years Anna had acquired an ability to analyze her past with equanimity. Understandably, she could never view anything that the Nazis did to her or to her life with evenness of mind, but there was a clarity she felt when recalling specific events from her last years in Poland.

"We were returning from derailing a train. What a sight that was. One of our men had been killed when we were surprised by an SS officer relieving himself on the side of the road. Can you imagine being killed because an SS officer had to take a leak? But it happened. It was also the night our camp burned down. Well, not the whole camp, just our little zemlyanka – that's an underground bunker the Russians taught us to build in the forest; perfectly camouflaged on the outside, but nice and cozy inside. We got very good at building these huts – we must have built five different huts through the course of that winter… because we had to move around quite a bit. But in the fire, we lost very little that we were unable to replace. We were lucky. I had these rings, and that very day I decided to hide them in the forest. I was very lucky."

Anna was only talking to the driver, but no one on the bus uttered a word as she spoke.

"Anyway, other than those two incidents, the rest of the mission went off wonderfully – without a hitch. It went so smoothly that my sister Ida never had to fire a single shot – outside of killing the SS officer. She enjoyed shooting any chance she got, but there was nothing to shoot at. We cut the railroad tracks and made the train run right off the track," Anna made a gesture with her hand like a plane taking off. "The eight cars behind it crunched together like an accordion and we all were so excited.

"Inside the cars, the only useful items we found were blankets. The rest of the cars were filled with spare parts for tanks, hay and some kind of wood paneling…for factories, I think. Since we could only carry a limited amount of material – there were only eighteen of us…no seventeen since one of our men had been killed – we just took the blankets. We decided, well Miriam decided, to bury the marksman who had been killed by the peeing

301

officer right where we fell. I was glad we had buried him and not tried to take his dead body back with us – it freed two pairs of hands to bring the blankets back to camp."

"So you derailed trains?" asked Rami.

"Oh yes. More than once. We did all kinds of things that winter: blew up bridges, kidnapped soldiers, derailed trains; it was a good time – even though it was as harsh as a Polish winter can be. Here in Israel, you have no idea what cold is. It snows in Jerusalem, but when was the last time it reached 20 below zero? We had months of that. But our zemlyanka was nice and cozy. The three of us, Miriam, Ida and I, loved spending time there. It was a good time."

Once again, Anna was silent and stared into space. She was thinking about how much she appreciated her time with the partisans. The ghetto had given her an appreciation for freedom. She knew that she could be happy wherever she was under two conditions: that no one was trying to kill her in her sleep and that she was with Ida. As difficult as the forests were for her, she was usually happy there – at least in retrospect. She and Ida had discussed that period often, and they both always viewed it fondly – even though some of their comrades had fallen.

"You were talking about when you realized that your son may be dead," said Yaakov.

"Oh yes, I was distracted. I do that to myself sometimes. So we were walking back from derailing the trail and I was carrying a few blankets. They were new and had a new blanket smell. You know that smell? I thought of Shimi, my first son because they smelled like a blanket I had bought him once. Then I felt like I saw Yehuda's head next to his. It was almost as if they were telling me they were together, but I understood it as they were both dead. I said something to Ida. I said, 'Ida, I think Yehuda is dead.' She said nonsense. It's all in my imagination. She said I was just panicking for no reason and that Hanna wouldn't let anything happen to him...."

"Hanna? That's the name of your friend?" said Yaakov.

"Yes, she was the one taking care of my Yehuda. She was the one that took him out of the ghetto. I mean, I sent him out with her...to his death."

"Hanna, that was my mother's name," said Yaakov.

Thirty-Five

During the summer of 1944, the Red Army successfully liberated all of Soviet Russia, Ukraine, Belorussia, the Baltic States and eastern Poland from the hands of the Germans who had occupied much of that territory for over two years. Word of the Russian successes continually flowed into the partisan camps, and it was becoming clear that soon the Red Army would expel the Nazis from Poland altogether. The operation that would eventually lead to the emancipation of Poland was called the Lvov-Sandomierz offensive, and it began on July 17, 1944.

Anna was one of the first in the camp, her sixth camp since leaving the ghetto, to hear of the planned attacks on Poland, and she, now a senior commander for the partisans – the only women commander in her unit – was set on assisting as best she could. However, their options were limited, and there was still much tension among the partisans. Throughout the winter, there had been numerous incidents where Polish Home Army and Armia Ludowa men had killed Jewish partisans. After all that they had been through together, old anti-Semitic sentiments outweighed the new cooperative atmosphere in the camps. The Home Army men would often drink and quarrel with the Jews, sometimes attempting to seduce the women and sometimes just beating defenseless young fighters who unwittingly wandered into the Polish area of the camp.

In April of that year, there was finally a battle in the forest. However, it was not between the partisans and the Nazis, but between Jewish Partisans of the Mordechai Anielewicz Partisan Unit operating in the Wyszkow area and their former comrades at arms, the Armia Krajowa Polish nationals. By the end of the fighting, the Poles had managed to murder three of the commanders and put an end to the Anielewicz unit for good.

Many of the Jewish fighters, at Anna's suggestion, had fled the area and had reestablished themselves in a northern region just before the April outburst. Anna had predicted the events and was quick to move as many of the Jews as would listen – and some of the more sympathetic Poles – far from the nationalists who had invaded her world. They had been used to moving around. This split in the camp also helped Anna establish herself as a local leader.

In addition, the Red Army had let down the Poles during the general uprising in Warsaw of the summer of 1944. Many of the survivors of the ghetto uprising had made strategic decisions to join the insurrection in

Warsaw, fighting side-by-side with the Polish Home Army and the anti-Semitic Armia Ludowa to gain home rule, only to die due to blatant disregard from the Red Army, who stopped their advance at the Vistula River, far short of what was expected of them. In August, after a successful four days when the Polish Home Army defeated German positions and took control of the city, the Germans began bombarding Warsaw. The Red Army withheld all assistance with the distinct intent of letting the Germans crush the Polish fighters, hence removing any potential opposition to Russian rule in Poland. The Russians did not only withhold the promised support greatly needed, but they prevented the western allies from assisting in any way. The Germans crushed the uprising and with it much of the Polish capital, expelled or executed thousands of Poles and cleared the way for an easy Red Army entrance and control of the country.

Once again, Anna had warned of this scenario, but as with most of her dismal predictions, this one was viewed as irrational and pessimistic. By mid-August, even the few remaining pro-Soviet Armia Ludowa fighters in the camps with Anna were able to see what was happening as the Germans continued to blast their capital. They inwardly praised Anna for her providence but outwardly criticized the commanders who let Anna, a woman and a Jew – albeit a socialist – take a leading role in the camp.

The winter had been long and harsh – as Polish winters tended to be. But the partisans, who had been forced to move camp twice during the winter, despite losses to illness, casualties on the battlefield and unnecessary infighting, managed to remain strong as a group. For those who did not take special care of themselves, frostbite was a danger that hindered many partisans' chances of surviving the winter. For others, attempting to avoid the bitter cold, burns from the fires were common. When it seemed in their best interest, the Red Army had assisted some, but the task of maintaining camp and a strong military front came from the partisans themselves. Among the assistance that the Red Army provided the partisans was airdropping from the sky. Supplies, including ammunition and food, were dropped into the forest at designated spots, and these supplies saved many of the partisan units from certain death in the winter. On one occasion, the camp was elated to find that the Russians had dropped Vodka and chocolate. The ensuing party ended with one Pole stabbing another in a drunken stupor, and several bad cases of stomach illness from over-indulgence in chocolate.

Anna had led several missions since the train derailment, and both Miriam and Ida had seen their share of targets destroyed. Ida, who was now able to practice her shooting, improved her marksmanship to a level unmatched of among the partisans. She was proud of her accomplishments, which included the shooting of seven German soldiers in three minutes from a range of over one hundred meters while it was snowing. Anna was proud of her too.

Anna had made it a point to remain close with the Red army commanders who would frequent their camps throughout the summer of 1944. One of her first encounters with such a commander was eye-opening for Anna, and she quickly learned from the experience.

Anna and her translator approached the commander who was pretending to be busy reading a map. The translator was a Polish boy who had lived close enough to the Russian border to learn the language. During those days in the forest, he was an important asset since the Russians enjoyed talking about the Jews behind their backs, believing that most of the Polish partisans knew no Russian. When the commander finally took note of her, he looked up nonchalantly.

"What does she want," he said in a condescending tone to the translator.

"She wants to thank you for helping the Jews," he said.

The commander set down his map and sat up in his chair. There must have been something in the intense way that she was looking at him that caught his attention, but that did not prevent him from being straight forward and crude.

"I don't care about the Jews. I don't care about the Poles. I only care about the success of the Soviet Union over the German pigs. If you can help me kill Germans, so be it."

Anna looked him in the eye as if she was the one in charge.

"I understand," she said. "But I would like to bomb the railway lines to the camps."

Over the previous year, it had become clear that the only way to stop the Nazi death machine was to prevent them from transferring more Jews to the camps. During the summer, between June and July, the Germans had expelled the remaining Jews of ghetto Lodz to Chelmno where they were brutally exterminated.

"I can't do that," he said coldly.

"Why not," she asked. "You can do whatever you want." She spoke as if she was the one giving the commands, but he was not about to listen to a Jew or a woman.

"It's not the plan. Now get back to whatever it was you were doing."

Anna glared at him for a second, shook her head and turned to leave.

"We have sent," he shouts after her, "numerous messages and requests to the Americans to bomb the railway lines. They just keep flying right over them and drop nothing. I think the Americans care even less

305

about the Jews."

"I doubt that," she whispered to the translator. "Don't translate that."

For Anna, Ida and Miriam, who no longer saw Poland as home, this was the time to begin planning their future in Eretz Yisrael. Miriam, who had spent the winter making plans with Nahum to leave for Palestine, could not fathom living in Poland another day. Anna had been waiting for the very Red Army operation that had taken place that summer to begin her moves to leave Poland and immigrate to Palestine. However, she knew that as long as the war was waging, any attempt to cross borders would be met with dangers she deemed unnecessary; the war would be over soon enough, she thought. There was no need to rush her departure.

Miriam's newly formed zeal to leave Poland was assisted by the arrival of an emissary from Palestine. The Zionist movement in Eretz Yisrael had been sending paratroopers to both fight the Nazis and to help the Jews escape. This particular man, Ze'ev Caspi, was the spitting image of the statue of David in Florence – not that any of the girls had ever actually seen the statue. He stood two meters tall, with blond wavy hair brushed back, a perfect build, and although he was thirty-two years old, he claimed to be twelve. "My birthday is the day I moved to Eretz Yisrael," he told them through a translator. "That would make me twelve years old next month." That was in October 1932. Ze'ev had left Germany before the Nazi rise to power. He told them that the writing was on the wall, but no one, not even the most pessimistic Jews in Germany could have fathomed what the future held for the strongest country in central Europe. He understood some Polish, having come from a small German village on the Polish border, but could not speak. He said he knew Yiddish but refused to speak it, stating that it was the language of exile; Hebrew was the only language the Jews of Eretz Yisrael should speak. Within a week of his arrival, he began giving the Jewish partisans Hebrew lessons, and Miriam was his number one student.

Miriam had told Anna that she thought there must have been something pleasant about their year in the forest to keep Anna from leaving. During the months they had been wandering the Polish wilderness, numerous comrades had been killed and captured, illness had taken the lives of hundreds, while others were forced to return to Warsaw to seek medical attention – at least better attention than the well-intentioned doctors of the forests were able to provide. But throughout the ordeals and hardships, Anna had been happy in the woods. So had Ida. Of the three, only Miriam had expressed impatience, which was why she and Nahum decided to leave the forest and head to the Mediterranean Sea. They thought that Yugoslavia would be their best departure point, and the night before they were to set out, Miriam broke the news to her two friends.

"Come with us," she said to Anna and Ida. "There is no reason to wait here any longer."

"Miriam," said Anna, "I will be the last person to tell you not to go, but I am not going to join you. Even if you can make it to the sea, the British will never let you enter Palestine right now – not as long as there is a war going on. They still need the Arabs' support and they won't let any Jews in."

Anna was using the geopolitical excuse not to go, but what she was not saying aloud was the true reason she wished to remain in Poland. She could not stomach the thought of leaving without finding out the fate of Hanna and Yehuda. She knew that it may take longer than she was willing to wait, but her logic was based on the premise that when the war was over, it would be easier to get information. Hanna and Yehuda were either out there waiting to be found or dead. In either case, someone knew about their fate, and she needed to know before she left.

She would not have to wait for long. In a stroke of freakish luck and eerie coincidence, Hanna, Anna's Hanna, was on her way to that very camp that very day and was to arrive the day after Miriam and Nahum departed to Palestine.

"I can't stay here anymore," said Miriam. "You know that. I have done all I can. If I am going to fight again, I want it to be for the establishment of a Jewish homeland in Eretz Yisrael. Don't you think they can use my skills?"

"I absolutely do," said Anna. "You must understand. I am just envious, that's all. I will soon join you, Miriam."

"You know where to find us," said Ida to Miriam as they bid farewell. Ida and Anna were crying – Miriam was not.

"You know where to find me," said Miriam.

Miriam had spoken often of living on Kibbutz Beit Alpha, the first kibbutz established by Hashomer Hatzair in the Beit Shean Valley. She often fantasized verbally about picking dates in the heat (it was often winter when she talked about the heat) and making the desert bloom. Anna would ask her to stop using stupid clichés, and they would then argue about semantics until Ida would intervene.

"Take care of her," Anna said to Nahum.

"Are you kidding," he said. "She'll be taking care of me."

Anna knew that most of the route was safer now that the Russians had pushed the Nazis back through a good part of Poland, but once she left Russian occupied territory, there was no telling what would happen. Safer was just a relative term, and Anna knew that no journey in Europe was safe. The movements had made some attempts to contact the Jews in Eretz Yisrael, but the messages were unclear and the White Paper immigration laws were being strongly enforced by the British. She feared that Miriam and Nahum would never make it out of Europe and would at best be sent to the internment camps that they had been hearing about – still a much better prospect than the extermination camps – although not by much. Anna was also concerned about Miriam's idyll with Nahum. If it didn't last, what would happen then? Would they split? She knew Miriam wouldn't hesitate to leave if she felt the need. She had a better chance than Nahum of surviving on her own.

Anna was not quite ready for the peripatetic lifestyle she would be forced to endure by prematurely leaving the absurd sanctity of the forest. Ironic, since her lifestyle after leaving the ghetto had been more nomadic than anything she would face on her way to Palestine. But she preferred to wait until she could simply make a bee-line from Europe to Palestine. Ida would follow her decision.

The zemlyanka felt empty after Miriam left, even though throughout most of the winter she had spent just as much time with Nahum as she had with the girls, leaving Ida and Anna alone in their zemlyankas. "We're not doing anything," Miriam would tell Anna and Ida about her relationship with Nahum. "I learned my lesson." But that was hard for them to believe. They were doing something; it just wasn't going to get her pregnant again.

However, the vacancy created by Miriam's departure would be filled the next day when Anna would experience the happiest and saddest moments of her year.

"Anna!" called a young man's voice the morning after Miriam had left. Anna had been with Ida inside the zemlyanka reading a copy of Nicolai Gogol's Dead Souls that she was given by an Armia Ludowa man who said he had finished reading it and had "despised" it. The man had said that it was inappropriate reading for him "at this time." Anna could only speculate as to what he meant but didn't value most of the Armia Ludowa's opinions anyway. The first thirty pages were missing, but that didn't bother Anna, since she had read it once before the war. It was difficult to get books in the forest, so whatever she could find was a blessing. She had recently finished a heavily soiled version of Quo Vadis by Henryk Sienkiewicz. Rumor had it that the book had been carried to the front by a Polish soldier who was killed at the outbreak of the war. It then found its way to Warsaw in the soldier's coffin, only to be removed before the burial. The cover had been torn, pages were stained to the point where Anna struggled to make out the letters, and the soldier had apparently been a poet himself and had lined the margins with prose that Anna found quite humorous. There was even a letter to his lover on one of the blank pages at the back of the book. It was incomplete and seemingly written just days before his untimely death. Anna enjoyed the fact that the paper itself had a history, as the story was already considered a classic, being one of the most translated Polish novels ever written. Sienkiewicz was even recognized with the Nobel Prize in 1905 for his work – the first Slav to be bestowed that honor. Anna appreciated that as well. But Anna's most satisfying literary feat while fighting the Polish winter nights in her tiny zemlyanka was when she came across a book by the Zionist thinker A. D. Gordon. She had read excerpts of his work before, but now her state of mind and surroundings made reading his thoughts more profound. Gordon wrote of the religion of manual labor and the creation of a homeland based on the new working Jew. Anna swallowed whole his assessments of the future of Labor Zionism, and as she read, she dreamed of working the land and building a country that was egalitarian and virtuous.

Hearing the call, Anna put down the book and gave Ida a questioning look. She stepped out of the hut and walked around it to the far side where she saw the man who had yelled her name pointing at her. The Red army uniform he was wearing was less than flattering, Anna thought. The fact that she was thinking about fashion meant that she was either getting healthy or stupid; for what Socialist thought about fashion? His shirt was unbuttoned on top, and the collar drooped down making him look like the Cossack his family had been running from for so long. He was wearing a cap that had once been yellow and now looked brownish-green. His odd appearance kept Anna from noticing that the person standing next to him rubbing her hands together was a very thin version of her friend Hanna.

The elation and the pain hit Anna at the same time. She smiled, cried and whimpered the words, "Oh no" all at once. Hanna was standing in front of her. The mystery would be over, but it was clear that no little boy – a would-be three-year-old – was anywhere in sight.

Anna closed the gap between herself and Hanna and they fell into each other's arms – Anna had actually lost control of the muscles in her legs and fell onto Hanna, whose thin, frail body struggled to remain standing with the weight of a fuller Anna than she had remembered.

"Ida! Oh, Ida!" cried Anna. Ida darted out of the hut and joined Anna and Hanna who were still embraced and weeping.

"I did all I could," sobbed Hanna. "I did. I really did. I did all I could. They surprised us. I did all I could."

Several of the other men in the camp came over to see what had happened. This was not an uncommon sight among the partisans. Many had lost family and only discovered their fates months and years later. However, few had witnessed the sheer horror of watching a woman hear her child was dead.

"I have to tell you," said Hanna. "I have to tell you what happened. I have to tell you."

"Okay," whimpered Anna. "Okay, just not yet." Anna was not ready to hear the details. She knew the outcome, and that was hard enough to endure. Hearing how her child died would not bring him back. She had lost her second son. She had lost Tuvia's little boy. "How did you find me?" she asked instead.

"You're famous. I made it to a partisan unit south of Warsaw. They knew who you were. They knew Ida and Miriam too. Where's Miriam? Oh no!"

"No, no," said Ida. "She left yesterday for Palestine with Nahum. She's okay."

"Thank God! I was so happy to hear you were alive," said Hanna through the tears, "They told me stories about the uprising. They told me everyone was dead. I knew that wasn't true. Then I met someone who said he knew you and where you were. He arranged to take me here. I had to find you, but I didn't know how I was going to tell you. I have run the story in my mind over and over. Now I have to tell you what happened."

It would be over several hours before the three would sit down to hear what had happened to Hanna and Yehuda on the Polish farm south of Warsaw. Anna insisted that Hanna eat something. She said she had been traveling for a week before reaching the camp in the south and then another two days to reach Anna. Anna thought how ironic it was that now she could leave Poland – there was absolutely nothing left to stay for – but Miriam had already left.

After drinking the tea Ida prepared for her, Hanna took a deep breath and started telling her story – the one she had been preparing for so long to tell.

Anna and Ida were crying before she even began.

"We were living with a Polish family on a farm outside of Warsaw. Before we found the farm, I had taken Yehuda to our neighbors – remember the Mazjelskis? I thought they would take us in. But they were too scared. She was hardly willing to open the door for me, but her husband made her give us a meal."

The girls were sitting in the zemlyanka, each wrapped in one of the blankets they had looted from the train one year earlier. Hanna, who had changed clothes into one of Ida's khaki shirts, was sitting up on what had been Miriam's mattress, and Anna and Ida were sitting on another blanket set on the ground looking over at her. Anna had thought about the moment she would see Hanna again for years, but this was not what she had dreamed of. She was struggling to comprehend that sitting where Miriam had normally been seated, in the small bunker that would soon be covered in snow, was Hanna. She had lost so much weight, thought Anna, who had now regained most of the body fat she had lost during her confinement to the ghetto.

"Then they sent us off toward the farms. They said there are some sympathetic farmers there. I carried Yehuda and one bag for two days. My arms hurt so much. On the way, we met a woman named Irena. She was so sweet. She liked Yehuda's smile. He always smiled. She took us to her brother's farm. Yehuda was happy there. He was safe, and he was happy. Irena and her family took good care of us. They watched out for Yehuda like he was their own. These were good Poles."

"The ones Nahum couldn't find," said Ida. "It's too bad you missed the chance to tell him about them."

"Yes, I'm sorry I missed them. Well, any time German patrols or Polish police would come they would hide us in the barn. Yehuda loved the barn. He was very good at hiding. I practiced with him all the time. He learned very quickly to keep quiet and still. Only once were we spotted; Irena tried to convince them that I was her niece visiting from Warsaw. They didn't believe her and wanted to see if we were Jews. They stripped Yehuda and looked at his penis. It was a wise decision not to circumcise him. He laughed when they pulled off his pants. He laughed." Ida began crying again. Anna too.

"We had to give Yehuda a Polish name, but he didn't mind. We were doing okay there. Really, okay. I tried to find out what was happening in the ghetto, but it was far too risky to ask questions. I knew nothing. Then, a few weeks ago, a retreating German garrison came by the farm. They took all the food and broke anything in their way. Irena's brother and wife tried to stop them, and they were beaten. Yehuda and I didn't have time to hide, but they didn't care whether or not we were Jews. They were going to kill everyone in the house anyway. They took all of us – Irena, her brother and his wife and Yehuda and me and put us in the back room while they ransacked the house. Then one of them came in and took Irena and me out into the kitchen. Two of them raped Irena right in front of me until their commander came and told them to stop, and then they threw her back into the room. They said something to me in German and laughed. Then two of them went back into the room. I heard screams, a bunch of shots and silence. The two came out smiling and one said to me in Polish, 'Your family is dead. Now you can come with us.'"

Hanna was trembling now. Anna was holding her right hand with both hands and Ida her left. Tears and whimpering filled the small hut-like background music to Hanna's tale.

"They threw me in the back of a truck. Then they burned the house

311

down…and the barn. We drove for about an hour to a field and one of the men had his way with me right there – it was the same commander who had told the others to stop raping Irena. But I didn't care. All I could think about was those screams and the shots and the flames and the smoke. They just drove off and left me there in the field. I walked back to the farm. The whole time I was terrified at what I'd see. When I arrived, the house was gone. All I found was Yehuda's shoe next to where the side door had been. They burned the house with Yehuda and everyone in it. Why would they do that? I sat by the house all night thinking about what I did wrong. Why didn't I hide Yehuda faster? What did I do wrong? The next day I tried to see if I could go into the house, but it was still too hot. There was nothing left anyway. I saw the lumps of bodies burned to nothing, and then I ran away. I've been trying to find you ever since to tell you."

As Hanna finished talking, Anna wiped her eyes and lifted herself onto her knees. She took hold of Hanna's cheeks with both hands and with eyes redder than the sun said, "You will never, ever blame yourself for Yehuda's death. Do you understand me?"

Hanna nodded. "But I lost the bet. I was so sure I was going to win this one. I lost the bet."

22 April 1945

Warsaw had not seen the sun for over three weeks, and when it finally came out on a brisk spring day, Anna let it warm her face knew she would be okay. The tiny Peugeot bounced around the dilapidated roads, and Anna and Ida continually bumped shoulders in the back seat of the small car. Abrasha cracked the window of the passenger seat and stuck four fingers out as if to test the air as they drove past fields and farms. There was a time when these same farms would serve as a refuge for the frightened Jews, but today there was little to fear. Anna looked at the farms differently now. It was on a farm like this where Yehuda had found his death, and that was all she could see while looking at the wagons, the meager animals and the unpainted barns deteriorating from years of neglect.

"Do you remember where we were this time two years ago," Ida asked Anna.

"We were fighting in the ghetto," said Anna smiling, while maintaining her view of the passing fields. "It was the day that Rachel sabotaged the German truck and it blew up with two SS officers inside. That was a good day, but it was the beginning of the end."

"The ghetto seems so far off. Do you think about it?"

"There are days I feel like I'm thinking of nothing else."

"Me too."

Abrasha looked back at them and started to speak, but the car hit an unusually large pothole and instead, he yelled at the driver.

Several weeks after Warsaw was liberated by the Red Army in January 1945, Anna, Hanna and Ida returned to the city from their forest home. Hanna had suggested that they first go to one of the many displaced persons camps that had been set up around the country, but Anna said that if she wanted to be caged again she would have never left the ghetto. They decided that between them they could find at least one Polish family that both survived and remembered them well enough to take them in. Hanna refused to return to the Mazjelskis, saying she would not honor anti-Semites with her presence. It was Ida who suggested going to one of her former school teachers, an elderly woman who had once been a scientist.

"Her name was Olesia," explained Ida. "She always insisted that we call her by her first name. She would say, 'My surname makes me sound old.' If she survived the war, she will surely take us in."

Olesia's husband had died in the early 1930s and had left Olesia with a generous sum of money. She did not need to work, but she viewed teaching as a calling and would often invite her favorite students, such as Ida, to her home to study. When the first decrees to place the Jews in the ghetto were released, Ida went to visit her for one last time.

"When this is over," said Olesia, "you will return to me and we will talk about your higher education. You tell your Jewish friends to stay strong. Some of us gentiles will pray for you. Remember, the Germans cannot remain in Poland forever, it will make them sick," she joked.

Ida led her friends to her old neighborhood in the northwest section of Warsaw. She went directly to the building she had last seen five years earlier – the day before she entered the ghetto. On many of her runs outside the ghetto walls, she had wanted to return but feared that the area was unsafe. Two buildings to the south of Olesia's five-story complex was a pile of rubble.

"That used to be Jolanta's house," she said. "She was the first girl I ever kissed." Hanna chuckled. Anna knew that she wasn't thinking about the destroyed property.

They entered the stairwell of Olesia's building. It looked as if a fire had burned in the hall, leaving uneven lines of black soot on the walls. They walked up two flights of stairs, Ida knocked on the door, and it promptly opened. Before them stood a thin, frail elderly woman, with cracked rimmed glasses and a flowered dress covered in an apron. She squinted up at Ida – the lenses on the glasses had not been corrected for some time.

"Yes?" she said.

"Olesia. It's me, Ida."

"Ida? ... Yes! Ida!" Olesia, whose stature had folded over the years, spread both arms out and embraced Ida. She was trembling as she held her and repeated several more times, "Ida. Yes, Ida." Anna watched and smiled as Olesia embraced her former student, finally releasing her. "So you've returned to discuss your future studies, have you?"

Olesia's flat had two bedrooms and a large living room attached on one side to the foyer and on the other to the dining room. Off of the dining room was the kitchen, where smells of boiling broth had filled the house.

"I had no idea who I was cooking for," said Olesia. "Now I know." Ida made the introductions, and Olesia gave both Hanna and Anna kisses on the cheeks as she invited them in and asked them to have a seat on the sofa while she checked the food.

"You're going to love her," said Ida. "She has a wit that I have missed dearly."

She returned without the apron and the glasses and sat down on the white armchair across from the three who had all sat on the velvet couch.

"So," said Olesia, who had placed her elbows on her knees and leaned forward to get closer to the girls, "how was the war?"

"See what I mean," Ida whispered to Anna.

"It's been five years."

"It was terrible, Olesia," said Ida.

"Yes, it was. I can only imagine what you have been through. May I ask where you are staying now?"

"That's just it," said Ida. "We have been hiding in the forests just north of here. We have nowhere to go."

"So you have come to old Olesia for shelter from the cold. That is an honor. I have heard of the atrocities the Jews have endured, and I know that not only the Germans made your lives miserable. My people are just as much to blame...well, not just as much. The German's are pigs. I can let you stay here under two conditions." She held up two fingers like a victory sign. "The first is that you help me around the house. I am older than I was when we last met, and it is getting more and more difficult to get on. Secondly, and I must admit that I am somewhat embarrassed that I must request this of you, but I must. It is for all of our good. You must never tell anyone where you are staying. Some people still are angry with the Jews. They blame the Jews for the German occupation, as ridiculous as that sounds, and they would not take lightly to my harboring you here. This neighborhood is safe. You can be seen coming and going – I'm sure many of the neighbors will not think twice about it – but don't tell anyone officially."

"We are used to keeping our whereabouts secret," said Ida. "Thank you."

"Oh don't thank me, dear. I am happy to have company. Now, before we eat, what would you like to read?" Anna's eyes seemed to pop out of her head.

The girls rested at Olesia's warm flat for the remainder of the day. Anna was so eager to read the wealth of material that Olesia had offered that she began to think she would never leave. Throughout the evening, Anna and Olesia discussed issues of common interest to the two bibliophiles, and Olesia would often rant on about completely unrelated topics. Anna suggested that it was Olesia's age that made her say some of the things she said, but Ida assured her that she had spoken that way for decades. She admitted to Anna her predisposition to collecting the classics but tended to regret ever going out of her way to acquire them. "They are pompous and crude," she said. Anna viewed her proclivity for acquisition as a blessing. It guaranteed that Anna would be well entertained while they rested with her.

The length of their stay was already a part of their causerie that evening. They knew that it could take months to find a safe passage to Palestine, and as cordial as Olesia had been, they were quite unsure whether she would be that hospitable. They also decided that they needed to make some visits "for purposes of closure," Anna had said, and their first stop would be the ghetto. However, when they finally ventured out to that part of the city, they were quite alarmed to find that there was nothing left to see. The entire area had been razed to the ground. It had been the German intention to build a park where the ghetto once stood. In an ironic gesture, Hanna picked up a small stone and placed it on top of a pile of rubble that remained at the entrance to Mila Street. "Jews are buried here," she said. "It should be treated as a grave." Anna and Ida stood holding hands, tears streaming down their cheeks as they thought about the death of their brothers and sisters in arms. The ghetto had been their home. Anna claimed that she grew more as a person in the ghetto than any other place. Everyone did, she said.

One week later, after contacting Abrasha, they decided they would return to the forest. Abrasha was surprisingly encouraging and told them he could supply both a driver and his own company.

"Will we find them?" asked Ida, while returning her stare to the fields outside of the car window.

"Where would they go?" answered Anna.

"Right."

"I just hope we can find the right tree."

"That won't be a problem. There are some things I don't forget. I'm good with trees. Besides, later that month I went back with Miriam and shot four holes in it – just to make sure."

Anna laughed.

Hanna had decided not to join them on their trip to the forest. She had not been feeling well and preferred to rest with Olesia, although she had told Anna that she was rather intimidated by Olesia's topics of conversation. Anna's attempt to mollify her by suggesting points of dialogue only made Hanna more nervous. Hanna did not read nearly as much as Anna.

"Stop the car," yelled Abrasha suddenly.

Anna and Ida looked in the direction he was facing and tried to see whatever it was that he was focusing on. As soon as the car came to a full stop, Abrasha ran out toward a large pile of dirt. He stood over the pile and removed his hat. Anna and Ida left the car as well, leaving only the driver to wait with his vehicle while the three stood over a lump of mud.

"This is the grave where five of my fighters are buried," he said as Anna and Ida approached. "There's nothing here anymore. No sign that five men fell in a battle to save this godforsaken piece of scum land from the Nazis. The whole country is scattered with these remnants. They curse the land for eternity. Poland will be cursed for its part in this mess. For as long as this world turns, Poland will be damned."

"Who were they?" asked Anna. "I mean, who was she?"

Abrasha turned abruptly and looked at Anna, then slowly returned his glance back to the tiny hill that was hardly noticed from the road.

"She was to be my wife. She and the four other men were on what was supposed to be a simple operation. But they were spotted on this very road. They were slaughtered – each shot at close range – and left here. The next day, after they had failed to return, we went after them. We found their bodies and buried them. We didn't have time to give them a proper grave, so we just threw them all together. The Nazi pigs took everything from them…even the engagement ring I gave her one week before this happened."

"You met in the camp? In Wyszkow? Did we know her?"

"Yes, you may have, she was often taking care of the sick. She participated in some of your raids, I believe." Abrasha stopped talking and looked at the mound again.

"Does she have a name?" asked Ida impatiently.

"Lenka."

"Lenka? Our Lenka?" said Ida.

"And how is it that you have ownership over her, may I ask? Oh, because she too was a ghetto fighter. Well, that only left her brave and scarred."

"How come we didn't know about this? Where were we?"

"My dear, there was a great deal you were unaware of back then. You had your unit and that was where your energy was focused. You may have been blind to the happenings around you. Besides, I left the camp for several months, remember? She came with me."

As they returned to the car, Abrasha turned and looked back at the remains of the love of his life. Anna thought about how lucky she was to have survived the war with two of her friends. She still had faith she would find more of them but her hopes weren't high. She had learned her lesson about maintaining unrealistic hope. The war had been far too cruel for her to keep illusions alive any longer than necessary. If Miriam was still alive, she was in Eretz Yisrael, and Anna would find her when she arrived there. Everyone else she had loved was dead.

"My mission here is complete," said Abrasha, "now on to yours. This package, is it close? Our camp was five kilometers north of here. I get impatient after I accomplish my tasks."

"Why didn't you tell us this was what you were coming for?"

"Would it have made any difference in the great scheme of this mad world? Would you have valued my presence more? Or would you have simply tolerated me with the reverence of a schoolgirl? It was of no consequence, my dear — none whatsoever. And do you think I have the slightest idea what it is you are after here? I do not, but unlike you, I do not pretend to care."

"I beg your pardon," said Ida.

"And my pardon you shall have. Now, may we move on to your menial endeavor?"

"Even for you," said Ida, "that was rude. Have some respect."

Abrasha shook his head and looked back at his Lenka. "Respect. It's overrated."

"Leave him be," said Anna to Ida quietly. "This has to be painful for him. We've never seen this side of him."

"You mean the grumpy side?"

"I mean the side you see when you watch someone yearn for what he's lost."

"You may speak of me in a whisper as if I am a freak," he said as he entered the car, "but I know you understand."

"We do," said Anna. "I'm sorry for your loss."

"Sorrow accepted. Now onward, Heinz."

The driver's name was not Heinz, but Fester. Fester was not his real name either — Egidiusz had been his given, Polish name, and before the war, most people had referred to him as Idzi. Idzi had been adopted by a military wing of the Red Army after fleeing Poland to Russia. In essence, he had volunteered to be their slave, doing whatever they wanted, whenever they wanted. He claimed to know the Polish countryside better than anyone and offered to help them navigate around German strongholds. When he first arrived at one of the Russian camps, the troops almost executed him on site, but one of the commanders agreed to hear him out and convinced them that somehow it was in their best interest to let him stick around. The Russian commanders, who started calling him Fester, meaning from the woods in German, figured he couldn't harm their cause and took him with them as they invaded his country. He never understood why they gave him a German name, but it later became rather handy when he was traveling in what he called, "German infested areas." When his unit arrived at Wyszkow, he met Abrasha, who decided that Fester would make the perfect wingman for Abrasha's plans. He would need someone as cheeky as Fester, who knew German, Russian and Polish fluently and who could work under the radar. Fester looked younger than he was; at twenty-five, he could easily have passed for a sixteen-year-old schoolboy. He had short, straight hair with bangs that reached past his eyebrows. His eyes were set tight together, and his small, pointy nose looked like it had been molded from clay.

Abrasha knew the story behind his names and decided just to call him Heinz. "We're off to find some kind of package in the woods. I couldn't for the life of me comprehend what could be its worth. But women are fickle that way, aren't they Heinz."

Heinz nodded keeping his eyes facing forward and both hands on the wheel.

Several weeks had passed since the last German soldier had fallen on Polish soil. The Red Army, with some meager assistance from the Polish Home Army and the partisans, easily repelled all attempts by German forces to hold their ground. Thousands of Germans died during the fighting, but as Anna would discover, thousands of Jews had died during the retreat as well. The Germans, determined to eradicate as many Jews as possible before the end of the war, worked hard to find creative methods of killing the remaining Jews in the camps. In some camps the living were firebombed; in others, men were killed and the women were forced to march hundreds of kilometers in the cold winter air towards Germany. On one such march from Auschwitz to Bergen-Belsen, over two thousand women started out. Only 150 survived.

As Anna looked out at the Polish landscape rolling by her window, she wondered what had it been that had saved her? What had been the key element to her ability to survive the war? Why her and not Tuvia or Rachel or Yehuda or Shimi or Peretz or Moishe or Emil or Leah or millions of others who had not lived to see post-Nazi Poland?

As the car turned a bend in the road that traveled along the lush forest, Ida yelled out to Heinz.

"Turn up there! That's it!"

"Are you sure?" said Abrasha. "I recall a much bigger entrance."

"You were smaller then," said Ida. "That's it."

The car turned into a muddy road that cut deep into the forest.

"We'll be able to get in," said Heinz, "but I'm not sure we'll be able to get out."

"Stop just up ahead, "said Ida.

The car came to a halt in what seemed to be the middle of a muddy road with no measurable landmarks. But Ida had seen what none of the others could have known existed. At eye level, carved into the trunk of a beech tree adjacent to the road, were the letters A M I. Moss had begun to grow in the inside of the letters, but their shape was clear.

"Who's Ami?" asked Anna once she finally made out the contour of the letters. "You've been keeping something from me."

"No," said Ida. "A. M. I. Anna, Miriam, Ida. I wanted to carve something to leave our mark on the forest."

"So camp is right there," said Anna, pointing just beyond the engraved beech.

The four walked into the forest, and at first, Abrasha expressed doubt that they were in the right place. There was no indication anywhere that there had been a camp of hundreds of fighters, but soon they were able to spot signs alongside the chunks of snow that had yet to melt. First, they noticed pits that had been dug for fires, with small stocks of firewood cut and ready beside them. Then they noticed remains of the first zemlyankas that the fighters had built in the Wyszkow forest.

"My memory deceives me. I recall everything to be much bigger," reiterated Abrasha.

It seemed to Anna that it had been ages ago. They had left camp in haste when rumors reached the Polish underground that German reconnaissance had spotted them. They had time to gather their belongings from around the camp, but nothing more. Anna had considered an attempt to collect the rings but knew that they were too far out of camp for it to be a safe venture. She was also content with their burial spot and felt it best they remain there until she could return for them when it was safe.

Now it was safe.

Walking through the remains of what had been their home for several months, Anna took Ida's hand. As they walked through the camp, they occasionally pointed at remnants of a grueling and severe time, but one that brought fond memories of days and nights spent in each other's company. They had survived bone-chilling winters, sometimes forced to huddle together throughout the night, all three in one bed, using only each other's body heat for warmth. They had learned that when they were all naked, they stayed even warmer, often perspiring from the contact of skin from head to toe, ignoring the smells of bodies that had not bathed in days, sometimes weeks. The one in the middle was always the warmest, and they switched positions continuously.

With Abrasha and Fester in tow, Anna and Ida led the group out of the camp and deeper into the cool, damp forest. Wildflowers were sprouting from their winter sleep, and the smell of fresh leaves blew across the forest floors. This had been everyone's favorite time of year. Spring signaled the end of the bitter winter, and each time April arrived, they allowed themselves to hope that next winter will be different – every time but once. When April 1943 arrived, winter had been the last thing on their minds.

Ida suddenly let out a small cheer when her bullet holes appeared in the distance. They were still almost thirty meters from the spot where Anna had buried her grandmother's rings, the rings of hope for a new life, when Ida began to run. She approached the tree and touched the bullet holes gently as if they were a piece of art she herself had sculpted. "See. I left a mark. I wonder who took the tractor."

"So it should be right...what's that?"

A full stride directly south of the tree with the bullet marks Anna noticed a large indentation dug out of the ground. It was as deep as they had expected to dig, and the soil, soggy from the recent rains, had been tilled recently – surely since the snow had melted.

"Someone dug here," said Anna. "Someone dug up the rings!"

"It could have been the Germans," said Abrasha. "Their damn muts frolic the countryside looking for mementos – usually us Jews. Perhaps they found your package. Could it possibly have had food in it?"

Both Anna and Ida ignored him. Anna was kneeling next to the hole and began groping around the edges. "Maybe this isn't the spot. Maybe..."

"Anna. I'm so sorry," said Ida.

"Wasted trip I'm afraid," said Abrasha.

"Would you just shut up!" said Ida.

"Let's dig around some," said Anna.

"You heard her," said Ida to Abrasha and Fester, "start digging."

"Don't know when to cut your losses, do you," mumbled Abrasha as he got down onto his knees and shuffled around some dirt as if looking for something. Fester was more cooperative and dug as if exposing a smothered human covered by an avalanche.

The four ended up digging a cavity the length and width of a grave – close to half a meter deep from the tilted tree southward. After over an hour, Anna shrugged. "Someone took my rings," she said softly. "Someone fucking took my rings," she said a bit louder. "Damn them! Those damn bastards!" she yelled at the top of her lungs. "What did you need them for! You took my husband! You took my lover! You took my two boys! You could have at least left me my damn rings!" she shouted at the trees.

Ida placed her arm on her shoulder and they returned to the car. The camp looked different to Anna on the walk back. Before it had seemed serene and inviting, bringing back memories of love and togetherness and missions and purpose. But this time, she saw the death and the fear, the despair and the grief.

No one said a word until they reached the car. As they were about to enter, Fester cleared his throat. "They knew it was there," he said.

"What?" asked Abrasha.

"They knew it was there. Whoever found the package, knew it was there."

"What do you mean?" asked Ida.

"They dug in one exact spot. They didn't just find it. They knew it was there."

"What about the damn German dogs?" asked Abrasha. "They could have started sniffing and found it that way."

"Those dogs were not trained to find objects, but people. It was a package. Someone saw you bury it and came back to get it."

Anna felt the blood rush to her head. She had felt sorry for herself, but now she was angry. She let go of Ida and made two fists.

"Do you think?" asked Ida. They were thinking the same thing.

"Sasha! That idiot who tried to seduce us. That bastard!"

"He must have followed us that night. He was still mad about the way you attacked him with that sandwich."

"Damn it!" Anna closed her eyes tight and grunted.

"Maybe we can find him?" said Fester. "Maybe he's still in the area."

"A Pole named Sasha," said Anna tersely. "That's all the information we have. If you run into him, ask him for my rings. He's probably sold them by now anyway. Who knows when he dug them up. That bastard!

"Well, if it's any consequence," said Abrasha trying to lighten the mood, "I'm sure they shot the old fool. Most of those poor souls didn't make it out of the forest alive."

"Thank you, Mister Happy," said Ida. "That helped."

"Don't mention it."

Thirty-Six

"Well, Hanna is a very nice name, but my Hanna couldn't save Yehuda. I'm sure your mother would have tried to save you too if she could have."

"She did," said Yaakov. "I'm here, aren't I?"

"Yes, you are. How did she save you?"

"I told you, I don't remember much. Why do you insist on prying?"

"You don't remember, or you don't want to tell me."

"Don't start with me again. I don't need to tell you anything."

"No, you don't. But I would be happy if you did. I told you so much already."

"You sure did," he said quietly as if he didn't intend for her to hear.

"Don't be cheeky with me! Tell me something. It's your turn to talk. I have talked enough."

"Yes, you...Okay. She tossed me out a window."

"Who tossed you out a window?"

"My mother...I guess. I don't remember exactly. I have vague images, not much more. I was living on a farm for a while with my mother. It wasn't our farm since there was another family there. I didn't go to school or anything – at least I don't remember going to school or kindergarten or anything. I remember that I used to climb on the bales of hay in the fields. And I remember that there was a man... he must have been the head of the household... he used to pat me on the head all the time. I didn't like it."

"What do you remember about your mother?" asked Anna.

"Almost nothing. She was blonde, and I remember when she took me aside one night and gave me something and said it was from my mother to keep always. I never understood what she meant and why she referred to herself as 'your mother.' Two days later she was dead."

"May I ask what happened?"

"I don't know exactly. Strange, but this part I remember more clearly – it must have been more from the stories I was told than actual memories. I remember soldiers, I can only assume they were Nazis, came and began hitting everyone. I must have been outside, maybe playing in the hay, when I saw them enter the house and point a gun at the man who used to pat me on the head. Then I remember being in a back room with my mother and everyone was crying. When the soldiers left the room, they threw me out the window and told me to run to the neighbors. As I was running away, I heard shooting coming from inside the house. My mother was there. She was killed. I ran to the neighbors, and the next day they told me that everyone in

323

the house was killed – except me. I don't know why they thought I would be safe there. It was the next farm over and I had once played with their daughter – but other than that I don't ever remember seeing them before that day. They adopted me as their own, and although I can remember leaving my real mother at one point, this became my family. I became Polish. In fact, up until the end of the war, I thought I was Polish. They called me Yanush and I even went to kindergarten with the little girl I had played with. They said we were brother and sister.

"Then, when I came home one day, there were two men and two women in the house. I had been there for about a year, maybe longer. My new mother took me aside and told me that these people were taking me to another country. I didn't understand. I asked if they were taking me to my old mother. Next thing I knew I was on a boat to Palestine. They brought me to a youth village filled with orphans like myself. They asked me what my name was, I said Yanush, and they told me that it used to be Yaakov, and from that moment on, they called me Yaakov, even though I never liked the name. I don't know why – it is the closest Hebrew name to Yanush."

"What was your last name?" asked Anna.

"I used to think I didn't have one until I got to kibbutz a few months later. They sent me to Yad Mordecai and I was adopted by a wonderful family. Theirs is my last name now – Halutz."

"Your story reminds me of what happened to my son. He too was met by the retreating Nazis while hiding on a farm. But he didn't survive. I guess he didn't have a nice girl next door to…."

Anna suddenly turned her head sharply toward Yaakov. There it was again, the flash of light reflecting off a passing car and elongating Yaakov's face. He did have Tuvia's chin. She noticed her lower lip was trembling as she said to Yaakov, "There's more about your mother you haven't told me, isn't there."

"No," said Yaakov. "There's nothing else. I remember very little. As I said, she was blond, a little sad, but…"

"What?"

"She was always singing, or humming. Nothing else. Oh, and she left me this."

Yaakov reached into his khaki-colored Egged shirt by his chest and pulled out a chain with a silver locket on the end. As soon as Anna saw the locket she gasped and put both hands over her mouth.

"Yes, it's nice isn't it," said Yaakov nonchalantly. "But there's a mistake on the inscription. They left out the H. My mother's name was Hanna and this just says…Well isn't that a coincidence." At that moment Yaakov looked down at Anna who was softly crying while staring up at the oblivious driver.

"It's no mistake. Yehuda. I'm…" but Anna was whimpering, making it hard to even take a breath. "Yehuda."

"What is it?" What, Anna?"

"Anna," said Rami. "Are you okay?" He was getting out of his seat, as were some of the other passengers on the bus. It looked as if Anna was not breathing. She was sitting straight up, still sitting on Rami's coat, her hands covering her mouth and her eyes wide open dripping tears. Yaakov had a frightened look on his face as he switched his head back and forth between Anna and the road. One of the passengers yelled that she was having a heart attack. Another passenger from the middle of the bus began moving toward the front of the aisle saying, "Move aside, I'm a doctor!"

But before he could reach her, Anna removed one hand from her mouth and stretched it out toward Yaakov.

"Yehuda…" she was trying to speak. Her mind was racing with thoughts she had never allowed herself to think. In the split instant that she saw the locket, her life without her child flashed in front of her. She thought about Tuvia, his life and his death, about Ida and Miriam and how much they had suffered together, about Hanna and her pain and how the worst moment of her life was when she heard how Yehuda had died. Anna had mourned the loss of her second child twice – once when Yehuda left the ghetto with Hanna, and then again, a mourning that had lasted thirty-one years, when Hanna arrived in the forest. Now she had to say the words she had dreamed of saying but knew were beyond the realm of possibility. And she had to say it while all these people were making a fuss over her, falsely thinking she was having a cardiac arrest.

"You're Yehuda. I'm your mother, Yehuda. I'm your mother."

Yaakov slammed on the brakes, and the people in the aisles moving toward Anna fell forward on to each other. He quickly pulled the bus over to the side of the two-lane road, drawing horns from the two cars behind him, and stopped on the dirt shoulder. Silence blanketed the bus like a thick fog. Everyone was watching Yaakov.

"Lady," said Yaakov. "What are you talking about? Are you having a heart attack or not?"

Anna's composure returned in a flash. He hadn't stopped the bus because of what she said but because he thought she was ill. Her voice steadied and her words were firm. She now spoke in the fashion those who knew her were accustomed to hearing.

"Did you hear what I said? I am your mother. I am Anna – the Anna from the locket. I gave you to Hanna so she could escape with you from the ghetto. I wanted you to get here."

325

"I…" Yaakov tried to speak.

Anna's voice was shaky as she spoke again. "I know it's hard to believe…Oh my god…But I have proof. If it is hard to believe that I am your mother, then it will be just as hard to accept that Hanna is still alive as well. She lives near me. Hanna thought you had died in that room…Oh god, oh god… You thought the Germans killed her there too. You both got out. Do you understand? She came back for you – Hanna did – she came back…she was sure you had burned with the house."

"How did you know the house had burned," said Yaakov. "I didn't tell you that."

"I'm telling you, I know your story. You also didn't tell me that you used to love to hide in the barn. But I know that too. Yaakov…Yehuda – your real name is Yehuda – I am your mother. I gave birth to you under the worst conditions imaginable to mankind, and I have been living the past thirty years thinking I had let you die. But you are here. You are with me here in Eretz Yisrael where I so often hoped you would be." Anna was crying again as was Yehuda. Her hand remained outstretched in his, and Rami, sobbing silently, was hugging her from behind. She lifted herself with his help and embraced Yehuda.

Like a wildfire, the events in the front of the bus spread through the questioning passengers of bus 405 from Jerusalem to Tel Aviv. As they began to comprehend the gravity of what they had witnessed, the murmur turned to tears, then to elation and smiles.

An elderly man forced his way to the front of the bus. Tears were rolling down his cheeks. He approached Yehuda and Anna and said, "I lost everyone there. My whole family. My parents, brothers and sister, grandparents. Somehow I feel I just got some of them back." Anna released Yehuda and hugged him.

"I still have to drive," said Yehuda.

"I still have to talk," she said. "I have so much to tell. If you think I was talking a lot before, wait until I tell you my story – the whole story – the story of the ghetto, the partisans and your family. Hanna may have a heart attack – a real one, not like the one you all thought I was having. She actually could die. There is so much you need to know, Yehuda."

"Yehuda. That feels right. That's it. Changing my name after all this time. Is that possible?"

"Women do it all the time – of course, it's their surname they change – but that too is part of a woman's identity, no?"

Thirty-Seven

25 September 1945

Throughout the summer, while making every attempt to contact Jewish emissaries from Palestine, Anna traveled with Ida to several communities around Warsaw looking for contacts. Following one such trip, where they had intended to meet with a Jewish Agency representative who never showed at their meeting spot, Hanna greeted them by the door as they entered the foyer.

"There was a message for you, Anna," she said. "A man named Gideon Sharrett from the Jewish Brigade. He said he wanted to talk to you. What's the Jewish Brigade?"

"I think it's the Jews from Eretz Yisrael who joined the British army. Maybe he has a way to Palestine. But what are they doing in Poland?"

"How did he find you?" asked Ida.

"I don't know. I left a lot of messages, but only with people I know are Jews. I hope he is who he claims and that we can trust him."

"Are we going? Do you think we're going?" asked Hanna. "I'm not sure I'm ready."

"What more do you need to be ready," asked Ida. "I mean, haven't you seen enough here? What are we waiting for?"

"It's not that simple," said Anna.

"Why not?" asked Hanna.

"Well, first of all, the British are controlling immigration, and they just don't want us there. We have to sneak in."

"We're quite good at that," said Ida.

"But not by sea. It's not as easy as it sounds. I heard that they're just taking the Jews and sending them back. That's why we need to talk to this Gideon. They have plans. But, yes, we may be going to Palestine."

The next day Gideon Sharrett returned, and he was with Abrasha.

"So you told him where we were!" said Ida. "We asked you not to tell anyone."

"I sincerely apologize, but you must hear this man out. He has a way to get me to Palestine and he needs something from you as well."

"He's not here to get us to Palestine?" asked Anna.

"First he is going to get me there. The rest he'll have to fill you in himself."

Gideon had been standing quietly listening as if awaiting a formal introduction. Anna had assumed that he knew no Polish and wondered how they were to communicate. The little Hebrew she had picked up was not enough to carry on a conversation about immigration – although she did know how to say immigration in Hebrew, and her English consisted of the three words her brother had taught her when they were children: "Good day, sir."

"I have a proposition for you," said Gideon in perfect, accent-free Polish. "I want you to come with me to the displaced persons camps that are being set up for the refugees. We are seeking qualified ghetto fighters and partisans – movement people really – who are willing to take on the new national mission. We know of your movement background, and you can help us set up kibbutzim and learning centers in the camps."

"You know Polish!" said Anna.

"I am Polish. I made aliyah in 1931 and now I live on Kibbutz Mishmar HaEmek. I grew up in Lodz. I joined the Jewish Brigade, and now I've returned to Europe to assist the needs of the refugees."

"So you've deserted?" said Ida.

"I'm on an extended leave, but I will return to Palestine soon. That's where Abrasha comes in."

"You see," said Abrasha, straightening his body in pride, "I have been summoned by Gideon to be, well, Gideon. I will become his double, allowing me to emigrate and Gideon to continue with his preposterous mission."

"Eh…Yes," said Gideon, "something like that. I need to find someone who will be capable of replacing me for a while – until I'm officially discharged from the Brigade. I have false papers for myself, which is how I got here, and Abrasha, soon to be Gideon, will receive my full identity – cards and all."

Anna hadn't noticed the resemblance between the two men until that moment; they were approximately the same height, had the same color hair and eyes and both looked like they had just learned to walk this year. The uncanny part of the picture was their identical smiles. They both had a smile that looked more like a plastered mold had dried before it had time to be removed.

"How's your English?" asked Ida rhetorically to Abrasha.

"Well," said Gideon, "we have a few weeks to work on that and a whole slew of other things. I have eight siblings and have been trained by the British military. There is a lot more than just some English that he will need to learn. But he will return to the Brigade with a 'buddy.' We'll have someone by his side at all times, and if there is ever a problem, he will blame it on his lacking language skills, and the buddy will feed him the correct answers. It's risky but no riskier than staying here."

"I suppose there are no women doubles," said Anna. "You should know that Ida here is a great shot."

"There are no women soldiers in the Brigade – at least not in Europe right now. Most of them are in the ATS – the transport corp. No, I have more important plans for you. We need you in the camps."

"The camps?" exclaimed Ida.

"Where are the camps?" asked Anna.

"In Germany. The one I am thinking about is in the American sector..."

"I'm not going to Germany!" said Ida. "I survived the war and now you think I'm going to Germany? No. If you can get me to Eretz Yisrael, I'll do anything, but I won't go to Germany."

"It's in Bavaria, not far from Munich. It is going to be an all Jewish camp, and we'll need people like you."

"Oh," said Ida, "Bavaria's not Germany? Still no."

"There are camps in Austria as well..."

"Same German scum."

"Listen," said Anna, "we appreciate the offer, but our hearts are set on Eretz Yisrael. Is there any way..."

"This is the fastest way for you to get to Palestine. You would work in the camp helping us prepare the refugees for the journey, which would prepare you as well. Then you would leave with the other refugees. It would both help us and help you, but most of all, it would help the refugees. Look, I don't want to force you to do anything. If it doesn't suit you, fine. But I must advise you to leave Poland as soon as you can. The situation here is volatile, and the Soviets are not going to make your life pleasant. At least the Americans are trying to make the Jews feel more comfortable. Get out of Poland. Get out of the Soviet-occupied areas. Leaving Poland, in turn, will make your move to Eretz Yisrael that much easier."

"I'm not going to Germany," said Ida after Gideon left the house.

"Then let's go to Greece," said Anna.

4 October 1945

"I'm terrified," said Hanna. I've never been out of Poland. I've never been out of the Warsaw area. What are we doing here?"

"Don't worry," said Ida. "Being out of Poland is nothing to be afraid of. Poland is a god awful place where Jews get murdered – even now that the Nazis are gone. We're safer anywhere but there. Hanna, we are the true heroines of Warsaw, and heroines of Warsaw can survive anywhere.... I can't believe I'm saying this. For god's sake, we're in Munich of all places."

"Yes," said Anna smiling. "Where Hitler got started."

The girls had been driven by an envoy from Jerusalem, an ex-Brigade corporal helping to bring Jews to Palestine. The ride had taken two days, and despite the length, it was easier than they had expected. For a full week, Anna had attempted to find passage to Eretz Yisrael via Greece, Romania and even Turkey but quickly realized that Gideon had been right. The fastest and easiest way for them to get to Palestine was through Germany. The irony was apparent to Anna and disturbing to Ida. Hanna was just frightened.

Gideon had told them that the Americans were making an effort to help the refugees feel safe. There was pressure from the Jewish lobby to send special missions to handle the influx of Jewish refugees from Poland and Russia into the West. One of the first decisions was to create all Jewish camps. The Americans had hoped to be able to return most of the refugees to their pre-war homes, but the Jewish agencies from Palestine had other plans. They would slowly take group after group out of the camps to boats waiting to cross the Mediterranean. Gideon told Anna that even if she was able to get to a port with a boat that would be traveling to Palestine, without the right support, the British would not let them in. Illegal immigration was becoming an art form for the Jewish settlement in Palestine, and they were getting quite good at it. Gideon had promised Anna that after working in the camp for a few months, he would personally guarantee that they would be promptly taken to the shores of the Holy Land. "I promise you the Promised Land," he said.

Ida had made the biggest fuss, saying that she may have a breakdown if she is confronted by Germans. Gideon could not promise that wouldn't happen but told her that most of the German speakers she would encounter would be Jews. The authority in Bavaria was the American military, and according to Gideon, "they are better than the British."

Gideon had also told them that as opposed to most of the refugees that had been making their way across the Polish-German border, Anna and her friends would not have to walk. They would be driven by a trustworthy and able driver. It was only Anna's promise to Ida that they would be in Palestine by the following summer that finally got Ida to agree to go to the DP camp in Germany.

Now, they were waiting in a three-story building that had previously been used by the U. S. military as a field hospital. There were cots with bloodstains, dirty rags in the sinks, a single stethoscope in the corner and the smell of antiseptic mixed with dust. The room was an entryway to the building, and they were sitting on a long bench facing two enormous mahogany doors that continuously swung open and closed, bringing in cold air and more people looking lost and alone. Since the girls had taken a seat on the bench, at least thirty people had come into the building and had either joined them on other benches or had been whisked away to corridors leading to more rooms and more people waiting to be helped. An elderly woman seemed to be in charge instructing three other women dressed as nurses. Only as they entered did someone tell them in Polish to take a seat and wait. That had been two hours earlier and they were growing impatient.

While Hanna remained bored, and Ida tried to nap on Anna's lap, Anna was deep in thought contemplating Ibsen's Enemy of the People, which Olesia had given her as a going-away present. What would Olesia say about the Mayor's attitude toward his brother? All Olesia had said to her about the book was, "The Polish translation is not as sharp as the original." Anna wondered how she would know since Norwegian was not one of her languages. Leaving Olesia had been harder than expected for all three. Anna had enjoyed the late-night discussions centered primarily around the arts and sometimes on the books that she was devouring. Olesia watched carefully as Anna turned page after page, and as soon as she saw that Anna was close to the end of the book, she would stand up, walk over to the bookshelf, look long and hard at the bindings and pull something out to be set by Anna's spot on the sofa. But Anna would never begin the next book in the queue without first discussing the previous novel with Olesia. Her insight always added something to the ending – like an extra epilogue written just for Anna. Sometimes it was a trite as the meaning of the name of a major character, while other times it was the historical context that the author had left out so as not to confuse the reader, who was expected to know the background. Anna would race through her books, sometimes just waiting to reach the ensuing discussion. At one point, she even tried talking to Olesia about a story before she had reached the end. "Oh no, it is not the time for this conversation," Olesia would say to her while shaking her head. "You must be patient, for you still don't know the meaning of chapter two." So Anna would hurry and read until the very end before approaching Olesia. When they departed, all Anna could say to her while accepting her parting gift was, "Who will tell me what Ibsen meant?" And Olesia replied quietly, "You'll know what he meant. You always knew more than I did anyway." Anna disagreed.

Hanna had found solace in the manner in which Olesia ran her small house. While Anna read, Hanna cooked. She loved Olesia's cooking and vowed to learn each of the recipes. However, there were no recipes. As Hanna asked to write down the ingredients and amounts of Olesia's cabbage stew, Olesia would tell her, "a dab of this, a dash of that – and then I just put in whatever is left around the kitchen." Hanna could not understand how the dish turned out the same each time it was made. But she enjoyed the cooking, and when they departed, Olesia gave her a card with a recipe for vegetable pie and said, "This is the only recipe I ever wrote down."

When Ida said goodbye to Olesia, she wept, holding her and thanking her repeatedly. "You didn't have to take us in, but you did." Olesia hugged her and said, "I did have to take you in. You were my student."

Anna was thinking about Olesia when Ida screamed.

"Miriam! Anna! Anna, it's Miriam!"

"Anna dropped Ibsen and looked at the giant door cracked ajar with a body blocking the opening. Before Miriam could enter the building, Ida was wrapped around her. Anna and Hanna were next to engulf her and soon the four returned to the relative warmth of the foyer.

"Your hair! What happened?" said Anna. Miriam's hair was now shorter than Ida's and Anna's. The long braid was gone, and her face looked thinner and pale.

"It's a story for another time."

"You must have many stories. You're here," said Ida.

Miriam looked at Hanna. "You must have stories too."

It suddenly dawned on Anna that Miriam was unaware of Yehuda's fate. She had left for Palestine before Hanna's arrival at camp. "Yes, there is a lot to tell."

"I hoped you would be here. A man named Gideon found me and told me that some women fighters were coming to this camp. That's why I came. I hoped it would be you. But where are we? And where are we going?"

"We're going to work in a DP, a displaced persons camp, until they can take us to Palestine," said Ida. "And we're in god-damned Germany."

"Nahum?" asked Anna.

Miriam shook her head. "I lost him to a mob of Polish nationalists last spring. The war was over." She once again looked at Hanna and then at Anna. A solemn look engulfed her face and her arms went limp. "She's here alone. I'm sorry, Anna. I'm so sorry."

Anna nodded. "I'm sorry you didn't get to Palestine."

"We got as far as the Romanian border. Then we were turned back by Soviet troops. So we tried again and again. Each time we tried to cross, we were caught. Each time another officer gave a stern warning, and we moved on to the next attempt. Finally, we ran into the same regiment a second time and they had no patience for us. They put us on a transport back to Warsaw. This was already in the winter. We had spent months on the border going from village to village, working a little, stealing a lot. By that time I thought we should return to the partisan camp. I didn't believe we'd ever get out of Poland. We got back to Warsaw and one night we were walking just outside of Kraszynski Square…."

"I thought you said that stories were for another time?" said Ida embracing Miriam again.

"Have anything better to do?" continued Miriam. "So we were walking just outside of Kraszynski Square. We could see the rubble from the ghetto – it was eerie walking there, looking back at that…that place. From behind one of the walls came these five men yelling nationalist slogans at us. We just kept walking. Then they guessed we were Jews and started hitting us with sticks. Nahum tried to fight back, and they cracked his head open. I tried to run, but one of them caught me and they decided to cut off my braid. It could have been worse for me, but not for Nahum. He bled to death, and there was nothing I could do. The next morning I tried to return to the forest. I thought, maybe there was still a camp somewhere. Maybe you would be there. I don't know what I was thinking. There was nothing there. The whole place was gone. I almost couldn't find it."

Miriam stopped talking and fiddled in her pocket.

"It's a good thing I went back, though. I brought you this." Out of the pocket of her large black overcoat, she pulled a soiled package tied shut with a string. "I checked to make sure they were still inside."

"My rings! It was you! It was you!"

"What do you mean?"

"We went back too," said Ida. "We went back to the forest just a few months ago to look for the rings. We dug and dug, even though we could see that they had already been dug up. Anna was quite upset. She yelled at the sky – you know how she can get."

"I'm so sorry," said Miriam. "I was sure that you wouldn't have had a chance to go back, so I took them for you. I didn't even know if you were alive… So many of the partisans didn't make it. I wanted to make sure that the rings stayed with one of us. I wanted to make sure that you got them if you did survive. I'm so sorry."

"Don't be sorry. You have made me happy. I had thought that they were gone forever. You brought me back something that I was sure I had lost and could never regain. You wouldn't happen to have saved my son, would you?" Anna's eyes swelled with tears as she held her rings.

Miriam looked up at Anna as a tear trickled down her right cheek. "He didn't…?"

Anna told her the story, occasionally checking with Hanna to make sure she was getting it right. As difficult as it was for her to tell Miriam how her son had died, she was not going to put Hanna through telling the tale once more. The first time had been horrifying for both of them, and she wanted to take on the burden herself this time. Hanna had already played mother and guardian to Anna's child. She no longer had to bear the weight of recitation. The time that had passed had not made it any easier for either of them, and Anna choked on her worlds as she tried to describe how Hanna heard the gunshots, returned to the burned house and later showed up at the camp without Yehuda.

When she was finished, Miriam's eyes turned to Anna and she asked, "What did we do to deserve this?"

"We are Jews," said Anna.

Thirty-Eight

July 4, 1976

The door opened slowly, and the wrinkled features of a woman showed themselves to the tiny group sitting in the living room of the three-bedroom apartment. The radio was on in the background, and the newscaster was excited and animated. His voice rang through the small room whose inhabitants could only listen to the elation in his speech.

"...is remarkable. The passengers are walking out the back of the military transport plane and directly into the arms of their loved ones. It's such a festive atmosphere here. There are signs and flags – lots of state flags – and people are cheering. I don't know if you can hear me well..."

"Hanna!" said Anna, who immediately stood to greet her friend.

"What's going on? What's that man yelling about?"

"They rescued the hostages," said Ida. "They sent planes to Uganda and rescued them."

"Oh my god. Oh my god! That's wonderful. Was it the IDF?"

"Yes," said Anna. "Our army did it again. They landed the plane and dressed up like the Ugandan army. The guards had no idea that it was us until it was too late."

"Like our rescue of the workers at the Melmann's metal factory in the ghetto," said Ida.

"Oh my," said Anna, "you're right. But Hanna, I have something even more important to tell you. You have to sit down."

"I have to sit down? Who died?"

"You mean, who lived?" said Ida.

Hanna's eyes were darting between Anna, Ida and the man sitting on the sofa between them. Yehuda was wearing a tan button-down short-sleeved shirt with short khaki pants and sandals. He was staring directly at Hanna and smiling. When she had walked in the door, he had moved to greet her as well, but Anna had shoved him back into his place. She knew that Hanna needed to be sitting down when she received the news. She was likely to pass out anyway.

"What's she talking about?" said Hanna.

Anna sat Hanna down at the end of the red sofa an arm's length from Yehuda. She stood in between them facing the couch and held both of their hands.

"Hanna, I have been trying to reach you since yesterday afternoon..."

"My phone was dead. I called someone to come fix it, but they said it

335

would take a week at least, and then I left for Tel Aviv. I just returned and saw your note. You said to come right away. I came right away. What's happening?"

"It's okay. You're here now. I want you to meet someone...well not exactly meet...you've met before...I guess re-meet would be a better word..."

"Anna!" said Ida.

"Hanna, Yehuda didn't die on that farm near Warsaw. This is..."

Hanna let out a screech that made Anna jump back and almost fall over the coffee table. She began shaking and then hitting Anna.

"This is how you tell me! This is how you tell me!"

"I made sure you were sitting down. Hanna, this is Yehuda. Give him a hug."

Tears dripped down Yehuda's nose, the nose that from Anna's vantage point standing above him now looked just like Tuvia's. He reached out with both arms and Hanna fell into them.

"How?" whispered Hanna.

"They threw me out the window and I ran to the neighbors. You remember the little girl that lived there, Kamilia. For that year, she became my sister. But how did you get out?"

Hanna told Yehuda the story of how she had been taken by the soldiers, dumped and later returned to find the carnage. She recalled how she had found his shoe near the side of the house. It hadn't made any sense before, but now she understood.

"I lost my shoe while running away. The first thing that the Gomolka's did was to get me new shoes."

"I had so often told you to tie your shoes, but you never listened. This time it cost you," she laughed. "Oh Anna, god must be happy with us."

"You know how I feel about that kind of talk," said Anna. She turned to Yehuda, "Your other mother has the Medieval Syndrome. She believes that only the supernatural can answer unexplainable phenomena."

"Your mother is an atheist," said Hanna.

"So who is my mother?" he asked looking back and forth between Hanna and Anna.

Hanna pointed to Anna.

"We both are," said Anna. "I gave birth to you, but Hanna protected you. And frankly, it doesn't matter."

"I think it does," said Hanna. "Yehuda, do you have a family now?"

"Yes, I have four children on Yad Mordechai. Three girls and a boy."

"Oh my! You live on Yad Mordechai," said Hanna. "That's

remarkable. Anna, they are your grandchildren. They will look like you, not me – I hope."

"They are beautiful children," said Yehuda. "Lilach is our oldest – she's eleven. Yasmin is nine and the sharpest kid you'll ever meet." Ida smiled at Anna. "Iris is eight and Ilan is four."

"Beautiful names," said Ida.

"Three flowers and a tree," said Anna.

"That's my wife's doing. I figured if she had to do all the work giving birth, she should be able to name the children. When can you come to visit them?"

"I don't know," said Anna. "It's quite difficult to find a bus from here to Yad Mordecai."

"I think I can help you out there."

"Maybe you'd like to have the whole family come here for Shabbat dinner," said Hanna.

"I think I'd rather have all of you come down to Yad Mordecai first. The children need to be in their environment when I spring all of this on them. I haven't told them anything. I told my wife…"

"What's her name?" asked Anna.

"Miriam. Well, Miri."

Anna jumped to her feet and clasped her hands together. "Miriam!" shouted Anna. "I completely forgot. I must be getting old. How could I forget something like that? I must start writing things down. Ida, you have to get me to write these things down."

"You know my wife?"

"No, no, no. It's nothing like that. I called Miriam and asked her to come here today as well. She was with us in the ghetto and now she lives on Kibbutz Megiddo. She was the reason I was so pressed to get on the bus yesterday. She was supposed to come down for Shabbat. But she missed her bus. Ironic, isn't it. She didn't have such an accommodating driver as I did. She's coming today and she'll be dropped off down the street by someone from her kibbutz. But I have to meet her there because she doesn't know where we live. She used to know, but we moved last month to this place. The other place was fine, but it had leaks in the rain and we had to get those pots…"

"Anna! Shut up and sit down," said Ida. "I'll go to meet Miriam. And I'll prepare her for your crazy state of mind." Ida stood up, looked down at Yehuda and rolled her eyes. "Your mother can lose it sometimes. I hope you didn't inherit the, you know," as she rolled her pointed finger around her ear.

Anna turned to Hanna. "I brought you something." She held a tiny cardboard box and a small glass bottle with a thick white liquid in it.

"Is that...?" Hanna started asking. "I won the bet? I won the bet!" Hanna was crying through the excitement.

Ida and Anna were laughing at Hanna's reaction, as Yehuda looked puzzled. Anna explained to Yehuda how they had bet for blueberries and cream and how Anna had always won.

"Should I serve it now, or would you like to wait for breakfast in bed?" asked Anna.

"Now!" exclaimed Hanna.

Miriam had grown her hair. She never cut it again after the war. "An occasional trim," she would say when people asked her how her hair got to be down to the tops of her thighs. It was white now, and she braided it less, but it was still a strong, full head of hair and she was proud of it. For thirty years, Anna would play with it whenever she would come down to visit – which wasn't often. Miriam was a busy woman.

Even in the egalitarian kibbutz, women factory directors were hard to come by. Miriam had arrived on Kibbutz Megiddo a few years after moving to Palestine. When the country gained its independence in 1948, she was where she thought she wanted to be, on Kibbutz Beit Alpha, the first Hashomer Hatzair kibbutz, but she would connect with a man who was planning to start a new kibbutz and he asked her to join him. Miriam not only joined the garin, the seed group that established Kibbutz Megiddo, she also married the man. During the first few years of her marriage, he had several affairs. Miriam was stunned by the discovery, and it changed her profoundly. Soon after finding out about his extramarital activities, instead of simply divorcing him, she had a few affairs of her own. Eventually, they split up, and he left the kibbutz following three years of unbearable collective punishment, living, working and socializing in the same space. While living on the same kibbutz, they would meet two or three times a day after they had separated. It became a game to her to see who would concede defeat first – who would leave the kibbutz. She won. She never married again, although she had many men in her life. Anna had said to Ida after returning from one of her trips to the north to visit Miriam, "Each time I walk into the room, a different man is holding her. You'd think she'd be bored by now." But older, single women were as rare on the kibbutz as female factory heads, particularly those with the drive, beauty and stature of Miriam. So it wasn't only the older and single men who courted her. She dated young and married men as well. She had told Anna, "It isn't my job to be the morality police. If these guys want to be with me, I'm not going to object." Anna had accused her of needing them out of loneliness. Her response was, "I was given a gift. I was given my life. We all were. It took me too long to realize that all I have in this world is my happiness. Intimacy makes me happy. I like the rush."

From the very onset, as a founding member of Megiddo, Miriam was active. She worked in agriculture for the first few years, and when they opened a plastics and rubber factory, Miriam jumped at the opportunity to reconnect to machines. She had confided in Anna once, saying that working with machines reminded her of shooting a gun and blowing things up. There was a rush there too.

When Miriam called Anna to tell her that she would not make it for Friday night dinner, Anna had just arrived home from the life-altering bus ride. Anna asked her to see if she could find a way to come anyway since there was thrilling news she needed to tell her in person. Miriam arranged it and was to arrive that morning just as Yehuda would be arriving. Yehuda walked in thirty minutes early, and Anna forgot about Miriam.

"She'll never let me hear the end of this one," said Anna. How can I forget Miriam? I love Miriam."

"You all seem so close," said Yehuda.

"We've been through a lot together."

Miriam's reaction to learning that the man sitting in Ida's and Anna's living room was Yehuda was to plop herself down in the green reclining chair and open her mouth. She left her mouth gaping and stared at Yehuda saying nothing for over five minutes while Anna told her the story. Yehuda began to fidget, as Miriam did not look as if she was going to take her eyes off of him for some time. Finally, after a long silence, she spoke.

"I understand why you forgot about me."

"I didn't forget about you," said Anna apologetically, "I just... fine, I forgot about you. I'm sorry."

"I said I understand," said Miriam, taking her stare from Yehuda and glaring at Anna.

"It's nice to meet you," said Yehuda. "I'd like you all to come down to Yad Mordecai and meet my family."

"At least you've picked the right movement," Miriam smiled.

Yad Mordecai and Megiddo both belonged to the Kibbutz Artzi movement, which is affiliated with Hashomer Hatzair. There was an ideological bond so deep between the movement kibbutzim that members could almost smell each other approaching. This encounter between Yehuda and Miriam would be the start of a special relationship that would lead to Miriam bringing Yehuda to work for the Kibbutz Atrzi Movement in Tel Aviv as one of her staff. Each kibbutz was required to send a certain number of members to do various jobs for the movement, and Miriam had been eyeing one of the positions for quite a while. She felt that it would be beneficial for her to work in the center of the country for a short time, which would allow her to spend more time with Anna and Ida as well. For a long while, Miriam had been planning the break from her job on the kibbutz to work for the movement, and she was going to tell Anna that weekend that starting the following week she would become director of the Economic Affairs department and move to Tel Aviv. Within a few months, Yehuda would be brought in as her southern coordinator.

"He's a bus driver," said Ida.

"Is that a childhood aspiration come true?" asked Miriam. "Your uncle, rest his soul, would have been proud."

"My uncle?" asked Yehuda.

"My brother," said Anna. "I told you about him on the bus. He was a bus driver in Warsaw before the war. Your half-brother, Shimi, used to play on his bus, and Moishe would get upset."

"Moishe never cared," said Hanna shyly. "It was you who got upset."

"I did not! Well, okay, maybe a little. I was afraid something would happen to him."

"What happened to him?" asked Yehuda.

"He died."

"I know that. You told me on the bus. It was one of the first things that you said to me. How did he die?"

"He caught a cold and didn't have the strength to recover."

"Did we look alike?"

Anna and Hanna smiled.

"Shimi looked like his father. You look like your father more than you look like me – only you have my brother's build."

"I guess there is still a lot more for me to learn about my family," said Yehuda.

"*Still* a lot more?" asked Anna.

"You talked quite a lot on the bus."

9 July 1976

That Friday afternoon, Yehuda drove north in one of the kibbutz vehicles to pick up Anna, Ida and Hanna. Miriam could not make it down that weekend as she was preparing for the move to Tel Aviv and would need the time to make arrangements.

They arrived at the kibbutz late in the afternoon, and Yehuda had arranged to have them spend the night in a guest room that had been prepared for them. They would have all weekend to get acquainted with Yehuda's family.

Yehuda steered the car into the central parking lot and parked in line with two other Peugeot 504 wagons.

"There they are now," said Yehuda pointing his chin in the direction of four children sitting at the bus stop in the lot.

"Those are your children?" asked Hanna.

"Yes," he said proudly. "Roll up your windows." The weather was hot in the south and it seemed that their proximity to the sea had increased the humidity considerably. After Yehuda shut off the engine, they exited the car and walked towards the four beautiful sandy blonde children.

"He looks exactly like Tuvia," said Anna. Anna looked at the smallest of the four, the only boy. She was overcome with the memory of Tuvia with his naturally sour face and filthy clothes on the day he first came to meet her in Warsaw at the onset of the war. Ilan, Yehuda's youngest, although only four, was a miniature Tuvia and just as filthy as Tuvia had been after returning from his travels. Standing behind him with her hands on Ilan's shoulders was the eldest, Lilach. She had bright blue eyes and hair down to the small of her back tied in a ponytail. Her skin was tanned from the Philistine sun, and she wore the same khaki shorts that all the children and their father were wearing. Her t-shirt had been cut at the collar and the sleeves, and the extra-wide neck opening made it fall off to one side exposing her right shoulder. Her grin disclosed her excitement. Flanking her and Ilan were Yasmin and Iris. Had Anna not been told that they were eighteen months apart in age, she would have mistaken them for twins. All four had the same skin and hair tones as Yehuda, but Yasmin and Iris had rounder heads and sharper facial features. Ilan was jumping up and down.

"Children, this is your grandmother."

"Didn't know we had a grandmother," said the youngest.

"There are a lot of things I didn't know," said Yehuda. "Like my name isn't Yaakov. I'll have to change that right away. And my real mother, and your grandmother, was called Anna, not Hanna. And my father was Tuvia."

"You told us, Abba," said Yasmin. "You don't have to repeat everything twenty times."

"That's Yasmin," said Yehuda. "And this is Lilach, Iris and Ilan."

"What beautiful children. What beautiful children." Tears were filling in Anna's eyes. "May I hug you?" All four surrounded her and placed their arms out. Anna tried to engulf all of them, but Ilan had to squeeze under the

341

group of arms to reach Anna.

"Let's go to the room," said Yehuda.

"Oh right," said Ida who was blowing her nose. "You call your home 'the room.' The children don't live there, do they?"

"We have our own home," said Yasmin, "in the children's house. You'll have to come to see our house. It's a great idea – the children's house, I mean. I have a friend, Avia, from Sderot who can't understand why we live like this. I always tell her that it's the best way to grow up. We get to spend time with our parents and then go back and be with our friends all the time. Then our parents are free to do whatever they want. Avia's Ema has to stay home all the time and cook and clean. My Ema can live a normal life. You know, they first built children's houses on kibbutzim for security reasons. Only later did they find all the educational reasons..."

"Okay, Yasmin," interrupted Yehuda, "You'll have plenty of time to explain later."

"She's only nine?" asked Ida.

"She reads a lot," said Yehuda.

"I think I know where she gets her brains," said Hanna looking at Anna.

"And her unrelenting verbal skills," whispered Ida.

They walked across the grounds until they reached a set of long buildings in the residential area of the kibbutz. Yehuda's wife greeted them at the door of their home. She had short brown hair, just darker than the rest of the family. She was tall and slim and had given Lilach her eyes. The size of the house justified calling it a room. There was one bedroom, a small living room that only had space for a sofa, an armchair and a large bookshelf filled with books. Attached to the living room, as if it was a design afterthought, was a small kitchen consisting of a sink in the middle of a two-meter long countertop, a refrigerator and a cupboard. On the counter was a gas unit with two burners. The walls of the room were filled with paintings with the name Miri signed at the bottom. For the most part, kibbutz families did not need to prepare food at home – other than hot drinks and an occasional cake.

Before Yehuda had entered, Miri had started the introductions.

"You must be Anna," she said as Anna entered. "I think Yasmin and Iris resemble you."

"In more ways than one," said Ida. "I wouldn't want to interrupt a conversation between Anna and Yasmin. Hi, I'm Ida."

"Miri. And...Hanna?"

"Yes. Very pleased to meet you."

"You have no idea what we have been going through this week. Finding family like that…"

"I think we know," said Anna. "I found my son." Anna started to cry and Miri immediately hugged her.

"I understand," said Miri.

"I know you do."

The children filed into the small room and all four ran directly to the couch and filled it up.

"I don't think so," said Miri. "Make room for your grandmother and her friends."

Reluctantly, the children slid off the sofa and onto the tile floor, where they sat facing the couch that was soon occupied by the three women.

"I brought some fresh bread from the dining room. A few months ago, one of the members decided that we should bake our own bread. It's quite good. There is also some fresh fruit. Please help yourselves."

"What do we call you," asked Lilach.

"Call me Safta. I am, after all, your grandmother. So call me that."

"But Safta lives in Nir Oz!" argued Ilan.

"He's talking about my mother," said Miri.

"It will take him time to get used to it," said Anna. She turned to Ilan. "Now you have two saftot."

"Wow! Like Avner. He has two saftot on this kibbutz. Are you going to live here?"

Anna chuckled and shook her head.

"So," said Yasmin. "You all fought in the ghetto, right?"

"Like Avner's saba!" said Ilan.

"This Avner has quite an influence on him," said Ida.

"It's his best friend," said Lilach.

"Yes, we did," said Anna. "But that was a long time ago. Your father was born in the ghetto."

"There are a lot of people here who survived the Holocaust," said Yasmin. "What happened to you after the war? You were in Warsaw? Did you leave the camps and have to take a boat here? Did you…"

"Slow down," said Yehuda who had just entered the house. He had been stopped outside by one of the neighbors inquiring about the entourage that had just entered the house. "Let's ask one question at a time. Ilan, Avner's in his parent's room and looking for you."

Ilan jumped up off the floor and ran for the front door.

"Hold it, say goodbye to your safta," said Yehuda.

"Bye Sa… Bye."

343

They all chuckled.

"So?" continued Yasmin impatiently.

"After the war," said Anna, "we all went to help out in one of the displacement camps. I was teaching Hebrew, even though I hardly knew how to speak. Ida started her medical training there. She was acting as a nurse…"

"Even though I hardly knew anything about medicine," said Ida.

"And Hanna worked…"

"I did whatever was necessary," said Hanna.

"What was necessary?" asked Yasmin.

"Cooking; taking inventory, caring for the sick…"

"Isn't that what a nurse does?" asked Yasmin.

"I would usually just sit with them and talk. The nurses did other things."

"We worked there for almost eight months," said Anna. "And finally, after such a long wait, we were brought by boat to Palestine."

"You mean Israel," said Lilach.

"It wasn't Israel yet," answered Yasmin curtly.

"Sorry!" said Lilach. "Don't chew my head off Miss Brainy-pants."

Iris got up off the floor and walked over to her mother who had removed a blender from the cupboard and was preparing ice coffee. She pulled her mother down and whispered loudly enough for everyone to hear. "Ema? When are we going to the dining room? Are they coming with us?"

"At dinner time," said Miri. "At seven o'clock, and yes, they are coming with us."

Iris smiled a huge grin and walked back to the center of the room to sit on the floor next to Yasmin who was still awaiting answers to her questions.

"There was a man from the Jewish Agency," Anna continued, "who put us on a boat. We arrived here late one night and had to sneak in…"

"So the British wouldn't catch you," said Yasmin.

Anna smiled, understanding Yasmin's acuity. "Right."

"Did you get seasick?" asked Lilach.

"What kind of question is that?" scolded Yasmin. "Who cares if they got seasick? They were making aliya and that's exciting."

"No, Lilach, I didn't get seasick. But some of the other passengers did."

Yasmin continued, "You must have been scared."

"Scared? Why would I be scared? After all that we had been through, it was the greatest moment of our lives."

"Even better than when Abba was born?"

"Yasmin!" said Yehuda. "Please control yourself. That's an inappropriate question."

"Why?" asked Yasmin.

"It's alright," said Anna.

"Yasmin," said Ida. "I think that you should take your safta for a walk around the kibbutz and talk with her alone. I'm sure you will get all the answers to all the questions your eager little mind desires. Anna loves to talk."

"So do I," said Yasmin.

"I hear you like to read, Yasmin. What are you reading now?" asked Anna.

"Today?"

"Yes, today. This week."

"Well, yesterday I finished Six Month Woman by Merav Snir, but I didn't like it. It wasn't very realistic. Last week I read one that I really liked, The Cost Struggle by Nadav Alon. It had a great ending. Today I started reading something, something, Bless the something...I can't remember, but it seems okay."

"I told you she reads a lot," said Yehuda.

"I know what that's like. I used to read anything I could get my hands on when I was her age."

"She's read everything I have on the shelves," said Miri.

"I know what to get her for her birthday," said Anna.

"I go to the kibbutz library to get more books...or borrow from friends," said Yasmin.

"Yehuda," said Anna, turning to face her son who had taken a chair from the kitchen area and placed it across from the couch in front of the bookshelves. "On the bus, before you tried to kill me..."

"He tried to kill you?" exclaimed Yasmin and Lilach together.

"No, no," said Yehuda. "I had to slam on the brakes to keep from hitting a crazy truck driver. I saved her life."

"From my perspective, you tried to kill me. Before you either saved my life or tried to kill me, you said I reminded you of someone."

Yehuda smiled and pointed to Yasmin. Yasmin smiled back.

"Let's go for a walk, child."

"I'll show you my house. We just build these strange sculptures out of cement outside. One looks like a lizard and the other like a squashed frog. I can also show you..."

"Go already," said Yehuda. "before she breaks into another homily

345

about something or other. I need a break. Yasmin, bring her back in one piece...and by 5:30. She'll want to freshen up before dinner. Isn't she amazing?"

"Anyone else want to come to see my room?" asked Yasmin.

"No!" said everyone in unison.

"Where did you go first when you got to Israel?" asked Yasmin as she held Anna's hand and left the room.

"The first few years I was on Kibbutz Ein Hashofet. I was a teacher in high school."

"I want to be a teacher too. Why did you leave?"

"I wanted to study, and the kibbutz couldn't let me at the time. They needed everyone to work and couldn't afford to let me go. There was a waiting list of people who wanted to study. I never was very attached to Ein Hashofet. So I moved to the center of the country with Ida and Hanna and studied Economics and Sociology. Then I taught at Tel Aviv University until a few years ago."

"Did you get married?"

"Not after I came here. I had been married in Poland before the war."

"To my grandfather."

"No, it was before your grandfather. Your grandfather and I never married."

Yasmin looked down at the floor as if trying to decide what the next line of questioning should be. Anna was worried she'd have to tell Tuvia's story.

"You know what?"

"What?"

"I wish it would snow here."

"It will never snow here," said Anna. "You're on the edge of the desert. You get forty-degree weather in the summer and it's usually close to twenty in the winter. I don't think you'll get snow. Besides, snow is overrated. You have to stay warm all the time, and if you don't, it stings."

"I would stand behind glass to keep warm from the sun."

"That may help a bit, but when it snows, there is no sun. In Poland, we would go weeks without seeing the sun – but a lot of snow. No, it won't snow here. It's against the laws of physics. You need an absence of heat to get the cold. That's science. Go to Jerusalem or the Golan for snow."

"My friend, not Avia from Sderot, but Lehi from Nir Oz, I go to school with her and she lives really, really close to my safta...my other safta...anyway, she said that she has a cousin who doesn't believe in the laws of physics. Her cousin believes in God. He thinks that God makes all the laws, not physics."

"Well, you could believe in both. There's no contradiction. He could believe in God and science."

"Do you believe in God or physics?"

"It's not that simple," said Anna and looked down at Yasmin. "I don't know if there is a god or not. I just know that the idea of God does not play a part in my life. I believe that God was created by people looking for answers. For me, science gives me much better answers than God."

"Then you believe in physics. Me too. I told Lehi to tell her cousin that his god did too many terrible things for me to believe in him... like the ghetto."

They walked on the dirt path leading from Yehuda's and Miri's room to the children's houses. A warm breeze blew through the one-story buildings coming off the sea. On the way, they saw a group of teenagers playing guitar and singing under a tree on the grass across from the dining room, and Yasmin explained everything she could about how the meals work on the kibbutz, which Anna already knew but loved to hear Yasmin explain. Already at age nine, she was a proud kibbutznikit and completely understood the workings of her collective community. She talked about equality of the sexes, working as a unit and taking care of the elderly. She had been taught well by the system.

"Here it is! See the smashed frog doesn't look very good. But I worked on the lizard. It looks just like a lizard, doesn't it?"

"It sure does. Good work," said Anna.

"Come inside," said Yasmin. She pulled Anna's arm toward the door.

"This is lovely," said Anna as she crossed the threshold to the white building. There was a hallway to the left with five pale green doors on one side and windows lining the other. To the right was a large room with a bookcase, a sofa and mattresses scattered in the center. A kitchen about the size of Yehuda's was off to the far right. Yasmin dragged Anna to the left and directly to the first door.

"This is my room. I share it with Maya, Yahav and Merav. Yahav and Merav are always together, so we call them Meryav."

"Where is everyone now?"

"This is family time. Every day from four in the afternoon until bedtime, we spend time with our parents."

Anna looked around Yasmin's room and didn't need the girl to tell her which area was hers. Each corner had a bed, a small dresser and a shelf above it. Yasmin had three shelves, and they were all filled with books.

"What's that book on the bed?"

"Oh, that's from school," said Yasmin. "Usually I don't like school books. This one's okay."

"I imagine you get good grades," said Anna.

"Grades? We don't have grades in our school."

"Oh, that's right. I forgot. It's been a while since I lived on a kibbutz."

"We just have meetings with the teachers. They always tell my parents that I talk too much. But they already knew that."

"It's okay to talk a lot if you have important things to say."

"Safta?"

"Yes, dear."

"Tell me about my grandfather."

Anna was falling in love. Yasmin was the same inquisitive, brilliant, active girl that Anna had been, and she identified with her unrelenting need to know. Already, during that first meeting, Anna was looking forward to the day she could tell Yasmin her whole story. Their meeting had conflated the past and the future into one unit that needed to be pampered. She wanted to tell her about the ghetto. She wanted her to know about what it meant to fight for freedom so that when Yasmin went into the Israel Defense Forces she would understand why she was there. She wanted to tell her about fighting with the partisans, and most of all, she wanted to tell her about her family – from her great, great, great grandmother all the way down to her grandfather.

During that first weekend listening to Yasmin ask question after question, Anna knew that Yasmin would be the one to inherit Anna's greatest physical treasure. For thirty years, Anna worried about who would be worthy of receiving the rings. Now, after less than two days with her, she was sure she had found the right person. It did not matter to her that Yasmin was not the oldest – there was always a chance that one of her sisters would get married first – but Yasmin was the one. Her grandchild, with a mind more powerful than the greatest of armies, was the person Anna had been hoping to find. And she was family.

Personal Note

This story is based on historical fact, mixed with fictional dialogue and encounters. The main characters are inspired by real people who fought in the ghetto as well as others who survived the war and lived to tell their tales. The story of the woman and the driver is true, and as far as I have been able to determine, it has never been told. It was told to me by one of the passengers. I heard it when I was 12-years-old from a young woman who had returned to the U.S. after a year in Israel. I never found that woman and would be grateful if I could.

I originally wrote this story to tell the tale of a woman's adventure on a bus ride from Jerusalem to Tel Aviv, but I soon found so many more incredible stories. My focus then became to tell the story of the role of women and youth movements in the Warsaw ghetto and the intimacy that developed between the fighters, both in the ghetto and as Partisans in the forests. The dialogues and personal encounters, as well as many of the details, are fictional.

As of course, I was not there, if I missed something or got something wrong, I would be very happy to receive new information and make the necessary revisions.